PRAISE FO

THE SWANS OF FIFTH AVENUE

New York Times bestseller

Los Angeles Times bestseller

National Indie bestseller

#1 *USA Today* "New and Noteworthy Books"

Top Ten LibraryReads pick

People Book of the Week

Entertainment Weekly's Must List

Us Weekly's Best of February Fiction

"The era and the sordid details come back to life in this jewel of a novel."

—*O: The Oprah Magazine*

"Highly entertaining."

—*The Washington Post*

"Shamelessly gossipy . . . a catty, juicy read that's like a three-martini lunch."

—*USA Today*

"Captur[es] the mesmerizing sparkle and scandal of New York high society in the 1950s."

—*Chicago Tribune*

"Benjamin reimagines the glittering friendships Capote so diligently cultivated."

—*New York Post*

"Tantalizing . . . Readers will fall into a world of glitz, glamour and the exciting life of the rich and famous. The details and conversations are so rich, you may forget you're reading a novel."

—Associated Press

"A scandal for the ages."

—*Cosmopolitan*

"This moving fictionalization brings the whole cast of characters back to vivid life. Gossipy and fun, it's also a nuanced look at the beauty and cruelty of a rarefied, bygone world."

—*People*

"Gripping . . . exceptional storytelling . . . teeming with scandal, gossip and excitement."

—*Harper's Bazaar*

"Benjamin recreates this world of glamour, cigarettes, alcohol and gossip. . . . Readers will enjoy—and be saddened by—this fascinating peek into the lives of the real people behind the society pages."

—*Historical Novel Society*

"Thoughtful, tragic, entertaining . . . Benjamin transforms these historical characters and their relationships into a vehicle for exploring multiple themes."

—Durham *Herald-Sun*

"Take *Gossip Girl* and move it to the 50's."

—*The Skimm*

"Benjamin has given us a compelling look at an American icon, a talented yet vulnerable man, and the complex woman he loved in his own distinctive way."

—*The Philadelphia Inquirer*

"Fans of vintage New York glamour who loved books such as Amor Towles's *Rules of Civility* will relish this chance to experience vicariously the lives (and fashion choices!) of the city's rich and famous. Benjamin convincingly portrays a large cast of colorful historical figures while crafting a compelling, gossipy narrative with rich emotional depth."

—*Library Journal* (starred review)

"Elegant Babe's thoughts, if not her lips, are unsealed at last."

—*Kirkus Reviews*

"A juicy story."

—*Bookreporter*

"Benjamin's fact-based narrative captures the era's juiciest scandals and wildest extravagances."

—*Publishers Weekly*

"The strange and fascinating relationship between Truman Capote and his 'swans'—Babe, Slim, Gloria, and the other social X-ray women of the era—is wonderfully reimagined in this engrossing novel where everyone behaves so badly and yet has so much fun. It's a credit to Benjamin that we end up caring so much for these women of power, grace, and beauty—and for Capote, too."

—SARA GRUEN, *New York Times* bestselling author of *Water for Elephants*

"A delicious tale of when society gossip became an art form, a spectator sport, and eventually a lethal weapon . . . Melanie Benjamin has turned Truman Capote's greatest scandal into your next must-read book-club selection."

—JAMIE FORD, *New York Times* bestselling author of *Hotel on the Corner of Bitter and Sweet*

"*The Swans of Fifth Avenue* is a deliciously spiky novel of love and betrayal in 1950s high society Manhattan. In prose as elegant as her real-life characters, Melanie Benjamin delivers a glittering but cautionary tale of the corrosive effects of celebrity. I loved every page of it."

—ALEX GEORGE, author of
A Good American

"*The Swans of Fifth Avenue* is a beautifully written story of friendship, love, and betrayal. It is a fascinating look at a gossipy, glamorous world filled with brilliant and vulnerable people. Every moment of triumph and tragedy is riveting, and Melanie Benjamin makes this gilded world come alive in a funny and moving novel that captivates from the first page to the last."

—EDWARD KELSEY MOORE,
New York Times bestselling author of
The Supremes at Earl's All-You-Can-Eat

"Reading *The Swans of Fifth Avenue* is like being ushered into a party where you're offered champagne and fed the sumptuous secrets of New York's elite—without having to pay the price afterwards. The swans are outmatched only by the elegance of Melanie Benjamin's prose—captivatingly earnest and sophisticated."

—VANESSA DIFFENBAUGH, *New York Times* bestselling
author of *The Language of Flowers* and
We Never Asked for Wings

"The beautiful people of the fifties and sixties glitter in this riveting tale of betrayal and greed, in which Truman Capote trundles toward his own ruin. . . . Irresistible, astonishing, and told with verve . . . not to be missed."

—LYNN CULLEN, nationally bestselling author of *Mrs. Poe*

"A delicious amalgam of wit, gossip, beauty, and scandal, *The Swans of Fifth Avenue* serves up a fictional roller-coaster ride through the chic mid-century world of Truman Capote and his high-society muses, meticulously researched and cleverly imagined. From Capote's devious charm to Babe Paley's tragic glamour, Melanie Benjamin conjures, in vivid detail, a lost world where secrets were currency, and antique pearls and a good martini were the only accessories that mattered. . . . The season's must-read guilty pleasure."

—MICHAEL CALLAHAN, author of *Searching for Grace Kelly*

"In a word—fabulous . . . *The Swans of Fifth Avenue* is a compulsively readable tale of friendship, betrayal, tragedy, and unconventional love. Benjamin skillfully reveals the duplicity, narcissism, charm, and vulnerability that defined Truman Capote, and how those closest to him paid the price for his love of celebrity."

—RENÉE ROSEN, bestselling author of *What the Lady Wants* and *White Collar Girl*

"Melanie Benjamin's heart-rending story about Truman Capote's betrayal of the women who adored him is at once gossipy, intimate, poignant, and astonishingly perceptive. Led along by Benjamin's enviable gift for spinning a tale, I devoured this compulsively readable book in two sittings. I've told everyone I know to read *Swans,* because Melanie Benjamin is at the height of her storytelling prowess, with no end in sight."

—ROBIN OLIVEIRA, bestselling author of *I Always Loved You*

By

MELANIE
BENJAMIN

. . . . .

Alice I Have Been

The Autobiography of Mrs. Tom Thumb

The Aviator's Wife

The Swans of Fifth Avenue

Reckless Hearts (short story)

THE

SWANS

OF

FIFTH

AVENUE

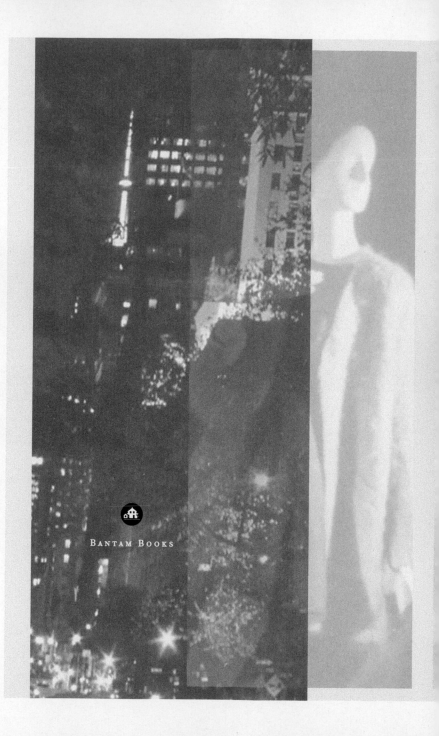

BANTAM BOOKS

THE

of

FIFTH AVENUE

. . . .

A   N O V E L

. . . .

MELANIE BENJAMIN

2016 Bantam Books Trade Paperback Edition

Copyright © 2016 by Melanie Hauser

Reading group guide copyright © 2016 by Penguin Random House LLC

Excerpt from *The Girls in the Picture* by Melanie Benjamin copyright © 2016 by Melanie Hauser

LIBRARY OF CONGRESS CATALOGING-IN-PUBLICATION DATA
Benjamin, Melanie
The Swans of Fifth Avenue : a novel / Melanie Benjamin.
pages ; cm
ISBN 978-0-345-52870-4 — ISBN 978-0-345-53975-5 (ebook) 1. Capote, Truman, 1924–1984—Fiction. 2. Paley, Babe Mortimer—Fiction. 3. Upper class—New York (State)—New York—Fiction. Title.
PS3608.A876S93 2016   813'.6—dc23
2014048099

Printed in the United States of America on acid-free paper

randomhousebooks.com
randomhousereaderscircle.com

246897531

Book design by Barbara M. Bachman

To my father,

Norman Miller

. . . . .

THE BEST TIME TO LEAVE A PARTY IS
WHEN THE PARTY'S JUST BEGINNING.

—*Diana Vreeland*

LANGUID, LOVELY, LONELY; THE SWANS ARCHED THEIR *beautiful necks and turned to gaze at him as he stood rooted to the shore, his feet encased in mud. They fluttered their eyelashes, rustled their feathers, and glided over to their leader, the most beautiful of all. There was no sound save the sigh of their graceful bodies drifting across the water.*

Watching from the shore, wringing his hands, willing himself still for once, even as he had a childish urge to hop first on one foot, then the other, he was filled with the old fear; that he wasn't good enough, brave enough, handsome enough, tall enough——enough. Still he hoped, he dreamed, he waited; holding his breath, he fixed his gaze upon the most dazzling of them all, the lead swan. Like he was making a birthday wish, he blew his breath toward her and her alone, praying the wind would catch it and carry it to her, a prayer.

As she bent her lovely head toward the other swans, she was seen to listen gravely, as if this was a most solemn rite; as if there was no other topic in the world that needed her attention, no wars and deaths and treaties and dilemmas. Only this, his happiness.

The other swans whispered, whispered; one hissed, but he could not tell which it was. Then they broke ranks; they swam into a preordained formation, a perfect arc surrounding their leader, who remained utterly still, her head bowed in reflection.

Then she raised her head, turned, and looked at him, still standing on the shore. They all turned to look; the swans, with one choreographed movement, beckoned to him with their blinding-white wings that were arms, he saw for the first time. Arms as white as snow leopards; whiter than the pearls around the swans' fragile necks.

The lead swan did not beckon. But her eyes, those dark, glittering pools of unfathomable loneliness, never left his as his feet took wing; as he skimmed the surface of the water, not a swan, no, never would he be one of them, and even then he knew it. He was a nymph, a hovering dragonfly—a sprite, landing among the swans with a burst of delighted laughter. They laughed, as well, all of them—except for their leader.

She only continued to watch him as he was passed about from one to the other like a new baby. When the swans were finished, when they sat him down on the water and took up their positions once more, he found himself between them and the lead swan. Uncertain, but dizzy with joy and belonging, he took a step toward her, still marveling at how the water was not water but the most polished marble beneath his feet, the feathers on the swans were not feathers but fur and cashmere and silk and satin, threaded together, hand-sewn to their disciplined bodies that were designed only for adornment.

And his swan, now—that was how he thought of her, and would forever, naming her, claiming her, forgetting already that it hadn't been his privilege to do the choosing—held out her hand, and he took it, as trustingly as a child. Mischievously as an imp.

Then the swans closed ranks about him.

And he was home.

La Côte Basque,
October 17, 1975

. . . . .

"H E KILLED HER. IT'S AS SIMPLE AS THAT." SLIM'S HANDS
shook as she spilled a packet of menthols all over her plate. "Truman killed her. And I'd like to know who the hell it was who be-
friended that little midget in the first place."

"It wasn't I," Pamela insisted. "I never did like the bugger."

"Oh, no, it wasn't me—I warned you about him, didn't I?"
Gloria asked rhetorically, those Latin eyes flashing so dangerously,
it was a good thing there were only butter knives on the table.

"I don't believe it was me," Marella murmured. "No, no, it was
not."

"It sure as hell wasn't me." Slim spat it out. "And if he's not
convicted for murder, I'm going to sue him for libel, at the very
least."

The table went silent; this was almost as much of a bombshell as
the reason they were gathered in haste, eyes hidden behind dark
glasses, as though that could disguise their famous faces. Odd, Slim
thought, how they'd all had the same idea: to hide, as if they were

the ones at fault when, really, it was Truman who should hide his face. Now and forever.

But defiantly, they had agreed to meet at the scene of the crime: the restaurant that had spawned the literary scandal of the century, as it was already being called. Slim Hawks Hayward Keith, Marella Agnelli, Gloria Guinness, and Pamela Churchill Hayward Harriman—not a shrinking violet in the bunch—had descended upon La Côte Basque, always the place to see and be seen, especially today.

"Where's C.Z.?" Gloria asked suddenly. "The honorable Mrs. Guest should be here, too. It only seems right. After all, she was here when it all began. Like it or not, she's one of us."

"C.Z.'s probably off digging a hole somewhere. Do you know what she did when I called and asked her if she'd read it? She laughed. She laughed! 'Oh, Slim,' she said. 'If you didn't know by now that Truman Capote couldn't keep a secret, then you're a much bigger fool than I am!' Of course, he didn't say a thing about *her*."

"But what about—?" Pamela asked, and they all glanced at the empty chair at the end of the table. "Wasn't C.Z. outraged on *her* behalf, at least?"

Slim finally lit the blessed, blessed cigarette and took a long draw. She leaned back in her chair and exhaled, narrowing her eyes at Pamela. Strange, how Truman could bring them together, how he'd made allies out of enemies with his pen. "She wasn't, not that I could tell."

"But Dillon, that odious man in Truman's story—it *is* Bill, isn't it? It's supposed to be Bill Paley?"

Slim took a big breath, but couldn't meet her friends' collective, searching gaze. "Yes. It is, I know it is. Don't ask me how; I just do."

Pamela, Gloria, and Marella gasped. So did the other tables nearby; when the four women entered the restaurant together, all heads had turned their way. Some in astonishment, some in out-right glee. Others in admiration. But all in curiosity.

Marcel, their favorite waiter, cautiously approached the table with the customary bottle of Cristal. He showed it to them, and Gloria wearily waved her hand in assent; he popped the cork, but without the usual flourish. He knew.

Everyone knew.

The latest issue of *Esquire* had hit the stands that morning, the cover a profile picture of a fat and pasty-looking Truman Capote, the headline trumpeting the acclaimed author of *In Cold Blood*'s newest, hotly anticipated short story. "La Côte Basque 1965," it was called. It was now one P.M. Liz Smith was probably already on the phone, frantically asking their maids if Madam was in or out.

Well, this madam is out, Slim thought to herself. And she might very well stay out, for the rest of the day. Hell, the rest of the night. Where was Papa when she needed him? For she would have hopped the next plane to Cuba, if that were still permissible. And if Heming-way were still alive, daiquiri in one hand, rifle or fly reel in the other, his big, virile, lecherous grin on his face at the sight of her, wondering when the hell he was going to get around to writing a book about her, the most fascinating woman he'd ever met.

Ah, but that was another story, from a different time. A different life.

Today, the story was different. And it wasn't really her story at all, Slim realized; she had been used, yes. But in the end, her secrets, mainly, remained intact. Still, that did not dampen her sense of be-trayal, her bitterness at what her True Heart—her stomach soured at the memory of that pet name!—had done.

The murder Truman Capote had committed, plain as day, by telling the stories he had told. Stories that he did not have a right to tell.

Stories they never should have told him in the first place.

"No one will return his calls now. No one will invite him anywhere. He's finished in society. Dead—as dead as—" Pam dabbed ostentatiously at her blue eyes, which, Slim couldn't help but observe, remained resolutely dry.

There was a lull in the conversation, a cloud that dropped over their table, dulling the brilliant light, throwing shadows on the gleaming cutlery, the sparkling crystal.

"Does anyone really remember when they first met him? Or did he just appear, like the plague?" Slim was in a reflective mood; one she did not allow herself often, and one that did not sit well with her companions, generally. Lunch at La Côte Basque was not for soul-searching.

But today was different. Today, they'd opened the pages of *Esquire* magazine and seen themselves—not merely themselves, but their kind, their tribe, their exclusive, privileged, envied set—eviscerated, skin flayed open, souls laid bare, ugliness acknowledged. Secrets betrayed and lives destroyed. By the viper in their nest; the storyteller in their midst.

But Truman Capote wasn't the only one who could tell tales, they decided over another glass of Cristal.

"So tell me," Slim cooed, her tongue comfortably loose, her throat deliciously numb. "How the hell did that southern-fried bastard get here in the first place?"

The four inclined their still-gorgeous necks, put their perfectly coiffed heads together in consultation. Beads and feathers quivered on gesticulating arms. Jewels and gold flashed on punctuating hands as they tried to piece it all together. From the very beginning. The story of how Truman Capote came to betray all his swans— but one especially. The one they all loved the most. Even Truman.

Especially Truman.

The problem with this particular story, however, was that Truman was the one who had told it to them in the first place.

THE

SWANS

OF

FIFTH

AVENUE

. . . . .

ONCE UPON A TIME—

It was the best of times, it was the worst of times—

There once was a man from Nantucket—

Truman giggled. He covered his mouth like a little boy, and tittered until his slender shoulders shook, his blue eyes so gleefully mischievous that he looked like a statue of Pan come to life.

"Oh, Big Mama! I am such a naughty imp!"

"True Heart, you are priceless!" Slim had laughed, too, she remembered, laughed until her ribs ached. Truman did that to her in those glorious early days; he made her laugh. That was it, really. The simple truth of the matter.

When he was young, back in 1955, when they were all young—or, at least, younger—when fame was new and friendships fledgling, fueled by champagne and caviar and gifts from Tiffany's, Truman Capote was a hell of a lot of fun to be around.

"Once upon a time," Slim had finally pronounced.

"Yes. Well . . . ," and Truman drawled it out in his theatrical way, adding several syllables. "Once upon a time, there was New York."

New York.

Stuyvesants and Vanderbilts and Roosevelts and staid, respectable Washington Square. Trinity Church. Mrs. Astor's famous ballroom, the Four Hundred, snobby Ward McAllister, that traitor Edith Wharton, Delmonico's. Zany Zelda and Scott in the Plaza fountain, the Algonquin Round Table, Dottie Parker and her razor tongue and pen, the Follies. Cholly Knickerbocker, 21, Lucky Strike dances at the Stork, El Morocco. The incomparable Hildegarde playing the Persian Room at the Plaza, Cary Grant kneeling at her feet in awe. Fifth Avenue: Henri Bendel, Bergdorf's, Tiffany's.

There was a subterranean New York, as well; "lower" in every meaning of the word. Ellis Island and the Bowery and the Lower East Side. The subway. Automats and Schrafft's, hot dogs from a cart, pizza by the slice. Chickens hanging from windows in Chinatown, pickles from a barrel on Delancey. Beatniks in the Village with their torn stockings and dirty turtlenecks and disdain for everything.

But that wasn't the New York that drew the climbers, the dreamers, the hungry. No, it was lofty New York, the city of penthouses and apartments in the St. Regis or the Plaza or the Waldorf, the New York for whom "Take the 'A' Train" was a song, not an option. The New York of big yellow taxis in a pinch, if the limousine was otherwise occupied. The New York of glittering opening nights at the Met; endless charity balls and banquets; wide, clean sidewalks uncluttered by pushcarts and clothing racks and children playing. Views of the park, the river, the bridge, not sooty brick walls or narrow, dank alleys.

The New York of the plays, the movies, the books; the New York of *The New Yorker* and *Vanity Fair* and *Vogue*.

It was a beacon, a spire, a beacon on top of a spire. A light, always glowing from afar, visible even from the cornfields of Iowa, the foothills of the Dakotas, the deserts of California. The swamps of Louisiana. Beckoning, always beckoning. Summoning the discontented, seducing the dreamers. Those whose blood ran too hot, and too quickly, causing them to look about at their placid families, their staid neighbors, the graves of their slumbering ancestors and say—

I'm different. I'm special. I'm more.

They all came to New York. Nancy Gross—nicknamed "Slim" by her friend the actor William Powell—from California. Gloria Guinness—"La Guinness"—born a peasant in a rural village in Mexico. Barbara Cushing—known as "Babe" from the day she was born, the youngest of three fabulous sisters from Boston.

And Truman. Truman Streckfus Persons Capote, who showed up one day on William S. and Babe Paley's private plane, a tagalong guest of their good friends Jennifer Jones and David O. Selznick. Bill Paley, the chairman and founder of CBS, had gaped at the slender young fawn with the big blue eyes and funny voice; "I thought you meant *President* Truman," he'd hissed to David. "I've never heard of this little—fellow. We have to spend the whole weekend with him?" Babe Paley, his wife, murmured softly, "Oh, Bill, of course you've heard of him," as she went to greet their unexpected guest with her legendary warmth and graciousness.

Of course, Bill Paley had heard of Truman Capote. Who hadn't, in Manhattan in 1955?

Truman, Truman, Truman—voices whispered, hissed, envied,

disdained. Barely thirty, the Boy Wonder, the Wunderkind, the Tiny Terror (this last, however, mainly uttered by other writers, it must be admitted). Truman Capote, slender, wistful bangs and soulful eyes and unsettling, pouty lips, reclining lazily, staring sultrily from the jacket of his first novel, *Other Voices, Other Rooms.* A novel that neither Babe nor any of her friends such as Slim or Gloria had bothered to read, it must be admitted. But still, they whispered his name at cocktail parties, benefits, and luncheons.

"You must meet—"

"I'm simply *mad* about—"

"Of course you know—"

Truman.

"I introduced you to him first," Slim reminded Babe after that fateful weekend jaunt to the Paleys' home in Jamaica; that startling, stunning weekend when Babe and Truman had found themselves blinking at the first dazzling sunrise of friendship, still so new that they didn't quite understand that it *was* friendship, this thing that had cast a spell over the two of them to the exclusion of mere mortals. "You just don't remember. But he was mine, my True Heart. It's not fair that you've stolen him from me." And Slim pouted and shook her blond hair, always hanging over one eye, looking more like Lauren Bacall than did Lauren Bacall, which was only appropriate, since Lauren Bacall had modeled herself after Slim. "Around the time he was working on the screenplay of *Beat the Devil,* Leland brought him home for dinner one night. Don't you remember?"

"No, it was I who first discovered him," Gloria insisted with a flash of her exotic dark eyes; that flash that always threatened to expose her real origin, concealed so nearly completely beneath the Balenciaga dresses and Kenneth hairstyles—and studied British accent. "I'm surprised, Slim, that you don't recall. It was soon after he adapted *The Grass Harp* for Broadway. I don't generally go in for Broadway, naturally," she said with an arch look at Slim, who bristled. "But I'm very glad I went to that opening night. I told you all about him then, Babe."

"My dear, no. I invited him for the weekend, in Paris, don't you recall?" Pamela broke in, her voice so veddy, veddy British that they all, instinctively, leaned in to hear her (and they all, instinctively, recognized the ploy for what it was, and the many times their husbands had done the same thing, only to encounter Pamela's magnificent cleavage displayed in a low-cut Dior). "Long before any of you—back when he had just published *Other Voices, Other Rooms*. Bennett Cerf, you know, the *publisher*"—and she could barely suppress a shudder; one simply did not like to admit one knew those types—"asked me if I could entertain this young novelist of his, as he was rather nervous about reviews. You were there, Babe. I'm certain of it."

"Ladies, ladies," admonished C.Z., unflappable and untouchable as ever, never quite "in" but never quite "out" of their world—simple and uncomplicated, a Hitchcock blonde with a sunny smile (and a clenched, exceedingly proper Boston drawl). But C.Z., they all knew, was happier puttering around in her garden, spade in hand, or tending to her horses than she was lunching at Le Pavillon. "I don't usually care about this sort of thing, but I do believe I was the one who introduced Truman to Babe. We were shopping at Bergdorf's. Truman is marvelous at picking out just the right handbag. You were there that afternoon, Babe."

"No, I propose it was on our yacht," Marella said in her uncertain English; her entire manner was shy and tentative around her friends, since she was much younger than they were, never entirely sure of her place, despite her fabulous wealth and exquisite beauty—and a face that Truman had pronounced "what Botticelli would have created, had Botticelli had more talent!" "Alec Korda brought him along, one summer. I believe you and Bill were there, Babe, were you not?"

Babe Paley, cool in a blue linen Chanel suit that did not crease, no matter the radiator heat of a New York summer, didn't reply; she merely looked on, amused, as she removed her gloves, folded them carefully, and slipped them inside her Hermès alligator bag. Seated in the middle of the best table at Le Pavillon, she surveyed her surroundings.

This was her world, a world of quiet elegance, artifice, presentation. And luncheon was the highlight of the day, the reason for getting up in the morning and going to the hairdresser, buying the latest Givenchy or Balenciaga; the reward for managing the perfect house, the perfect children, the perfect husband. And for maintaining the perfect body. After all, one generally dined at home, or at a dinner party; why else employ a personal chef or two? But one went out for luncheon, at The Colony or Quo Vadis. But especially Le Pavillon, where the owner, Henri Soulé, displayed his society ladies like the *objets* of fine art that they were, seating them proudly in the front room, spreading them out in plush red-velvet banquettes, setting the table with the finest linen, Baccarat glasses, exquisite china and silver, and cut crystal bowls of fresh flowers. They drank their favorite wine, pushed the finest French cuisine around their plates (for in order to wear the kind of clothes and possess the kind of cachet to be welcome at Le Pavillon, naturally one could not actually eat), gossiped, and were seen.

Photographers were always gathered on the sidewalk outside, waiting to snap the beautiful people inside, and Babe, tall, regal, a gracious smile on her face, was the most sought-after of all, to her friends' eternal dismay and her own weary disdain—although the most observant, like Slim, might notice that Babe would pause, imperceptibly, if no photographer happened to be around, as if looking, or wishing, for one magically to appear.

Why was Babe Paley such a favorite? Why was she the most fussed over, the most sought out for a quick, reverent hello by those not privileged to be seated with her? She was not the most beautiful; that honor must go to Gloria Guinness, with her exquisite neck, lustrous black hair, and flashing eyes. She was not the most amusing; that was Slim Hayward, with her quips and her quick wit, honed at the feet of men like Ernest Hemingway and Howard Hawks and Gary Cooper. She was not the most noble; no, that would be a tie between the Honorable Pamela Digby Churchill, daughter of a baron, ex-daughter-in-law of a prime minister, and Marella Agnelli, a bona fide Italian princess, married to Gianni Agnelli, the heir to the Fiat kingdom.

It was her style, that indefinable asset. It was said that the others had style but Babe *was* style. No one noticed Babe's clothes, for instance; not at first, even though she was always clad in the chicest, most exquisite designs. They noticed *her*, her tall, slender frame, her grave dark eyes, the way she had of holding her handbag in the crook of her arm, the simple grace with which she pushed her sunglasses on top of her hair or unbuttoned a coat with just one hand, allowing it to fall elegantly from her shoulders into the always-waiting arms of a maître d'.

What they did not notice was the loneliness that trailed after her, along with the faint, grassy scent of her favorite fragrance, Balmain's Vent Vert. The loneliness that, despite fabulous wealth, numerous houses, children, the most vibrant and powerful husband of all her friends, was her constant companion—or, at least, had been. Until now.

"It doesn't really matter," Babe finally pronounced, settling it once and for all. "I'm simply so very glad to know him. To Truman!" And she raised a flute of Cristal.

"To Truman!" her five friends all echoed, and they toasted to their latest find, excited and hungrily anticipating fresh amusements galore, nothing more.

"To Truman," Babe whispered to herself, and smiled a private little smile that none of her friends had ever seen before. But the Duchess of Windsor had just entered the restaurant, her harsh little face turned first to the left, then to the right, as if she really were royalty, igniting a small wildfire of catty conversation— *"Isn't the duke the most boring man you've ever met? But those jewels! The one thing he's ever done right!"*—and none of Babe's friends was even looking at her.

Except for Slim, who narrowed her eyes and bit her lip. And wondered.

THERE WAS ANOTHER YOUNG WOMAN WHO DREAMED OF New York; another young woman who knew that if she could only find her way there, she could live happily ever after—with or without her young son. Her name was Lillie Mae Faulk, and she was from Monroeville, Alabama. She came to New York, too.

Once upon a time.

"My mother's name was Nina," Truman told Gloria, told C.Z., told Slim. His eyes gleamed softly, reverently. "Nina was beautiful—a real lady. She was too much for Monroeville, Alabama! She always told me, 'Truman, my little man, I'm going to take you to New York one day.' And she did, when I was eleven. That's when my life really began—because it's New York! Not sleepy little Monroeville, where nothing ever happened. Although I did get bit by a cottonmouth once, and nearly died. Nearly—oh, my goodness, I was one foot over the line! But they saved me. Nothing can kill me, not even a snake!"

"Oh!" Slim gasped. Then she grinned. "Let me see the scar!"

"Big Mama!" Truman wagged a finger at her but obliged, rolling up his shirt to reveal a thin, supple arm, paler than the moon, covered with a fine down of silken blond hair, as white as the hair on his head, the hair brushing his eyes, always falling, falling over his face like a curtain or a veil. "See?"

Slim did see: two faint punctures on his forearm, barely visible.

"These are my scars, my only scars," Truman told her, triumphantly. "I don't have any others!"

"My mother's name was really Lillie Mae," Truman revealed to Babe. It was early in their friendship, those days when they had to catch each other up on everything that had happened to them, so that they could mark their lives—Before. And After.

"Lillie Mae Faulk. And she was a selfish bitch," Truman said, his voice flat for once. He wasn't trying to captivate or ensnare; he knew he had Babe, knew it in his heart. Knew it as a dream come true, for that was what it was.

A beautiful—an exquisite—woman. Loving him, Truman. *Needing* him, as he needed her. For what, neither could precisely express just yet. They only recognized each other, not as a reflection in a mirror, but as a reflection of a deeper, darker, murkier sore, or hole, or something gaping but always, *always* hidden. Until the moment they locked eyes on the CBS plane, each so startled their masks fell, and Truman was, for only a fragment of a moment, no longer the startlingly self-assured prodigy but a lost little boy, forgotten. And Babe was, beneath the couture and makeup, a shy, unsure woodland creature, hugging herself for comfort.

Two souls, exposed like raw wounds. Visible only to each other, they firmly believed.

"My mother hated me. *Hated me!* Despised, loathed." Truman gnashed the words with his teeth. "She abandoned me to those horrible cousins in Monroeville, and I thought I'd never see her again. She used to lock me in hotel rooms, did you know? Lock me in while she went off with her 'gentleman callers'—thank you, Tennessee!—and I'd cry and cry, but she'd left instructions, you see. Told the staff not to let me out, no matter how I hollered. And I did! But then I'd finally tire myself out and fall asleep, never knowing when—if—she'd come back for me."

Babe was shocked; she wanted to fold her new friend up in her arms, hug him to her heart, which was pierced on his behalf. But she did not; she knew the effort it took to keep one's exterior self together, upright, when everything inside was in pieces, broken beyond repair. One touch, one warm, compassionate hand, could shatter that hard-won perfect exterior. And then it would take years and years to restore it.

So Babe did not hug Truman, who looked, in that moment of confession, as if he were still that six-year-old boy abandoned by his mother in Monroeville, Alabama. Forgotten by his father, too— "Arch Persons! What a farce *he* was. Is. Someday I'll tell you about him, but not today, Babe, dear. I'm a little weary today." And he rubbed his eyes tiredly, with his two small fists.

"But she did bring you here, Truman. That's the good thing. The blessed thing."

"Yes, Lillie Mae did get here, after all. She married my stepfather, Joe Capote. She changed her name to Nina and she had a fabulous apartment on Park Avenue, just as she'd dreamed. She finally sent for me and put me in military school, to butch me up. She hated who I was. Called me a fag one moment, then asked me when I'd marry a nice girl the next. She never was proud of me, never. I could have written the Bible, and she'd still call me, to my face, the greatest disappointment in her life."

"Never! You're no disappointment, Truman. You're a beautiful person, a great artist. You must know that!"

"Well"—and Truman did grin up at her, a sly, satisfied little boyish grin. "I will admit to overcoming my childhood, anyway. The hell that it was."

"I HAD THE MOST MARVELOUS CHILDHOOD!" Truman exclaimed to Slim, to Gloria, to C.Z., at their parties, where they would surround their new discovery, these glamorous wives of glamorous men, while their husbands looked on in confusion, for they'd never seen a Truman Capote before, and hoped, at first, never to see one again. This tiny, effeminate creature dressed in velvet suits, red socks, an absurdly long scarf usually wrapped around his throat, trailing after him like a coronation robe, who pronounced, after dinner, "I'm going to go sit over here with the rest of the girls and gossip!" This pixie who might suddenly leap into the air, kicking one foot out behind him, exclaiming, "Oh, what fun, fun, *fun* it is to be me! I'm beside myself!"

These men, titans of industry, old money, heirs to fortunes, looked on, agape. And told one another, "Well, at least we don't have anything to worry about from *him*," as their wives fluttered and cooed and preened and fought to sit next to him.

But Truman, watching them, recognizing the sneering disdain—and the barely concealed fear—in their eyes, smiled to himself, even as he kept chattering to their wives. "These eccentric old cousins who raised me—such material! You've read *The Grass*

Harp, of course. Sook was such a wonderful, crazy old lady! She adored me. They all did—I was the pride of Monroeville, Alabama! The star! And you must meet my friend Nelle. Nelle Harper Lee. She's in New York now, working on a novel about our childhood, apparently, although I'm sure she'll need my help, poor thing. She's bright, but not quite as *gifted* as *moi*—but shh, you didn't hear that from me!"

"NELLE WAS MY ONLY FRIEND in Monroeville," Truman told Babe, bitterly. They were in her bedroom, her sanctum of sanctums, at Kiluna Farm. That was her home—oh, of course the Paleys had many homes; an apartment in the St. Regis, a summer house in New Hampshire, the beach house in Jamaica. But it was the sprawling estate—"Eighty acres!" Truman exclaimed to his lover, Jack Dunphy, who only grunted and said "So what?"—on Long Island that was their constant, their true north. After the fateful plane trip, during which the two of them had immediately tumbled into a conversation neither could recall, except for the fact that it seemed to bind them together with an invisible golden thread none of the others present could unravel, Babe immediately invited Truman out for the weekend. She had installed him in a guest room equipped with a personal valet, fresh flowers, the finest Porthault linens, and a view of her spectacular gardens. Truman—after first allowing himself to roll around the plush carpet like a puppy, bounce on the bed like a ten-year-old, and bury his elfin face in the flowers—knocked on her bedroom door and walked right in without waiting for a reply, as if he'd been there a thousand times before.

And Babe—who rarely allowed anyone into her bedroom—

smiled and patted the bedspread and found herself, to her amazement, sitting cross-legged next to Truman Capote, who studied her anxiously, his eyes big and blue and innocent. He was like a child at times, she decided, as so many people did upon meeting him. A child who needed reassurance and shelter from the capriciousness of a cruel world. And so she surprised herself by sharing confidences as she had never done before, not even, really, with her two sisters back in Boston.

"Nelle was a tomboy—tough as nails and she didn't have too many friends herself, plus her mother was crazy as a loon. But she wanted to be a writer, too. We had that in common. No one else in that dusty Alabama town knew what a writer was. But we found an old typewriter in her father's office and we oiled it up and got some ribbon and would take turns pounding out stories and dialogue and anything that came to mind. We called it 'going to work.' Nelle and I wrote ourselves out of Monroeville, since we couldn't very well leave on our own. Lillie Mae went off to New York, divorced my father, married Joe Capote, and still she didn't send for me. Not until I was eleven. So I was left to be raised by these kooky old cousins, mocked for my good manners, my nice clothes that Nina sent. Mocked for being me, smaller than any other boy, prettier, too." There wasn't a trace of bitterness in Truman's voice; he lolled about the bed, grabbed his knees, and laid his head upon Babe's lap.

"MY MOTHER DIED OF PNEUMONIA," Truman whispered to Slim, to Gloria, to C.Z. To their husbands, now joining their wives by the fire, a cozy, bejeweled, hushed little group surrounding this charming male Scheherazade with the barest traces of a southern accent, the odd, enchanting lisp, the dreamy eyes. And that hair! Fairy hair, spun gold, with long bangs. Men did not have bangs; men wore their hair slicked back with Brylcreem, no-nonsense.

But Truman wasn't a man. He wasn't a woman. He was an unearthly creature, a genius—or so those who weren't inclined to read had been told by those who were. A genius whose eyes were now wet with tears. And their hearts opened to him, as of one accord. "My mother was very young, still beautiful, you know. It was only a couple of years ago. I was in Europe and couldn't get back in time. She died of pneumonia and she was all alone. And so now I'm an orphan."

The wives wiped their own tears. The husbands said to themselves, "Well, he's not so bad, after all, the little fellow. I've never been friends with a fag before. What the hell."

"MY MOTHER KILLED HERSELF," Truman told Babe. His eyes were dry and frighteningly clear. "Killed herself with booze and pills. She'd tried before but always chickened out. But not this time. Old Capote lost all his money, you see. She had nothing—she was back to being Lillie Mae Faulk, not glamorous Nina Capote. She couldn't bear it. She couldn't bear *me*. I was in Europe, working on the script for *Beat the Devil,* and I had her cremated because she would have hated that. It's so sordid, disgraceful. But now you know."

He frowned, and sighed, and seemed lost in memories; Babe thought his face most beautiful in repose, when the delicate features—the small, yet lusciously red-lipped mouth, the flushed and freckled cheeks, the surprising cleft in his determined jaw—weren't working so hard to beguile.

Suddenly he opened his eyes wide and peered up into her face.

He smiled that mischievous smile, patted her knee, and cooed, "So now you know about me. All about me. Tell me about *you*."

And Babe felt she had no choice—and didn't want one, anyway. This was communion, something of a nature so deep she couldn't articulate it, only feel it rumbling beneath her ribs, tickling her heart. Surface, surface, surface—that was her life, and it had been, for as long as she could remember. But here was someone who had bared his soul to her. He had shown her his wounds, his scars; the real ones, the ones that never healed. The ones that weren't visible to the naked eye.

So naturally, she felt she should show him hers, as well. A scar for a scar; an eye for an eye.

A story for a story.

. . . . .

"ONCE UPON A TIME . . ." WITH BABE, THERE WAS NO question. She was a princess, a walking fairy tale. There was no other way to begin her story.

"Once upon a time, there was a beautiful Babe," Truman said, prompting.

"Once upon a time," Babe admitted, smiling shyly, ducking her head. "I suppose."

It was that—her reticence, he decided. That was what elevated her from woman to goddess, from merely stylish to perfection itself. Her stillness, her grave smile, her quiet voice, her beautiful dark eyes that glittered only to show understanding or reveal some secret hurt, never pride or flirtatiousness. Or even, he thought sadly, wit. No, Barbara Cushing Mortimer Paley was not a great intellectual.

But then, she hadn't been brought up to be one.

"I was raised to marry well," Babe finally said, with a simple, elegant shrug. "My mother was a force of nature, although not like yours. She would never have abandoned us. We were her life's work."

"What was she like?"

"Gogs. That's what we called her, after our own children were born. Gogs Cushing. I loved her. That's all."

"But what was she like?"

"She loved her family. She made a wonderful home for my father, who was always away at work—he was a brain surgeon, you know. He pioneered it, actually. And she taught my sisters and me that if we all stuck together, nothing could stop us. Or harm us."

"But, Babe—what was she *like*? A pill-popper, like Nina? A whore, like Gloria's mother?"

"Truman!" Babe frowned, disapproving, as was only proper—but then she grinned slyly. "Gloria? Gloria Guinness?"

"Oh, don't pretend you don't know all about that! Honey, La Guinness was not exactly legitimate, shall we say. Her mother worked the streets in Mexico. Of course you know that!"

"Truman, Gloria's my friend. My dear friend," protested Babe with a gentle shake of her head.

"But, Bobolink, darling—you don't mind if I call you that, do you? I have pet names for all my dearest friends! I can't stand formality when the heart is involved, can you?"

And Babe—who had not been called by her real name for years, yet despised the nickname by which she was so well known—shook her head, touched. And delighted.

"Now, Bobolink, how can we be friends if we don't gossip together? Just a little? Isn't that the most fun ever? Of course we love Gloria—La Guinness! She's divine! But isn't she just a *trifle* more interesting, knowing that her mother was a whore? Don't you admire her just a bit more when you see how far she had to come to get here?"

"Truman, I've always admired Gloria. She's—well, she's—"

Detecting the slightest bit of hesitation in Babe's not-quite-so-sympathetic eyes, Truman pounced. Like a kitten, dainty claws unsheathed, on a caterpillar. "What? She's what? Oh, do tell, Babe-a-licious—oh, that's even better! Do tell! What did Gloria do to you? What did she say?"

"Nothing. Gloria's a dear friend, as I said. But—well, she does have a habit. It's endearing, when you think of it. It shows she's still a trifle uncertain of herself. But when she invites Bill and me to join her and Loel on their yacht, every summer, she plays this little game."

"Yacht! Oh, take me! Take me!" Truman bounced on his knees, clapping his hands, rumpling the perfection of the satin bedspread so that Babe bit her lip and practically sat on her own hands to prevent them from immediately restoring it to order.

"Of course! We'll take you this summer! You'll go with us, Bill and me. It will be tremendous fun."

"What game? What does Gloria do?" Truman immediately sat back down, serious.

"It's nothing. It's amusing. But she'll tell me, a week before we go, 'Babe, dear, this year we're going to be completely casual. No dressing for dinner. For anything! We'll be windblown and fancy-free!' So that's how I'll pack. Only casual clothes, leaving most of the jewelry behind. And then, the first night, there I'll be in linen pants and a silk blouse, and Gloria will arrive in the latest Balenciaga gown, draped in jewels from ear to ear. Stunning, of course. And she'll announce that we've been invited to a very formal dinner onshore. And I'll feel like a hobo. Then the next year, I'll fool her. I'll bring only formal clothes, and sit down to dinner so elegant, you could die. And Gloria will show up in pants and a blouse, her hair tied back with a scarf, and she'll say, 'Why so formal,

Babe? It's a yacht, not Maxim's! Where do you think you're going?' " Babe laughed, a good, hearty chuckle, completely at odds with her porcelain perfection.

But Truman detected the exasperation in her eyes. And his own gleamed with catty delight.

"That's priceless! And horrid! Yes, it shows how insecure she must be, despite all of Loel's fabulous wealth."

"Gloria's my friend," Babe reminded him. His heart thrilled to her voice; it was so low, gentle, soothing. Nothing could ruffle it, he thought. Nothing could ruffle *her*.

But then the clock on her mantel struck seven soft, discreet chimes. And suddenly Babe Paley was not unruffled. Panic flared in her eyes as she turned in horror to the clock. Her hands reached out in the first abrupt, involuntary gesture he had seen from her.

"Oh! It can't be seven! It simply can't be!"

"So?"

"But Bill will be home any minute. And I'm not ready to greet him." Babe slid down from the bed and walked—gracefully, with her shoulders squared and straight, her long legs as strong yet supple as a ballerina's—to her dressing room. Truman jumped down off the bed and capered after her.

"Oh, Babe! What an Aladdin's cave!" He looked around in awe; Babe Paley's dressing room was nearly as big as her bedroom, and decorated in the same pattern of chintz from ceiling to floor. Her vanity was enormous, draped in beautiful pink fabric that echoed the chintz, and covered with crystal perfume flacons, powder puffs, mirrored trays, bottles of makeup devoid of any trace of fingerprints or smudges, silver-plated brushes (both hairbrushes and makeup brushes), several mirrors of different sizes—handheld, upright, lighted. Babe was seated on the vanity stool, studying herself in the largest mirror with the intensity of an artist assessing his just-finished painting.

"You look perfect," Truman soothed her, sensing his role.

But Babe shook her head. "I always remove my makeup and reapply it just for him. But now I don't have time."

"There's no need," Truman insisted, putting his hands on her shoulders and peering into the mirror, gazing at the apparition before him. *She must be forty,* he thought. But her face did not give away such sordid secrets.

Babe was not a natural beauty, although you sensed that she had the potential to be. But something—some insecurity, Truman felt, instantly determined to locate its source—prevented her from showing it. No, Barbara Paley's style, her beauty, her legendary polish, was artificial, cultivated over a lifetime of discipline and discernment, and she did not take pains to hide the fact. She was heavily made up, eyebrows perfectly groomed and brushed and colored, those glittering, deep-set eyes coated in subtle, complementary eye shadows and liners and mascara. Those high, sculpted cheekbones were further enhanced, with the precision of a professional, by blush, several shades artfully blended together. And her skin, while luminous, was that way due to foundation, thickly applied yet somehow not appearing to be; buffed completely, no lines of demarcation, dewy-looking, fresh.

But still, it was makeup. Beautifully, painstakingly applied; you could gasp at the mastery of it, and appreciate the skill and time necessary. Babe was no blank canvas; her face was a work of art, and she, not God, was the artist. Her hair, too, so perfectly, yet naturally, sculpted and waved to give the appearance of insouciance, thick and brown but with silver streaks weaving through it, catching the light, so chic, and unexpected. Yet again, one sensed the effort that went into it, while marveling at the result.

And the clothes, the accessories! A still life, artfully arranged. Taken separately, they were not spectacular: black Italian loafers, perfectly tailored khaki slacks, a crisp white linen shirt. A glittering diamond necklace. But it was the way they were arranged, the shirt tucked in the front, not the back; the diamond necklace not worn about the throat, but wrapped casually about Babe's left wrist. Expected, yet not. Recognizable, yet unattainable.

And here was this woman, this icon whose face had graced the pages of *Vogue, Harper's Bazaar, Life,* peering worriedly into her mirror, taking a small brush and blending something beneath her eyes, blotting at her nose with a powder puff, a delicate blue vein on her forehead beginning to dance with tension.

"I hope he's not home yet. Oh, if I'm not there, standing in the hall, to greet him, to look wonderful for him——"

Suddenly there was a pounding on the bedroom door. Two brisk knocks, then the handle turned and he was there, striding into the bedroom, shouting, "Babe? Babe?"

Babe jumped up from her stool, swiftly swiped her lips with a lipstick, not a smudge or a smear, smoothed her shirt, and gazed at Truman with heartbreakingly helpless, uncertain eyes.

"How do I look?" she whispered.

"Perfect," he replied. For it was only the truth.

Grasping his hand for confidence, a gesture that touched his heart, she sucked in her stomach and took a big breath.

"Bill, darling!" she cooed in that soothing voice. She walked unhurriedly into her bedroom to greet her husband, as if she'd been sitting in a beauty parlor for hours, idly paging through a magazine. "Oh, I'm so glad you're home! I've simply been bored all day without you. Would you like a drink, darling? I know you would! I'll get it in a jiffy. Meanwhile, you remember Truman, don't you? You two go downstairs and wait for me in the drawing room. I'll just change quickly for dinner, and get you that drink before you know it."

Truman smiled, put out his hand. "Bill. I hope you don't mind that I borrowed your beautiful wife for the afternoon. But I return her to you now, no strings attached!"

William S. Paley, founder and chairman of the board of CBS, adviser to President Eisenhower, the man who discovered Bing Crosby, and Edward R. Murrow, and the zany redhead and her Cuban husband who were currently the most popular stars on that still-new medium called television, squinted down at the graceful, lily-white hand extended to him. He frowned at his wife, who stood before him, gazing worshipfully at him as if he were Zeus himself come down from Mount Olympus. He pulled himself up, all six feet, two inches of him, and grunted.

"I'm starving. What's for dinner?"

"Lamb chops—so tender you can eat them with a spoon!—and these adorable baby vegetables I found in the city, and brought out with me today in a little wicker basket. And potatoes, new and succulent, with butter and rosemary picked fresh just an hour ago." Babe narrated the upcoming meal with the crisp yet poetic professionalism of a food stylist, or a critic from *The New York Times*.

"All right." Suddenly Bill Paley smiled; it was an enormous, cocky, glad-to-see-you grin that crinkled up his eyes and made him seem, Truman thought at that moment, like a man who had just swallowed an entire human being. (Oh, that was very good, Truman said to himself; that was a keeper. *A man who had just swallowed an entire human being*——he filed it away in his photographic memory, to be used at a later date.)

Yet the grin was infectious, changing Bill Paley's whole demeanor; Truman couldn't help but grin back. "Come on, Truman, nice to see you again. I'll show you around. Don't take too long, Babe."

"Of course I won't, darling!" Babe laid her hand on her husband's arm and tiptoed up to give him a kiss on the cheek; she was only a couple of inches shorter than he, and Truman noticed, for the first time, that she was wearing flats. And that she always wore flats.

Bill Paley, still grinning, rubbing his hands together in anticipation of the meal ahead, turned on his heel, striding quickly out of the room. Not even turning to see if Truman was following, but something in the sureness of his gait, the way his arms swung, like a general's, indicating that he knew that Truman was. This was a man obviously used to barking out orders and having them followed.

And Truman did. With a quick, sympathetic glance at Babe, who rewarded him with another glimpse behind her mask of perfection——a small, involuntary little grimace.

But when she reappeared, not ten minutes later, in the perfectly appointed drawing room full of exquisite antiques, rare paintings, yet somehow so comfortable that sinking into one of the upholstered chairs was like sinking into a nap, she was as serene as ever. Wearing a column of silk, draped about her tall form like an exquisitely tailored toga, the neckline a deep slash to her sternum, a slim black belt encircling her nonexistent waist. Her makeup was perfect; not a hair was out of place. She looked as if she could glide into the Plaza ballroom.

Except for her feet. They were elegant, arched and bare, toe-nails glittering with a ruby-red polish. Brushing the top of her surprising pale feet, the hemline of her gown tinkled softly.

"Jingle bells!" Truman cried, so delighted he clapped his hands. The creature had sewn jingle bells into the hem of her couture gown!

"Shhh!" Babe put her finger to her lips, sharing the secret with a conspiratorial grin. And so she chimed, softly, faintly, Tinker Bell in Givenchy, wherever she glided—to and from the bar, handing Bill his drink, getting one for Truman, offering them both a silver plate of hors d'oeuvres that had magically appeared, making sure the fire was just the right temperature, turning on lamps that shone with the most amazing, flattering light—faintly pink, not white. Finally settling down at her husband's feet, her skirt rustling a musical crescendo, to remove his shoes, massage his insteps, and suggest, "Now tell me about your day, my darling. I want to know every detail. You look as if you've been through the wringer, poor baby."

Bill Paley, his tie off, his Italian shirt opened at the neck, a Manhattan in one hand, a crisp, bacon-wrapped fig in the other, didn't respond. He didn't even glance at the gorgeous creature kneeling at his feet. He did, however, study Truman with heavily lidded, reptilian eyes.

And Truman, watching the scene, frowned. His goddess, turned into a mere housewife.

If this was what her mother had trained her for, then God damn her soul.

"DARLING! YOU DON'T *KNOW*! YOU SIMPLY CAN'T UN-
derstand how glorious they were, those girls! They still *are*! But
when they first arrived, you simply can't appreciate the *sensation*
they made, all three of them—Betsey, Minnie, and Babe!"

"Then tell me, my pet, my divine one," Truman cooed, sitting,
with his legs tucked beneath him, on a fragile-looking yet sturdy
Oriental chair.

"Truman, I do have a job, you know. Although God knows
Hearst pays me pennies to do it."

Diana Vreeland, fashion editor, thrust her chin out and smiled
her monkey smile, a big, scarlet-rouged grin that made her ears
stick out even more prominently than usual. Her yellow teeth,
framed by viciously red lips, tore into the words with gusto. Her
black hair, so lacquered you couldn't see the individual strands, was
brushed severely back and held in a blue-black snood. An incon-
gruous wide satin bow corralled the front of her hair back from her
forehead. As she spoke, her long, tapered fingers flew and beckoned
and pronounced, punctuated by pointy red talons.

Truman was in her office at *Harper's Bazaar*. On her desk, on the credenza, flickered the jewel-toned, richly scented Rigaud candles every rich woman he knew favored. There were photos, drawings, bits of fabric in every hue and weight, hats, gloves, all pinned to the walls. As he sat, he had the distinct impression that hovering outside were armies of emaciated mannequins clad in the latest styles, waiting to be told "Yes—*divine!*" or "God, no, that's *ghastly!*" An entire world of fur and satin and cashmere and chiffon and silk, hemlines of dizzying lengths, exquisitely impractical shoes, nervous designers and languid models, all awaiting Mrs. Vreeland's pronouncement. Which she would surely give; she gazed at the world with those myopic, glittering, slanted eyes and passed judgment, editing, always editing—even life itself.

"But I wasn't quite aware then, you know," Truman reminded her. "I wasn't yet fully formed. An embryo, that's what I was! You must tell me. I have fallen in love, you see. Fallen in love with the most glorious creature and I simply must know more about her."

"Fallen in love?" Diana raised a perfectly arched eyebrow.

"Oh, yes! Truly! Not in the physical sense, of course, but if I could, she would be the One. Even as the idea is simply revolting. But, somehow, less revolting with Babe."

"You have no *idea* what you're talking about." Diana snorted.

Truman's eyes, usually so wide and sparkling with mischief, hardened. He set his jaw in a way few people ever saw—few of his society friends, anyway. Others were very well acquainted with that shrewd, determined look: His lover, Jack Dunphy. His friend from Monroeville, Nelle Harper Lee. His mother, Nina/Lillie Mae, certainly, had been on the wrong end of it in her lifetime. As had various schoolmates who went one step too far in their teasing and bullying. As had Humphrey Bogart, when he challenged Truman, on the set of *Beat the Devil*, to an arm-wrestling contest.

Humphrey Bogart, his wrist nearly snapped off his arm, never teased Truman Capote again.

"Yes, I do know what I'm talking about, as a matter of fact," Truman replied evenly.

Diana Vreeland shrugged. She refilled her cigarette holder from a silver box on her desk, struck a match, lit the cigarette, puffed, and leaned forward.

"Darling, it was like this," Diana began in her sandpaper bleat. And Truman smiled, closed his eyes—the better to imagine—and listened to

The Story of the
Three Beautiful Cushing Sisters

First, I suppose, we have to start with the mother. Gogs, that's what she was called by the girls—the most ordinary *woman, darling. Not a spark of anything to her, at first glance. A matron from Ohio, plump. Correct in every way—the* most *beautiful manners, which you see in the girls to this very day. But a hausfrau, a total* geisha *to that husband, Harvey Cushing. He was a genius, of course. Di-vine! Quite handsome, a surgeon. A* brain *surgeon! He absolutely invented brain surgery! And the mother, Gogs, she waited for him* forever *until he felt he was established. And, once married, provided him with the most serene house and life. Everything run perfectly, a real salon, in Boston, where he went to work, you know. (What a* ghastly *place is Boston, isn't it, darling? No imagination. Colorless. The clothes—well, let's not speak of the clothes.)*

And Gogs, she was shrewd. She knew that her two boys could fend for themselves, but her girls would never be truly accepted by Boston

society simply because she and Harvey weren't from there, and you know those Brahmins. It takes generations *to get in! And old Gogsie, she was determined that her three beautiful girls would marry the best. The very best—princes and shahs or, at the very least, mountains of money. Gobs and gobs of it. Betsey was the most like her mother; rather a mousy little thing, I sometimes think, until she gives you that imperious look down her nose. Betsey's the most mannered, in her way. As if she truly was the queen of England. She was the first to marry, to James Roosevelt. Son of FDR! The president's daughter-in-law! A brilliant match, of course! Except that James couldn't keep his pecker in his pants, and all but abandoned Betsey and their two little girls. But FDR adored her—adored her! Eleanor, of course, detested her. She didn't like Betsey taking her place by FDR's side, but then Eleanor was never there herself. What a dreary woman she is.*

("And a big ol' lez," said Truman.)

("Oh, darling, that's old news," said Diana. "But why *are* lesbians always so dowdy? I would love to know. It simply doesn't make sense—why, women dress for women, *anyway*! Everyone knows that.")

("Well, *I* don't know," Truman said, and sniffed. "It's not like we all have a club or anything.")

Anyway, Betsey's wedding to young Roosevelt was quite the coup, of course. It brought the Cushings into old New York—leapfrogging over stuffy old Boston!—the Roosevelts and the Knickerbockers and all that fabulous old musty society, which still counts, you know! Not as much as it used to, but it still does, good God, I would say so! And due to sister Betsey's marriage, Babe's coming-out party was held at the White House—so you'd think that Gogs would be satisfied. But she still had the other two to launch, and Betsey's marriage was in trouble. But I'll give the old girl this much—she always told those three girls to stick together, no matter what. And they did—they were a triumvirate! All slender, with those cutting cheekbones, like a ship's prow, although Minnie is too much of a scarecrow for my taste. A girl should have a little meat *on her bones, so the clothes will hang! But the most beautiful, of course, was Babe. Beautiful Babe: That's what they called her from the instant she was born. And the other two simply never were jealous of her, to hear them say it, but I think Betsey secretly is. Not Minnie—she's not got a jealous bone in her bony body. But Betsey used to be the queen, and now she isn't.*

But Babe had a dreadful car accident when she was nineteen, did you know?

(Truman, his eyes wide with horror, shook his head.)

Oh, yes! Legend has it the young man was so besotted *by her beauty, he turned to gaze at her and ran smack into a tree. Babe's face was horribly disfigured, apparently. But her father brought in the very best surgeons and patched it all up—you can't even tell! She's as beautiful as before. Maybe even more so.*

Betsey divorced Roosevelt. Then Minnie started her affair with Vincent Astor. The Cushing girls were truly in New York now—appearing at all the nightclubs, the charity functions. Gogsie didn't much like this, at first—Mother Cushing was Victorian, you see. From the time when a lady did not go out, get photographed, have her name in the papers. But this was in the forties when Café Society was really in*, of course. Cholly Knickerbocker's column—if you wanted a man, a real* catch*, as those girls did—as they were brought up to do!—you had to be seen in the right places, be in the newspapers. So those girls stuck together, and brother, what an entrance they made! The three of them entering the Stork Club—Golly!* What *a sight! Regal Betsey, the former Roosevelt; tall, kind Minnie, whom everyone knew was sleeping with Vincent Astor on top of simply piles and piles of money. And Babe. The beauti-*

ful, sweet Babe, whom I've never heard say a cruel word about anybody. And in New York! Babe was always wearing the latest fashions, not that she could afford them; brother, she could not! *Pops Cushing lost all his money in the Crash. But Babe was given these* gorgeous *clothes by simply everyone, because she made exquisite clothes look heavenly and they all wanted her to wear their fashions, knowing they'd be photographed and in the newspapers. Babe even worked here at the* Bazaar, *for a time, then at* Vogue—*as a fashion editor. She was quite the little career girl. She even had an affair or two—I do sometimes think she was happiest then. She took her work very seriously, unlike most of those society girls who are hired just for their names and connections. Babe had those, of course, but she worked hard, that girl. She went on shoots, modeled some herself. But with Gogs pulling the strings, it was only a matter of time before Babe married, too. And she did, to young Stanley Mortimer. Standard Oil heir. Tuxedo Park—you know, that true old-money Protestant background, good* golly!

And Babe quit her job then, and had two children. Gogs finally threatened Vincent Astor, and he married Minnie. Then Betsey got the catch of them all—Jock Whitney! So Gogs had a Mortimer, an Astor, and a Vanderbilt-Whitney in the family.

Then Babe divorced Stanley Mortimer. Well, she had to! *He came back from the war an absolute* wreck! *Not that he was all right even before. There were rumors that he hit her, plus all his money was tied up in trust, which Babe didn't know before the marriage. But Babe, true to her mother's training, never let on. Those girls were* bred, *you see.* Bred! *Like show horses! Appearance matters most. Loyal families. No troubles. Stick together, put on a happy—perfectly made-up—face! Never air your dirty laundry. So you'd see Babe, impeccably dressed, so beautiful, going about as usual, but still, there was a sadness in her eyes—*

("I see it still," Truman whispered.)

("Well, she has pots of money now and I've never heard of Bill hitting her, so I don't know why," Diana scoffed.)

Anyway, divorce. I really think Gogs did not approve of divorce, and yet all three of her daughters have had one. Gogs probably thought, Well, if I had to put up with a sorry old so-and-so who never cared about me except for how I ran his house and made him comfortable, so can they! *But those sisters are more modern, of course. And in the end, except for Minnie, they each traded up—Cadillac for Rolls-Royce! Betsey traded a Roosevelt for a Whitney and all that divine cash. And Babe, well—good God! William S. Paley! He runs everything—the world! Of course, he's Jewish. That's the puzzling thing. Babe, marrying a Jew. It killed her mother, truly. Poor old Gogs died a couple years after. Oh, by then I think she was reconciled to the money—good God, who wouldn't be? Rich as* Croesus, *Paley is! But the Jewish thing . . . well. But Babe doesn't mind. I think she takes it as a challenge. You don't want us? Well, then we'll make our own society, even better. And she has! Although she was dropped off the Social Register, of course,* tout de suite. *And there are clubs that simply won't have them. But Babe is* determined. *Rot in hell, those who won't have us! Although Babe would never say such a thing. Too well bred. Too damn nice.*

After Gogs died, Minnie divorced Astor. Well, who wouldn't, really, except for all that money? Vincent Astor was one cold fish, only interested in his toy railroads, if you can believe that*! True to form, though, Minnie found him his next wife before she left. Those women do know how to take care of their men! Now Minnie's married to Jim Fosburgh, the artist. Although he's queer, isn't he? You would know.*

"Darling Mrs. Vreeland," Truman cooed, with just a hint of ice behind his lisp. "As I told you, we are not all members of one big club. Believe it or not, I do not know the name, rank, and serial number of every homosexual in Manhattan."

"But you do know about Jim Fosburgh, don't you?" Diana asked serenely.

Truman sighed. "Yes, I do. He is."

"Of course. I think Minnie's a bit of a lez, too, if you ask me. But that breeding and training. Never would she admit it, probably not even to herself."

"I have no patience for people like that," Truman snapped.

Diana looked at him, her eyes gleaming in admiration. "No, I see. True to yourself, that's who you are, Truman. And God bless you. You are a *champion*! Now, when are you going to give us another story here at the *Bazaar*? You know I don't run that particular show—God, I barely even read!—but circulation is always up when we run one of yours."

"Darling, you'll be the first to know. In fact, I'm working on something now. A delicious story. But I'm not going to share a word of it yet. It's too soon." He rose, stretched, way up on his tiptoes, glimpses of his crimson socks peeking out beneath the turned-up hem of his plaid pants. He wrapped a scarlet scarf around his throat with a flourish. Then he leapt around the desk to hug Mrs. Vreeland, who did not generally allow hugs, but with Truman, of course, exceptions were made.

"You are a dear dragon lady. The dearest! And I mean it in the most *admirable* way. I happen to love dragon ladies. They are fiercely protective of those they love."

"Truman, you could charm the rattle off a snake," Diana Vreeland pronounced. "I'm going to lunch at Le Pavillon. Will you join me?"

"No, my dearest dragon lady, I'm going to work now. On that story. Another time. And do not gossip without me, do you hear? Don't go to any dives or pick up any sailors. No naughtiness without me, Mrs. Vreeland!"

Diana laughed, her great, echoing "ha ha," every guffaw as articulated as every syllable she spoke. Truman turned to go, hands in pockets, golden head bent in thought. So lost in contemplation was he, he didn't even notice that, indeed, hovering outside of Mrs. Vreeland's office were hordes of emaciated mannequins clad in the latest fashions, nervously awaiting their reckoning.

He got into a cab and told the driver, "Brooklyn Heights." And the cab carried him across the bridge, up up up and then down down down, away from Neverland, from Mother Goose, from Oz.

It pulled up in front of a canary-yellow townhouse on a quiet, tree-lined street. Truman paid the fare and walked down into a basement apartment.

And then he went to work.

TRUMAN
AT WORK

S O MANY WANTED TO CATCH HIM AT IT! WATCH AS GE-
nius burned! Not his fellow authors, of course; *they* were far too
blasé and jaded to care. But his swans, in particular, all longed to see
Truman Capote write. They went out of their way to offer him
help—for if they weren't patrons of the arts, then who were they?

They weren't patrons of the arts.

But Gloria offered him his own beach villa at her place in Palm
Beach. Slim provided him with hampers of food from 21 so he
would be properly nourished. Pamela offered to sit at his feet, literally, a muse. Marella invited him to work on her yacht, bobbing up
and down in the Mediterranean.

Truman refused. As much as he loved and appreciated their
lives, their comforts, their wealth and bounty, when it came to his
work, he displayed a monastic discipline none of his new friends
could have suspected. Work was work; play was play. And never
the twain shall meet.

Except—

Well, perhaps there was a time ahead when they could; he wondered. There were marvelous stories here, ripe for the picking. And if Truman wasn't a storyteller, then who was he?

Truman was a storyteller.

But for now, the story he was telling was not theirs, although he already knew they would all want to lay claim to it when it was done. But this particular story was entirely of his own invention; he resented the implication by so many that he could write only from his own life. *Other Voices, Other Rooms*—why, that wasn't autobiographical at all! It was a story. Made up in his own mind. The story of a young boy without a family, without a home, seduced into darkness, born into light—but the darkness beckoning, always beckoning.

No, his first novel wasn't autobiographical at all.

And this new story; he had an idea for a title. He'd heard a sailor on leave, during the war, tell another sailor that he'd take him to breakfast at the most expensive place in town. Where did he want to go?

"Well," the naïve sailor had replied, "I always heard that Tiffany's was the most expensive place in New York."

Breakfast at Tiffany's. It was a great title, that much Truman knew. Beyond that—

Truman gathered up a notebook. A simple composition book with lined paper. He sharpened his pencils, settled in on a velvet sofa beneath a window, and propped up the notebook on his knees.

His forehead furrowed, he read what he had written the day before, the words in his tiny, squared-off handwriting, meticulous, spare.

"Listen, Fred, you've got to cross your heart and kiss your elbow—"

And Truman was lost in the words. Awash in sentence structure, agonizing over punctuation. Studying the picture on the page; rearranging paragraph breaks so that there was just enough white space. Going back and forth, in his mind, between the words *approximation* and *facsimile* until finally choosing *approximation*.

Perhaps contortionists can kiss their elbow; she had to accept an approximation.

Truman worked through the entire afternoon, then stopped. Some internal alarm inside him, as nascent as the primordial switch that turns winter to spring, simply said, "Enough. Enough for today. One more word and you will question everything you've written so far." And he put the notebook and pencil away on his desk, scratched himself in those patient places that required scratching, having been ignored all day, and went into the kitchen, where Jack was flinging pots and pans about, preparing dinner. Gruffly. Which was how Jack approached life.

Gruffly.

"Good day's work?" Jack grumbled, viciously grinding pepper over a flank steak.

"Hmm-mmm." Truman reached for the cocktail shaker with one hand, the vodka with another. "I'll read you some tonight, if you want."

"Sure."

"And you?"

"It's rubbish. It always is."

"It's not. And you just want me to tell you that, so stop fishing. By the way, the Paleys invited us both to Kiluna this weekend."

"I don't want to go."

"Jack."

"I don't like those people."

"Jack, you've not even met them."

"Yes, I have. In various guises over the years. They're all the same. Phonies."

"No, they're not, Holden Caulfield. The Paleys are different. Babe is, for sure. And Bill, well, I think he might be, too. There's something about him."

"They distract you," Jack growled. "They're not worthy of you. I have no idea why you're so fascinated with the rich and famous and pretentious."

"But they're beautiful, Jack! Their lives are so quietly beautiful, devoted to graciousness, taste, decorum. I admire that—I think that's the epitome of living, to be able to create art out of your life. It's what we do, in a way, isn't it? In writing?"

"Hardly." Jack flung the pepper grinder down with a snort. Jack, tall and freckled and lean, reddish-blond hair balding, glared down at Truman, short and pale and lean, blond hair receding. "I can't bear the thought of you comparing yourself, with your talent, to them. It's ridiculous. And I thought you said you despised Paley, after that weekend with those parasites."

"Well, I barely know him. I should be fair."

"Men like that don't deserve your charity, Truman. People in general don't."

"Oh, my misanthropic darling." Truman sighed, putting his arms about Jack's waist, allowing one hand to slide between the waistband of his pants and warm, yielding flesh. "What would you do without me to shine light on your dark and dreary world?"

"I did just fine without you, before," Jack growled. But he did not throw off Truman's embrace. The two leaned into each other for a moment, surrendering to blissful, ordinary domesticity—oil sizzling in a pan on the stove, fragrant rosemary in a pot on the windowsill, their two dogs warming their ankles with their heavy, stupid dog breathing. A quiet meal ahead, a martini or two, reading in bed before the lights were out. Familiar yearnings satisfied by familiar bodies; Jack had been a dancer, which never ceased to thrill Truman as he traced those muscles still retaining their disciplined sculpture, those battered feet with their astonishingly high arches. Truman's body was much less disciplined but still wiry, with a surprising hardness of the abdomen and biceps, so slender that lanky, raw-boned Jack could almost put two hands about his lover's waist—"like Scarlett O'Hara," Truman liked to boast. Then sleep, in their ordinary basement apartment in ordinary Brooklyn Heights, Manhattan and all its tempting glitter safely across the bridge, for now.

It should have been enough, Truman knew. Enough to be with Jack, wrapped in his arms, satiated and sleepy, a good day's work behind him, another ahead. He had projects galore on his plate, because he was Truman Capote, literary darling: a trip to the Soviet Union with a touring company of *Porgy and Bess* paid for and the resulting story to be published by *The New Yorker,* his old employer (and his first real publishing disappointment, long ago but never forgotten). *House of Flowers,* based on one of his short stories, was still running on Broadway, even though it was only a matter of time before it closed. *Breakfast at Tiffany's* was simmering, percolating, proceeding one agonizing word at a time.

He was at the top of his game, he knew. He'd never doubted he'd be there, not even when he'd been fired from *The New Yorker.* And he loved a darling man, who loved him in return—in his own gruff way.

But it wasn't enough, and late that night, as Truman turned away from a softly snoring Jack, there was a dancing flame inside of him that would not be extinguished, could never be extinguished no matter how many sleeping pills he took. No matter how many times he told himself that it could be lit again by the morning sun. But there was always *more*. More beauty to be seen, more places to travel, more acclaim to be won. More love to earn, to barter, to exchange or withhold. To miss, always.

Outside, looking in. Why did he always feel that way, every moment of every day?

Even when he was at the center of attention, standing at a lectern reading, slicing into a cake with the cover of his book depicted in the icing—it was never completely his. There were always other things going on; two heads bent in conversation in a dark corner of the room; a secret smile between lovers; a peal of laughter prompted by a joke he hadn't heard. People exchanging telephone numbers— not his. A whispered "I'll get a taxi for us all," and suddenly a group of four had vanished with a hurried waggle of their fingers in his direction, blown kisses in perfumed air that never quite reached his cheek.

Leaving him behind. He was always left behind.

So he had to try harder. Be more. Be better, more sparkling, more vibrant—a spotlight shining up to the heavens, lighting the dark, drawing everyone to his brilliant beacon. If he only dressed a little more outrageously—why not a velvet cape to go with a velvet suit? If he only danced a little more vigorously—doing the Charleston when everyone else was doing the two-step. If he only leapt into a room, arms outspread, legs kicking up behind him, instead of merely walking into it.

If he only told the best stories, dished the most delicious gossip, dropped the grandest of names.

Then, perhaps. Then. Would he truly belong?

Would Mama come get him so that it would be the two of them, finally? And he would be loved, embraced, and see only pride and understanding in those eyes, those shining, shining eyes, brown, almost black, peering out of a face sculpted out of marble, high cheekbones, aquiline nose, a slender neck, a swan's neck, black, black eyes like a swan, feathers ruffling, arms beckoning.

Babe's eyes. He began to relax, finally, thinking of Babe's eyes, and how they looked at him, and only him; how they shared a hurt deeper, maybe, than his own.

And how they might shine with love. True love. True Heart.

Truman.

And finally, thankfully, he was asleep.

BABE, IN HER LOFTY pied-à-terre at the St. Regis hotel, Fifty-fifth and Fifth Avenue, the epicenter of glittering Manhattan, was not.

Bill, in bed beside her, had taken up the entire mattress with his tall, restless body. Hard, unyielding—and a stranger to her now. Two children together, and that was enough; she didn't mind that. Two with him, two with Stanley; Babe was a mother of four. Yes, that was enough.

But Babe, idealized and idolized, perpetually on the "Best Dressed" lists, always mentioned in columns that began, "The most beautiful women in New York," was not desired by her own husband. Oh, yes—coveted, perhaps. Prized. Displayed, like one of his Picassos. "Mr. and Mrs. William S. Paley," dazzling together at charity events, balls, highly sought after at dinner parties.

But Babe was not *desired.* Holding herself still, so stiff and light she wondered if she even made an imprint on the mattress, she knew only rejection, colder than the air conditioner blowing stale Manhattan air over her body. Bill hadn't reached for her tonight, as he hadn't last night, nor any night that she could remember. It wasn't as if sex was something she craved; frankly, sex with Bill was strictly a one-sided affair. She couldn't even remember it, to tell the truth—no real details, no exquisite rapture, no lovely, sated feeling after. But rejection is rejection is rejection, as Gertrude Stein might have said. And the truth was that Bill Paley rejected his own wife's body, if not her needs. Babe! Beautiful Babe! Rejected like a common wallflower by her own husband, whose roving eye was legendary.

She thought bitterly of those who had wanted her. Condé Nast, back when she worked for *Vogue*. How many times had he chased her around his desk? And he was quite handsome for his age, she could now realize. Very trim, sharply chiseled features. But at the time she thought him absurd, old enough to be her grandfather.

And Serge! Serge Obolensky! She'd adored Serge, loved his passion, his exoticism—a real Russian prince!—yet he was so courtly. Quite old-fashioned, yet so dashingly handsome with that little brush of a mustache that tickled; suddenly Babe couldn't keep still on her side of the bed. She squirmed, flexed her toes, stretched her hamstrings, turned over so that her pelvis pressed into the mattress, remembering how Serge kissed her one day, the two of them lying, entwined, upon a gorgeous velvet swooning couch in his apartment. A kiss so deep, stirring so many yearnings. And she would have given in to them, too, had she been able to stifle her mother's voice in her head.

But that she could never do. "Sit up straight." "Don't fidget." "Write a thank-you note the minute you receive a gift or return home from a party." "Always have fresh flowers, no matter the cost." "Clean gloves and shoes are the sign of a lady." "Never let the help get the upper hand." "Be discreet." "Be above gossip."

"Be a perfect little angel for Papa, because he's so rarely home, and when he is, he wants to see only the very best of you." "Be a perfect little debutante because sister Betsey is now married to the president's son." "Be a perfect little wife to Stanley, because he's old money, Tuxedo Park."

"Be a perfect wife to Bill, even if he is a Jew. Because that's what he's paying for, and if you're not perfect, he'll replace you so fast your head will spin, and then where will you be? Divorced twice, with four children and no money of your own."

"Be perfect. Because that's what people expect of you now. Because what are you, if not that? *Who* are you?"

Perfect. Babe must be perfect, in every way. She had been born to be a rich man's wife, decorative, an asset. She never remembered being allowed to dream of anything else. When she was very small, Betsey and Minnie—Minnie nine years older, Betsey seven—allowed her to play at being a flower girl for their fabulously staged weddings. It was the only pretend play that her mother sanctioned. "Now let Babe catch the bouquet," her mother would admonish her older sisters. "Babe has to catch the bouquet, so that she'll be next."

Babe didn't want to catch the bouquet. She wanted to pretend that she was someone else—Odeal, that was the name she told her brothers and sisters to call her, while she pretended to be an ordinary scullery maid, dirtying her hands, calling them "m'lord" and "m'lady" in a terrible cockney accent. Odeal was an orphan, admired by all for her pluck and wit.

But her mother was so furious, she forbade anyone to talk to Babe while she was pretending to be Odeal. "Do not encourage her," her mother hissed. "We can't have that kind of behavior. What will people think?"

Babe gave up being Odeal, after a while. She couldn't remember just when her imagination left her, flew away like a bird; she just knew she was happy being alone, in her own dreamy world, for a time. And then she was not; she missed her sisters telling her what to do, her brothers coaxing her along in their games. She burned with shame at the dinner table, when no one would speak to her or pass her the salt. So she gave it up, and accepted that she was Babe, only Babe. She would never be anyone else, anything other than what her mother wanted for her. She willed herself not to imagine or dream, because there was no profit in it. The only profit was in being the best, most perfect little girl in the world, then the best, most perfect debutante, then the best, most perfect wife. Because if she wasn't perfect, precisely who others expected her to be, no one would talk to her. Or even acknowledge her existence. She would simply wink out, disappear like a vapor.

All that energy she'd had as a child, as Odeal—she remembered running just to feel the wind blow through her hair; she recalled rolling down a hill, miraculously not getting grass stains on her dress, and she was so thankful for that, she never did it again, but oh, the dizziness! The delicious head rush, the scratching of twigs against her cheek, the feeling that the sky was on the bottom and the earth was on top but she remained where she was, by some mysterious force called gravity—all that energy, she learned to channel into the one thing she could count on, as her mother drilled her over and over. Her face, her appearance, her decorative quality. Her mother never stinted on praise when it came to how Babe looked, if her clothes were neat and pressed, if her skin was clear and her cheeks flushed and her hair glossy. If she attracted the stares of the rich young men she met at her sisters' parties and dances.

Even now, now that she was forty and Gogs was dead, she felt the heavy weight of her mother's admonitions, her quick disapproval, her religious appreciation of beauty and grace and manners. The pulse-racing terror that if she didn't live up to everyone's expectations, she would be shunned, abandoned. So Babe had to rise early, long before Bill, to put on her makeup and take out her hairpins, so he would see her at her absolute best when he awoke. As he always had, and always would. And to tell the truth, she was dependent on her cosmetics as others might be dependent on alcohol, in a tactile, pleasurable way. She loved the faint, flowery smell of her favorite blush; she delighted in the heavy silver of the brushes, the silkiness of the bristles against her skin. She enjoyed applying foundation, personally mixed for her by Elizabeth Arden herself, taking the sponge and dabbing it on her skin, each dab like a scale of armor, of power. She never grew tired of seeing her cheekbones come into sculpted glory with each swipe of the brush; she stared into the mirror as she blended and stroked and dabbed, and little by little, like pointillism, her face, the face she knew and depended on, emerged into a complete portrait. Perfection.

No one had ever seen her without makeup. Not even Bill on their wedding night. Just the thought of showing a bare face to the world—Babe squirmed again, turning away from Bill as if he could read her thoughts and might wake up, despite the fact that he was still snoring steadily. This was one reason why she didn't like the tiny apartment at the St. Regis; she and Bill had to share a bed, as there were only three rooms. At least at Kiluna, and the summer house up in New Hampshire, and in Round Hill, their place in Jamaica, they had separate bedrooms. So there was never a chance he might awaken in the middle of the night and see her naked, exposed: imperfect.

Had she ever loved Bill enough to show him her true self? Had she ever loved anyone? Or was this another of her defects, something else to hide from the world beneath the latest Chanel jacket? She didn't know if she loved her husband, although she appreciated him, and enjoyed his company, and ached to be touched by him, noticed, wanted for something other than being a very glamorous concierge.

Which was what Babe was, really.

And so, every morning, her makeup and hair immaculate, clad in a fresh negligee and fabulous quilted housecoat, she sat at her desk and compiled her lists. First, she planned all the day's meals, resigning herself to hours of scavenging in the most obscure markets for some new, exotic vegetable or fruit to tempt him. Bill loved food, had a voracious appetite, ate several meals a day. She had to make sure they were memorable, each and every one. Seated at the dinner table, she took notes in her custom-made palm-sized notebook from Tiffany's, jotting down Bill's comments about the food, what he liked, what he didn't. So that next time, she would not repeat any mistakes.

She had lists pertaining to clothes—Bill's blue suit needed its buttons tightened. His shoes needed polishing. Her coats needed storing. The lace on her negligees needed repairing.

Her mind, even knowing how early she had to rise, was a list now, as she rolled back on her side, gingerly, so as not to disturb her husband. Tomorrow night was dinner at Quo Vadis with the Guinnesses. Bill wanted her to pick him up at the office before. She must send the chauffeur out to buy supplies to take back to Kiluna this weekend: mundane, necessary supplies such as toilet paper and cleaning sprays and new hand towels for all the guest bathrooms—supplies Bill would never imagine needed to be procured. His hand reached—for a bar of soap, a paper clip, a length of toilet paper to wipe his ass. And it was there. Because of her, Babe, concierge extraordinaire. And he never, ever thanked her for it.

She began to grind her teeth, even as her mind raced on. Her hair needed to be done by Kenneth tomorrow, before the weekend. The Agnellis had had to cancel their visit to Kiluna, so she must find a replacement couple, because Bill couldn't stand it if the house was less than full, the weekend less than jam-packed with activities. If he despised anything more than pontificating newsmen and disgruntled advertisers, it was boredom. Which reminded her, she must buy a new pair of tennis shoes because she'd torn her old ones playing softball last weekend. Every Saturday, either the Paleys or the Whitneys—sister Betsey and her husband, Jock, whose weekend home was adjacent to the Paleys' in Manhasset, Long Island—hosted a softball game for their combined guests.

Softball. Babe wrinkled her nose. She detested the sport, but Bill didn't know. He'd never know, for she played it determinedly, a serene smile on her face, taking care not to get dirt on her pressed dungarees or muss up her makeup, which she had to set with a spritz of water to ensure it would last outside. How she'd torn her tennis shoes, she had no idea, but after the game, as they all sat out on the veranda with tall, cool drinks—Pimm's Cups—she'd noticed it and quickly excused herself to go change, before Bill or anyone else could see.

Truman had immediately followed her, though. He'd played surprisingly well, fielding balls with a fawnlike grace, and Bill had even given him a rare "atta boy!" when he'd hit a home run. But she'd known that Truman had detested playing as much as she had; they'd exchanged looks in the outfield. He'd made such a funny, wry face that she'd laughed out loud.

Truman.

He'd join them again this weekend; he'd promised, crossing his heart as solemnly as a child. And the realization finally allowed her to relax her limbs, so stiff her joints ached; her jaw, too, was released so that she was no longer grinding her false teeth, a necessity after that long-ago car accident—Babe shuddered at the memory, still. Always. Her hand reached up to trace a line along her jaw, where the skin was just slightly tougher, imperceptibly raised; her neck began to throb, reminded of how long she'd had to hold it still in that hospital bed, not move a muscle, or else. *"Don't you want to look as beautiful as before, Babe? Hold still, or you'll scar even more. And we can't have that, can we, dear? Your face is your fortune."*

Who'd said that? Papa or Mother? It was so long ago. The scars remained, though. Only Babe had ever seen them. And her teeth—oh, how she hated having false teeth! It was so cruel to be reminded of the inevitability of old age, teeth in a glass, when you're only nineteen, as she had been. And no matter how much she spent, how many new dentists she saw, the teeth were always the same. They ached incessantly, rubbing against her gums, forcing her to nibble at food; she'd not bitten into an apple since before the accident. She had no choice but to sleep in them, whenever Bill shared her bed.

But, of course, he didn't. Not in the most intimate sense, the most coveted, beloved sense. And no one knew this. No one. She was lonely in her own home, in her own bed—in her own skin— and she couldn't tell a soul. "Don't air your dirty laundry outside the family," Mother had said a million times.

But Truman. Did he suspect? The way he looked at her, adoringly—but more. Or was it less? Sympathetically. Under- standingly. He'd actually taken the time, that first weekend at Kiluna, to write down a reading list for her—suspecting the truth. That Babe was unfinished, as most decorative objects are; scratch the surface and all you see is a blank piece of porcelain or a canvas. And that she was ashamed of it, deep down.

"Just for you, Bobolink. I think you would enjoy these books. A mind, a heart, can't be neglected."

How did he know? They'd not discussed much of anything, beyond his childhood. After Bill had come home, and she hadn't been ready for him, the rest of the weekend had passed in a blur of company and arrangements, meals and games and drinks and minor crises, like the mystifying disappearance of one of the game cups for the Parcheesi set, a dress strap of Slim's breaking, requiring a last-minute stitching before Saturday's dinner. She and Truman hadn't had another opportunity for conversation, although she had longed for it the entire weekend.

And yet, before he left, he'd presented her with this reading list; *Madame Bovary* had been underlined twice. His eyes, behind the thick black-framed spectacles he wore while reading, were preternaturally wise and solemn, studying her as she scanned the list. Seeing right through her—the makeup, the clothes she'd picked out so carefully. He didn't notice all that, didn't care for it, except to admire her artistry. But surface wasn't what mattered, not to Truman. Was it?

She wished that it wasn't. She shut her eyes, determined to dream that it wasn't. For Babe longed to confide—her true self, her hopes, her fears, yes, even her imperfections, Odeal in middle age—in someone; she yearned for it so desperately that her heart swelled with pent-up fears and frustrations to the point where she wondered if it could be seen beneath her tailored shirts and couture dresses, this pulsating, swollen, disgusting sac of desire. If the world only knew! Perfect Babe. Full of ugliness on the inside, teetering on the side of her bed, unable to sleep; unloved, unwanted.

Except by Truman. She had known it from the first moment they'd met, on the plane. Someone had arrived. Someone very important to her. How does one know that, before the first hello? It's a heaviness in the air combined with a lightness of step. It's a slowing down of the past, and a speeding up of the future. A desire to both giggle and cry. A table for two, not one. But tucked away in the darkest corner of the restaurant, curtains drawn tight about it, the table groaning with enough wine to loosen tongues and hearts.

"Don't air your dirty laundry," her mother whispered in her ear, one last time, as Babe's mind finally slowed down, welcoming blanketing, numbing sleep.

"But Truman doesn't count," she protested softly, even in her drowsiness taking care not to disturb a sleeping Bill.

"Truman. He might be a friend, I think. And I haven't had a friend in so long."

And Babe finally went to sleep.

. . . . .

TELL ME ABOUT—YOUR FIRST KISS.

"A boy in second grade." Babe grinned slyly. "He told me I was too pretty not to kiss, so, of course, I let him! Mother sent me to private girls' school after that."

"A boy in second grade," Truman said, and cackled. "Me, too! He didn't tell me I was too pretty. He had no idea what I was doing to him. Neither did I! But I saw his lips, his rosy lips, and I simply had to taste them, to see if they tasted like roses or cherries— something candied. Something sweet. I was hungry for that, for sweetness. In my life."

"And did they? Taste sweet?"

"No. They were lifeless, stunned. Flat as old champagne. It was the greatest disappointment of my childhood."

Tell me about—your favorite pet as a child.

"My dog, Bobo. I loved that dog! He was a black poodle. He wasn't supposed to sleep with me, but I always snuck him up when no one was looking. Betsey knew, and once, because I'd borrowed a sweater from her and ruined it, she told Mother. Bobo was banished outdoors after that, for good. I guess he ran away. Like most dogs do." Babe, whose gaze had been so grave and thoughtful, suddenly smiled. "I haven't thought of Bobo in years. We have English bulldogs now. Bill thinks they're very chic. Purebred, of course, kept in heated and air-conditioned kennels. I don't even know all their names. Someone else takes care of them, and brings them in once a day to be petted, maybe walked, if I'm about to take some exercise. It's not the same, though, at all." And her eyes widened, as if realizing this for the first time. "We have dogs. But we don't have pets."

"We had so many animals back in Monroeville! Sook had a fat old bird she kept in a cage in the kitchen. I always had a lizard or two in a shoe box. Cats simply draped themselves about the house, on the porch, the windowsills, the eaves and rain barrels. Most everyone had an old hound dog, just because. That's how the South is. I don't know that I had a favorite, though. I finally persuaded Jack to let me have a dog about a year ago. Now the dog loves Jack more than he loves me—typical!" Truman laughed, but there was a hollowness to it that made Babe impulsively grasp his hand in sympathy.

"Why do they always love the one that doesn't love them?"

Truman shrugged. "Bitches. We're all the same, after all."

Tell me about—your guiltiest pleasure.

"Sex," Truman said immediately, his eyes sparkling. His pink tongue darted between his white teeth, and he licked his lips, as if tasting candy on his own flesh.

"That doesn't count," Babe retorted, squirming slightly even as she managed to look very prissy. Like the most fabulously dressed Puritan, her Roman nose tilted very high, her fastidiously lipsticked mouth pursed. Truman noticed her discomfort. And said nothing, for the time being.

"All right, then," he drawled. "Chocolate milk shakes. I adore chocolate milk shakes, with whipped cream and sprinkles."

Babe's eyes widened. "I do, too! Ice cream of any kind! Oh, we should go to Berthillon in Paris sometime!"

"Paris would be too *magnifique* with you! We could go to the Latin Quarter and see the most divinely decadent shows, and then go backstage and talk to the girls and boys. I love talking to them. They have the most fascinating stories, you know."

"I, well—" Babe frowned. Of course, she could never do that! Bill would have a fit! What if someone recognized her and took her picture? What on earth would people say? Oh, but it would be fun, wouldn't it? Although entirely out of the question.

Tell me about—your most amazing accomplishment.

"It's not yet happened." Truman tilted that stubborn chin, steeled those blue eyes. "But it will. The Pulitzer. Of course."

"Of course," Babe agreed, thrilled. That her friend, her intimate new friend, would win a Pulitzer Prize! That she should know someone—be sitting by the side of her pool at Round Hill with him, their bare feet cooling off in the silky water—who was an intellectual, a writer of such stature! How had this happened? No one in her life, save her father, had ever been what you could call an intellectual. Not even Bill, for all that he had accomplished. Bill moved through life like a shark, fueled by sheer instinct. His instincts were sound—miraculous, even—but still. One of his most endearing traits was that he was the first to admit he did not have the kind of mind of, say, an Ed Murrow. That was why Bill worshipped Murrow so, had tried to emulate him to the point of wearing the same trench coat and hat, London-made, when they first became friends during the war.

But Truman, with his shrewd eyes, his interest in everything yet an ability to home in on the most intriguing, unusual aspect, his talent for understanding people and what made them tick, his vast knowledge of literature and craft, his precise, yet expansive vocabulary—Truman was an intellectual, she was certain of it. An intellectual with a love of gossip and high society and low life, to be sure. But still an intellectual. And he was her friend.

Hers, not Bill's. She'd seen him first.

"My greatest accomplishment?" Babe repeated the question. "My children, of course."

"No. That's bourgeois. No woman should mistake nature for an accomplishment. It's distasteful, this emphasis on reproduction. It's biological, and that is all. Besides, I've never met your children, so how can you be so proud of them?"

Babe colored. "I am. All mothers are."

"Yet you let others care for them? You leave them all week, while you're in the city or traveling, and they stay out at Kiluna with their keepers?"

"It's better that way, Truman. More stability. And there's no room for them in the apartment, you know."

"And whose idea was that? To live in such a tiny little space with no room for anybody else?"

"Bill's," Babe admitted, her throat suddenly tight, unwilling to allow the disloyal words. "Bill wanted that. It's close to his office."

"What about you?"

"You don't understand. Bill needs me, and women always go where they're needed. I have to take care of him. I have to make sure he eats well, and is entertained, looked after."

"Your children need you. They need you to take care of them, even with all the nurses and nannies. Children need their mothers, Babe. Oh, honey, that is one thing I do know!"

"Stop!" Babe held up her hand, her breath coming heavily, gearing up for flight. "I don't—how dare you say these things?"

"I say these things because I'm your friend," Truman replied with a shrug that threw off her anger and bewilderment—and with a smile that melted the ice threatening to encase her.

And then she knew, with a clarity that echoed some long-forgotten childhood sense of justice, of knowing right from wrong, because it was the simplest thing, because it was *true*. She knew that he was right. And that he *had* the right to say this to her.

Because Truman is your friend. Truman is a real friend, the only one who has ever talked to you like this. The only one who cares enough to tell you the truth. The only one who wants to see past the surface. This moment is important. It is the template for the rest of your life. Don't run away from it.

"I'm not used to having friends," Babe finally confessed, kicking a foot up so that it broke the surface of the water, like a porpoise. "I have acquaintances."

"Not anymore," Truman said solemnly. He crooked his little finger and held it out to her. "Best friends. Pinkie swear."

Babe smiled, and crooked her own finger through his. "Pinkie swear." Then her heart—that swollen sac of regret—tore, and she felt something slide down her cheek. She swiped away a tear, as astonished to see it as she would have been to see a lizard floating in the clarion-blue pool, as blue as Montego Bay itself, just down the lush, verdant hill. The air was silky, warm on winter-parched skin; Truman was paler than smoke, while Babe's flesh was tawny, from years spent following the annual migration of her flock—several long stays each winter in the Caribbean, summers in the country, an annual yachting trip in the Mediterranean. A year spent chasing the sun, in golden chariots. "I've never done that before—pinkie swear, I mean. Not with my sisters. Not with my children."

"There are a lot of things you've never done before, but that you'll do with me. I just know it. We're good for each other, Bobolink. Perfect, actually. We're so alike."

And Babe, searching the face of her new friend, so brash and confident, yet because he believed in that confidence, touchingly vulnerable, wasn't so sure. And then, suddenly, she was. Because, of course, that was how she'd recognized him in the first place, when he, all five feet four of him, wrapped in an absurd plaid scarf, his hands nonchalantly in his pockets as he stood in the front of her plane, blinked to adjust his eyesight from the dark outside to the light within.

He was exactly like her. Rare and exotic and yet so completely messy and ordinary. Disgustingly ordinary. So ordinary that great pains must be taken to disguise the fact, to protect the feelings of those who invested so much in exoticism and perfection.

How could anyone else but the two of them ever know the cost?

"Let's get out of here." Truman stood up, shook his tiny white feet, and helped Babe rise. "I want to buy you something. A present—it's only proper. Your hospitality, as advertised, is legendary and I have to pay you back."

"No, Truman, you don't have to. You have already given me more than you can know."

Truman threw his arms about her.

"Of course you'd say that! But still, isn't there some divinely picturesque market around here? I've heard so much about the colorful Jamaicans—I want to see some! It's exquisite up here on your mountain, but a tad—well, you know."

"A tad isolated and exclusive?" Babe laughed; just down the hill from their cottage was Noël Coward's. And up the hill, Oscar Hammerstein sometimes vacationed. "Yes, there's a lovely little market down the hill in Montego Bay. I'll drive—it will be fun. I so rarely get to."

Babe went inside the luxurious villa—all filmy white curtains and palm fronds and wicker, but weighed down by English antiques, a nod to the colonial history of the island—to "freshen up." She emerged minutes later in the chicest pink linen sundress, not flouncy, but a cool column. She had on white leather sandals, carried a straw bag, and had subtly adjusted her makeup so that her lipstick now complemented the pink. She'd brushed some kind of iridescent powder on her cheekbones, to catch the sun. Truman clapped his hands at the sight of her, causing Bill Paley to look up from a hammock on the veranda and grunt.

"Darling Bill, we're just going down to the market for a bit. Would you like me to get you anything?"

"How about some conch? Do we have any of that around? I like those little conch balls that the cook makes, rolled up and fried in that batter."

"I'll make sure you have some for dinner! We'll be back before then."

Babe leaned over to kiss her husband, who said, "Don't wreck the car," before he closed his eyes and resumed his nap.

The warning was not unfounded, Truman soon discovered. Babe was a terrible driver; he found himself clutching the dashboard and squeezing his eyes shut as she took the hairpin corners down the mountain to the bay. They roared past palm trees so fast, they were just blurry giants with fuzzy green hats; the dusty road was full of ruts, which launched the car into the air before it landed with a jolt that caused Truman to bite his tongue, hard, and wince in pain.

But Babe was jubilant; she had a fierce grin on her face the whole time, and when she roared to a stop outside a small courtyard in the middle of the town of Montego Bay—a collection of cobbled streets and brightly painted buildings—she brushed her hair out of her eyes, adjusted the Gucci scarf about her throat, threw back her head, and laughed.

"My, that was fun!"

"I'm glad one of us enjoyed ourselves." Truman grimaced, gingerly tested his tongue, and Babe instantly stopped laughing. She whipped off her sunglasses and laid a hand on his arm, her gaze grave, a pucker between her eyes.

"Oh, was my driving terrible? I suppose it was—I don't get to do it very often. Bill doesn't think it's fitting. I'm so, so sorry, Truman. Bill's right. I never should have driven, because I scared you, and oh, that's the last thing in the world I want to do!"

"No, no, it was fine. Really. Just fine."

But Babe seemed troubled, and stayed that way as they strolled through the market. It was small, a cluster of stands made out of wooden crates or palm fronds, piles and piles of the most tempting fruit—bananas and papayas and kumquats and peaches and limes and lemons and oranges, ruby grapefruit, pineapples as big as Truman's head. There were adorable little Jamaican children, their clothes vivid white against their dark skin, dancing around for money. Women in brilliantly colored dresses, turbans on their heads, sat at their stands, spreading their wares; there were scarves and straw hats and bags, gauzy cotton dresses in vivid tropical colors, leather sandals.

But Babe's mood remained downcast, despite Truman's running narrative—"Oh, my, I've never seen such fruit, not even down in the Village!" "These little children are simply gorgeous—look at how graceful the girls are, the way they carry themselves, so tall and proud. Mrs. Vreeland would want to collect them all!" "Do you hear that music? It's Calypso, isn't it? It reminds me of Harry Belafonte—who is divine, by the way. A gentleman, and a true artist. I'll introduce you to him."

Then Truman stopped in his tracks; they'd come upon a stall overflowing with colorful paper flowers. Blossoms burst out of baskets, carpeted a small rattan table, were pinned to the grinning vendor, covering her so that she looked like a float in the Tournament of Roses Parade.

"Oh, Babe—look!"

Babe did; she smiled, but her eyes were dull with remorse.

"No, I mean really look." Truman reached up and grabbed her by the shoulders and marched her right into the middle of the stall, so that they were surrounded by cheerful, vibrant flowers. "Now, how can you stand here and not be simply awash in happiness? Just try to frown right now—I dare you, just try it!"

And Babe did, finally, grin; she began to touch all the flowers, picking them up one by one, and then Truman was doing the same. He proceeded to scoop up huge, messy bouquets and pile them into Babe's arms, showering her with the delicate, vivid blossoms—there were paper roses and orchids and tulips and impatiens and begonias and poppies, reds and purples and oranges and yellows and greens and blues. Babe began to giggle, and then she was glowing with happiness, her cheeks as colorful as the blossoms. They spilled out of her arms, stuck to her shoulders, her skirt, her shoes, even.

"Voilà! You are a work of art, darling!"

"Oh, Truman!" Babe gasped, her eyes wide, crinkling up in pure pleasure.

"Oh, look—look at this one!" Truman plucked a snow-white rose from her arms. "Do you know what this reminds me of?"

Babe shook her head.

"When I was a little boy. Back in Monroeville. One Christmas, we had a parade of all the children. We all had to dress up—Nelle and I were stars, twinkling little stars. My cousin Sook made me a white jumpsuit, and she fastened pasteboard points on my head, my arms and legs—the five points of a star. She painted them snow white, as white as this flower. And I was so thrilled, because Sook whispered that my mama and papa were going to come see the parade. Oh, Babe, you don't know how much that meant to me—I hadn't seen them, you see, in months! Most of the brats in school didn't actually believe I had parents, to tell the truth. And so I spent the entire week leading up to the parade telling everyone my parents would be there—why, they were even bringing a talent scout from Hollywood! Just to watch me! Or so I told everyone." Truman studied the flower in his hands, twirling it.

Babe stood still, afraid to move. She didn't want to spill any of the flowers. She didn't want to break Truman's spell.

"Well, anyway," Truman continued, "the day of the parade, Sook walked me and Nelle to the school, where we were supposed to line up. 'When will they be here? When?' I kept asking, and Sook kept shaking her head and saying, 'Truman, I just don't know. Soon, I hope. Soon.' She left me with the teacher, who lined us all up, and then we started walking down Main Street, toward the old courthouse. The high school band was playing Christmas songs, and there was a Santa Claus, and ranks of angels, and then, finally, us stars. I didn't really concentrate on what I was doing. I just walked along, searching the sidewalks for any sign of my parents. Finally, I saw Sook and Jennie—the other cousin who cared for me. Jennie was scowling, as usual. I never saw that woman smile! But Sook, she just looked so sad, and when she caught my eye, she shook her head. So I knew that my parents weren't coming, after all."

"Oh, Truman!" Babe, her arms still full of flowers, felt helpless to comfort her friend, who looked so young, so vulnerable, a golden wisp, as he twirled the flower, his blue eyes soft, mired in sad memories.

Then he shook his head and looked at Babe. He smiled, brilliantly; a beam as vibrant as the flower he held. He started spinning, his arms outstretched; he whirled about, faster and faster.

"So do you know what I did?" he called out, still beaming, his head turned toward the sun, his arms reaching out to the sky. "I *twirled*. I stuck out my chin and I twirled and twirled, the best, the biggest, the most beautiful star in the whole damn parade! I wasn't going to let those brats see me cry. I wasn't going to let Sook know how devastated I was. I wasn't going to let my parents break me, in any way. I was simply going to be the very *best*."

Truman stopped, stumbling a bit as if he were dizzy, and his breath came in quick bursts.

"And do you know what? I was. I was the very best star that day. I had the best time of any of them. And then I went home with Sook and she made me my favorite cake, a lemon cake, and we ate it together, every last crumb, in the kitchen, when it was still warm from the oven, a little drizzle of bourbon sauce on top. And I didn't think of my parents at all. Not at all."

Truman took that white flower, and, gently tiptoeing up, he tucked it into Babe's hair and kissed her on the cheek.

"So there. Now you know. Something I've never told anyone before. Something I don't want anyone else to know. A gift to you, from me."

"Truman, I—I'm so sorry. Earlier, I mean." Babe gazed down at the flowers in her arms. "I used to love to drive, you see. I had the cutest little roadster, when I met Bill. But then, well—we had a car, and a driver, and that was the way it was. Befitting our position, naturally. So I'm rusty, and I apologize for scaring you. I'll be more careful, going home."

"Babe, my darling Babe, don't you see? I don't care! I loved seeing you that way, giddy, free—having the time of your life! It was so unlike you, the you that you present to the world. I felt privileged, to see that side of you. I was just making a joke. It's such a little thing, my dearest girl! Please forget about it, and enjoy yourself, and drive like a maniac on the way home. Forget Bill. Forget what's expected of you. Just *enjoy* yourself—*twirl*!"

"I am enjoying myself now," Babe confided, touchingly shy. She tried to conceal the sudden flush in her cheeks by burying her head in the flowers. "I know it's silly, to be so worried all the time, but I—well, I just don't want to disappoint anyone, you see."

"You could never disappoint me. Now, I'm buying you all the flowers. The entire stall! Madam." Truman turned to the woman vendor, who had been watching them this whole time, her mouth open, her lap full of flowers. "All of your wares, please! Pack them up, every last one of them, and allow me to pay."

"Oh, thank you, Truman!" Babe dropped the flowers she held into a basket that the woman hastily provided. Then she grasped Truman's hand. "Thank you, for everything. For all."

"My pleasure, my darling heart!"

The two of them hauled basket after basket of bright paper flowers out to the car. Babe drove very carefully back up the mountain, so the flowers wouldn't spill. And that night, at dinner, there were flowers everywhere, tumbling out of small baskets, cascading out of vases, a paper flower on every plate.

Truman pinned his—a sunny orange poppy—to his lapel, and Babe wore five, clustered together in a corsage, on her shoulder. She kept the snow-white rose in her hair.

Bill didn't seem to notice any of the flowers. Although he did compliment Babe on the conch fritters, wondering why the two of them suddenly started to giggle like schoolchildren when he did.

TELL ME—WHAT IS YOUR greatest fear?

There was a long silence. No sounds but the low hum of the pool filter, the faraway grazing of a lawn mower, and the determined *clip clip* of a gardener on the other side of some tall azalea bushes, trimming away.

"That someone will see," Babe whispered, while at the same time, Truman murmured, "That someone will find me out."

"That no one will love me," Truman added after another moment. While at the same time, Babe admitted, "And that I'll never be loved, truly."

They didn't look at each other. They only sat quietly, kicking at the water. Two pairs of bare feet, vulnerable, occasionally bumping into each other, tickling, nudging.

Two paper flowers reflected in the pool water. Comforting.

. . . . .

"Now I'm going to be very serious. So listen, please!" Truman banged a butter knife against his champagne flute.

The swans fluttered and sighed, turning toward him. Slim rummaged around in her purse for her glasses. Pamela adjusted her cleavage and leaned over her plate toward Truman. C.Z. burst into giggles. Marella frowned, hoping she would be able to keep up with the conversation; Truman's accent was so foreign to her ears. Gloria smiled one of her *Mona Lisa* smiles: a secret tickle of the lips, designed and perfected in front of a mirror countless times.

Babe adjusted the napkin on her lap and settled back into her chair, turning to her right. Truman grasped her hand beneath the table, giving it a little squeeze; she detected the private twinkle in his eyes, just for her.

"Do I have everyone's attention? Good. I would like to announce that we're going to play a little game. That's why I invited you all here, you know. Not just because I wanted to see each and every one of you after my time in the Gulag, but because we need to have some real fun."

"I heard your time in the Gulag was simply divine, and you had caviar and vodka every day," Slim called across the table.

"It was, and I did, but that's beside the point. And you can read all about it when the book's published—oh, didn't I tell you?" Truman turned coy, tucking his chin into his chest, assuming that breezy, "oh, this old thing?" attitude he always assumed whenever he talked about his work. "Bennett said when I'm finished with the article—and the writing is going divinely, thank you very much!— he's going to bring it out in book form, too. I already have a title. *The Muses Are Heard*."

Babe led the applause, which Truman grandly allowed; she was thrilled that only to her had he told the whole story. How he'd been so amused by the whole experiment of taking *Porgy and Bess* to Soviet Russia that he simply had to tag along and write about it. How disappointed the entire company had been when, in fact, they were not served caviar and vodka every day. How absurdly the producers had behaved, believing themselves to be great ambassadors of the arts and not just wealthy dilettantes, looking for glory. How curious the Russian audiences had been about the black actors and singers, how they'd asked about lynchings and other things no one really wanted to discuss. How one night Truman found a bar full of Soviet drag queens, hidden in the basement of a basement of a basement; hidden from the police. And how hideous the men had been, yet how they'd touched him with their bravery, their tattered dresses so tacky, but obviously cherished.

Everyone at this table at Le Pavillon was Truman's friend—at times, each could claim he had whispered that she was his very best friend, ever. But only Babe knew that for sure. Their friendship was a fact of her life, as she knew it was a fact of his. The best fact of her life, as she'd recently told her analyst. Who'd nodded and written this down and made no comment, other than, after the session was over, to ask if she could get Truman to autograph a book for him.

"Now, ladies." Truman raised his hands, like a conductor; like a well-rehearsed orchestra, they all turned to him, breathless. "Thank you. But that's not why I asked you all to lunch with me today. Lift up your plates and see what's there!"

Puzzled, Babe did so, like the rest. This was a surprise, then! Even to her. And she had a momentary pang of pique. Why hadn't Truman let her in on the joke first?

"What is it?" C.Z. waved a small, elegant envelope, sealed. Each exquisitely manicured hand held an identical one.

"Open them," Truman cried, a very impish gleam in his eye that Slim, at least, caught. And that made her hold her breath as she opened her envelope.

Inside were four calling cards. *Face-lift* was printed on one card; *Breasts* on another. *Tummy tuck* and *Nose job* were printed on the last two.

Everyone tittered nervously, surveying the cards. Slim squinted through her glasses at Truman. "True Heart, dear, what deviltry are you up to now?"

"Well," Truman drawled, his eyes still sparkling. "Everyone's had it done, haven't they? At least once? One kind of plastic surgery?"

Pamela pulled her neckline up. Gloria reached for her bag, ready to manufacture some kind of excuse for leaving. C.Z. laughed.

Slim watched Babe, who had paled, even as she continued to gaze smilingly at Truman. Trusting him, Slim realized. Completely trusting him not to humiliate her, or anyone else at this table. Yet

Slim could not quite do that. Truman was fun, so much fun—God, who else would show up at Kenneth's while she was getting her hair done with the unpublished memoirs of a Paris gigolo and read them aloud to her in his most resonant voice while she was helplessly trapped by the hair dryer?—but there was always a dark undercurrent gurgling at his feet, threatening to suck under those who got too close.

"Now, I'm going to call out a name, and I want you each to hold up the appropriate card. Let's start with something easy. Marilyn Monroe—a darling girl and a dear friend of mine, but oh, what a mess she is! Do you know"—he lowered his voice to a whisper—"that while she was married to DiMaggio, she was terrified of his mother? The most beautiful woman in the world, according to some—not me, though"—and once again, Truman squeezed Babe's hand beneath the table—"spending her days in the kitchen trying to make spaghetti sauce just like Mama DiMaggio used to make?"

"No," C.Z. squealed. "No! Are you serious?" And then she held up her *Nose job* card, and Truman put his finger to his own nose, and they both giggled.

They leaned in to hear more gossip about the Hollywood star, whom no one would ever have invited into their homes, but in whom they were all voraciously interested, anyway.

"And," Truman drawled, relishing the spotlight, the beauty of his swans, their glorious heads all turned toward him, "she really is a mess, the poor girl. An insecure mess, and, honey, you wouldn't believe the hygiene! Nonexistent. Truly. She smells. Marilyn Monroe reeks! That's why none of her leading men can stand her."

"Oh!" A collective, superior gasp, champagne flutes lifted, jeweled throats exposed.

The game continued—"Mamie Eisenhower!" And Truman, his face red with merriment, as each and every one had held up *Breasts*, except for Slim—who called out, "Ike!"—took a sip of champagne, leaned back in his chair, and sighed contentedly. "Oh, you are all so gorgeous! I could sit here and look at you forever and ever." And they knew they were safe from the game, safe from exposure; this wasn't about them, not at all. This was about the *others*. And so they could play it unreservedly, and did; even Babe, who normally did not stoop to such lows. No one had ever heard Babe Paley say a catty thing about anyone else, and here she was holding up her *Face-lift* card and giggling like a twelve-year-old.

Good for her, thought Slim, watching. *She needs something like this, for all that she has to put up with*. And in that moment, Slim decided not to be jealous of the relationship between Truman and Babe, after all. She had been; everyone was. It was the talk of the town. *What is going on with the Paleys and Truman?*

Because Truman was suddenly there, not just in Babe's coveted orbit but in her Givenchy pocket, her Hermès handbag, her Wedgwood teacup. And Bill Paley, notoriously stingy with his wife's company even as he had so little regard for it, didn't seem to mind at all; in fact, he welcomed Truman's presence in his wife's life, and seemed to enjoy it in his own. They were a trio, a peculiar little trio made up of the most powerful man in television, the most beautiful woman in New York, and the most darling, fey—and bitchy—of all the literary darlings. Truman had his own room at all their homes; he had an open invitation to use the CBS jet. It was known that Bill had given him some advice concerning money and investing; it was whispered that, on more than one occasion, Truman had even managed to coerce Bill Paley into singing "Danny Boy" around the fire after dinner, and had taken him down to the Village one evening to see a drag show.

Who was who in this relationship? Was Truman the child, and Bill and Babe the parents? Were Truman and Babe naughty siblings? Were Truman and Babe maybe—more?

Or was it Bill and Truman?

Oh, the possibilities! Slim's head buzzed to think of them. She decided, for now, only to be happy for her friend. Who had never, in all their years of friendship, pounded her fists on the table and laughed as girlishly, as giddily, as she was doing right now.

And if anyone deserved that, it was Babe Paley. Slim, more than anyone, knew that.

"Oh, look!" Truman did not lower his voice, and Gloria frowned regally, in disapproval. But Slim looked, and her pulse quickened, the corners of her mouth began to tickle. Oh, this was good. This was very good, indeed!

For who was walking in the front door of Le Pavillon but Elsie Woodward and her murderess daughter-in-law, Ann?

"Can you believe it?" Truman's voice finally did drop. "Oh, girls, tell me all! I was out of the country when it happened, but you were here! I only heard the barest, driest, dullest of facts. Is it true? Did Ann shoot Billy Woodward in cold blood?"

"Yes!" Gloria hissed, shaking her head. "She most certainly did!"

"And she claimed it was a prowler!" chimed in C.Z.

"She said it was in self-defense!" Slim piped up.

"She claimed it was too dark to see," Pam added throatily.

Babe didn't say a word; she merely arched an eyebrow.

"Oh, someone tell! Tell it all," Truman begged, throwing his napkin down and climbing up on his knees, so that he was bouncing up and down like a little boy. And they all laughed to look at him; who could resist such an audience?

And so, with an imperceptible nod from Babe, Truman's swans fluttered their bejeweled hands, swarmed about him, and began to hiss:

The Story of the
Murderer and the Martyr

We all remember when Ann started showing up.

("I don't," said Gloria, "because I was still living abroad.")

("Doing what?" asked Slim, with a malicious grin that Truman couldn't help but notice; his ears practically bristled like a cat's.)

("Never mind," said Gloria, waving her hand regally.)

Anyway. It was during the war. Ann, Ann—what was her name then, anyway? Cryer? Crower? Something like that. It didn't matter. She was from Kansas. So it just didn't matter.

Ann was a radio actress—not bad, either. And a showgirl, of all things! But she started showing up with Bill Woodward, the father. Just popping up wherever he was. Elsie, the dear ("Poor Elsie," Marella whispered), *turned a blind eye, as one would imagine. We all love Elsie* ("Poor Elsie," Gloria murmured). *Who doesn't? She's truly beloved. She really does take her charity work to heart, her position in society.*

Well, you know the Woodwards are old money by now. Not back in the days of Mrs. Astor, no, they wouldn't have quite passed muster; Ward McAllister would have run them out of the ballroom.

("Well, hell," Slim interjected, stabbing out a cigarette and lighting another. "The old snob would have thrown all of us out, come to think of it.")

("Really, Slim," Gloria scolded. "There's no need to be vulgar.")

But now, with the banking fortune and that terrific stud farm, the Woodwards are officially old money.

("Oh, the farm is terrific," enthused C.Z., wrinkling her freckled nose. "Have you been there? It looks like a Red Door spa for horses! Manicured lawns and gardens, and the stables so clean and gleaming!")

Anyway. Bill and Elsie Woodward had the one son, Billy. Well, Billy is a charmer, but, you know, there were rumors. . . .

("Gay," Pamela whispered apologetically to Truman.)

("There's nothing wrong with that," Truman replied, with just a hint of ice.)

("No, no, that's not what I meant—oh, well—")

Anyway. Billy married Ann. Just like that! Out of the blue. She was the father's mistress and then she became the son's bride. Well, Bill, even if he had been the one to fall for whatever charms she had—

("Now, now, Ann is attractive," Babe protested, inclining her head toward the corner table where Ann, in black, wan and very blond and very slender, sat staring into her lap while her mother-in-law removed her gloves and placed them next to her plate. Neither woman seemed able to look at the other.)

Yes, attractive, sure, if you like 'em cheap and blowsy, which she was back then—

("How much weight do you think she's lost?" Slim mused. "Because I should try it. Although I don't think I want to kill Leland. Yet.")

(There was an uncomfortable silence; Pamela dropped a knife on the floor, and bent to retrieve it. The hairs on Truman's neck stood on end, like fine-tuned antennae.)

Anyway. Attractive Ann may have been, but still—a radio actress, marrying a Woodward? Bill and Elsie ("Poor Elsie," whispered Pamela) *were not pleased. But they tried to make the best of it, for Billy's sake, and to stave off any gossip.*

But gold digger Ann wasn't so happy, once she married into the family. She and Billy began to have operatic screaming matches. It was because no one—absolutely no one—would be seen with them. Not even for poor Elsie's sake. Ann was very vulgar, very crass. She simply couldn't be taught—or wouldn't learn. Elsie had to be taken to her room the evening Ann wore red shoes with a blue evening gown at one of her dinner parties.

(Babe gasped. Truman sighed. "Tacky, tacky," he said.)

But for some reason, you know, the Duchess of Windsor took a shine to her. Of course, vulgar *knows* vulgar. *The Duchess of Windsor liked Ann, and had Ann and Billy over frequently. In fact,* it *happened the night of one of their dinner parties. Apparently, Billy and Ann were drunk and tearing into each other and it got to be so bad that even Wallis asked them to leave.*

Now, this was out in Oyster Bay, you know. And there had been some talk of prowlers around. Somebody breaking into people's houses even when they were there. Not even taking much, just there, in the house, making a mess and then leaving. People were a little jumpy.

("I remember it so well," Gloria whispered. "Billy and Ann weren't the only ones who slept with a gun in the bedroom.")

("Yes, but honestly, Gloria. Did you sleep with a loaded gun?" asked Slim.)

("No, but I did put my jewels in my pillowcase. I didn't get a wink of sleep, it was so lumpy!")

("Like the princess and the pea," Truman exclaimed, clapping his hands.)

Well, even though we all knew about them, Ann made a point that evening to mention the prowlers several times, and how nervous they made her. It was almost as if she was preparing her alibi.

So that night, then, after she and Billy went home early, banished by Wallis because of their fighting—

("Bang!" whispered Pamela.)

(Truman, his eyes round as an owl's behind his glasses, jumped in his seat and squealed, clutching Babe's hand to his heart.)

Ann shot him. She shot him in the dark, turned on the light, called the ambulance—and called her lawyer, too. And sat there, working herself up to some convincing hysterics by the time the ambulance arrived. Oh, my poor Billy! Oh, my poor dear! I heard a noise and thought it was that prowler, that horrible prowler! Oh, what have I done! *Apparently, the actress was quite effective. The police later said she ought to have been in movies.*

("She'd calmed down by the time the lawyer arrived," Slim observed, lighting up a cigarette. "She was perfectly clear-eyed, and wondering how quickly Billy's life insurance might pay up.")

Now, Elsie ("Poor Elsie," Truman said), *the grand dame—Bill Senior died a couple years ago, remember?—was heartbroken. Not just for herself but for her grandsons, Ann and Billy's two boys. So Elsie did what any respectable grand dame would do. We can't imagine Mrs. Astor could have done it any better. Elsie opened up the vault and paid everyone off—we mean everyone! The police, the judge, the jury, the reporters. Ann gave a statement to the grand jury, and—miracle of miracles!—they determined there was no reason for a trial. It was an accident, pure and simple. Ann mistook her husband—who slept in a bedroom down the hall, away from her, conveniently so in this case— for a prowler.*

And so now Ann and Elsie are the two Woodward widows, and Elsie makes a show of inviting Ann to dinner, to lunch—

All of them turned to stare at the two women in black, seated across from each other, barely eating, not speaking. There was the sense that some invisible alarm clock was set, and the two were only waiting for it to ring before they could escape their shared ordeal.

Elsie takes her everywhere, parades her about, and Ann is utterly miserable—oh, she hates Elsie ("Dear Elsie," acknowledged Babe), *of course—but what can she do? She's forever in her mother-in-law's debt, if she doesn't want to go to prison.*

("I do wonder," Slim mused, narrowing her feline eyes, "what they talk about. Don't you? What in heaven's name do those two talk about, sitting at the best table for all to see, putting on such a happy—well, at least inscrutable—face?")

(No one had an answer to that.)

Soon, though, Elsie's sending Ann to Europe. Away, leaving those two little boys with Elsie. Ann may have escaped trial by jury, but trial by mother-in-law is just as damning. Meanwhile, here they sit, just like us. Lunching at La Pavillon. Putting on brave faces for the photographers. A united front. So no one will gossip.

"I understand that," Babe said with a quiet sigh. "I really do. I don't know if Ann is guilty or not. I've never been close to her. But I think poor, sweet Elsie did the right thing."

"I think Ann should rot in jail," Slim declared. "Elsie should think about justice for her son, not about how the family Christmas card will look."

"No, but think how painful it would be for Elsie to admit that—that her son had made a mistake. That *she* had made a terrible mistake. To know that everyone is talking about you in that way—"

"But we are, anyway, Babe! Elsie may drag Ann along to lunch, and keep inviting her over for dinner and family gatherings, but we all know what happened, and we're still talking about it, so why even bother? Why not let Ann get what she deserves?"

"I don't know." Babe frowned, her eyes darker than usual. She put a cigarette in her long ebony holder with a shaking hand, allowing Truman to light it for her. "It's not easy, you know, trying so hard to—to act as if everything is just fine. To put on a united front in the face of such gossip. I simply admire Elsie so much, for trying to keep it all quiet, for being loyal, in her way, to her daughter-in-law, who, after all, is family, the mother of her grandsons."

"Even if that daughter-in-law murdered her son?"

"Of course that's terrible and tragic, and I'm not sure—I don't think—it's a private matter. That's all. Between them. None of us should see anything untoward in Elsie's behavior. No one should suspect the truth between them, because it's only that. Between them."

Truman put a warm hand on Babe's arm, soothing her.

"Bobolink, you're a dear. A sweet, naïve dear, and I love you." He kissed her cheek, and Babe put a hand to his face, briefly, claiming him. "We'll talk later," he promised quietly, but Slim heard, and bit her lip, studying how grateful Babe suddenly looked, the eagerness in her eyes as she nodded at Truman and grasped his hand, like a lifeline.

But then Truman grinned slyly at the rest of them and held up a card. "Breast job," he whispered, nodding toward Ann, and the table erupted into laughter once more. Even Babe smiled wanly.

However. After lunch, on their way to the powder room, they all stopped by Ann and Elsie Woodward's table to say a kind word to Elsie, and to cut Ann cold. Except for Babe; Babe alone put a hand on Ann's shoulder in greeting.

Truman, too, acknowledged Ann, as Slim, hanging back and rummaging in her handbag for some change, happened to see. After Babe and the others passed on, Truman turned around. He and Ann locked gazes; Ann's lip curled up sardonically. Truman pointed his fingers at her and whispered, "Bang! Bang!"

Slim gasped; Truman heard her. He shrugged nonchalantly as they continued on their way toward the lounges, where they parted and Slim pulled Babe aside, ostensibly to see if she could borrow a dollar for the matron.

"Babe, dear, be careful."

"Why? What do you mean?" Babe handed her five dollars with a slightly scolding frown. "Always five dollars, Slim, dear. It's nothing to you, but quite a lot to them."

"Thank you. I know how private you are. I know how discreet, always—it's not like you to gossip, and we all love you for it. It's what makes you Babe and the rest of us mere humans. So with Truman, just—be careful. That's all. Be careful what you talk about. We all should."

"Slim, you are sweet." Babe smiled and kissed her friend on the cheek. "I so appreciate your concern. But Truman—why, he's family. I rely on him more than I do Betsey or Minnie, even. He's a true friend. I have to say, one of the dearest friends I've ever had."

"Yes, well, I hope so, Babe. For your sake, I hope so."

"Slim, Slim, Slim." Babe shook her head and tucked her arm through her friend's as they walked toward the ladies' room. "So kind, so concerned and thoughtful! Are you and Leland coming out to Kiluna this weekend? I do hope you'll wear that divine gown I saw you trying on at Bergdorf's. You looked stunning. Like a tall glass of champagne."

Slim smiled. "Babe, they broke the mold with you."

"Well, I certainly hope so!"

And the two women laughed. They were still laughing when they joined the others in the lobby. Truman was surrounded by C.Z., Marella, Pam, and Gloria; he was in the midst of one of his stories. But when he saw his two favorites approaching, their heads bent together in intimacy and laughter, he stopped right in the middle of a sentence. Hopping up and down, rubbing his hands, his voice raised to stratospheric heights, Truman squealed.

"Ooh, what's so funny? What are you two talking about without me? Tell me! Tell me, do!"

"Nothing, True Heart. So don't strain yourself. It's nothing."

"Really?" Truman looked up, first at Slim, then at Babe. His wide eyes narrowed; his jaw set. "Really, honey? Because you know me. You know I just can't stand secrets, unless I'm the one telling them!"

Slim didn't join in the general laughter. She looked worriedly at Babe, who didn't return her gaze.

She couldn't. Babe Paley was staring at Truman with the indulgent, yet hungry look of a proud mother.

Or was it a lover?

. . . . .

"YOU KNOW, I TRIED TO WARN HER."

Slim ground out another cigarette; the crystal ashtrays were overflowing now with lipstick-stained butts, piles of ash spilling over the edges onto Monsieur Soulé's fine linen tablecloth. There was even a small burn mark, which Gloria had covered up with a wineglass. The sun was lower in the sky; so was the champagne in the bottle (the third bottle, to be precise).

"What, darling? What do you mean?" Gloria tried to stifle a yawn; she couldn't remember sitting in one place for so long, not even at La Côte Basque. Her ass, quite honestly, was a little numb. And she had to pee.

Instead, she raised her glass once more, and it was miraculously filled. Oh, being rich was simply lovely, when it came right down to it. Hold out a glass, and it was filled. Hold out an arm, and it was thrust into a satin-lined fur coat. Hold out a finger, and it was encrusted with jewels.

Yet even as Gloria smiled to herself, her eyes half closed, the memories of her childhood and early youth were not far away. They never were; they were always lapping at the edges of her consciousness, persistent waves of fear and loathing and humiliation: *Solo el que carga el cajón sabe lo que pesa el muerto.*

Just the other day, trying on a new pair of Ferragamo pumps, her narrow foot stretching out luxuriously in the supple leather, testing the cushioned sole, she'd felt a burning, stabbing pain in the pad of that foot, so acute that she'd cried out, startling the Bergdorf salesman. It was the phantom pain of having to walk barefoot on bad days, or in the thinnest huaraches on good, on the burning gravel streets of the village in Mexico where she had been born, sixty-three years earlier: Veracruz, to be precise. But she hadn't said the name of her hometown aloud for years, decades. She'd hypnotized it out of her mind, for fear of blurting it out at an inopportune moment, one reason why she rarely drank much—*del plato a la boca se cae la sopa*, her father had often reminded her when she was a girl. But other details, stories, of her youth remained. That searing pain, for instance; how her feet never could get clean, how the gravel would disintegrate into a rough powder, grinding into her soles until they became ugly, thorny pads, not feet at all.

How the first thing she did, once she had a little money from working in the local dance hall, where a man would grab the first available girl like he was catching a *pollo* in a yard, was to buy cream to rub into her feet every night, so that someday, when she slept with the kind of man who would notice, they would be smooth, soft as velvet: aristocratic feet.

How the first time she did sleep with the kind of man who would notice, he didn't. But he did notice her hands, her nails, and so then she started spending time on them, too. Pinching pesos—stealing pesos—to buy more creams, a pumice stone. How she learned to view her body then as a man would, by sleeping with many men, many different men. The other girls dressed and preened for one another, but Gloria soon recognized there was no currency in that. She must stand out, be the one men wanted, because men, at their most vulnerable (in bed, with their soft spots exposed and used up, red and tender, the curling tendrils of their upper thighs matted with secretions), would *pay*.

Women never let themselves be that vulnerable. And women never had enough money, anyway. She knew women who slept with other women, saying it was easier, but she never did. Maybe it was easier, but it simply didn't pay. So Gloria concentrated on the men, learning from each individual. There was the one who liked to lick her teeth, laughing at how crooked they were. There was the one who put his two hands about her waist and pinched at the roll of baby fat above her hips with a scowl. So she began to save, squirreling away the money to have the teeth fixed; she stopped buying sweets.

They all were entranced by her neck, that long, lovely pipe stem holding up her flower of a head. A few even wanted to hold it in their hands, chokingly, during sex, which she allowed only once. That was enough; she'd blacked out, the bastard had stolen from *her*, and it set her back for months.

But finally she found a man, a different man. A man who came to the dance hall one night and seemed entranced by the colored lanterns, the terrible mariachi band with the mismatched outfits, the dogs sprawling lazily around the edges of the dance floor, as hungry as the girls themselves were, but only the dogs could look forward to any scraps of food. A man who took his time to choose, and he chose her, Gloria Rubio y Alatorre, daughter of a journalist with lofty ideas and no money, and of a seamstress whose only useful piece of advice to her child was that she must learn how to sew a straight line with tiny stitches, and be nice to men.

The man—his name? Gloria honestly couldn't remember anymore—married her and took her away, and that was all that mattered. He took her to Europe, where she promptly left him at a train station in Paris, deciding that was where she wanted to be, not some village on an Alp. She took one look, one whiff of Paris—the scent of fresh cut flowers and warm bread, the saturated colors, even the grays were beautiful—and she planted her feet firmly on the train platform and said *"Buenas noches"* to her hapless German. Because Paris was where she belonged; instinctively, she knew that was where the wealthy men were. And her German, she had discovered on the boat over, when they'd settled for steerage and had to share a suitcase, was not wealthy. *Bastard!* Gloria detested men who lied more than she detested women who did. Women, after all, were trained to do nothing else from birth. We lie about pain, we lie about happiness, we lie about how happy men make us, how good they make us feel when really all we want is to sleep in a clean, warm bed. Alone.

Suddenly Gloria cringed, remembering something she'd told Truman not long ago, her head muddled by the false intimacy fueled by too much champagne and not enough food. "Loel farts," she'd pronounced with a tipsy giggle. "Like a farm animal, all night long—pooh, pooh, pooh! That's why I can't bear to sleep with him. Who on earth could? And why do men fart, anyway?"

"Honey, if I knew the answer to that one, I wouldn't have to rely on Seconal," Truman had commiserated.

Oh, God. What if that made it into a story or a book someday? *La Guinness confided that she couldn't stand to sleep with Loel due to his uncontrollable flatulence. . . .*

What if something worse was made known to the world via the poison of Truman Capote's pen? Her mouth tightened, the muscles in her lovely long neck strained. Even now, after all these years, she felt the raw, animal fear of all she had to lose, should someone find out.

Gloria felt a grip on her arm; she looked up to see Slim's cat's-eye glasses askew, her lipstick smeared.

"I also made that little bastard a shitload of money," Slim slurred, beckoning to the waiter. "Vodka, baby. Champagne gives me the trots, to tell the truth, but we don't normally do that, do we? Well, hell. Today, we do!"

Slim turned back to Gloria, who steadily, silently downed an entire glass of champagne, her gaze never leaving Slim's, as if to prove her superiority of constitution.

"I made him the deal. The film deal for *In Cold Blood*. I did! Not Swifty, not anyone else. And so what does he do? He makes *me* the bitch in his story. The blabbermouth. Lady Ina Coolbirth. What the hell kind of a name is that, anyway?"

"I think," Pamela whispered, "there was a real person by that name, a long time ago. . . ."

"Shut up, Pam!" Slim grabbed the crystal highball glass full of vodka out of the waiter's hands before he could set it on the table. She sipped, welcoming the icy-hot alcohol down her throat, and it brought tears to her eyes. Tears and memories, both.

Because it had been so long since she had just been Slim. Nancy. Whoever. It had been so long since she had been herself, and that was a laugh. A hell of a laugh. "Oh, Slim! You're such an original! No one's like you! You're true, the truest I know!"

God. Truman had said that, hadn't he? The little creep. The wise old soul. The friend who had broken her heart—and friends who betrayed other friends were simply the—the—

Take Pam, for instance. Slim's heart was already broken long before Truman's deviltry, crushed and ground beneath the stiletto heel of one Pamela Churchill (Hayward). She gazed at Pam now, tempted to throw some ice water down that cleavage. God, Pam really was getting too old to dress like the slut that she was; her cleavage was a bit leathery, wrinkled. But Slim didn't douse her rival with ice water; Leland was dead now, anyway. Dead, dead, dead, like all the other men who'd loved her.

Almost all, that is.

But she had been an original back then, hadn't she, once upon a time? She'd reveled in it, rejoiced in it, chuckled to herself about it at night. All those men, those Hollywood men, those legends—how they'd all fallen for her, every one, and she'd pretended to be embarrassed or shy or confused or surprised. But she wasn't; she'd made them fall in love with her by being her truest self to the point that it became a costume she put on in the morning, a mask she slipped over her head. The all-American girl, the blond California goddess, the outdoorswoman who could ride and shoot and fish, seemingly not caring about how she looked—secretly spending quite a lot of time, indeed, brushing that golden hair and buffing those natural nails and plucking those untamed eyebrows, choosing those clothes, unusual and tailored and clean when everyone else was wearing snoods and lace collars and giant hats with feathers, jersey dresses with jewel clips.

Not her. Not Slim.

Who'd called her that, in the first place? Bill Powell? Probably. He was the first movie star she'd met, when she was barely fifteen, escaping, running, charging away from a tyrant father who tried to control her even after he left, a sad, broken mother, a bitchy sister; the ghost of a dead brother hovering over the entire town of Salinas, California. So as soon as she could, she vamoosed, driving away in a convertible, heading toward a resort in the desert, already starring in the movie of her life. There, she found herself—her young, golden, slim self—surrounded by actual, honest-to-God movie stars: Bill Powell, for instance. Men who took her under their wing, at first, waiting until she grew up. Just a little.

And when she did, she met Howard Hawks, another daddy. God, how she had a thing for the daddy figures! She didn't have to pay an analyst fifty bucks an hour to figure out why. Classic story: Daddy left. Little girl spends her life trying to replace him.

Howard brought her into Hollywood finally, firmly, where she discovered, to her own surprise, that she didn't want to star in movies. It was so much more fun to be involved in the making of them, on the arm of one of the best directors in the business, Howard Hawks. Howard fetishized her, to tell the truth; he was fascinated by how she spoke, her chin tilted down, eyes looking up, her voice throaty and full of answers to unasked questions. Howard made her read his scripts, rewriting the women characters' dialogue as she would say it. He made sure their costumes were tailored, like her own wardrobe, even sending her out sometimes to buy an actress's clothes herself. That's how much he trusted her taste.

And he introduced her to more men, and what the hell was he thinking, doing that? She was so young—barely nineteen, then twenty. In love, but not in lust, and Howard knew that and so did she. And he surrounded her with Gary Cooper—rather stupid, but gorgeous as a mountain, those dimples! That surprised grin! Clark Gable—not stupid at all, although he dared you to think he was. A barrel of a man, broad-shouldered and -hipped; Clark never looked quite right in a tux, but he was a woman's own wet dream in a flannel shirt and jeans.

And Papa. Finally, always, Papa. Had she ever been sexually

attracted to him? Not in the conventional sense; the man was a mess. You could see how he'd been gorgeous when he was young; the bones were there, like archaeological ruins beneath a wind-blown canvas tent. But when she'd met him, back in the forties, Ernest Hemingway was no longer interested in things such as grooming and hygiene. He'd found a look—safari shirt; baggy, ratty shorts or pants; scruffy beard—and kept it, no matter the season or occasion. And he so rarely bothered to bathe, or wash his clothes, or trim his toenails, or clean his fingernails.

Yet. He was so muskily, powerfully masculine. More than any other man she'd met, and that was saying something when Clark Gable was a notch in your belt. So it was that, and his brain, his heart—poetic, sad, boyish, angry—that drew her. And he wanted her. Slim could see it in his hungry eyes, voraciously taking her in, no matter how many times a day he saw her; each time was like the first time after a wrenching separation. He made no bones about it, not even in front of Howard.

And Howard got a kick out of it. To tell the truth, it turned him on. It made him tear her clothes off at night, knowing that Papa was just in the next room, or tent, brooding about her, dreaming about her. To tell the truth, she got off on it, as well.

Well, why not? Sex is great. Sex is all. Was, anyway.

Oh, hell. When did it vanish, sex? When did it leave, pack up its bags, and take up residence elsewhere, leaving only a polite thank-you note for your gracious hospitality?

"I'll have another," Slim whispered, waving her glass, then tipping it for one last drop. The ice slid down and rattled her teeth.

"Your lipstick has come off," Marella observed sleepily.

"So's yours."

"I'll reapply it." And Marella opened her purse and actually brought her lipstick out, before all four realized what she was doing and gasped. Gloria slapped her hand in horror.

"Babe would never do that," Slim admonished her. "Babe Paley would never apply lipstick at the table."

"She never had to," Pam marveled. "How is that possible? I've never seen Babe's lipstick ever smear or fade." Slim, she noticed, had apparently applied her makeup with a trowel, and now it was sliding down her face, like melted frosting. Poor Slim. She did look like the wreck that she was; the bitter, resentful wreck who still behaved as if she was Leland's rightful widow.

But Pamela simply was not to blame. Men, the dear boys, did need to be taken care of, and American women were particularly bad at that, so intent on having their own fun. Babe really was the only American woman of her acquaintance who knew how to keep a husband. Whereas British women, well, they were born knowing how to take care of men, their own—and everyone else's.

Pamela had grown up possessing the gift: how to soothe and flatter and caress and purr and then ignore, just when the flattering and caressing got to be a bit too much. She knew how to cast a wide net and keep things friendly, no matter how distastefully they might end, so that she would be able to use one lover to help another, politically or in business. These men were grateful to her, and had paid her handsomely, set her up very well, and for a long time, after that disaster of a first marriage to Randolph Churchill (*Oh, Randy, the only thing you ever gave me of any value was your name!*), that had been enough. But then, one day she realized she was well into her thirties and known only as a courtesan, not a wife. And in the twentieth century—the prosaic, unromantic twentieth century—wives were more highly prized than mistresses. So she looked around and saw a husband who wasn't being cared for, and determined to rectify that. Yes, well, it *was* rather a shame that the husband happened to belong to a friend of hers. But that was water under the bridge, in her opinion.

Oh, these Americans. They did tend to carry on and on about such things. Yet, of course, they did have the most money, the best houses, and the finest food, the most divine restaurants. She'd not regretted throwing in her lot with them, not once. Not even now, with wretched Truman causing such a row. It was still preferable to living in a drafty flat in London or Paris with her veiny hands and crepey bosom, wondering how she was going to pay her bills, clinging to the Churchill name like a tiara, a tarnished, dusty old tiara long out of fashion.

"Babe puts her lipstick on," Gloria was saying, rather fuzzily. "Then she powders it. Then she puts it on again. Oh, and before she puts it on, she puts something else on her lips. I forget."

"But even if it did fade," Slim slurred, "she would never, ever apply it at the table. Babe Paley would *die* first."

Marella gasped; no one spoke for a long moment. Gloria glared at Slim, whose eyes, behind those cat's-eye glasses, were now brimming with tears.

"Oh, damn," Slim said. "Damn. I didn't mean to say that—I didn't mean—"

"I hate Truman," Gloria snarled. "I despise him. But I don't want to lose him. I don't want to lose them both—oh, what hell it is, Slim! What hell it is to grow old! Men don't ever grow old, they just get more and more distinguished, desirable, even—look at some of these old farts, our husbands, still on the prowl! Babe is lucky—yes, I said that! She'll never grow old. Old and undesirable. Like me. Like all of us." Gloria's voice quavered; her hand was trembling as she raised her champagne flute to her lips. She never voiced these fears, these demons that chased after her with flaming daggers.

"I wonder," Slim mused, as if she hadn't heard Gloria at all, and perhaps that was for the best. "Speaking of men, I wonder." Her hand shook as she adjusted her eyeglasses, so that she could see properly again. "What do you think Bill Paley's going to do to the little homicidal maniac? What on earth do you think Bill is going to do to Truman, after this?"

Pam shuddered, her cleavage bouncing; Marella grimaced.

"Whatever it is," Gloria growled, those Latin eyes gleaming dangerously, "I do hope I'm there to see it."

. . . . .

WILLIAM S. PALEY WAS HUNGRY.

William S. Paley was always hungry; his mother never failed to remind him how exhausted she had been when he was a baby, feeding him 'round the clock, until finally she just couldn't take it anymore and weaned him early. She also never failed to remind him how she hadn't had to do that with his sister, who was a much more reasonable child in every way.

Bill couldn't remember a time when he didn't rise and think, first thing before his feet hit the floor, *What am I going to have for dinner?* And, of course, before dinner there was breakfast, lunch, snack after snack, dinner after dinner, even; invariably, he was ravenous again around midnight, and Babe had installed a separate kitchen off his bedroom in all their homes, completely stocked with eggs and cheeses and salamis and breads, cookies, sliced vegetables, whole roasted chickens in the refrigerator.

He was a big man, that was true; not heavy, but tall and raw-boned. His stomach was simply the part of his body that claimed most of his thoughts. He didn't pay much attention to his hands or his feet, or his broad shoulders or even his graying hair, beyond ensuring that the whole machine was always encased in the finest: custom-made shoes and suits from Savile Row and silk ties. But his stomach was always on his mind. Craving everything, fearing emptiness.

So he rolled his chair away from his desk, the chairman of the board of CBS, and wandered into a little kitchenette off his office; this, too, was always stocked by someone. Maybe Babe; he didn't really know. He rummaged through the shelves, opened the refrigerator, and questioned his stomach carefully. Did he want a sandwich? Foie gras? Scrambled eggs? Something was required to fill him up again, give him the fuel he needed to get through the day— even though he'd had lunch only two hours ago at 21 with the head of Frigidaire, one of CBS's biggest advertisers.

He hated 21. He detested the whole artificial clubby atmosphere of it, the dark paneled rooms, low ceilings, the cast-iron jockeys lined up in front. But he was supposed to like it, he knew; it was one of the places he was expected to frequent—and advertisers expected to be taken—and so he did. He knew how to play the game, when it had to be played.

Bill decided on a sandwich. Opening up a breadbox, he eyed a large rye bread from Carnegie Deli, not even sliced. There was also an unsliced baguette. He chose the baguette, laid it out on the bread board, and, taking a bread knife, sliced the long loaf lengthwise.

He hated *society,* to tell the truth. Even as he yearned for it, collected it, wore it about his neck like a medal. He craved acceptance; he craved the sensation of knowing that he was the most sought after; he and Babe, that is. The Paleys. Mr. and Mrs. The richest, most beautiful, most glamorous couple in New York. That's what he wanted. He just didn't want to have to put up with some of the exhausting exercises required to attain his desire, that was all. He left most of it up to Babe, and simply waited for her to tell him what was required of him. Like this evening, for instance. After a long day at work, he'd have to change and go to the Plaza and mix and mingle.

But that was why he'd married Babe in the first place, wasn't it? Because she knew society, she knew how to navigate it easily, not clumsily; Babe knew where to go and with whom to be seen. Although it wasn't as if he'd been some rube off the turnip truck when he'd met her; he was already William S. Paley, chairman of CBS. His first wife, Dorothy, had polished the rough edges, shown him how to dress, where to live, introduced him to art, to performers, politicians, artists; he'd selected her for the job, just as he'd selected Babe, later on, and Fred Friendly to run the news division, and countless other employees, even the most admired faces in the land. They were all his employees, wives included; the famous men and women of CBS, whom he could call on whenever and wherever and they'd show up: Bing Crosby, whom he'd discovered, drunk but singing like an angel, and then turned into one of the first radio crooners. Jack and Mary Benny, personal favorites of his; Jack could make him fall down on the floor laughing with just one flick of a wrist and a long, steady slow burn. George Burns and Gracie Allen; Gracie was a doll, literally. A tiny thing with that crinkly little voice, although he didn't much care for George. Too sly, too condescending. But he had to admit he'd given the cigar industry a boost.

Cigars. He didn't smoke them anymore, but they were still part of who he was: the rich smell of tobacco in his clothes, the slimy feel of the palm leaves in his hands, the small rings declaring "La Palina." The brand of cigars his father and his uncle Jake had founded and turned into a thriving business. The business he, Bill, was expected to go into as a youth, and he had, learning it from the bottom up, rolling the cigars himself along with the laborers in the beginning, because that's how his father had first started out. But then he'd heard about this new thing called radio, back in the twenties, and one summer, when he was left in charge of the business in Philadelphia while his uncle and father were on a buying trip to Cuba, he'd approached one of the local radio stations about sponsoring a show—*The La Palina Hour.* Some bad singer, he recalled, was the star of the show, but it didn't matter. People listened; people listened to anything broadcast in those days. Sales went through the roof, and he realized there was a lot more to this radio business than he'd thought.

How did he know? Instinct. Gut instinct, from deep within that stomach he so carefully attended. He couldn't analyze it, not if he tried—and he'd been begged to try, many times over the decades. He just *knew.* He wasn't the only hungry person out there. Everyone was hungry for something—food, for sure. But sometimes it was for laughter, sometimes for tears. Sometimes to recognize themselves, sometimes to be jolted into awareness of something novel and even frightening. Hungry for other people, mostly, and radio did that; it brought people together, made them feel less lonely. And so he figured out this radio thing, bought a struggling little network of a few stations around Philly—Columbia Phonographic Broadcasting System. He got rid of the *Phonographic* right away.

And what he, Bill Paley, did was realize fairly quickly that the money was in advertising, not in forcing the small affiliate stations to pay for the programming, the way it had been. He would offer the programming for free, in return for advertising time on each station, and the advertisers would pay for the privilege. And that's how it worked, even in television. Once he figured out the system, he was eager to move on and let others run it. He still had a hand in programming—he knew what people wanted, and he always felt the privilege of that knowledge—and he'd been lucky enough to figure out that network news could be a powerful force during the war. He'd been damned lucky to have had Ed Murrow already in Europe when war broke out, ready to assume the ultimate mantle of "right man at the right time."

But the running of the company, the day-to-day demands, he left to others. Oh, he was in the office all day, signing papers, attending to big decisions, paying surprise visits just to keep people on their toes. He was still Mr. CBS, the face of the company, and he sure as hell knew how to live that life.

With Babe on his arm, of course.

Babe.

He still couldn't think of her, after how many years now—they'd married in '47 and it was '58, so eleven. Eleven years now. And he still couldn't think of her without shaking his head at his luck. He didn't have to be told—as he was daily, by total strangers, even—how lucky he was to be married to her.

How lucky he was that Barbara Cushing Mortimer, the ultimate Boston shiksa, had said "yes" to him. A Jew from Chicago.

Bill opened the small refrigerator—of course, a Frigidaire—and pulled out several packages of thick white butcher's paper; he unrolled each and surveyed the contents. Pastrami? Thin Genoa salami? Slices of Angus beef, bloody red at the center?

He chose the Genoa salami, wrapping the other packages up tenderly, putting them to bed back in the refrigerator. Then he opened a jar of brown deli mustard.

Cognizance of his Jewishness was right up there with his cognizance of his stomach. It was always in his thoughts, his plans, his schemes. Not paramount, and not in any sort of religious sense. He couldn't remember when he'd last been to temple. But every time a door closed, the slam he heard was a word, and the word was *Jew*. Real or imagined, there it was. Clubs he could never join. Schools his children could never attend. Women he could never have.

Yet one of those women had said yes. Was it love that prompted this act of bravery on Babe's part? Or was it money, all his piles of money?

Yes. No. Maybe.

Bill Paley was nothing if not pragmatic, and so was his wife. It was that pragmatism that drew them together in the first place. Oh, God, yes, Babe was beautiful and stunning and fabulous and all that—she lived up to her advertising, that was for sure. But when they met, she newly divorced, he nearly so (well, that counted, right? His intention was to be divorced, anyway. He'd just not gotten around to telling his first wife), whatever passed for physical attraction between them was utterly trumped by shared pragmatism. With her society pedigree, she could get him into places he couldn't go alone. And he could give her financial stability for her children, and entrée into something more exciting than that staid society she was groomed for. Radio and television, the entertainment industry. This was new, and exciting, and Babe was curious.

He noticed that right away about her—her curiosity. He appreciated it, to a point. He also had no intention of having a second marriage like his first, a marriage in which the wife taught the husband, and didn't care who knew it; in fact, took pains to let others see how much she had taught him, how much more she knew about art and politics and all the rest. That had been Dorothy Hearst Paley's fatal flaw, one she recognized too late.

Babe was more astute. She soothed where Dorothy had nagged; she waited where Dorothy would leave impatiently on her own. She anticipated—everything. His hunger, his moods, a tickle in his throat that worried him, and that she couldn't possibly know about, but she did.

His boredom. She anticipated that, as well, and did her best to alleviate it. Truman, for example; she'd brought Truman into their lives, and damned if he didn't like the little queen, after all.

He certainly made life more interesting, that was for sure.

Bill opened the refrigerator again and grabbed an onion, peeled the skin, sliced it paper-thin, so quickly his eyes didn't have time to water. He thought of that first night at Kiluna, when he'd arrived, stunned, to find that Babe wasn't waiting for him downstairs, a drink in her hand, and at first he was angry, petulant as a child. Truman stayed the weekend, along with the usual suspects, Slim and Leland, Gloria and Loel, Minnie and Jim Fosburgh. During dinner Truman had been amusing, arch, gossipy, but not too; he'd told funny stories about John Huston and Humphrey Bogart, and he'd made Babe laugh. Not in that polite way she did whenever Bill told her a funny story, but hearty guffaws that made her shoulders shake, her eyes tear up. And Bill hadn't seen Babe laugh like that in, well—ever.

After dinner, when usually they'd all retreat to the drawing room and play quiet games, Truman insisted on dancing. He'd actually brought some records—all CBS, which Bill of course noticed, and gave him points for—and they'd played them out on the terrace. Truman was an astounding dancer: lithe, light on his feet, knowing all the latest moves.

At one point, he grabbed Babe by the arm. "Dance with me, Bobolink," he sang. And Babe, who never danced because he, Bill, hated it, blushed like a schoolgirl. But with a ready eagerness that took Bill by surprise, she leapt to her feet, those damned little bells tinkling as she did so. And Bill Paley watched his wife, the graceful, reserved goddess, the refined Mrs. Paley, jitterbug with Truman Capote with utter abandon. She twisted her hips, licked her lips suggestively at Truman, rewarded the astonished onlookers with drowsy come-hither looks, before finally closing her eyes and abandoning herself completely to the music. Then she followed Truman as he led her into a sexy rhumba, the two of them melting into each other's bodies despite the absurd difference in height; Truman's head came up to Babe's collarbones, but somehow she was the one resting in his arms, and the two of them, bodies supple, slender, bending to the music and to some other rhythm palpable only to each other, had stirred in Bill such a feeling of longing, of unaccountable sadness, that he'd found himself blinking away a few tears.

When the dance was done, everyone but Bill had burst into applause. Slim leapt to her feet and shouted "Bravo!" And Babe, an enormous grin on her flushed face, her hair uncharacteristically tousled, but somehow this only made her look even more beautiful, bowed deeply, graciously, and then allowed Truman to lead her back to her seat with a light-footed grace worthy of Fred Astaire.

Bill had never seen his wife look happier.

"That was quite a show," was all Bill could say. Babe didn't reply; she only flashed him a shy smile, put her hand on his arm, and motioned for a butler to fill his wineglass. He hadn't even realized it was empty.

After everyone went up to bed, Bill remained on the terrace for several moments, flummoxed about what had just happened, why he had been stirred to such emotion simply by watching his wife dancing with a fag—a graceful, lithe fag, but still a fag. That his wife could look so radiant! So girlish! Babe was cool, calm, and collected. Always. When he proposed—"Of course, Bill, I'll marry you. There's nothing else I would like more," followed by a kiss on his cheek and one quick flash of gratitude from those doelike eyes. When she presented him with a son—"Bill, darling, I'd like you to meet your namesake, William S. Paley Junior."

The few times they'd had sex, in fact: "Oh, darling. Yes, that's wonderful. You're a marvel. You know just what to do to make a girl feel—oh." And the last just a small gasp of surprise. But she never broke a sweat. Never even mussed her makeup. Just looked at him adoringly, with gratitude, then after an appropriate amount of time, wrapped herself up in a sheet and went to fix her hair.

But Truman, the little fairy—*he* was the one to put a shine to her, make her sweat, glow, muss her hair. Just by dancing?

Bill had gone upstairs feeling as if his equilibrium was off, but not knowing entirely why, when he'd heard a small, childish lisp. "Oh, Bill! Come sit with me. I can't sleep." Startled, Bill found himself peeking into one of the guest rooms. Only to behold a tousled blond apparition in silk pajamas, tucked into bed with the covers up to his chin, patting the mattress beside him.

Bill froze. Was this a proposition? Surely the little fag knew he wasn't like that? By God, he'd throw the twerp out of the house first thing in the—

"Oh, don't look so terrified. You're not my type, I assure you. I just thought you might like to talk. I know I would. I can never go right to sleep after a party. I'm always too wound up."

And so Bill Paley walked into Truman Capote's bedroom and

sat down on the bed, and ended up talking for three hours, during which the two of them repaired to his small kitchen to scramble some eggs and uncork a bottle of champagne. Truman's breadth of knowledge impressed Bill; he asked very intelligent questions about radio and television, and art. He asked advice about having one of his short stories made into a teleplay. He never once propositioned him, or made any inappropriate or lewd gesture or remark, and by the time they both had to admit they couldn't keep their eyes open one more minute, Bill had come to look at Truman as both a peer and a waif. Because there was such an innocence to him; he was so certain of his future, of his place in the literary world, in posterity, even, that Bill could only shake his head. Had Bill Paley, even in his confident youth when everything he touched turned to gold, ever been that certain?

He didn't think so.

The sandwich now assembled, Bill closed his eyes, almost in reverence. His big white teeth bit into the crusty, yet doughy bread; he savored the bracing crunchiness of onion, the saltiness of the salami, the thick brown tang of the mustard. He chewed and chewed, spilling crumbs everywhere, pausing now and then to pick them up with his greasy fingers, licking them between bites.

And when he was finished, when his hands were dripping with oil and mustard, littered with crumbs, his stomach temporarily silenced, he remembered that there would be food tonight at the party; Babe had promised him that, reminding him before he left for work in the morning. "Don't worry, darling, I'll take care of you. We'll have something more substantial than party food!"

And now he wasn't even hungry!

Bill consulted his watch, picked up the phone on his desk, and called his driver. Then he went into his private dressing room; no mere executive bathroom, but a real dressing room with rows of extra suits and shirts and ties. Quickly he shed one wrinkled shirt—he merely dropped it on the floor, never for a second wondering who might pick it up and have it laundered—for a fresh one and put on a different suit jacket, tied a new tie. He splashed some water on his face, combed his hair—cut closer than he used to wear it, to disguise the thinning—and then strode out of his office toward an elevator at the end of the hall. His secretary called out a sincere "Good night, Mr. Paley!" and before him, dozens of other secretaries and vice presidents and directors scraped and bowed, raising hats, wishing him the fondest of good nights.

Bill didn't even notice them. He was thinking of the evening ahead, and gritting his teeth until he realized, with a jolt, that despite the ordeal before him, he was looking forward to seeing Truman. Even though he'd seen him last weekend and would see him this one coming up.

And he hadn't had a friend like that in—well, had he ever? Someone whose company he truly enjoyed, who didn't bring with him any headaches, past or present (like Murrow now; Ed used to be the debonair, bon vivant reminder of the glamorous war years when he and CBS were *the* voice of the war, of dashing correspondents, righteousness, bravery. Now Ed's very presence only reminded him of angry sponsors and President Eisenhower calling him on the phone, asking him why one of his own employees—the face of CBS News, no less—was so intent on being a Pinko?).

So where once he and Ed Murrow had dined at Claridge's while the bombs rained down on London, toasting to the triumph of good over evil and bedding grateful English girls—including Pam Churchill, that tasty little British dish—now he and Truman Capote hobnobbed in Manhattan. With Babe, of course; Bill had to forcibly remind himself of his wife's presence tonight. She would look beautiful, as always. Tall and elegant and coolly perfect. An asset, just as prized as the new Picasso he'd hung in the foyer of the St. Regis pied-à-terre. Just as valuable. Just as essential to his sense of self.

Bill suddenly remembered the sandwich. Did he have any bits of salami stuck between his teeth? He peered at himself in the mirrored elevator wall, baring his teeth, as the uniformed elevator boy tactfully examined his polished black shoes. No, nothing amiss. He looked good—and not just for his age, fifty-seven this year. He was still tall, no sloped shoulders, still flat of stomach although no one who saw how viciously he ate could ever understand how. He still had that grin; that devouring, yet boyishly infectious grin. He looked good. Damn good.

Hmm. Maybe that friend of Truman's that he'd met at another one of these parties, that cute little Carol Marcus, would be there tonight. She was a blond cream puff, a Marilyn look-alike, just his type. Bill grinned, thinking about pink, pert nipples against creamy, filmy silk, writhing hips beneath his hands, softness, suppleness, buoyant boobs slapping against his chest—

And just like that, Bill Paley was hungry again.

"BILL! HAVE YOU EVER SEEN anything like this?" Truman approached him, a martini in one hand, a cigarette in the other. He was red of face, flustered, sweat plastering his thinning hair to his forehead. But he surveyed the room with the satisfaction of a potentate. "Oh, I *love* the Plaza, don't you? It's my favorite place on earth. I just adore how even the bellhops look down their noses at you, as if you might take a shit in the potted plants. How wonderful of Babe to throw me this little shindig!"

"You deserve it, even though I don't want to think about what this little shindig is costing me. What's the new book called again?" Bill downed the last warm drops of watered-down bourbon and signaled for a fresh glass. One magically appeared.

"It's a novella. *Breakfast at Tiffany's*. Random House published it while I was in Europe, but what a nice treat to come home to. And Babe, of course—she simply insisted on throwing this little fete, even as I begged her not to." Truman shook his head, but he did not appear to be too put out.

This little fete was taking place in the Oak Room at the Plaza; for Mrs. William S. Paley and her friend, the bestselling author Truman Capote, naturally management had closed it to the public on this night. The vaulted ceilings, the gleaming oak walls, the heavy square bar at the end of the room; the old baronial atmosphere of the place was lightened somewhat by cozy little round tables filled with flowers and copies of Truman's book. The red cover, emblazoned with the words *Breakfast at Tiffany's, a Short Novel, and Three Other Stories by Truman Capote*—Bill could see a copy of it wherever he looked, for Babe had bought out Brentano's. Bennett and Phyllis Cerf, holding court at the other end of the room, must be counting the profits even while they were making small talk.

But Bennett was only the publisher. Truman was the writer. And Bill respected artists, creative types. He was like Bennett himself—arbiter and procurer of talent—so he had no great awe for the founder of Random House (and besides, there was no money in books, anyway. Television was where it was at). But around someone like Truman, especially tonight, Bill could sometimes be uncharacteristically shy. For Bill Paley truly admired artists, and he had to admit that Truman, swishy and flamboyant, was a complete professional at his craft, taking it very seriously, secreting himself away from even Babe for long periods of time to work on it. And he was good. Talented. Respected by those who should know, his peers and critics. And so Bill had to respect him, too. And sometimes, just like when Jack Benny and George Burns bent their heads together and dissected a joke with the cold precision of surgeons, Bill got a little tongue-tied.

He hadn't read this book, mind you. And Truman didn't appear to have expected him to—another thing Bill appreciated about him; Truman simply seemed happy to see his friend, to involve him in his celebration. Before he'd joined Bill at the bar, Truman had been swanning about, gliding through the other guests, accepting accolades with humility, poking and provoking—"So what did you think of Holly? The only completely honest character I've ever written, hand to God." Or, wagging his finger at Slim, at Gloria, at C.Z., at Marella and that dishy little Carol and her equally dishy friend Gloria Vanderbilt—"Now, you don't think I modeled Holly after you, do you? She's my own creation!"

But now, with Bill, he seemed to relax, shrug off the famous-author mantle, and appeared happy to talk about anything other than himself.

"Babe said you were about to buy another Degas. I'd love to see it."

"Yeah, yeah, my broker has a lead. I don't know where I'll hang it yet, though. That's always the thing, isn't it?"

"Problems, problems," Truman said with an impish grin, and Bill had to laugh at himself and take a swig of ice-cold bourbon on the rocks.

"Christ, I know, that sounds so pompous. I would have given my left nut to have these kinds of problems, back in the day."

"Don't I know it." Truman narrowed his eyes, looking out at the party. The two men were leaning against the great oak bar; from across the room Babe, tall and impossibly beautiful in a red wool Charles James cocktail suit with a portrait collar, stood out even among this rarefied crowd of millionaires and models, actors and authors. "Now, you see, I have to think about what I'll write next. What can possibly trump this last book? It's always on my mind. Do I keep writing short stories? Journalism? What about another novel? I just don't seem to have the stamina for a novel, though. But it does seem as if it's expected of me. I have ideas, of course—I record them all. But I don't know, honey, I just don't. And there's so much pressure, you have no idea! Bennett may smile and say, 'Take your time,' but he runs a business and I make money for that business, and so I'm a bit like a sharecropper. Indebted to the company store."

"But you're talent." Now Bill felt more comfortable; he was on familiar ground here. "Talent has to be made some allowances. I couldn't let Jack Benny work fifty-two weeks a year. He needs a hiatus. And when he's off the air, or we're in reruns, I lose money, believe me. But he needs the time off to recharge. The show would suffer."

"What about that Lucy show?" Truman arched an eyebrow and rubbed his forehead with his pinkie finger. "I wouldn't call that quality television, Bill."

"No, you're right. It's not. And she's showing some age—the show, that is."

"Lucy, too." And Truman sat his drink down, put both hands to the side of his face, and pulled the skin back, tight.

Bill laughed again. "But people—pardon the pun—love Lucy. Shows like that make money. They allow me to put on other things, more highbrow—Leonard Bernstein's concerts, for example. *Playhouse Ninety.*"

"What's your favorite show, Bill? Tell me, I'm curious. I know a patriarch isn't supposed to have favorites, but you must. And don't just blurt out the show that makes the most money."

"*Gunsmoke,* " Bill replied without a moment's hesitation.

"Oh, my God!" And Truman threw back his head and laughed; he clapped his hands, as delighted as a boy at the circus.

But Bill wasn't at all embarrassed by the reaction; he was accustomed to it.

"*Gunsmoke* is America. It's good versus evil. It's like it used to be—like it used to be in the war." But he did surprise himself by this comparison; he hadn't thought about it that way before. But by God, that was it, probably. Why he loved the show so damn much. The simple heroism of Marshal Dillon—Ed Murrow during the war, but in a ten-gallon hat instead of a trench coat. The comic relief of Chester. The gruff wisdom of Doc. The too-good-to-be-true whore with the heart of gold, Miss Kitty.

And evil, every episode, in the form of outlaws and bandits and speculators and Indians. Uncomplicated evil. Bad guys who needed their comeuppance, and thanks to him, Bill Paley, by way of Marshal Matt Dillon (played by James Arness, the sweetest, dumbest lug he'd ever met), they would get it. They'd get that bullet in the heart, or a scalping by the Indians, or be run out of town forever. Because they deserved it.

Just like Hitler, just like the Nazis, just like the Japs.

Today, the enemy wasn't so clear. Sometimes Bill was just so heartily sick of all he had to contend with: instilling loyalty oaths, a few years back. God, Ed Murrow had given him an earful about that. There were Commies, Pinkos, those Rosenbergs, giving him one more reason to try to forget he was a Jew. There were always problems with affiliates, griping about the programming; there were always sponsors threatening to withdraw (like Alcoa, pulling out of *See It Now*). Color television—well, he'd lost that battle. David Sarnoff and RCA won. It was their technology, not CBS's, that the government determined to be the industry standard.

"I like the show, Truman, that's all. It appeals to me, for reasons I'm sure you'll never understand."

But Truman surprised him. Truman always managed to surprise him.

"Bill, I am the last person on this earth who would criticize your taste. I believe that the most creative, forward-thinking personalities are those with a healthy dose of lowbrow, mixed with high-brow. That's your genius. As it is mine, I'm not too modest to say. Modesty bores me. I hate people who act coy. Just come right out and say it, if you believe it—I'm the greatest. I'm the cat's pajamas. I'm *it*!" And Truman clinked his own glass—a martini—against Bill's. "So are you, Bill Paley. You are *it*. We both are. Two titans, astride their world."

Bill grinned and relaxed. He had to hand it to Truman; he was the only fairy in New York who knew how to talk to men. Real men.

"Oh, Truman, you naughty, naughty boy!" A dishy blonde—not that Carol, but someone who looked a lot like her—wriggled up to them. She was wearing a very low-cut, very tight red satin dress. Immediately, Bill thought that if Babe saw her, she'd wrinkle her nose and decide the fabric was too shiny, the cut too extreme, the overall effect cheap. Sometimes he couldn't help but see women through his wife's superior eyes, but it never clouded his overall vision.

"What, Mona?" Truman gazed at the girl with a calm, bemused expression.

"You know, she's me! I mean, I! Holly Golightly! I'm her! I know you based her on me!"

"Mona, my dearest, most vapid girl, I assure you that I did not. Holly Golightly is entirely my own creation."

"Oh, no!" The girl inched closer, and looked up at Bill. Her eyes widened, and she squirmed, as if someone had just dropped an ice cube down her back. "Now, I want you to tell this gorgeous man here—"

"Bill Paley, Mona Cartwright. Mona Cartwright, Bill Paley."

"Oooh! So nice to meet you, Mr. Paley! Anyway, Tru-Tru, I want you to tell Mr. Paley that I am the model for Holly Golightly! The things I've told you, over too many cocktails—and then I read them on the pages of your story! The South American—that Brazilian! You know I told you all about that!"

"Mona, you may believe what you like. If it helps you sleep at night, by all means, go to bed thinking you're Holly Golightly. Now, be a good little Marilyn and wriggle off somewhere else."

"Truman!" Mona leaned over to kiss Truman on the cheek— and flash Bill her creamy, heaving cleavage. Then she did sashay off, with only one sleepy-lidded backward glance.

"Honestly." Truman turned to Bill with a chuckle. Even a less keen observer of the human condition than Truman Capote couldn't have helped to notice the hunger, the desire, in Bill Paley's eyes as they followed the blonde through her maneuvers. Truman noted, but made no reference to it. He simply stored it away. For now.

"Everyone wants to be in a book," he drawled exaggeratedly. "I've simply been deluged by women who believe they're the model for Holly. Carol Marcus, Gloria Vanderbilt, Gloria Guinness, Marella, Slim, even. They all think that some part of Holly is based on them."

"I don't want to be in a book," Bill said with a grunt. "I have no desire. I think it would be terrible, actually. To have people read something and think it's about you."

"Well, you're an exception, then."

"An exception to what?" Babe had suddenly inserted herself between her husband and her friend. With one arm behind Bill's back and the other tucked into Truman's arm, she surveyed her party with a beatific, satisfied smile.

"An exception to mere mortals. Bill, that is. He claims he'd hate to be written about in a book."

"Oh, Bill!" Babe tilted her impeccable head up to him and laughed. She was exceptionally beautiful tonight; she seemed to have her own spotlight following her around, illuminating her features, making her eyes even darker, her cheekbones even more pronounced, her hair even silkier. Just to look at her—Bill smiled the satisfied grin of ownership; Truman, the incredulous grin of appreciation. Their gazes met behind Babe's back; Bill's eyes widened, as did Truman's. So they had something else in common, too.

"But I think he's right," Babe continued, unaware of the slight jousting occurring on either side (Bill's arm encircled her waist; Truman gripped her arm more tightly). "I would detest being in a book. Promise me that, Truman? Promise me you won't ever do that? I know every woman here tonight thinks she's Holly Golightly. But I—" And she shuddered.

"I don't know how I could," Truman said, and he knew it to be honest and true, as honest and true as Holly Golightly herself. "Any words of mine could never do you justice, Babe, dear."

Babe blushed, a rarity. Bill could count on one hand the number of times he'd seen his wife blush, and each one was because of Truman. With Bill, she was so composed, always. Composed, and dignified, and untouchable. Impervious to abandonment or real emotion.

But that little blonde . . . now, there was a woman who a man—a real man, like Bill Paley, not some little homo like Truman Capote—could make blush. Pretty pink, from her cheeks to her little round—

"Bill, dear, I know you must be famished. They'll bring in a buffet in a moment, full of your favorites, I made sure of it. I also reserved a table for you and for Jock and Betsey, so you don't have to talk to anyone you don't want to—"

"Never mind. I'm not hungry. And I think I'll disappear now, Babe. I had a hard day."

Bill, his eyes following that little blonde as she sashayed her way around the room, did not even glance at his wife's face. "Truman, will you see Babe home? I give her to you. For now. And congratulations again. I'm sure it's a terrific book, and Babe will make me read it someday."

Truman laughed and grasped Bill's hand in his own surprisingly strong grip. Babe, after an imperceptible intake of breath, kissed her husband on the cheek and whispered sincerely, a worried expression in her brown eyes, "You go home and go right to bed, poor darling! I'll sleep in the drawing room when I come in, so I won't disturb you." Then she watched her husband stride through the room, his arms swinging in that commanding way of his, his grin, as he was greeted by everyone in his path, incandescent enough to light the room all by itself.

Truman turned Babe around, toward the bartender, just in time. Just in time for her not to see Bill Paley follow a writhing, red-satin-clad bottom out of the Oak Room of the Plaza.

"Now the fun will really start," he whispered in her ear, delighted to see her wary eyes turn girlish, just at the promise of his voice. "Now we'll have the best time ever, just the two of us!"

And Babe, hastily erasing the frown that had puckered her forehead, put her hand in Truman's, trusting him.

Bill didn't give either of them another thought. He was too busy convincing the little blonde to go upstairs, allowing her her maidenly protests, playing the game as well as any other man in his position, with his wealth, his appetites, his power. It didn't take very long.

It never did.

. . . . .

Babe was up before Bill the next morning, as usual. After a short but heavenly night's sleep on the drawing room sofa (she'd been able to take her teeth out, thank the Lord!), she'd risen with the sun, determined to call her florist's private number and arrange a special early delivery. Then she'd rushed into the bathroom, made up her face, and rung for some coffee, delivered to her, naturally, by St. Regis room service, the waiter pushing in a mahogany cart with her own Wedgwood coffeepot and cup and saucer, and a silver vase with a peony in it, not a rose. As soon as she and Bill redecorated this small apartment and made it their city residence, she'd gone down to the kitchen and introduced herself to all the staff, thanking them in advance for their care and consideration. And asking them, if they pleased, never to put a rose on her tray. They understood, surely, that she and Bill wanted to think of this as a real home, not a hotel, and she so looked forward to doing just that, with their help.

And of course, she asked her secretary to record all their birthdays, and she never missed a one, sending a card with a little extra gift of money to each. She and Bill both were generous tippers, each week sending out little envelopes full of cash to those who made their lives easier. When she was out shopping, she often brought something back—something small, like a flattering lipstick or a silk-flower pin or a cigarette case—for a maid, or a particularly attentive bellman.

Thus, the peony and her own china, not the official St. Regis pattern. And the newspapers ironed, without her even having to ask.

"Thank you so much," she told the waiter, a new boy with a complexion like a lobster, so skinny his Adam's apple was as pronounced as his nose. "Andrew, isn't it? I so appreciate it."

And Andrew—Andy to his friends and family, but not here, not at the St. Regis where nicknames were not allowed—blushed, his face turning even more mottled and scarlet; he tripped over his own comically large feet on the way out, and thought to himself, as he took the service elevator back down to the kitchen, that he'd never seen a more beautiful gal than Mrs. Paley first thing in the morning. He thought of his own mother, probably just getting up in their apartment in Queens. In her scruffy old quilted housecoat, her hair still in curlers, no makeup on, her eyes puffy from sleep, creases on her face as if she'd slept on chicken wire instead of a lumpy mattress. Drinking her coffee out of a heavy mug while she watched the small TV in the kitchen, picking away at the chipped Formica on the table.

But Mrs. Paley! She looked as if she didn't need sleep at all! She was wearing some kind of silk gown with a tie around her waist, and slippers that looked like real shoes, only with little puffs of fur on the end, and her hair was all done, and he thought, although he wasn't sure—because he never could tell about these things, just ask his girlfriend, Sue—that she even had lipstick on. And her eyes weren't the least bit red and puffy, not at all! Not a crease of sleep on her face, either.

Babe smiled after Andrew the waiter left; she'd read the awe, the appreciation on his face. And even if he was just a young man, a waiter, she enjoyed that, of course. What woman doesn't enjoy being appreciated? To know that, first thing in the morning, was very special, indeed. And she savored the moment, lighting a cigarette, inhaling through her ebony holder, watching the closed door through the haze of smoke, half wondering if Andrew would pop back in for another glimpse, on the pretext of forgetting something.

But then she shook her head sternly. *Oh, Babe! Stop being such a common girl.* And she poured her coffee and dialed the phone.

Three hours later, after Bill had risen, showered, shaved, shoveled his food down his throat, kissed her cheek, and left for work with a grunt, there was a knock at the door. And Babe ran to answer it, her heart beating wildly. What was wrong with her today? She really was acting like a teenager!

"How did you know?" Truman had tears in his swollen, red eyes as he held out his hand; in it was a small vase of lilies of the valley, their sweet, bell-like flowers still creamy white against the dark green foliage. "How on earth did you know?"

"I just did."

Truman fell into Babe's arms; she grabbed the vase from him just in time. They walked into the drawing room, Truman's head on her shoulder, tears streaming down his face.

"I am so blue," he sobbed quietly as they sat down on a small sofa. "Just so blue. And you knew. You knew!"

"Yes. I knew you would be, the morning after. I had a feeling."

"It's so hard. Why does it always have to be so hard?" Truman's shoulders shook with a suppressed sob. "And Jack doesn't understand at all. He's so tyrannical, in his way. He has absolutely no sympathy for me. He just doesn't know. How—how empty I am! Even after last night—especially after last night, and nights like it. How the hollowness just gets to you. The loneliness. The special loneliness of being in a room full of people who are there just for you. God, he has no idea!"

"I do," Babe whispered into her friend's ear. "I do, dearest Truman. Because Bill—oh, I was so furious with him last night! He didn't even see me, did he? Not once did he compliment me. I had that suit made especially for him, because he once said he liked that color. And he didn't even eat a bite of all that food I arranged just for him! He didn't say a word to Betsey and Jock! He has no idea how hard I work to make things just right for him, to give him what he wants, to look how he wants me to—he just takes it all for granted. Why, even the waiter this morning who brought up my coffee took more notice of me!"

"And that's why I brought you some of my flowers." Truman pointed to the vase that Babe had set down on an end table—not just an end table, of course, but a priceless Louis XVI commode. "You sent me these flowers because you knew I'd be blue. I brought you some because I knew the same thing. We don't even have to tell each other, do we, Babe? We just know. It's so rare, what we have. Come here, my darling girl." And he held out his arms.

Babe stretched out on the sofa (not just a sofa, naturally, but a Louis XVI settee completely re-covered in an antique silk upholstery re-created and woven just for the Paleys) and put her head on Truman's lap; he smoothed that throbbing vein on her forehead, pale blue against her creamy skin. She closed her eyes and let a few tears fall. "I hate him sometimes, you know. I really do. I don't know what time he came home last night. I didn't check to see if he was in bed when I got home. I don't do that anymore. I just don't want to know."

"But you love him, too," Truman whispered soothingly. "Just like I love Jack. We hate them, but we can't live without them."

"Jack loves you back. Bill doesn't love me. Jack is prickly and fierce to everyone because he wants to protect you, because he values you. Bill wouldn't throw me a life preserver if I was drowning."

"That's ridiculous. He loves you, Babe. He just doesn't know how to show it. Not like I do. And you love him, too. Admit it."

"I want him to love me. Is that the same thing?" Babe's eyes remained closed. She thought back to when she first met Bill, after having been told, through mutual friends, that he admired her. Babe was newly divorced from a Tuxedo Park blueblood (who had hit her on occasion, but that was what makeup was for, Gogs had sternly reminded her when Babe came running home for comfort; funny, though, how vehemently her mother argued for divorce after the blueblood revealed all his money was tied up in trust). She was, she recalled, emotionally bruised and battered, feeling as if she'd been found wanting in judgment and taste. Even though she had absolutely no memory of ever choosing Stanley Mortimer, only of being forced to sit next to him at debutante party after party, dinner after dinner, until she found herself sitting beside him in a bridal gown at their wedding lunch.

Despite her emotional fragility, Babe Cushing Mortimer had been at the peak of her desirability. Beautiful, more sure of her taste and fashion sense than ever before, still ripe—and with no money to speak of, but a fabulous lifestyle to finance. Because what else could a woman like her, of good breeding, a finishing school education, and coveted looks, do but live well and decoratively? And that took money, of course.

And Bill. Not quite divorced, although later they both conveniently rearranged the timeline and insisted that he had already jettisoned the first wife. But Bill, that evening she first saw him at one of Condé Nast's hilariously crowded parties, was certainly the most vibrant man in the room, with that blustery grin; Stanley, her first husband, had so rarely smiled. The grinning, brash young head of CBS was also by far the most important man present, even more important than the host; this was evident by the way all the guests circled about him, eager and obsequious, while Condé sat alone in a corner, munching on canapés.

And then Bill raised his head above the sycophants and saw her, Babe, standing tall beneath a chandelier, a silver fox stole over her shoulders, and he chose her. She saw it in his eyes, the way they widened, the way his shoulders squared, his head snapped up, and there was nothing more she wanted but to be possessed by him, reassured of her worth in a world where feminine beauty and refinement were currency. Someone whispered that he was Jewish, but in that heady moment of being acquired by someone as powerful and handsome and wealthy as he was, it didn't matter. Or— perhaps it did; her mother had picked out Stanley Mortimer. Gogs would never have picked out Bill Paley. That was Babe's decision alone; perhaps the first she'd made in her life.

But was that love?

She hurt when Bill hurt, that was true. Once, she'd walked over to a new swim club being built across the road from Kiluna North, in lily-white New Hampshire. She thought the children could join; it would do them good to make friends. She introduced herself as

Mrs. William S. Paley, filled out the forms, was polite and sincere in her hope that the Paleys could enjoy the club. But she never heard back; later, a neighbor told her it was because Bill—and his children—were Jewish. But that she, Babe, could join if she liked.

She'd never told Bill this. She had seen him so wounded, so forlorn, when similar rejections had occurred. His blue eyes would fill with tears and his chin would tremble as if he were a little boy and not one of the most powerful men in all of broadcasting. Then the hurt would drain away to wrath, to steely determination, another house or another Picasso or another television station, or another designer dress that Babe didn't really want but that Bill insisted on, insisted on her looking so unattainable that those who rejected him would surely gnash their teeth in despair, to look at what he owned. Whom he owned.

Whom he married, that is.

But love?

She'd never felt her heart race in anticipation, knowing she would see Bill. Yet every time she was going to meet Truman, she felt so excited, so certain of delight that her skin tingled with adrenaline and she found herself laughing, all alone, even before he arrived. She always looked her best for Bill, but she went out of her way to find some new twist or flare to delight Truman: bells on her skirt, a whimsical brooch on an otherwise tasteful, expensive blouse. Because to make Truman gasp, to make him clap his hands, dance with joy, be struck dumb with awe, was simply the greatest delight she knew.

Pleasure, she realized, joy, anticipation—none of these had anything to do with how she felt about her husband, or even her children. But they had everything to do with how she felt about Truman.

"Do you know what?" Babe sat up, reached into her pocket, and dried her eyes with an embroidered handkerchief, careful not to smudge her mascara. She gazed at Truman, who was holding her hand tenderly, caressing it, loving it. Claiming it.

Claiming her.

So Babe took a deep breath, and decided to take the plunge. To be loved was not something she ever expected for herself, not anymore. But to love someone—oh, yes. Oh, God, yes. No one could deprive her of that.

"My analyst said something ridiculous to me the other day." She couldn't prevent a nervous laugh; she couldn't look Truman in the eye. "He said—I can't believe he said this!—he said I ought to have an affair with you. That you were obviously my obsession, and an affair would be a good thing, a healthy thing. For me, that is." Babe felt unsteady, even though she was seated on the sofa; the room, red fabric walls, the silk hangings on the window, the most charming antiques money could buy, seemed to press in on her, tighter than the most unforgiving ball gown, the most constricting undergarment. Nothing was as it was supposed to be. The room was no longer a diorama of money and taste, arranged by the best decorators in town, Billy Baldwin and Sister Parish, but rather, now it was a circus tent. A *hideous* circus tent—oh, why hadn't she seen this before, all that fabric on the ceiling and the walls?—and she was the freak show on display, all her needs and wants spilling out of her, pooling into the sawdust at her feet.

She couldn't breathe. Although she was aware, acutely, of the sound of Truman doing just that, sitting next to her.

Suddenly she pulled her hand away from his and buried her face in a pillow. She simply couldn't bear to hear what she knew he was going to say.

"Oh, Babe." And his voice was soft, sad. "Oh, my Babe. Do you know, do you have any idea, how dearly I would love for that to be possible?"

Babe shook her head, the silk tassels of the pillow tickling her cheek. If she could only stay buried; if she never had to look at Truman's face.

But that was impossible; she felt his hands, strong and masculine and soft and feminine, pulling her up, turning her toward him. He pushed her hair out of her eyes, and finally she had to look. His face was naked, completely vulnerable; he'd taken off his glasses, an act of intimacy that made her heart race with hope. He leaned in to her, carefully, and holding his breath, just like the most tender, most unsure of hopeful lovers, he kissed her, his lips tickling hers.

But then he pulled away, although he kept his hands on her shoulders. There were tears in his beautiful eyes.

"But it's not possible. I am who I am, and I'm not ashamed of it. I like men. I always have. I've never even been tempted by the thought of being with a woman. But now, this moment, is the first time in my entire life when I have wished, just for the teensiest bit, that I was. You must know that, and remember it. *We* must remember this moment forever, because it is love we feel for each other. And we're so lucky to have it."

Babe took a deep breath, let the air fill her lungs almost to bursting, holding it in, like a child desperate for a wish to come true. If it had been anyone else but Truman, she would have run, hidden herself. If it had been anyone else but Truman, she wouldn't have said this in the first place, would never have exposed herself so thoroughly, allowed herself to be seen as someone real with raw needs and desires. If it had been anyone else but Truman whom she did love, just as he said—she released her breath. If it had been anyone else, but Truman.

But it was Truman, wasn't it? Now, and always. He was still the same soul who saw her, and appreciated her, no matter how she allowed herself to be seen: vulnerable or impenetrable, exquisitely clothed and coiffed or with her hair unkempt, her eyes pink and runny.

It was Truman.

"It's ridiculous, I know. I told Dr. Cameron so. It's just that—" and Babe suddenly found herself with her friend again, not rejected at all; and best of all, most startling of all, loved, even if it wasn't quite the way she longed to be. But sometimes one had to make the best of things. Hadn't her mother taught her that, all her life? Bill might not see her, might not love her. But Truman, in his way, did.

So Babe indulged herself, pouring out that swollen sac of loneliness and regret, spilling it all over his lap, knowing he wouldn't mind the mess of it, after all. "It's just that I do get lonely, you know. For love, in that way. Bill won't be that for me again, if he ever was. Oh, but I do miss it! I long for it. I long to be touched, and desired. I don't know how I can live the rest of my life, knowing that my husband doesn't want me. And I've never told anyone that before. Not even Dr. Cameron. Not even my sisters. I don't know why I told you, even. But I'm glad. I'm *so* glad that I did!"

Babe closed her eyes and laid her head back down in Truman's lap; he didn't say a word for a very long time. He only continued to stroke her hair, bend down to kiss her on the lips—chastely, but lovingly. She could have gone to sleep; she could have slept better than she ever had, no need for a Miltown. She felt sated, physically. As if they had, indeed, consummated their passion.

And, perhaps, they had.

After several minutes, she opened her eyes. Truman was gazing down at her with such love, such sincere concern. She smiled and sat up.

"Goodness, I must be a mess. Let me fix myself up and let's go out. What would you like to do?"

"You look absolutely breathtaking, but do what you have to do, my love. I'd like to see a movie. Let's do that."

"Do you want me to ring up CBS and reserve the screening room? Or we could have them send something out to Kiluna and watch it there, in the little theater."

"Babe, oh, my Babe!" Truman laughed, but it wasn't cruel. "Don't you ever go out to the movies, like real people? To an actual theater?"

"Well, no, not since, well, not in a long time." Babe blushed; sometimes she did forget how rarefied her life had become. Bless Truman for not making her feel utterly ridiculous!

"Well, I meant we should go see a movie. In a movie theater. With popcorn and everything. Not caviar. And it will be my treat."

"Of course, that sounds wonderful." And Babe rose, herself once more; she felt her spine straighten, her breathing slow down, and the room once more was a gorgeous thing to behold, a testament to her taste and breeding and wealth. Bill's wealth. She was Barbara Cushing Mortimer Paley.

And right now, this moment, maybe, perhaps, she was loved.

Babe quickly changed into a Dior day dress, white silk with soft blue polka dots, tight at the waist, with a bow to the side and a portrait collar—she supposed that was appropriate for a movie theater—reapplied her makeup, and selected a deeper blue Hermès bag. She put her gloves on, surveyed herself in the full-length mirror, turning around, craning her neck so she could see over her shoulder. One slight adjustment to her stocking, and she felt ready to sail out and face whoever might be looking her way: maids, waiters, salespeople, photographers, Gloria or Slim or Marella or C.Z. People—friends, families, strangers—looked *at* her, and they looked *for* her. They always had. It was a fact of her life. She must be ready, then. She must make it worth their while.

"Before we see the movie, I have a surprise for you." Babe rejoined Truman in the drawing room. He had reverted back to being rather melancholy; he had not moved from the sofa to fix himself a drink, or to ooh and ahh at the paintings or antiques; he hadn't followed her into the bedroom to sit and gossip while she got ready, so unlike him. No, he was still seated on the sofa, his spectacles off, his face in his hands; when he looked up at her, she could see he had been rubbing his eyes, as they looked small and tired.

"A surprise?" Now he did put on his glasses; she saw an interested little gleam in his eyes, and she was thrilled to have sparked it.

"A surprise."

"Where are we going?"

"You'll see!"

And soon enough they were sailing through the marble lobby of the St. Regis, with its clouds and cherubs on the ceiling, inlaid floors, gigantic floral arrangements, and crossing Fifty-fifth Street, turning right on Fifth Avenue, and entering Tiffany's. The top-hatted doorman's eyes widened in recognition; he held the door open for them with a properly awed "Good morning, Mrs. Paley! Mr. Capote! What an honor!"

Truman's face was truly gleaming now; he seemed to grow five inches.

"Oh, I do love Tiffany's." He sighed as he followed Babe's lead;

she strode surely down the center aisle, not stopping to look in any of the cases, for naturally, Mrs. William S. Paley did not shop like mere mortals; there were private rooms and corridors for her, employees whom the regular shoppers would never see. Hidden doors, soft chairs, teacups, and jewels brought out on velvet trays, just for her. Truman had never known this world, until he met her. "Oh, Truman, one never buys jewelry in public. It's so dear of you, though, to think of it," she once told him, when he wanted to pop into Van Cleef to buy her a trinket. And far from being offended, he was grateful for the advice. He'd told her that she was the "best finishing school in the world," and she'd beamed.

"Tiffany's is like a country club for the gods," Truman said with a sigh. "I always think that, when I'm here." And Babe smiled; the wooden paneling always did remind her of a club. A rarefied, exclusive club.

"Third floor," she instructed the elevator man, who nodded and pressed the button. "I told you, Truman, dear, that I'd been asked to design a little display upstairs?"

"No, you didn't, Bobolink. How thrilling!"

"Not really," Babe said with a wry smile. "They asked several 'society ladies,' as I believe they refer to us. Gloria did one, and so did Marella."

The elevator opened and they stepped out; in the display cases were exquisite place settings of china and crystal and silver, all tastefully illuminated. There was a room off to one side, where a young woman, clad in a dress, hat, and gloves that made her look forty, not twenty—already dressing for the role, Babe decided— sat with her mother, obviously registering for wedding gifts.

Babe slowed down and took Truman's hand in hers; she was

already smiling, anticipating his reaction, when she led him into another room and pointed to the display.

There, amid several boring, uninventive set pieces (Marella had set a wicker table with a china pattern of yellow roses and grapevines—"How typically, revoltingly *Italian*," Truman whispered, while Babe shook her head in admonishment; Gloria Guinness's table setting was equally uninspired—"La Guinness can't disguise the peasant in her," was Truman's pronouncement even as Babe tried to shush him), was a flowered chaise longue that Truman recognized from Babe's bedroom at Kiluna. Next to the chaise stood a round table holding a full place setting of bone china with a lattice-worked border, along with a silver coffeepot and a crystal glass filled with orange juice.

On the chaise longue, half-opened, was a copy of Truman's book.

"*Breakfast at Tiffany's!*" he squealed, his face pure joy; he laughed so delightedly, from his belly, that the smattering of hushed, earnest shoppers all turned his way. But Babe didn't care; she had done it. She had surprised him, delighted him. Given him something back—given him back himself, the assured, triumphant self that had fled him the morning after, leaving him hollow and empty and so sad.

"Oh, Babe, you dear! You love, you perfect creature! I'm utterly delighted. Tickled to death, spank my bottom and call me Daddy!"

"I'm so glad you like it," Babe said, her face flushing with accomplishment. She couldn't help but think of how much time she'd put into this "silly little thing," as she'd pronounced it to one and all. How she'd racked and racked her brain to come up with something different from the expected, and how pleased she'd been when she'd hit on the idea. She'd longed for weeks to tell Truman about it, but now was satisfied that she'd waited until just the right moment to share it with him.

"Now, let's go see that movie," she said, and he nodded as they left, pausing only to sign one or two autographs from patrons who had finally recognized him. With each signature, his eyes sparkled just a bit more.

So did Babe's.

THE MOVIE TRUMAN CHOSE was *Pinocchio*. That old Disney cartoon. She was mystified as to why; as to why he dragged her downtown, somewhere around the Bowery, and insisted on hailing a cab instead of phoning for a car. Babe pretended to enjoy riding in the big yellow taxi, making sure that a game "let's see what happens next!" expression was arranged on her face. But she was fearful the entire ride that she'd sat in something dreadful, like gum, or a squished candy bar. Or worse.

The theater was in what she would euphemistically call an "interesting neighborhood." There were many young Negro children playing in the street, all by themselves, no parents or nannies in watchful attendance. Rusty cars and delivery trucks dominated the landscape, and the apartment buildings were all in dreadful condition, some of them with broken windows, torn awnings; all had filthy, crumbling stoops.

But she followed Truman into the theater, which was surprisingly clean and spacious and empty. They had an entire row to themselves. The lights dimmed and the movie commenced, the old story about Geppetto, longing for a son, and the Blue Fairy, who granted the wish, and Jiminy Cricket, who yearned to be a conscience—and Pinocchio, the wooden puppet who comes to life.

Babe hid a yawn, not very interested in the movie, although she hadn't seen it before. She was more interested in Truman's rapturous face as he gazed at the screen, the movie's images reflected in his tortoise-shell eyeglasses. He laughed delightedly when Pinocchio went to Pleasure Island, and by the end, when the Blue Fairy granted Pinocchio his wish and turned him into a real boy and Jiminy Cricket was crooning "When You Wish Upon a Star," Truman grasped her hand and began to sob uncontrollably.

The lights flickered back on, and the few others in the theater rose and filed out, gaping at the two of them, Truman crying, Babe bewildered. She was terrified someone would recognize her; she instinctively ducked her head, averting her famous face. But then she realized that no one would recognize her, not here, not in this neighborhood, and the realization was both a stab of annoyance and a warm bath of safe anonymity. For a giddy moment, Babe longed to run up and down the aisle screaming and waving her arms, or to do something equally scandalous and out of character. No one would ever know it was she.

But she was brought back to reality by her gasping, sobbing friend, clinging to her arm as if he were drowning.

"Truman, what is it, dear? What's wrong? It's a happy ending! Truman, it's a happy film!"

Truman shook his head, the tears still streaming, his face very red, anguish in his eyes. Finally, he collected himself a little; he took a deep breath, let out an enormous sigh, and mopped his eyes with a handkerchief.

"The first time I saw this, my heart broke, it just gave way inside me. Because, you see, that was always my dearest wish, too. To be a real boy for my mother, so she would love me, so she wouldn't be ashamed of me and say hateful things to me and try to pretend I was something I wasn't. I just wanted to be a real boy, you see. Not always, you understand—oh, no! But when I saw this movie, all I could think of was how pleased Mama would be, how she'd finally love me, if only I was."

"Oh, Truman!" Babe's own heart twisted in sympathy; she wanted to fold him up in her arms and take him home and give him the childhood he so deserved, the love that he had missed. She wanted to be his mother, and his lover, both in one day, and the different emotions, jaggedly different, *biblically* different, made her disoriented, dizzy once more.

"And now, today, what you said to me earlier. Babe, right now, this minute, I wish I could be a real boy for you, my heart. So I could give you what you need, all you need and desire. So I can give you what Bill won't, that bastard. That's what I want so much. Only this moment, you understand. But it's true, it's real, it's the realest thing about me when I'm with you."

Babe blinked, surprised tears in her eyes. She looked down at Truman's manicured little hand in hers, and she looked at the rest of him, the short legs, barely touching the floor; the tweed trousers he was wearing, his soft belly just beginning to strain against his cashmere sweater vest. She thought of the hidden rest of him, the parts she'd never seen, and was overcome with desire to see them, touch him, arouse him, challenge him to do the same to her, to overcome his true nature, to be a real boy—a real man.

But then he wouldn't be Truman, would he? For that otherness, that uniqueness—goodness, let's just say it, Babe, all right, his *queerness*—was the gossamer, quirky thread stitching everything else together, the intellect and talent and confidence and thirst for beauty. His seriousness—that's what she always told people she admired most about him. How serious and dedicated he was about his work, about people, about life.

But if that was all he was, he wouldn't have made it into her orbit. It was the "other" quality that made it safe for Bill to approve of their friendship, to invite him into their lives as fully as he had. Truman straight just wasn't Truman. And even she, Babe Paley, goddess among mere mortals, couldn't bring herself to believe that she could be the one, the only woman in his life, while he continued to sleep with men on the side. That just wasn't possible, and she knew it.

"Truman, dear, don't distress yourself about me. It's just a thing my analyst said, a passing fancy, and a measure of how much I love you. A physical affair couldn't bring us any closer." And as Babe said this, she recognized it as the absolute truth.

"I know." Truman's eyes were dry now, but his hand was still in hers. It remained there as they got in the taxi, and—sensing that neither wanted to go back to the world that expected too much of them, at times—Babe impulsively asked the driver, "How much will you charge to drive out to Long Island?"

It didn't matter what he answered, of course. Babe would pay it, without question.

AND SO, RETREATING, Babe and Truman entered the house at Kiluna feeling rather like runaway children, which they were. The staff was surprised to see them but rose to the occasion, as Babe had selected and trained them to do. She and Truman had a cozy, intimate little dinner of quail and potatoes before the fire in the library, and they didn't say much at all; Babe was content merely to be with him, after all the emotional upheaval of the day, resting her eyes on his sensitive pink face; feeling his hand reach for hers on occasion, but also rejoicing when he let it go and was lost in his own thoughts, but still, somehow—with her. That he felt that comfortable, that natural, so that he didn't strain to impress or amuse; that was a gift.

"Good night, dearest," Babe told him as they went up the stairs, hand in hand; they stood in the hallway outside her room. "Everything should be ready for you in your usual room."

But Truman shook his head.

"No, not tonight, Babe. Tonight, I'm sleeping with you. In your bed, next to you. It's what I want, to be close to you in the only way I can be."

For a moment, Babe couldn't think straight; a swirl of thoughts buzzed about her head and she actually swatted at them, as if they were flies. What did he mean? He'd just said he couldn't have an affair with her. Did he mean, just to sleep? In her bed? Then she'd have to sleep in her makeup, for he could never see her without it. She'd have to keep her teeth in. She wouldn't be able to set her hair. What would Bill say, if any of the servants whispered?

Would Bill even care?

"I don't know, Truman, it's just so—"

"Easy. It's just so easy. Come." And Truman opened the door for her, held her by the hand, and led her across the threshold.

"Oh, I—do let me, let me change in the dressing room, and I'll be out in a jiffy, and if you want—do you need pajamas? I'm sure we have some extra, I'll just ring for some—" Babe was pacing, lighting up a cigarette. Her hands were shaking; her skin felt tight, hot, as though a foreign substance were coating her pores, suffocating her.

Truman shook his head. He walked over to her, the most solemn expression in his eyes; they weren't twinkling, they weren't lighting up with ideas and schemes and plots. They were big and blue, as solemn as a child's. As serious as a man's.

"Stop." And he took the cigarette from her, put it in an ashtray on the table next to her enormous bed.

Trembling, she stood before him. His hands were on her shoulders; he was reaching around her back, undoing the zipper on her dress, letting the fabric fall away so that her back was exposed, and she shivered, her suffocating skin now an icy glaze. As the bodice fell away from her, she put her hands up, covering herself even though she was still in her girdle, bra, panties, and stockings.

Truman undid his own shirt. His eyes never left her face; he was studying her, intense yet wistful. Searching for something. Babe didn't know what. She didn't know what to do, what to say, where to look. So she focused on his chest. She'd seen his chest before, of course: swimming, cavorting around the pool here and in Jamaica, on the Agnellis' yacht last September. She'd even rubbed suntan oil on it, marveling at its smoothness, so unlike Bill's torso with its clumps of hair, swirls of it dotted with odd bare patches.

But now Truman's chest looked like an angel's, innocent and fair, a fine dusting of those golden hairs all over it giving him an ethereal glow. His biceps were surprisingly defined, and he would have looked like a young Adonis, with that pouty, dreamy face, were it not for his stomach, which was a tad poochy. He didn't even try to hold it in as Babe was holding hers, drawing every inch of flesh and muscle inward toward her spine, tightening her buttocks, clenching her teeth, trying to disappear, to be nothing but wisp.

Then Truman guided her over to the bed. "Shhh. Wait here," he said, and he stepped out of his trousers so he was only in his boxers and his socks. Babe wanted to giggle at the red garters holding up his dark stockings; he must have sensed this, because he quickly removed them so that his muscular, perfect legs were completely exposed, and then she wanted to gasp.

Truman went into her dressing room; she couldn't imagine why. Was he drawing her a bath, perhaps?

He returned with some cotton pads and a bottle of astringent.

"Look at me," he said, settling next to her on the bed. "Look at me, only at me. And let me look only at you, Babe. You, just as you really are, beautiful. Real. Mine."

Dabbing a pad with the astringent, he reached toward her face. She sucked in her breath, tears filling her eyes, and she began to protest, squirming.

"Oh, Truman, no, no, please, no—"

"Yes." And he dabbed at her right cheek, taking away. Taking away her makeup, her mask. Exposing—everything. All the ugliness.

She turned away, letting him, but unable to look at him, unable to bear the expression in his eyes when he saw, finally, all she had to hide. She felt him trace her scar, the one along her jaw, tenderly, lovingly.

"It happened," she replied, to the unasked question, "when I was nineteen. A car accident, with some boy. Do you know, I can't even remember his name? We were talking, he was drinking from a flask, and suddenly the car left the road and slammed into a tree. That's what they told me, after. I don't remember; it happened so fast. That's what people always say, don't they? That it happened so fast? Well, it's true. We were driving and then there was a loud bang, like an explosion, and then I woke up in the hospital. My parents—my father, even—they were there, and my face was completely smothered in bandages. I couldn't move; there were harnesses, straps, and rods holding my head and neck completely still. My arms, even my chest, were strapped down. And my mother kept saying, 'Your face! Your face! Your perfect face! What on earth will you do now, my darling, without that face?' "

Babe swallowed as gingerly as she used to back in the hospital, completely immobile, a captive of her looks, of her future. Truman had stopped dabbing and was holding his breath, the astringent in one hand, the cotton pad in the other. Babe found herself staring at his pooch of a stomach, slightly overhanging his plaid silk boxers.

"Do you know, it was the most attention my father ever paid to me?" She laughed, but it sounded, even to Babe's own ears, insincere. "For the first time in my life, my father was with me day and night, bringing in all the best plastic surgeons, ones who had learned from the war. And it was all because of my face. Never mind all those years when I yearned for him to pay attention to me because of my grades, or a funny joke, or simply because I loved him. Finally, I had him, all of him, and it was only to save my face. My 'calling card,' Mother kept saying. And I thought—I really did think this—that if, when the surgeries were done and the bandages removed and I didn't have this face anymore, they wouldn't love me. They'd leave me there in the hospital forever, if I didn't have 'that face.' "

"Darling Babe," Truman breathed, and she finally looked into his eyes; they were beautiful and full of tears and pity and love for her, scars and all.

"The surgeries were so painful," she continued, emboldened now to tell him all, tell him everything, because he wouldn't leave her, he wouldn't hurt her, no matter what she looked like, no matter what imperfections she confided. She had never told her sisters about all of it, had never mentioned it to Serge or to Stanley, her first husband, or, God forbid, Bill, who had no patience for anyone's troubles but his own, who did not care about the provenance of anything except for the paintings he collected. "Little surgeries, one at a time. Tiny little stitches sewing me back together. Some without anesthesia, so my face wouldn't go slack, so the scars would be minimal. I couldn't move for months; I had to lie flat on my back and not stir, not laugh or cry or anything at all, while they restored my face, my perfect face. And my teeth—" Here she did hesitate, still so ashamed that her hand flew to her mouth. "I have false teeth," she said simply. "My own had to be removed."

"Oh, sweetheart!"

"At least I don't have to worry about cavities," Babe replied with a smile. But then she didn't know what else to say; she felt odd, half exposed, with one side of her face made up, the other not. And she was still only wearing her underclothes.

Truman must have sensed this, because he continued his dabbing, swiping away the rest of her mask. Exposing the other scars: The one near her upper lip. The tiny one at the corner of her right eye.

And when he had finished, he turned her toward him. She lifted her head and steeled herself to see her reflection—unadorned, unaltered—in Truman's eyes.

"You are beautiful," he said. "Beautiful. I don't see scars. I only see you. Babe. Perfect—not just because you still are absolutely gorgeous without all the makeup. Good God, those cheekbones! Those eyes! But you are perfect because of who you are, inside. I love you, Babe. I love you for that. For who you are, not for what you look like."

Babe realized she was no longer covering her half-naked torso with her hands; her skin no longer felt cold, raw, unsheathed. She was completely relaxed. Comfortable, for the first time since she was a little girl, in just her own skin. Literally. Because of Truman.

Truman put the astringent and pads on the nightstand. He turned off the light, and they both pulled back the bedcovers and got into bed. They lay on their backs, side by side, for a long time not saying anything, not even when Truman guided her head toward his shoulder and put his arm about her.

Babe held her breath, listening to his heartbeat, so sturdy, so faithful. Finally she heard him begin to breathe deeply, and she knew he was asleep.

But Babe was wide awake; despite the comfort of being held so closely by someone she trusted so completely, her body still ached for more. She knew she'd never have that gift, not from him, and the loss did sting, although not like the rejection with which she was so familiar, from Bill.

But mostly, she was grateful for this moment. Because tomorrow, she would put on her makeup again, strive to find just the right outfit, organize Bill's days and weeks and years, live up to her mother's expectations, her father's very conditional love. "That face" would be hers once more, to put on, hide behind, wield like a weapon, use like the sun, coaxing and beguiling and charming and turning to stone those who could not believe its perfection.

But there would always be one person who knew what she looked like, without it. Who had seen her scars and loved her, anyway. Who would never wound her with his words, like Bill, or with his absence, like her father.

And that person was now, and would be forever, Truman.

. . . . .

Things with the Paleys were getting complicated,
he mused. And interesting; oh, so deliciously, delightfully interesting!

Truman still gasped whenever he first saw Babe after time away
from her. Her beauty did not fade; it only became more finely
honed with each passing year. His obsession with her still burned,
for he craved beauty as he craved love and approval, and if he could
have both in one gorgeous, glamorous package, then what more
could he ask for?

And her vulnerability, her touching confessions; he could—and
sometimes did—weep at the memory of that day they spent together, that night in her bed when he had lain beside William S.
Paley's wife and known her more completely than her husband
ever would. He'd meant it when he said that she was the one woman
whom he wished he could love physically. But even as he'd said it,
part of him—the part he despised when he was hungover and re-
gretful on certain mornings after—had suppressed a laugh, hearing
himself already rearranging the story so he could tell it to those

who appreciated his stories, especially the ones about the rich and famous, just like them. Cecil, perhaps—Cecil Beaton, to the masses; or Margaret—that is, Princess Margaret, to most people.

But they were just Cecil and Margaret to him. As were Liz and Grace and Marlon and Marilyn and Audrey and Humphrey and Betty.

"Well," he'd begin, as he always began, that southern drawl that never failed to hypnotize, like a snake charmer's tune. "You will not *believe* what happened to me the other day! Me, the queen of the fairies! Propositioned by a woman—and not just any ol' woman, mind you. But the fabulous, the one and only, Babe Paley!"

Oh, it would be a delicious story! He could dine out on it for simply weeks—years, even! But he did feel an uncomfortable stab of loyalty for Babe, a rush of love and protection—feelings so unfamiliar that he scarcely knew how to process them—except for the fact that somehow, he knew he couldn't do that to her. Not to Babe. He couldn't expose her that way, after she'd so trustingly exposed herself to him. He couldn't humiliate her vulnerability, her despair.

But Bill—well, that was another matter. And where things began to get complicated.

He liked Bill Paley. Most people didn't, actually. Oh, sure, Slim was always very loyal to him, when the girls began dissecting one another's husbands—although Babe never played that particular game. But oh, God, poor Slim! Oh, the poor dear—but Truman couldn't think about her right now. No, Bill was the more pressing problem.

Bill Paley was a wily chameleon, warm one minute, dangerously coiled and unpredictable the next. He had no patience, none at all! The way he barked at Babe whenever he wanted something; it did make Truman's blood boil. Truman knew how heroically Babe

worked, he knew how desperate she was to be loved and appreciated, and to see how churlishly Bill treated her stirred up the most
inconveniently uncomfortable feelings in him. He actually hated
Bill at times, for the hurt, the neglect, he heaped upon exquisite,
treasured Babe, whom Truman loved. And who loved him back.

But it was not in Truman's nature to openly despise people of
wealth and taste and privilege. And he had to admit that Bill possessed all of these. The wealth—well! The man ran an empire!
Television, radio, CBS records; he invested in Broadway plays, he
owned buildings, he shaped the way people thought. The taste—
God, what taste! For a man who sometimes had the unraveled edges
of a New Orleans pimp, he had an exquisite eye for art and beauty.

Well, the man had picked Babe, hadn't he? That alone elevated
him in Truman's eyes.

And power. Back to the empire again. And the political connections; he'd had Truman's—the other Truman, the president—ear.
Eisenhower's, too. His brother-in-law, Jock Whitney, Babe's sister's husband, was the ambassador to Great Britain. But power is
always tied most directly to money. Bill Paley knew that.

So did Truman Capote.

When Bill asked him to perform that particular—function—the
first time, Truman had hesitated. Out of loyalty to Babe, he'd stam-
mered, pretending not to understand the question. Bill retreated
hastily, changing the subject to boxing, a sport they both enjoyed.

But the very next night, Bill invited Truman out for a drink at
the Links Club. Truman, always eager to invade these hidden bas-
tions of overt masculinity, had accepted. And he'd not been disappointed. The Links Club was a testosterone riot of leather and
wood paneling and pictures of golf, golf, and more golf—golf
courses, golf clubs, men in ridiculous golf gear. It was full of small

rooms where hushed games of backgammon were being conducted, or phone calls to brokers being made. The drinks were all strong and neat, no garnishes. No less than three shoe-shine men—darkies all—waited patiently just outside the lounge.

Truman spied a couple of men he had last encountered in different kinds of clubs, farther—much farther—downtown. One had been dancing with a swarthy Puerto Rican boy dressed like Carmen Miranda in the back room of one of those clubs. He saw the man pale at his entrance, but Truman didn't break a smile, didn't raise an eyebrow, didn't slow his stride at all as he followed Bill to a cozy corner of the main room, decorated in a Scottish nightmare of dark paneling and painting after painting of men in kilts gripping large wooden clubs.

No, no compensation here, not at all.

"Truman, I need you to do me a favor."

"Anything, Bill," Truman had replied with a sinking heart. One didn't refuse—or pretend not to understand—Bill Paley twice in a row.

Bill pressed a hidden buzzer beneath the table between them, and from a concealed panel in the wall, out popped a liveried waiter. Bill ordered two whiskey and sodas and drummed his fingers against the mahogany tabletop; the chairs were well-worn leather, comfortable, with high backs, giving at least an illusion of privacy. After the drinks were delivered, Bill sipped his, then placed it down on the table. He immediately saw the water ring it left, and grinned a suddenly charming, boyish grin.

"Babe and her coasters. At home, every table has dozens. She thinks I'm a slob if I don't use them."

"Women!" Truman grunted and pretended to spit on the floor. Bill guffawed.

"Yes. Women. Here's to them all." And Bill raised his glass in a toast. Truman did the same. "Now, to the point. You know that little blonde, that Carol something, a friend of yours? I think she's just a terrific little gal. I bet she's a real tiger in bed. I'd like to find out, at any rate. Could you arrange it?"

As he had been before, Truman was shocked by the directness. No prevaricating, no warming up to the subject. But he also admired Bill's methodology. Here was a man who knew what he wanted, and didn't see the need to waste any time in getting it.

"Bill. I'm flattered that you'd think I'd have any sway over the wonderful women in my life."

"Cut the crap, Truman. Will you or won't you? I can get anyone I want, you know." Bill's legs were jangling now; he was always restless, always in search of more. At the house, he'd pace and roam. On the plane, he couldn't sit still, either, always drumming his fingers, crossing and uncrossing his legs, pacing the aisle, driving Babe and Truman to distraction. His big hands were always clasping and unclasping, scratching, rubbing, drawing doodles on pads of paper.

"Then why don't you?" Truman felt he had to at least pretend to be affronted. Bill wouldn't respect him if he didn't.

"It's distasteful to be direct in this matter, I've found. Girls don't like it so much. They like to be wooed, to think they're special. And they need time to come around to the idea themselves."

"Bill Paley. The world's greatest lover." Truman arched an eyebrow, and Bill laughed.

"Okay, okay. I just fancy that little blonde. I like blondes, all right? I like them dishy and squishy and blond and pale. And earthy. I like earthy, in bed."

"Same here. We're a lot alike, you know."

"What?" Bill was startled; he nearly spilled his drink as his face paled.

"Well, for instance. Clubs." Truman cocked his head and gestured around him. "There are certain clubs neither one of us can get into. Am I right?"

Bill's face hardened, but he nodded. Truman had heard about the awful debacle after Phil Graham had nominated Bill for membership in the F Street Club in Washington; Graham had been told, in no uncertain terms, that they did not accept members of the Hebrew race. Not even those in charge of immense media empires.

"And we both enjoy earthy—lovers."

Bill again nodded. Carefully.

"And we both love Babe. Or, at least, I do."

"Of course I love my wife." Bill sipped his drink slowly, deliberately placing it back down upon the ring of condensation. "I don't want you to make a big deal out of this, because it's not one. If you don't want to, fine. But we're friends, and friends do each other favors."

"There are favors, and then there are favors."

"Look at it this way. If you take care of this, find me a nice girl who won't make a fuss—as I've unfortunately experienced in the past—it would make everyone involved happy. *Everyone.* We would be keeping it in the family, in a way. And I'm sure you know how much that means to us. Keeping it quiet. Not inviting a mess."

"Yes, I know how much that means to—us."

"Truman, you're a levelheaded man. You also know some interesting people, particularly women. You have a lot of influence over them. And I'm very generous; I'm always eager to help those who help me. But as I said, it's up to you."

Bill's eyes had taken on that reptilian look; he leaned back and gazed at Truman steadily, coldly. Truman had no idea what the man was thinking.

Then Bill leaned forward and clapped Truman on the shoulder. "I just thought of another way we're alike," he said with a conspiratorial grin. And despite himself, Truman was thrilled to see it; thrilled to see that William S. Paley thought of him as his equal. His pal. A real boy. The old experience in military school, the old wound of never being man enough—God, it was tiring, wasn't it, how these things took roost and never, ever left? Like squatters. Yes. The traumas of childhood were like squatters. They took advantage of negligence, weakness, until the point where you couldn't imagine your life being whole without them.

"How?" Truman asked with a melancholy sigh. "How are we both alike?"

"We're both collectors. Collectors of women. You and your— what do you call them, Babe and her friends? Your swans?"

"Ah, but this is where we're different," Truman replied with a cool smile.

"In what way?"

"I don't treat them like shit."

Bill, who had been about to take another drink, froze. He sat for a minute—an eternal, bone-rattling minute—staring at Truman, his eyes betraying no emotion, no anger—but no friendliness, either. Then Bill rose abruptly, told him he had to meet a sponsor for dinner but Truman should take his time and linger, if he wanted. And then he was gone, with a quick but crushing handshake.

Truman watched him stride out of the room. Then he did take his time finishing his drink. He wasn't going to be hurried by any insufferable waiters' stares or whispers by shocked members. Right now he belonged here, with them, with men who controlled empires, who hobnobbed with presidents and kings. Men who needed him. Men who asked him to do them manly favors.

But then he felt his face burn; he was being ridiculous. He didn't want to be these men, not really, for their lives were much more deceitful, full of darker corners where no light ever shone, than his. He was better than them, yes, he was; he had a desperate urge to jump up on the table and scream, "Yes, I'm a homosexual! And I've invaded your clubhouse, and you can't do a damn thing about it! Does anyone want to take a picture, you men with your obsession with giant clubs and little balls?"

He chuckled to himself, wishing with every outrageous cashmere fiber of his being that he could do so. But he couldn't—no, he *wouldn't*. It was his choice, not theirs.

But he did take his time with his drink, inciting the maximum amount of discomfort possible. And on his way out, he whispered in the ear of the man he had seen dancing with the Puerto Rican, "Your secret's safe with me, darling."

But when he left, he had asked himself the question he hadn't quite asked Bill Paley.

What about Babe?

Was it a betrayal to help her husband cheat on her? Well, yes. At its essence, it was.

But Bill was his friend, too. Bill was going to cheat on Babe with or without Truman's help; he'd been doing it for years. Babe knew it. Hell, the entire city knew it.

Bill cheated on Babe and Slim cheated on Leland and Gianni cheated on Marella and Gloria cheated on Loel and Loel cheated on Gloria—and Loel had cheated on Gloria with Pam Churchill, come to think of it—and Truman, yes, cheated on Jack and Jack cheated on him. But it wasn't cheating for the two of them because they both knew about each other's conquests, discussed them in detail. The thing is, though, everyone stayed together. Everyone, for the most part, behaved, kept it quiet, out of their social circle—don't shit in your backyard, Slim had once advised to him cryptically, her eyes red.

Everyone came home to each other, at the end of the day, and sailed out into the world and had their photographs taken together—*Mr. and Mrs. William S. Paley at the Metropolitan Museum of Art, celebrating the opening of a new wing.* Because that was what mattered, that was what counted.

And if he, Truman, could keep Bill happy so that he would keep coming home to Babe, who would be devastated if he ever did anything so old-fashioned as to divorce her, as Leland was apparently going to do to Slim, then wasn't Truman performing a good deed?

Wasn't he being a real man, helping out another man?

Wasn't he being a true, loyal friend to Babe, ensuring that at least Bill wasn't going to get the clap, and wouldn't he be there for her, always, whenever she needed a shoulder to cry on, someone to pick up the pieces of her shattered heart and glue them together in a beautiful mosaic, something as glittering and gay and gorgeous as she was, giving her back her heart as a present? One that she would cherish forever, and be reminded of him—Truman—every single day that lovely heart beat gallantly, and never, ever hurt or leave him? And love him, love him as he deserved to be loved, finally?

Yes. Yes, that was it. He was doing it for Babe.

So he called up his longtime friend Carol Marcus Saroyan Saroyan (for she'd married Bill Saroyan twice) Matthau and invited her to lunch at 21. And after they had finished their salads, he asked her, "Do you know Bill Paley?"

Carol, an ice-cream blonde, all melting curves, creamy skin, and big, brown little girl eyes, shuddered. She and Truman had been friends ever since they were children, neglected children of Manhattan mothers clawing to gain a foothold in society. Carol was built for men; she was a vessel for every lustful thought, sentimental notion, they possessed. Truman was quite upset that she'd recently married some poor actor—Matthau what's-his-name—instead of marrying into money. It seemed a colossal waste of assets, pure and simple.

"Bill Paley?" Carol pouted. "Yes, I know him. Slightly. He chased me around a table once."

"Every man with a pulse has chased you around a table once, baby doll."

"That's true."

"You must have made an impression, because Bill asked me about you. He wanted you to know that he thinks you're extremely special. His ideal, I believe is how he put it."

"So?" Carol barely touched the Manhattan in front of her, other than to suck on the cherry, like Lolita.

"He would be quite honored if you'd consent to be his guest at dinner some evening. Soon. Just the two of you, of course. A quiet tête-à-tête."

"He wants to seduce me?"

"Well, I'm not sure Bill is much of a seducer, darling. He's more of a 'launch an offensive' kind of man, I suspect. After all, he's friends with Eisenhower."

"Those World War Two men! They never stop preparing for battle."

"No, they don't. But to get to the matter at hand, dearest Carol, I know you're just mad about this actor of yours—although, for the life of me, I can't understand why—but I thought this would be good for you. Bill can pull some strings, of course; he's a very influential man in the industry. And really, he's quite enamored. You're just his type."

"Married?"

"Silly! No, blond and dishy."

"*He's* married to Babe, for God's sake! Babe Paley! I couldn't even come close to her—look at me!" And Carol gestured to her frilly peasant dress, the type she liked to wear in order to emphasize her femininity. Truman was tired of trying to get her into more tailored, stylish clothes; he'd simply given up on it.

"Darling, Babe is perfection. And my dearest angel of a friend, so you must know how this pains me. But between you and me, Babe and Bill—well, they aren't exactly intimate in that way. You know these jet-setting married couples! They are very his and hers. It's in their blue-blooded DNA."

"No, Truman, I won't do it. Tell Bill Paley to—well, tell him to do whatever you think he should do, but I'm not going to be his conquest. I like Babe. I *admire* her."

"Yes, I foresee that's going to be the trouble," Truman agreed sadly. "Most of the women I know do. What about your dearest friend Gloria? Gloria Vanderbilt? She's not exactly Paley's type, but she might do. Do you think she'd be interested?"

"Truman, dear, listen to me." Carol rose, reaching for her handbag, leaving Truman the check. He was very generous to his longtime friends, those whose star hadn't risen to his heights. He was always happy to pay.

"Yes?"

"Don't be a pimp. It doesn't suit you. You're too short."

Truman clapped his hands delightedly and reared his head back, roaring with laughter.

"Oh, Carol, you are divine!"

He was still laughing as Carol traipsed out of the restaurant. But he also still had a problem. Until he saw Pamela Churchill enter the room and spot him seated alone at his table. She broke into her fake smile, her British teeth perfectly capped, courtesy of one lover or another. Truman couldn't help but appreciate her porcelain British complexion, but that dress! Satin in the daytime? God, the woman really was just a common tart dressed up in sheep's clothing—he couldn't believe that anyone would be serious about marrying her. She'd been kept by every important man alive—Gianni Agnelli, Averell Harriman, a Rothschild or two. Even Paley had paid for her, during the war, or so the rumor went—when he wasn't sharing her with Ed Murrow. And now, Leland Hayward—

She saw him, waved regally, and started his way.

"Pamela! Darling! You look divine!"

"Oh, Truman, you love," Pamela murmured in her posh British accent. She exuded her famous charm; she fluttered her eyelids at him like a baby lamb, blushed like a schoolgirl, made him feel as if he were the only man in the world for her.

Truman appreciated the effort; he had to admire the woman for putting on the full act for him, knowing quite well he'd never take her to bed. Or buy her a piece of jewelry.

"I was just going, sweetheart of mine, but do have a wonderful lunch, won't you?"

"I'm meeting Leland," she purred. "He simply can't allow me out of his sight for a minute! The poor man was absolutely neglected by Slim, who is a darling girl, but a trifle flighty."

"He's a wise man," Truman replied, wagging his finger at her naughtily. Pamela giggled, and he paid his check, kissed her on the cheek, and left.

It was raining, a chill fall afternoon, the kind that made even Fifth Avenue look sordid and cheap, the sidewalks slick and carpeted with matted, moldy newspapers and trash. People were in a hurry to be anywhere but outside, so he found himself bumped by passing shoulders, poked at with umbrellas. But he walked slowly, his hands in his pockets, his head bowed, glasses blurry, streaked with rain. And by the time he got to the Waldorf, his mind was made up; he removed his coat, shook his head like a spaniel, dried his glasses, and took the elevator up to a top floor. Then he knocked on a door.

"Truman!"

"Big Mama! You poor darling!"

Slim Hawks Hayward looked awful. Simply awful. She had lost weight—living up to her nickname for the first time in years—but it made her look haggard, and not sleek and feline, as she'd been in her youth. Her hair was quite unkempt: stringy, and not freshly colored, so that you could see the darker roots coming in. She wasn't wearing sunglasses, as she did most everywhere these days, and so he could see that her eyes were puffy and bloodshot.

"Now, Big Mama, you haven't been crying, have you? Over that son of a bitch? For shame!"

"No, I haven't. Not since breakfast, anyway. And by the way, come in."

"Dearest, I just had to tell you. I saw Pamela at lunch. I cut her *dead*, of course. Out of loyalty to my Big Mama! I just cut that thing dead. Dead as a doornail."

"Were that the literal truth." Slim, clad in an oversized man's shirt with the initials LH embroidered on the pocket, and dungarees that hung on her, walked over to the sofa and picked up a cigarette that was burning in an ashtray.

"Oh, Slim!" Truman's eyes filled with tears, to behold what she was reduced to. Living in a suite at the Waldorf, wearing her soon-to-be ex-husband's clothing. It might as well have been a hair shirt.

Slim was always the most vibrant of the swans. She had such a sense of humor, such a genuine love of life. She'd traveled with him back to the Soviet Union a couple years ago, when he was thinking of writing a follow-up article to *The Muses Are Heard*. She'd managed to rustle up Cary Grant to come along, too. Cary Grant! Slim Hayward! Truman Capote! A merry band of travelers!

Except that Cary Grant proved to be too preoccupied with people recognizing that he was Cary Grant. If ever someone didn't stop and do a double take at that famous puss, he'd do something to his face that somehow made the cleft in his chin even deeper, and say something very loudly in that distinctive cockney voice of his. It got so that Slim and Truman couldn't suppress their giggles at the absurdity of it, and Cary Grant had decided to sulk the rest of the trip, until he got off the train abruptly in Finland and went back to Hollywood.

But Slim was absolutely without vanity. She didn't care if Truman saw her first thing in the morning or last thing in the evening; she didn't fix her makeup constantly. She wrapped herself in a fur coat and sunglasses and faced the world head-on, and she never stopped telling him stories.

And Truman, like most storytellers, enjoyed listening, almost as much as he enjoyed doing the telling.

Slim told him of the time Hemingway's wife—the latest one, whom nobody liked—tried to drown her in a swimming pool after Papa was too openly flirtatious. She told him about her one-night stand with Frank Sinatra—"He sang when he came. Honest to God. I thought I'd die laughing but I didn't dare. He has that Sicilian male thing going on. I had to tell him he was the best I'd ever had." She told him about the tryouts of *South Pacific*, which her husband Leland had produced; how so many people told them all, very seriously, not to take it to Broadway because it was "too damn good and nobody would ever understand it."

One time, the two of them had gotten very drunk and decided to call Babe, long distance, and tell her something shocking, something very un-Babe-like; they'd asked the operator for the trunk line, waited for the connection—drinking vodka shots all the while—and when Babe finally was on the other end, Slim had slurred a lurid little tale about having her period while having sex one time, and how horrified the man was, and then Slim started giggling so hard she was suddenly crying, so that Truman took the phone and told a shocked Babe that Slim must be on her period now, the poor baby, so please forgive her and kiss kiss, Bobolink, you're my one and only and I miss you!

And then he hung up and begged Slim to tell him the story again.

Slim had been on top of the world then. Secure enough in her marriage to leave her husband at home while she traveled. Stupid enough to believe that she could have an affair or two—and tell him about it, the fatal mistake, and one that he, Truman, had begged her not to make—and believe that it wouldn't matter. She took off soon after for another trip, this time to Italy with Betty Bacall. More drunken phone calls to friends in the middle of the night, but nobody minded, because it was Slim! And she was keeping Betty company, making her laugh, which she needed, since Bogie had so recently died.

But that Italian trip was when it happened. And now, look at her.

"Darling Slim, I just want to carry you around in my pocket all the time and take care of you. I have a wonderful idea! Let's make something up about Pamela and start spreading it around! I could make up some dreadful disease or something!"

"How about the clap?"

"Perfect!"

Slim smiled wanly. But then she turned her head away, and Truman knew she was crying.

"Babe is devastated, of course. You know that, right?"

"Yes, yes. Babe comes here every day. She cleans up, has food delivered, makes sure I bathe. She invites me to Kiluna every weekend, said I could stay at Round Hill, in Jamaica, anytime I want. Babe is, well—Babe. The kindest friend I've ever had. And I don't deserve her."

"So you don't blame her?"

"No! How could I! She did what I told her to do—she looked after Leland while I was away in Italy. She made sure he wasn't lonely. God, what a damned fool I was! I am!"

"What was it you told Leland, again, when he called you? It was so perfect, Slim! So completely cutting and truthful!"

"I told him, when he said he wanted a divorce, I told him— 'Leland, nobody *marries* Pam Churchill!' And nobody does! How many affairs has that tramp had?"

"Dozens. Hundreds. Hence the clap!"

"But wouldn't you know it. My husband. The last of the great romantics. He wants to marry the bitch." Slim got up, kicked at the foot of the coffee table, and went to the bar. She opened a bottle of Scotch, raised an eyebrow at Truman, who nodded, and poured them both two tall glasses, not even bothering with ice.

"Babe had no choice but to invite her. Pam was a guest of Jock and Betsey's, and Babe needed an extra woman for dinner one night, and Leland was there, and so—"

"I know, I know! And it's not as if Leland didn't know Pam before! Why that time, that particular dinner, I'll never understand. And she was so nice to me, when Betty and I were in Europe! She kept sending me flowers, telephoning to see if there was anyone she could introduce us to! That a friend—that someone who called herself a friend—could do that—" Slim's hands began to shake, and she had to set the Scotch down. She seemed on the verge of more hysterics, but then she took a deep breath, clenched her fists, and picked up the drinks, handing him his.

"But that's that, I guess. Some might say it's only what I deserve. Leland wants a divorce. I'm not going to contest it, not anymore."

"So get back at him. Have an affair of your own."

"Well, you know. I did. Sinatra. Peter Viertel." Slim glanced at Truman, bit her lip. "Others. And yes, I guess that—I *know* that's part of why he was susceptible to that British whore's charms. But for Christ's sake, Truman—that's what marriage is, of course. You take care of what you need to on the side, but for God's sake, you *stay* married!"

"Naturally. Unless you're some poor sop from the Midwest, with enchanting midwestern notions about marrying for love. Where was Leland born again? Nebraska?"

"I do love him, True Heart! I do! That's the thing! I love the man, and I thought—oh! Oh, my God, that's it!" Slim looked stricken; she set the glass down without having taken a sip.

"What?" Truman didn't wait; he took a long gulp from his Scotch; he was still a bit damp, raw from the rain. Then he grimaced; this was not the good stuff, not the usual Johnnie Walker

Black. He didn't know what it was, but he heroically hid his distaste from Big Mama, who continued to stand, stock-still, as if she'd taken a good long look at her unkempt self in a mirror.

"Oh, my God. I married the last old-fashioned man in New York, didn't I? That poor, dumb, softhearted bastard! Leland simply can't imagine sleeping with someone unless he marries her. He was that way with me, with Maggie Sullavan before me. Even with Kate Hepburn, now that I think about it. Leland wanted to get married and Kate didn't, because she wanted to focus on her career. And now Pam. He slept with her, and so he has to marry her."

"She's wasting no time making sure that he does, I hear." Truman took another swig and gestured that Slim ought to do the same. "She's picking out china at Tiffany's."

"God. China. As if that's what defines a marriage—the china pattern. The silver. None of that matters in the end. I took care of his children, you know! Those poor kids, Maggie Sullavan's children, so messed up. I arranged his life. I picked out his socks and shirts and threw his opening-night parties and traveled with him to every tryout of every show, staying up late, ordering sandwiches and coffee when they stayed up all night trying to fix things. That's marriage. And he's throwing it all away." Slim's eyes watered again, and she even let one big tear roll down her patrician nose and drop into her drink, but she didn't appear to notice.

"Now, Big Mama, listen to True Heart." Truman patted the sofa. Slim sat down. He had the feeling that she was a marionette and he the puppet master. Right now, he could get her to do anything. Which was what he was counting on.

"You understand marriage. Marriage, as it's done among our crowd. That stupid little Carol Matthau doesn't—she's a dear girl, but she marries for love. Not practicality. She's just like poor Leland. But you are much more intelligent than that. And I wonder if you have any idea how much you might be able to help out a friend? A couple of them, to be exact?"

"What? What could I do to help anyone now? Without Leland—I'm nobody. I'm a divorcée with no money of her own. Marella and Gloria and C.Z.—they'll drop me in a minute."

"No, they won't! I'll stab them in the heart!" And Truman was absolutely fierce in his conviction that he would do it; that he would champion Big Mama, who loved him. Not as much as Babe; no, never did he think that. Always Slim seemed to be looking at him with one eyebrow arched in anticipation of something. Slim was smart; Slim knew how to protect herself. And so she would never love him like Babe did—but then again, she didn't need him as much as Babe did. Nor did he need Slim as much. And they knew that about each other, which was both comforting and not.

"True Heart," Slim said with a whiskey-soaked sigh. She patted his hand, took a sip of her drink, and hiccuped. "I love you. I really do. Tell me a story. Something amusing. Cheer me up, for I'm blue."

"No, you don't." Suddenly Truman was sick; sick of these people and their dramas and their selfishness, their favors. Their very wealth and privilege, which they used to get what they wanted, used to get *him*, ensnare him, make him feel ugly and dirty and sordid—more so than usual.

"I don't what?"

"You don't love me, Big Mama. Nobody does."

"Of course we do! We all love you!"

"No, you don't. Nobody does—except maybe Jack. Look at me. I'm a freak to you, all of you, aren't I? A distraction, an impulse, some big joke. Someone to be used."

"No, no—what are you talking about?"

Truman leaned back into the sofa and hugged a pillow to his chest. He looked up at his Big Mama, now standing before him, stricken, lost. Forlorn. But she was a woman, she would be all right. She'd find someone else to marry, soon enough. She was tough, Big Mama was. Tough as nails; tougher than him.

Tougher than Babe; the one who did love him, he remembered, his stomach souring at what he'd already done—and what he had been about to do. To Babe, and Babe alone, he was something other than a jester, the flavor—the fairy—of the week.

"True Heart, what do you mean? Did I say something wrong? I'm sorry, I'm—I'm just not myself today."

"No, Slim, no." He sighed. It was too hard, to tell the truth to these people, to speak honestly, seriously, and not in witty one-liners, bitchy repartee. They simply couldn't see him any other way; he was too small, too different, too precious to be taken seriously. And good Lord, none of them were in any way literary! No, he would never have been admitted to their circles on the basis of anything so drearily ordinary as talent or truth. So he only shrugged, and smiled wanly at Big Mama.

And decided that, at least for today, he would not be Bill Paley's fairy pimpmother.

"Now, where were we?" Truman patted Slim's hand. "Weren't we going to spread that rumor about Pam?"

Slim pushed her stringy hair back from her face—her profile no longer youthful and firm, the poor dear; she might have a tough time of it, after all, finding someone new at her age—picked up the phone, and handed it to him.

"You do it, True Heart. More people will believe it, if it comes from you."

"Yes," Truman said slowly, drawling it out, turning up the lisp, the camp, the dazzle. "Yes, Big Mama, you wise, sly thing. Of course. How brilliant of you! Now. Who should we call first? Who's going to have the privilege—oh, wait, I have it!" He dialed the phone, winking naughtily at Slim.

"Gloria? Darling! It's me, Truman! Did you hear about Pam Churchill. . . ."

And Slim began to giggle.

. . . . .

C.Z. HUNG UP THE PHONE.

It had been Truman, of course. Crying, outraged, petulant, remorseful.

"I don't understand!" he had raged, but in the next breath, he was sobbing pitifully. "What did they think? I'm an author! I write what I know!"

C.Z. had let him rage on, whispering only murmurs and soothing, clucking sounds, much as she would to an outraged child. She'd told him that she didn't hate him, that she understood, that people were really quite naïve, that yes, now that he asked, the writing was spectacular, truly. This new short story was the best thing he'd ever written.

"La Côte Basque 1965" was not the best thing he'd ever written, however. C.Z. actually had to suppress her laughter as she read the thing. The short story was just a play, really. A dialogue, running commentary, bitchy gossip. Certainly it was nothing like his best work, which for her remained *In Cold Blood*.

C.Z. didn't take too much seriously. She never had; she'd been born with a silver spoon in her mouth, but had removed it at her first gurgle and flung it across the nursery. But when she'd read *In Cold Blood* almost ten years earlier, she, like all of Truman's swans, had been stunned into an uncomfortable bashfulness around him. Suddenly their gay, gossipy little friend, arm candy, pocket change, was another creature entirely. A giant, a literary sentinel. She wondered how she'd ever imagined that they looked at the world in the same way, thought the same thoughts, shared the same vices and delights and interests.

Truman simply stopped being Truman. For a while, anyway.

She remembered the writing of that book, how it had taken years and years. He still, during the time of the writing, went to their parties, took them dancing at the Peppermint Lounge when their husbands refused. He still sat around the fire and gossiped with them. Only once in a while, C.Z. supposed, he would have a far-off look; she would see his lips move, he'd take a notebook out and jot something down, or more often, he'd suddenly become very downcast, and still everyone continued their merry dance about him, like a maypole. But he always snapped out of it and jumped right back in.

But then the book came out and everyone read it (and they really did this time, as opposed to his other books) and the name *Truman Capote* began to be spoken in hushed, awed tones, and every television, newspaper, and radio personality with an ounce of self-importance wanted to interview him. Truman had been famous before, of course, and even during the writing of *In Cold Blood,* the movie of *Breakfast at Tiffany's* came out, further catapulting him in the limelight—

Oh, C.Z. laughed and laughed, a throaty, sexy laugh so at odds with her crisp Brahmin drawl, remembering how she'd seen the movie with him. Not the first time he'd seen it—that he'd shared with Babe, of course—but later, during a matinee, the two of them sneaking into the back row of the dark theater, munching on Cracker Jack. Truman had whispered such catty things, a running commentary of bitchiness, during the whole movie—*Audrey Hepburn is a nice enough little thing, but she's not my Holly. Marilyn Monroe is who I wanted. But poor Marilyn—no one would work with her. Oh, look—isn't it terrible what they've done to Mickey Rooney? It's offensive. Not to mention a crime, the way he's chewing the scenery— it's a wonder he didn't gain fifty pounds! Patricia Neal—marvelous woman, but why did they have to add her character? I think Fred's much more interesting if he's just a common male gigolo, more like Holly. Now, watch for the scene when Audrey has to sing that song.* "Moon River"—*well, it's a nice enough little tune, but it's not the one I wrote in the book, which—I have to say it—was much more appropriate. But look at how nervous Audrey is; she's shaking as she holds the guitar. You can't really see it in the final cut, but trust me, I was there on the set that day. And, darling, let me tell you about Audrey's husband, Mel—*

She'd had to go back and see the movie again, alone, because she hadn't had a real chance to with Truman by her side.

So Truman had been famous before—and if he hadn't been, he wouldn't have been part of their circle—but nothing like what happened to him after *In Cold Blood*.

And no one—not even Babe—felt entirely comfortable with him, once they realized that he had done something truly important and groundbreaking in literature. C.Z. was the first to admit she knew nothing about writing. Other than that the author was someone to be respected and revered—and until then, she'd never thought of Truman as an author, believe it or not. He was simply an ornament, a bauble to be collected, enjoyed, and appreciated, but not really admired.

C.Z. opened the doors to her spectacular terrace. She felt the setting Florida sun bathe her skin, warm every follicle, open every pore. She inhaled profoundly, remembering how her father always taught her to breathe deeply when outdoors, the better to clear the lungs. She sniffed the salty ocean spray and the candy sweet perfume of jasmine in pots all over the terrace. The blue of her pool was bluer than the ocean, which was just a short stroll across a lawn that was so manicured, it looked as if you might cut your feet on it. But you couldn't; it was soft, like rainwater, something no visitor could ever understand, given how coarse and sticky Florida grass was everywhere else.

Days like this, when the air hummed with insects, and flowers were so abundant as to look almost comical, like a movie set from an old MGM musical, reminded her of her youth. She had made mistakes then, as poor Truman seemed to be making them now. Or, rather, had already begun to make them, years ago, once *In Cold Blood* came out. That was really it, C.Z. decided; that's when he began to fuck up.

But who hadn't fucked something up at some time in her life? She certainly had. How eager had she been, as a young debutante, to distance herself from her privileged life? She remembered how she'd cringed to see her name added to the Social Register—*Miss Lucy Douglas Cochrane,* and nobody called her that, ever; from childhood she was C.Z., because her idiot brother couldn't pronounce *Sissy*—and to see her real name, her proper Bostonian name, printed like that had been like having a brand ironed into her flesh, like she was simply part of a breed. A special, rarefied, privileged breed, but still. So she'd vowed to do something, anything, to be kicked out of it, to be different, to stand alone as brave as a solitary dandelion in a well-tended lawn.

So she ran. With her money, her youthful bravado, and her good looks—in those days, she did tend to linger in front of mirrors more than she should (and as, she had to admit, most of her friends still did). She admired her profile the most, that sharply etched cameo, all her features both strong and delicate at the same time. Her hair was always a champagne blond (although, yes, she used a rinse now to maintain it). She was tall and leggy, and she made the most of *that*, first by appearing in the forties as a showgirl in one of the last editions of the Ziegfeld Follies—oh, Christ, how Mama and Papa had seethed! But not to the point of disinheriting her, which, she had to admit, would have brought her home in a flash. C.Z. loved money. She just didn't love the pretentious crap that went along with it.

After the Follies—where she had enjoyed being pawed over by stage-door Johnnies—she'd fled to Hollywood; she'd taken some acting lessons, landed a contract at Twentieth Century–Fox but ultimately never appeared in anything. Movie work wasn't for her, the lights and costumes and makeup and all that. She felt as if her skin couldn't really breathe; she felt fake and more pretentious than she had as a debutante. Plus, as she soon discovered, being a movie star required discipline. She'd been dismayed to find that no party lasted past nine or ten P.M., as everyone had to go home and get enough rest to appear fresh in front of the cameras early in the morning.

So off she went to Mexico. *That* was a time! Bullfights and languid, sultry nights full of festive music and carpets of bougainvillea, vivid even under the stars. Drifting and dancing and fishing and drinking, losing herself, shedding her patrician skin, her stiff clothes and calfskin shoes replaced by peasant blouses, skirts, and huaraches. Abandoning herself altogether; C.Z. grinned as she bent over to pull up an impudent dandelion from her lawn, remembering how she had reclined on a dusty couch in Diego Rivera's study for a couple weeks, letting his lascivious gaze wash over her as he painted her nude form, preserved it for posterity.

The portrait now hung in her Florida home, in a room no one ever used. For C.Z. had found, to her horror, that she could not completely shed her pedigreed skin, after all. After those wandering couple of years, she'd hightailed it home, back to the safety of money and privilege and class, married Winston Guest, much older but so damn handsome, a polo player of international renown and possessor of a great fortune and even greater pedigree, and she'd resumed the life mapped out for her from birth. Rather happily, she thought. As long as she could still have a little—proper—fun.

But she'd sown her wild oats, at least. She couldn't say that for everyone in her acquaintance—Babe, for instance. The poor soul wouldn't know a wild oat if it were wrapped in a Louis Vuitton handbag. She never had the chance, C.Z. supposed. Something in her personality, something closed off and timid. The wildest oat Babe had ever sown, C.Z. mused, was in allowing herself to become so besotted with Truman that she dropped her guard, for the first and now, probably, last time in her life.

Oh, Truman! The little devil! C.Z. plopped down in a chaise longue and stared at her long, narrow feet, toenails painted a vivid fuchsia. Dammit. C.Z. still liked Truman, would even if he had used her in that damn story, which he had not. But he had gone off the rails, rather. He'd always been charming, amusing, gossipy, but never downright bitchy. His self-importance, his astonishing self-confidence, had been benign.

Until *In Cold Blood*.

Yes, it all came back to that, didn't it? His greatest achievement. His greatest failure. Because the only thing he'd written since was *this;* this bitchy little story in *Esquire* that apparently was bringing hellfire and brimstone down around Truman's pudgy little head. And that had murdered one of her tribe, if all the gossip was to be trusted. At least that's what Slim had said this morning when she'd called, furious, to ask if C.Z. had read it.

"La Côte Basque 1965." Christ. Even the title was dreadful.

Well, she'd have him down here when he was finished shooting that terrible movie in California, make a fuss over him, coddle him, protect him. For a while, anyway. But he'd have to sink or swim on his own, as she had, as she'd taught her children to do. She rather doubted that he'd swim, however.

He didn't have the breeding, the pedigree. He wasn't a thoroughbred. It was a damn shame, but there it was.

C.Z. shook her head, rose, and went off to find the gardener.

That dandelion simply didn't belong.

. . . . .

BABE PUT DOWN HER SIGNED COPY OF *IN COLD BLOOD*, which Truman had pressed into her hand only last night. His own hands had trembled; his entire body had pulsated with pride, accomplishment, and, perhaps, a touch of fear?

"I do hope you'll like it, my dearest Babe," he'd whispered, gazing up at her with his solemn eyes after he dated his inscription *January, 1966.* "Your opinion means the most to me, truly."

And she had been touched, as always; touched, and made to feel special and needed and important, and those were feelings that she cherished, clutched to her heart, polished up, and took out to marvel over with more pride of ownership than her finest pearls.

Babe had stayed up all night to finish the book—when it had first appeared in four parts in *The New Yorker* last fall, Truman had implored her to wait until it was published in book form, so she could read it all in one sitting. And so she had, although before settling down with it, she'd first tiptoed around the house to make sure all the doors and windows were locked, for she was sure it would be rather a frightening book to read alone, at night. And while it was, initially, soon that wore off and she became simply fascinated by the character studies. Yes, the portraits of the killers, Perry and Dick, were mesmerizing, but it was the characterization of one of the victims—Mrs. Clutter, Bonnie—that Babe couldn't get out of her head.

For Bonnie Clutter was something of a mess, in Babe's opinion. Frail and neurotic. Unable to cope with life, beset by doubt and inadequacy and fear. Bonnie Clutter hid in her room, slept all day, didn't run the house—all that was left to her daughter, poor doomed Nancy. And the thing is—everyone in Holcomb, Kansas, apparently knew all about it! And accepted Bonnie, and worried over her, and didn't seem to judge Bonnie Clutter for being who she was—weepy, fragile, depressed, withdrawn.

All traits that had threatened Babe, in her darkest moments when she felt she couldn't put up with Bill, with her high-profile life, with the image she herself had spent so much time perfecting. But never, not once, had she given in to the temptation to do what Bonnie Clutter had done right up until the night she was murdered—allow the mess, the darkness, to triumph.

Babe picked up the book again and turned to the photograph insert; there was a picture of Bonnie Clutter in better days. A plain, unfortunately bespectacled woman in one of those dreary Mamie Eisenhower getups, with the full flowered skirt, the enormous corsage pinned to her shoulder, the unflattering, lacy hat perched on tightly permed curls. Bonnie was smiling, with a beguiling dimple. She looked happy.

But Truman's portrait was of a woman who was anything but; a woman who once explained to a friend that she regretted not finishing nursing school despite the fact that she was no good at it, "just to prove that I once succeeded at something."

Oh, how Babe could relate to that! She had a diploma, but it was merely decorative; Gogsie had decreed that all her girls attend Westover, a finishing school, rather than a college. And while Babe had graduated at the top of her class, still—it was just a finishing school. Her years as a fashion editor had given her a taste of accomplishment at something other than being her own fabulous self, but they'd been fleeting. Marriage had been her destiny, as it had been Bonnie's, as it was for most women. At least Babe had succeeded at that, in the only way her mother defined success: marriage to wealthy, desirable men. But Bonnie had done that, as well; Herb Clutter, as portrayed by Truman, had been the alpha male of Holcomb, Kansas, a leader in the community.

But Bonnie couldn't keep up, couldn't cope, and while Babe understood this more than anyone but Truman ever suspected, she didn't give in, she didn't allow anyone to see her life as anything but a triumph. That was how Babe would be remembered, at least; unlike poor Bonnie, who was now immortalized, vanquished by the life determined for her. How did her surviving daughters feel about this? Did Bonnie Clutter herself somehow know that Truman had stripped her naked, bare? Exposed her for who she really was?

But Bonnie Clutter was dead. No, of course she didn't know.

Babe shuddered, stamped out her cigarette, lit another. She was alone at Kiluna; Bill was in Los Angeles for business. The children were at school, but even if they'd been home, she wouldn't really know it. They were housed in a separate little wing of their own. And so, isolated, Babe indulged in dark thoughts; it was as sinful, as clandestine, as if she'd eaten an entire cake by herself, and just as satisfying. And disgusting.

Would her children mourn her, were she to die suddenly, horrifically? Babe was no fool; she knew they would not, and it was her own fault. She was close to her oldest son, Tony, now that he was an adult, but she hadn't been when he was a child. She didn't like children very much, she had to admit; her arms simply didn't ache to hold her babies; she wasn't tolerant of the odors and stains of childhood. And as the children grew, each with their special problems—Amanda terribly shy; Bill Junior hyper, afraid of his father; poor Kate so permanently stressed she'd lost her hair as a child, something Babe could never fully accept despite the fact that she and Bill had had every specialist in to examine her, and the finest, most natural wigs made—Babe found herself letting each one of them down, incapable of fixing them, molding them, as her mother had molded her. So she withdrew from her own children, and hoped others could do it for her. She employed the very best nurses and nannies and governesses and tutors, interviewing them herself, treating the help like family, making sure they were well compensated—she'd even had a separate pool put in just for these helpers, away from the main pool, so they'd have some privacy, some release. She saw that her children attended the best schools. She oversaw their playmates, invited them to stay at Kiluna or Kiluna North; she filled the children's wing with all the newest toys and record players and televisions and games. She made a point of dropping in once a day, spending time with each child when they were small, reading or playing board games or applauding swimming prowess, new dance moves.

And then she left them—oh, what was that line in Truman's book? Babe scurried over to the bed and picked it up; yes, there it was. Bonnie was talking about her youngest son—*"And how will he remember me? As a kind of ghost."*

Babe shook her head, lit another cigarette. She'd never have thought she'd have so much in common with a plain neurotic housewife from Holcomb, Kansas.

Yet surely that was how she was to her four children: a ghost. A fabulously dressed, unattainable ghost. She left them to their own devices so that she could tend to herself, and to Bill. So that she could tend to her guests, her house, her gardens, her clothes, her charitable organizations. And so that she could tend to Truman; she let him into her heart as she'd never let her children, and she knew it, and they knew it, and so she understood that if she were murdered in the middle of the night as Bonnie Clutter was—messy, imperfect, frail Bonnie Clutter!—she would not be mourned half as much.

Except, of course, by Truman. Astonishing, great little Truman. Who had written an astonishing, great big book that had taken the world by storm, and now she had a new fear—oh, she was afraid of everything, wasn't she? She was just like Bonnie Clutter! Only a few cigarettes away from retreating to her room, never to emerge in the daylight. Her parents had not raised her to be afraid, but she was; she was constantly beset by uncertainty, nibbled by doubts. If only the world knew! But Truman did know; he knew everything about her, every tough scar and tender wound, except this—

He did not know that she was terrified of losing him.

Despite her education practically at his own knee—the reading of Dickens, Proust, Faulkner—she honestly didn't know how she was going to talk to him now. Sharing her doubts and dreams with this great man seemed absurd. Tickling him, dancing with him, exchanging confidences and gossip—how on earth could she continue doing that? Now that she had read this book, this book by someone else, not her confidant, not her soul mate. This was a book written by a man—and she had ceased to think of Truman as that. He had become an extension of herself: her analyst, her pillow, her sleeping pill at night, her coffee in the morning.

The phone rang, jolting her out of her reverie. Babe padded over to the gilded French provincial phone on her bedside table, not waiting for the staff to answer. For she knew who it was.

"Bobolink! Darling! So—tell me! Tell me what you think!"

Babe almost gasped with relief. Truman sounded just like—Truman! Her heart, her soul, her twin. And not the great man of letters.

"Truman, dearest one, I loved it. I devoured it, every word. I'm in awe of your talent—I always have been, but now! This really is it. Your masterpiece."

"I know!" Truman giggled, and Babe did, too. She wished he were with her, so she could see his expression, even as she knew what it was—she could picture his pink face, his eyes crinkled up, his pure, cat-that-ate-the-canary grin; she knew he was dancing up and down, hopping from one foot to the other in delight. Truman enjoyed himself more than anyone she knew; he luxuriated in his success, did not attempt false modesty, did not attribute it to others, or to luck, or to anything but his own talent. And you had to love someone like that.

"Oh, Babe," he continued, his voice still a riot of delight, a bubbling, babbling river of joy, "I'm so, so happy you think so! What was your favorite part? Tell me, do. I really want to know. Everyone keeps telling me it's Perry and Dick, but especially Perry. I captured Perry perfectly. I wanted to show the soul of a killer, but also that of the wounded little boy who had a choice, and made the wrong one."

"Yes, of course, Perry is brilliant. Your characterization of him, I mean."

"That's not your favorite part," Truman said instantly. "I can tell."

"No, it was Bonnie. Poor Bonnie."

"I knew you'd like her."

"You did?"

"Yes. Because you identify with her, my Babe. Don't you?"

"Yes." Babe blushed; how could she feel this way, as if he'd X-rayed her over the phone? "Oh, how did you know, Truman?"

"Because I know *you,* dear. I know the you no one else can see, not even Bill—especially not Bill—because you don't let them. And they don't deserve to! I know the real Babe. The loveliest Babe of all. And the loneliest."

"Can you—would you like to come out?" Babe wound the telephone cord about her finger, feeling as shy and giddy as a teenager. "I'm all alone out here. I wanted to be, in order to read your book, to be able to really concentrate. But now I'd—I'd like to see you, Truman. If you can, that is. I know you must be so busy."

"Oh, Babe, dearest, I can't! Can you believe I'm being interviewed for television? Not CBS, unfortunately. But Lee Bailey wants to come out to my place in Southampton with his cameras."

"Oh." Babe would not admit her disappointment, would not diminish her friend's obvious, deserved excitement in any way—would not be Bonnie Clutter. "Oh, Truman! How wonderful! What will you wear, for the cameras?"

"Well, I was thinking my orange cashmere turtleneck, and some plaid pants. Very colorful, but not too much for the cameras. What do you think?"

"Yes, that sounds right." Babe didn't voice her opinion that the sweater would do a good job of camouflaging his tummy; he had grown rather more soft during the writing of this book, the long years of waiting for Perry Smith and Dick Hickock to meet their deaths by hanging so he could finally write the ending. All the delays, the stays of execution, had pushed Truman to indulge himself in food and drink and dejected inactivity. "I always think a turtleneck is proper, for most occasions."

"And I think I'll get a manicure before. And a facial. In fact, I have to run right now, if I'm going to work those in."

"Of course, Truman, you must! You'll look simply wonderful on camera! I can't wait to watch the program—will you, will you watch it with me? I mean, let me watch it with you?"

"Babe, I promise. I won't watch it with another soul, not even Jack—who is simply livid, by the way, at all the attention. Jealous, too. Poor dear boy, he's such a *good* writer." Truman sighed, and Babe could picture him shaking his head. "Though it's hard on him to see my success, especially now. But I can't be expected not to enjoy it just because of him, can I?"

"Of course not!"

"I knew you'd understand, Bobolink! Now I must fly. I'll see you soon!"

"When?"

But Truman had already hung up the phone.

Babe paced around the house for a while, at loose ends. She could go talk to the gardener about the new trees she wanted for the pond this spring, although she couldn't wander the garden; it was January now. While there was no snow on the ground, she shivered just to think of the bare limbs, dried-out stalks, matted-down leaves, and patches of ice. She really disliked New York in winter; lately, the cold had started to take its toll. It was more difficult to catch her breath in the frigid, dry air. But Bill was in Los Angeles; that was the reason they weren't in Jamaica, as they normally would be.

Restless, Babe walked into her closet, that Aladdin's cave of racks upon racks, cloth-lined drawers, hidden compartments, garment bags full of treasures, shoes stuffed with tissue and placed in color-coded cloth bags. Bonnie Clutter had lived in housedresses and nightgowns and thick white socks.

But Babe Paley stood in the middle of designer glory, surrounded by beautiful gowns, stylish day dresses, suits of every color and weight, and decided, with the contrariness of a fretful child, to go into the city, to Bergdorf's, and buy some more. Because that was something that she could do, and Bonnie Clutter could not.

For that was what Babe did, after all; it was her primary occupation. Acquisition. She sometimes thought of herself as a museum curator, only the museum was herself, her homes, her way of life. That was what she had learned to do at Westover, and so she did it extraordinarily well. Surrounding and draping herself with luxury and beauty was her profession, and it was a nicer one than most people had to put up with, and yes, she did enjoy it; it was her outlet, her chief pleasure. Until she'd met Truman, that is.

But Truman was busy. Soon Babe found herself tucked into the backseat of a huge black sedan, settling into leather seats, an array of the newest magazines in a rack before her, a little wooden caddy filled with a carafe of water and a split of champagne on the floor next to her feet, a cashmere throw over her lap, classical music piped softly from hidden speakers. And then she was being whisked away from Long Island and into the city, where she was deposited in front of Bergdorf Goodman; she exited the car without giving a thought about where it would have to be parked, or how much it might cost. Someone would take care of it for her.

And so she pushed herself through the revolving doors of Bergdorf Goodman, not stopping to marvel, as others might, at the polished marble floors and walls, the gleaming display cases that looked like priceless antiques themselves—ancient armoires, French china cabinets; the towering ceilings, gold fixtures, blazing crystal chandeliers, delicate little settees and armchairs and stools placed around at intervals. Bergdorf's was as familiar to Babe Paley, and as luxuriously appointed, as any of her many homes.

"Oh, Mrs. Paley!" A floor manager was approaching, wringing his hands. "Mrs. Hughes isn't here today. We didn't know you'd be stopping by!"

Mrs. Hughes was *her* salesperson; Babe, like all of Bergdorf's favored clients, had her own personal assistant to fetch and carry and suggest and praise.

"It's quite all right, Mr. Stevens. I'm feeling rather impromptu today. I think I'll just wander a bit, if you don't mind? Yes, that's it. I'll just be a shopper today, a tourist, just like anyone else!" *Just like Bonnie Clutter*, Babe thought, even as she smiled kindly at the worried little man in front of her with a bead of sweat on his brow, obviously fearful that he had made a mistake, that the powerful Mrs. Paley might be angry with him for not being ready for her. He could lose his job for much, much less.

Babe smiled kindly at him, to put him at ease; he was only doing his job, which was to make women like herself feel privileged and pampered and come back for more. She allowed Mr. Stevens to take her coat from her shoulders, and thanked him.

"Of course not! Please let me know if there's anything I can get for you." And Mr. Stevens bowed, backed away, but did not re-move himself from her sight, and would not for the rest of the af-ternoon, Babe knew. She stifled a sigh, put on a pair of sunglasses—she was attracting stares now—and had a fleeting wish for anonymity, for being able to wander, touch, feel, try on, without anyone bowing and scraping and fetching and carrying. Or envying.

But she also longed for Truman to be with her, and the two of them together would have attracted even more attention. Aching inside from a familiar emptiness, Babe determined to fill it. She went to the hat salon, where Halston himself—wiry, nervous—was only too happy to show her several new models; she sat in front of an ornate gold mirror while he helped her arrange them on her elaborate coiffure. He had the rare talent of being able to do so without mussing the hairstyles of his clients. Babe smiled, put up with his obsequious small talk—"Oh, Mrs. Paley, you look divine in anything, but I particularly like the red turban"—and she agreed, and the red silk turban with a jeweled brooch was promptly whisked away to be wrapped and boxed. Babe thanked Halston profusely, complimented him sincerely—the man was an artist, there was no denying it—and then decided she needed a new pair of white loaf-ers.

She wandered over to the shoe salon, the busiest part of the store, the air humming with chatter and gossip from customers and salespeople alike, yet the teeming space was divided into cozy, inti-mate little areas where one could almost feel as if one was sitting in one's own dressing room. She sat down, someone brought her tea in a Spode china cup, and then she was being shown dozens of white leather loafers, some with tassels, some with gold hardware, some with slippery leather soles, some with ridged rubber driving soles;

all made of luxurious calfskin leather, soft and malleable, already conforming to her long, narrow feet. After much consideration— walking carefully, weighing each step, studying how her feet looked in the little slanted mirrors—Babe chose three pairs of Ferragamo loafers, identical, so that she could have a pair waiting for her at Kiluna, at Round Hill in Jamaica, and at Kiluna North, in New Hampshire. While she didn't quite subscribe to the Guinnesses' method of having identical wardrobes at all their various homes, so they didn't have to carry luggage with them, she felt that she was being very prudent in this case. Italian loafers were a staple, just like loaves of bread. She was only exhibiting common sense.

The shoes, too, were whisked away to be wrapped up and shipped to the appropriate locations; after thanking the salesperson, Babe resumed her wandering, feeling very odd, light, as if she might float off the ground, like a balloon breaking free of its tether. Generally, Babe did not meander; she did not approve of it because her mother had not approved of such wasteful effort. Babe always had a plan, a list, and spending an afternoon at Bergdorf's to fulfill it restored her sense of self, of worth and accomplishment. But today, it wasn't working. So she found herself, uncharacteristically, picking items up just to feel the slippery fabric of a silk dress, or the cool weight of a gold belt, in her hand, then placing them back down again, picking up, placing down, over and over, touching, touching, touching—silk and satin and gold and silver and crystal and leather and wool—and she knew she looked ridiculous; she could glimpse Mr. Stevens trying not to stare at her. Babe Paley simply never made an empty gesture, and here she was, assembling a parade of them. But her feet, her hands, her mind, her heart, were all restless.

Truman. It was all because of Truman. The things that used to keep her occupied and amused, now that she had grown to rely on him so deeply, did not. She was not the same person she'd been, before him. So what would happen to her if she lost him now? Now that he was vaulted into the celebrity stratosphere? Now that he was appearing on talk shows, on the covers of magazines, with his pick of royal admirers, debutantes, movie stars?

Now that, for the first time, he didn't need her as much as she needed him?

Oh, what did it matter if she bought something new, something designed to make her look beautiful and desirable, today? Truman loved to admire her clothes—he could spend as much time in her closet as she could, happily taking inventory; he delighted in watching as she arrayed herself for an evening out or in, sitting at her feet, applauding and gasping and praising as she put on a private fashion show for two.

But now the world was at *his* feet. And nothing would be the same. And she had recognized herself in the pages of his master-piece, in the guise of a plain—downright ugly, even—murdered housewife from Kansas.

Babe lit up a cigarette; she knew she smoked too much lately, lighting up one after another in her long ebony holder. Her doctor, worried about a persistent cough, had suggested she cut back, but that was impossible.

"Babe! Darling!"

Babe quickly inhaled, desperate for the smoke in her lungs; closing her eyes in an almost sexual pleasure, she exhaled and finally turned, a welcoming smile on her face before she even knew who had called her name. When she saw that it was Slim, she smiled even brighter, genuinely happy to see her. Surprised, as well.

Lady Keith, as she was now known after her marriage to a dusty, dreary British nobleman, had a title, that was true. But titles were a dime a dozen in their world, especially those titles without the cash to back them up. And that, unfortunately, was the title that Slim had hastily married, on the rebound from Leland, a few years back.

"Slim, dear, I'm so happy to see you! What are you doing here? I mean, what are you shopping for today?"

"Stockings and lingerie. Those Brits don't know what they're doing in that way. Now, they are brilliant with riding boots and hunting jackets, I'll give them that. But anything for the boudoir simply isn't in their wheelhouse, or imagination."

"Boudoir?" Babe arched an eyebrow.

"Oh, Babe, not with my husband! How dreary! No, I have an assignation later on." Slim looked her friend square in the eye, and Babe felt a flood of relief. So, not with Bill. Thank God. Slim would never do that to her, unlike some of her other so-called friends.

"You don't have to tell me who." Babe patted Slim's arm. "I'm simply happy that you're finding a way to have a little fun. Kenneth is . . . well, so very British."

"You mean so very dull and hellishly snobbish. Well, I married him, so what's that say about me?"

"It says you never have gotten over Leland," Babe answered. Slim's blue eyes filled with tears, her nose reddened, and she nodded, before turning away to look at a pair of brown suede gloves. "What an idiot I was, to have fallen in love with my own husband," Slim whispered, blinking furiously. "Tell me about Truman. Have you seen him lately? Is the little guy insufferable with success?" And just like that, Slim was once again her fun, breezy self; she tucked her arm in Babe's and the two headed to the elevator, where Slim instructed the boy to take them up to the lingerie floor.

"Yes, two days ago. He gave me a copy of *In Cold Blood* to read, and it was fabulous. Wasn't it, Slim? Simply stunning?" For despite her tutelage under Truman's watch—the mountains of books he made her read, some enjoyable (Jane Austen, for instance) others not (goodness, she simply loathed the Proust, which had disappointed Truman to no end)—Babe still was unsure of her judgment where literature, politics, the arts were concerned.

"God, yes. He's brilliant. The book's brilliant. I couldn't put it down. And he knows it, too, the little devil. But I have to say he's done me a great favor. He wants me to handle the film rights to it, because he knows I haven't a penny, really, to call my own. Or should I say a shilling? Anyway, that's very generous of him."

"Oh, it is!" And Babe felt herself glow from within, proud of Truman and happy for Slim.

"I wonder," Slim mused, freshening up her lipstick, quickly, before the elevator stopped. "I wonder if he'll still have time for us, the little people. Now that he's such a big fat famous star. And I mean that, literally. He's putting on weight."

"Oh, Slim," Babe automatically admonished. But she didn't say anything else, and Slim, snapping shut her gold compact and slipping it back in her purse, caught the pucker of a frown between Babe's beautiful eyes.

The elevator stopped and the two of them exited it, finding themselves in a discreet boudoir—the lights were even subtly dimmed—full of lace and satin and silk. Antique chests with drawers overflowing with garter belts, black silk stockings. Armoires opened to display stunning pink peignoirs trimmed with dyed rabbit fur, wispy little negligees of delicate lace, so fragile-looking, like the most intricate spiderweb. An entire trunk full of a make-believe bride's trousseau—ivory satin negligees, matching robes, silk panties in every pastel, frothy bed jackets. Over in a corner were a few sensible cotton pajamas, men's style, hung on scented padded hangers.

And discreet young saleswomen everywhere, withholding judgment, assisting, measuring, fetching.

"My treat," Babe announced, tucking her arm in Slim's. "I'm completely at loose ends today, but I can't think of a thing I need. It would bring me great happiness to buy something for you, Slim. There's nothing more I'd like to do today. Truly."

"No, Babe, I couldn't." Slim shook her head vehemently. "I'm perfectly fine."

"I insist. Please, Slim, please." And Babe dropped her friend's arm; there was a look of quiet desperation in those brown eyes that Slim hadn't seen in a very long time, since before Truman. "Please let me. It would mean so much, you see. To help, in any way—"

"I see." And Slim did see; she saw that her friend was panicked, terrified, although Slim couldn't begin to think of the reason. Babe was at the peak of her beauty; just to look at her made one feel restful, refreshed. Those sculpted cheekbones, the deep-set eyes; her jawline was still firm, her skin creamy and unlined. Even her hair, more silver than black now, looked striking. And she was as trim as ever; she never seemed to put on a pound. Indulgence was not in Babe's nature, and she was reaping the benefits now, unlike Slim, who automatically patted her chin, feeling the flesh give way, even wiggle a little.

Was Slim jealous of Babe? She told herself she wasn't; she told herself that Babe was her one and only female friend, the only one she'd never felt in competition with, because there simply was no comparison. Babe was in her own class. And Slim always saw how that could be a lonely existence, one that she herself didn't really covet. She saw it in sharp relief today; Babe had been overjoyed to see her, but not before Slim had caught a glimpse of raw fear in her friend's eyes.

"Then thank you very much, dearest Babe."

"Oh, good!" And Babe beamed; the pucker between her eyes relaxed. "Let's pick something out that's perfect."

"Yes, perfect." Slim followed Babe, who now strode through the department with confidence, her exquisite taste unquestionable as she sorted through hangers, delicately picked through piles. Soon she had a small but absolutely breathtaking assortment of gowns in Slim's exact size—God, for the days when she was a six!—and Slim found herself in an elaborate dressing room filled with more furniture than most small apartments, trying them all on.

"Now, do not look at the price tags," Babe instructed in a soothing voice through the closed door. "Promise?"

"Promise," said Slim as she studied herself in a mirror, turning so she could see her backside, lifting her breasts with her hands and frowning as they fell back into middle-aged place. "Babe?"

"Yes, dear?"

"I didn't mean what I said, earlier. Of course Truman will still have time for us. We're his swans, remember? I was only being flippant. He's still our True Heart."

There was a long pause, then Babe murmured, "Thank you."

"Now"—Slim threw open the dressing room door with a grand gesture, just like Claudette Colbert in a movie from the thirties. She swept around the little parlor where Babe was perched on a chair, enjoying another tiny cup of tea. Posing, posturing, Slim modeled the most exquisite—and expensive—of the gowns, a white silk one with delicate black embroidered flowers across the cups and straps;

it plunged down in the back to just barely above her tailbone, and the silk felt like cool lips on her skin. "What do you think?"

"I think whoever it's for will be unable to resist you for a second."

"Then I'll take it. And thank you, my dearest friend." Slim ran to Babe and threw her arms about her, kissed her on the cheek, then fled back to the dressing room, leaving them both breathless and slightly dizzy from the unexpected physical contact.

They simply didn't do that, normally. Friendship among their set was sedate, wry, at arm's length.

But something about Babe today—how pale, how uncertain she had looked before Slim called out to her, her hesitancy in discussing Truman—touched Slim to the core. In taking Babe's gift, Slim felt she was giving, instead. Giving Babe something she very much needed.

"Let's go make sure Truman doesn't forget us," Slim urged, after Babe had paid for the gown. "Let's go buy him the kind of present that he likes. Something shiny and garish and too damn expensive for him to ignore."

"That's a wonderful idea!" Babe's eyes lit up. "Something for his new apartment; I know exactly what he needs—he saw the most exquisite foo dogs at this little antiques store on Seventh Avenue."

"Seventh Avenue it is!" As the two women exited Bergdorf's, the CBS limo was already waiting for them. Mr. Stevens had done his job well. They handed their purchases, wrapped up in the signature Bergdorf purple, to the driver, who carefully placed them in the trunk.

Then they sank down into the seats, and were driven two blocks west.

"It's fun, sometimes, pretending," Babe said.

"What do you mean?"

"Oh, today. Today, I just pretended I was someone else. It was fun, in a way. Not to be me, just to be a person. A normal person."

Slim gnawed her lip, watching her friend settle happily into the plush leather of the sedan. She looked outside the window; they were stuck in traffic, people walking briskly by. They could have strolled to the shop faster than their luxurious car was moving.

"Darling Babe," Slim murmured, taking her friend's hand.

"What?"

"Nothing. Just don't pretend too often, please. I love you just the way you are. And so does Bill. And so does Truman."

Babe blushed and folded her arms; she looked outside and didn't say a word. But Slim glimpsed a tear rolling down her cheek, reflected in the discreetly tinted windows of the Town Car.

New York loved a parade.

For war heroes, baseball players, prizefighters, presidents, holidays. Ticker tape raining down from the tallest buildings; ridiculous giant balloons floating down Broadway for Thanksgiving. Fireworks over the Statue of Liberty on the Fourth of July.

But as much as he wanted to, longed to, ached to, Truman Capote could not give himself a parade. Or erect a statue in his own honor. Or name a park after himself. Or rent the Statue of Liberty.

Second to parades, statues, and parks, then, New York loved a party. A really splendid soiree. *The* Mrs. Astor's famous Patriarch's balls, admission only to the Four Hundred as determined by her little lapdog, Ward McAllister. Mrs. Vanderbilt's costume ball to christen her new mansion, the one that *the* Mrs. Astor deigned to attend, thus allowing those upstart Vanderbilts into real Society and ushering in the excesses of the Gilded Age. The Bradley-Martins' infamous Louis XIV party, given in the middle of one of the worst recessions in American history. The Bradley-Martins felt it necessary to leave the country soon after. But every single guest thought it a fabulous time.

Then there were the more recent parties before the war, given by the legendary Elsa Maxwell, that corpulent darling of society. Elsa invented the scavenger hunt: heiresses in their evening clothes accosting hobos for scraps of food, canned goods, whatever was on the list, screeching with laughter, running off with prizes. Treasure hunts in the ballroom of the Waldorf Astoria, millionaires elbowing one another viciously for tin trinkets and plastic whistles.

Then there were the charity galas and openings galore, one practically every night during the season; socialites and their reluctant husbands dressed to the nines. But it was always for a good cause! It was work, really. One simply had to do her part, no matter how tiring it might be, planning a wardrobe for an entire season, spending hours before the mirror ensuring that each gown was flattering from any angle, because, really, one could not trust those photographers to capture the most beguiling aspect.

But there hadn't been a truly grand party, an honest-to-God, "Honey, let's get Grandmama's tiara out," fancy-dress party in decades. And Truman decided it was his duty to rectify this.

All summer long—the summer of 1966, the golden summer, as even then he knew he would look back on it; the summer of his ascendancy to the very top of the world, literary, popular, social— Truman sang a little tune to himself.

Well, didja evah, what a swell party, a swell party, a swellegant elegant party, this is. . . .

For Truman was going to throw himself a party in lieu of a parade. A party so grand, so exclusive, it would keep him in the headlines for months. It would make those who weren't invited weep and flee the country, or change their names and go into hiding. It would go down in history as the *most,* the cherry on top of the sundae, the caviar on top of the toast. The diamond as big as the Ritz.

And so that golden summer, as Truman lounged poolside at his friends' mansions, sunned himself on their yachts in the Mediterranean, even on the rare occasions it was only him and Jack, silent but companionable on the beach between their adjacent houses in Southampton, he planned (when he wasn't clipping reviews for his scrapbook, or giving interviews, or posing for photographs). He schemed. He was never without his notebook, a plain, black-covered lined notebook, and he wrote down and crossed out names, over and over and over again. For he was Ward McAllister and *the* Mrs. Astor and himself, Truman Capote, literary giant/social arbiter, all rolled into one.

He had the power now. And the money.

As he lay on the Agnellis' yacht that summer—refusing to go off on their exhausting little excursions to some ruin or another, smirking when they all trooped back, dusty and footsore while he had spent the day being served champagne by swarthy stewards, bobbing up and down in the turquoise Mediterranean, admiring the scenery from afar—or lounged by Babe's pool, or danced with Lee Radziwill (Jackie's sister, don'tchaknow, the newest addition to his swans), Truman, on the outside, was the same as ever. The same jokester, prankster, entertainer. The same lapdog, pocket fairy, jester.

"I want to pay you all back," he drawled, when questioned about his notebook, which he guarded fiercely, joked that he kept it locked up in a safe at night. "You've all been so kind to me, giving me parties, dinners, vacations, even! Marella, your yacht, it is to die for! A floating palace! So it's the least I can do, to throw a little ol' party in return!"

Yes, I want to pay you all back, he said to himself. *I want to make you jump through the hoops. Amuse me, amuse me! I want you to remember just who I am now. Truman Capote. The acclaimed author of the acclaimed* In Cold Blood, *the book that everyone is talking about this summer of 1966. The book none of you shallow idiots could ever have written. I'm not just your little True Heart, your favorite dinner guest, your token fag. I'm just as powerful as you!*

And just as glamorous. And just as headline-worthy.

And infinitely more interesting.

Still, as rich as he now was from the proceeds of the book—rich enough to make Nina/Lillie Mae spin in her urn, rich enough finally to move from dreary Brooklyn into a stunning Manhattan apartment at the new UN Plaza, an apartment that Babe helped him decorate, with heady views of the East River, the Brooklyn Bridge, lower Manhattan; rich enough to buy Jack's Southampton house for him, in his own name, and give it to him as a present, possibly the most generous act of his life, and thinking about it still brought tears to his eyes; rich enough to throw this party—still, he wasn't rich enough to own a yacht. Or a plane. Or a television network.

So he bit his tongue and planned his party gleefully, telling all his swans that of course they'd be invited—why, they'd be the very top of the list!

Still, it wouldn't do to throw the party for himself. Far too tacky, even for him. And he couldn't throw it for any of his swans—dear God, what a tangle of shredded feathers, rent designer gowns, torn jewels that would be! No, best to throw it for someone else, someone rather small and dreary; someone not nearly as fabulous as him, if he was going to have to share the spotlight. Someone like Kay Graham.

Poor Kay!

Poor plain Kay, wife of Phil Graham, a tragic suicide. Poor Kay, left with pots of money and a newspaper, *The Washington Post*, to run. Poor Kay of Washington, D.C., that dowdy little town where women did not dress for lunch, where they did not get their hair done by Kenneth, where the parties were soggy with politicians and other earnest drabs who talked more than they drank.

Poor Kay, whom Babe had introduced him to, and whom Truman had immediately liked, because of her very plainness. Just as he'd been drawn to Alvin and Marie Dewey of Kansas, whom he'd met while researching *In Cold Blood* (Alvin was the lead detective on the case); just as he was drawn irresistibly to truck drivers and appliance repairmen and dumb, brawny dockworkers. Truman knew he had a fascination for the ordinary that almost overshadowed his fascination with the rich and famous. He truly couldn't live without either. He'd left many a dinner in a penthouse apartment on Fifth to go down to the docks and pick up a Teamster.

So, Kay. Dowdy, pitiful Kay, who, he insisted in a phone call that summer, needed cheering up.

"No, not really," she'd replied, puzzled. "I'm just fine, Truman."

"No, you're not. I'm going to give you a party. Just a little party, to put a smile back on your face."

"You don't have to, but if you want to, I'd be honored."

"Fine. It's settled, then. Just an intimate party with dear friends."

By August, that intimate party had swelled to five hundred "dear friends." Only five hundred. Maybe five forty. No more. Because that was all the Grand Ballroom at the Plaza Hotel could comfortably hold. And that was to be the setting for this intimate little cheering-up party for his good friend, poor Kay Graham. He, Truman, was giving a party at the Plaza! *Mama, Mama, look at me now!*

"Now, Marella, don't feel put out. I couldn't have you as the guest of honor because everyone else would be jealous! But I will need you to host a pre-party dinner, sweetheart, if you don't mind. I'm only asking a very few of my dearest friends."

"Now, Slim, Big Mama, darling! Of course you'll be tops of the guest list, but I couldn't have you as the guest of honor—can you imagine how furious La Guinness would be? Knives would be thrown! Daggers! But I'm saving the first dance for you, my darling!"

"Now, Gloria, don't get furious, but you couldn't be the guest of honor. That's going to be Kay Graham, poor Kay! But you know, don't you, darling, that you're the guest of honor in my heart of hearts? And I'm instructing you to wear your finest jewelry because it's going to be fancy, fancy, and you'll be the belle of the ball, anyway!"

"C.Z.! My pet! What fun we're going to have! I know you won't mind if you're not the guest of honor—you know Kay Graham, don't you? Poor Kay! I decided she needed some cheering up so she's going to be the center of attention, because she needs it. But really, who'll be looking at her, poor dreary soul, when you're there, the golden goddess of all time?"

"Babe! Bobolink, my heart! Of course, I thought of you right away when I wanted to throw a party. I longed to give it for you, in your honor, after all we've been through together! But can you *imagine* how Slim would feel, the poor dear? Her life with that dreadful English lord is dreary enough. But I absolutely will rely on you for help in planning! And would you be the dearest of dears and host a pre-party dinner? I'm asking only a few really special friends, so that some of the guests who won't have escorts won't have to arrive alone. Everyone can dine together, and arrive en masse!"

And Marella, Slim, Gloria, C.Z., Babe, all that summer while they indulged their favorite, showed him off, now even more in demand than ever, a true prize at the dinner table, an intellectual feather in their jeweled caps, all murmured and agreed and felt special, singled out, and superior to poor Kay Graham. Who was a dowdy, dear soul.

And so Truman cackled and rubbed his hands with glee, a Machiavellian party planner, and dangled and withheld, delighting to see all Manhattan dancing at his feet, begging to be invited to what was already, that summer, shaping up to be the biggest event of the season. Truman dropped hints in the press. He called up his famous friends and drawled into their famous ears, tantalizing, purring— "So Tony, Tony Curtis, my favorite actor of all time! You'll be in Manhattan in November, won't you?"

Tony Curtis, his favorite actor of all time (that day, anyway), cleared his schedule. And waited for an invitation that never appeared.

"Carson, darling! My pet, my favorite author! You'll be in town in November, of course?"

And Carson McCullers, former friend and champion of a then-unknown writer named Truman Capote, waited. Until she heard, via Norman Mailer, that she wasn't invited. Then she grandly announced she'd be giving her own party that same night. But no one paid any attention.

All summer long, Truman schemed and planned and finalized. The guest list was the major work, and he spent as much time agonizing over it as he had any of his manuscripts. It had to be perfect. It had to be a unique mix of the beautiful people, the wealthy, the respected, the new and exciting, for this was 1966! Nineteen sixty-six, and the Beatles were absolutely *it*, and people were dancing the go-go at the Cheetah, and Andy Warhol was holding parties of his own at his workspace, the Factory, and skirts were up to *there*, and hair down to *here*, and Frank Sinatra had just married Mia Farrow!

Frank Sinatra. Mia Farrow. Truman scribbled their names down. Along with Aly Khan. Lynda Bird Johnson—but not Lady Bird, God no; he didn't want any dreary Secret Service men invading his party. Candice Bergen. Henry Fonda. The Windsors, for the expected touch of royalty.

Cecil Beaton. Henry Ford II. McGeorge Bundy. Norman Mailer. The Deweys and their friends from Kansas. Bennett and Phyllis Cerf, of course. The doorman at his new apartment building. Jack.

Margaret Truman—but not Bess or Harry. Alice Roosevelt. The Whitneys, *naturellement*. A couple of Vanderbilts and Astors, just for nostalgia's sake.

Should he invite the Beatles? Nah. But Andy Warhol, definitely. Christopher, of course—Christopher Isherwood. And John Knowles. He thought, briefly, of the entire Pulitzer Prize committee, sure to award *In Cold Blood* the prize for nonfiction in the upcoming year, but decided against that as too calculated, even for him.

Greta Garbo, Marlene Dietrich, the Harry Belafontes. Tallulah Bankhead—who was apt to show up naked, please, God! Think of the publicity. Rudolf Nureyev, definitely! George Balanchine. There would be dancing, of course; better book Peter Duchin now.

Betty Bacall. Pamela and Leland Hayward—well, hell, of

course he had to invite *them;* surely Slim was over that whole thing by now! The cabdriver who took Truman home for free one night because he'd had his wallet stolen at a dive bar. Rose Kennedy. Ethel and Bobby, his neighbors at the UN Plaza. Jackie, naturally. Although Truman had taken to whispering, to anyone who would listen, that she looked like a drag version of herself, in person.

For every name added there were two crossed out, perhaps to be added later. Or not. Truman was God. And not a benevolent one, either. Old grievances were dredged up—of course, Carson McCullers wouldn't be invited, the sow. The bitchy, envious sow who had turned on him ever since he became more acclaimed than she was. And forget Gore Vidal, that bitch. Ann Woodward could forget it, too, and not just because she was a murderess. They'd met at a party at the Windsors' not too long ago, where the other guests were giving her a wide berth. Ann was standing alone, one arm on the fireplace mantel, surveying the crowd. Truman strolled right up to her.

"Well, if it isn't Miss Bang Bang herself," he had greeted her. "Seen any burglars lately?"

"Well, if it isn't Truman Capote, literary asshole and garden-variety fag," Ann had slurred back. She was stoned. Her eyes were glazed over, her lipstick smeared all over her face, and Wallis was surveying her grimly, visibly regretting having invited her. But some people had started to feel sorry for her, trapped in Elsie's golden grip, and she was starting to make the rounds again.

Then she threw her drink in his face, chest heaving, pupils dilated. She had a twisted grin of triumph on her cherry-streaked lips. "You don't fool me, you little queer. You're just as pathetic as I am. Maybe more pathetic."

"You'll regret this," he assured her calmly, as she was hastily ushered away, cackling wildly, by one of Wallis's lapdogs. He was already starting to plot his revenge. . . .

But that was for later. *After.* Right now, the only thing he wanted to work on, could work on, was his party. Throwing this party meant he didn't have to worry about what to write next. He'd worked himself raw, scraped his soul to the marrow, writing *In Cold Blood.* At first it was just a diversion, a small article in the *Times* about a murdered Kansas family that piqued his interest. He thought it might make a nice little piece for *The New Yorker*—something about a murder in a small town, the shocking randomness of it, the reverberations. So he convinced William Shawn, the editor, to send him out to Kansas so he could report on it. That was all.

But from the moment he laid eyes on Dick—stupid, blustering Dick—and Perry—mesmerizing, charismatic Perry—at the tiny Kansas courthouse, the night the two men were arrested for the murders of the Clutter family, he knew that he had something more. His masterpiece. A case study, a brilliant piece of journalism, written with the lyricism of a novel. "In fact, I've invented a new genre. The nonfiction novel," he never tired of telling anyone who would listen, back in 1959, when the whole thing started. He spent endless weeks in Holcomb, Kansas, gathering the material, interviewing the townsfolk, trying to understand the doomed Clutters, getting cozy with the lead detective, granite-faced Alvin Dewey, and his adorable wife, Marie, getting even cozier with the arrested and then convicted murderers, Dick Hickock and Perry Smith—and understanding the latter better, more intimately, than he ever did the Clutters.

When he returned to New York and settled down with his notebooks to write, it had been easy, for a change. The manuscript flowed from his fingertips on its own, and he told absolutely everyone about it, and soon everyone in New York was salivating to read it, and he would give them glimpses, little performances of certain scenes, at parties and dinners. But then the waiting; the everlasting, tortuous waiting for the end. *The End*—oh, how he longed to write it, but he couldn't, not for years, agonizing years that dragged on while Dick and Perry were granted stay after stay, pleading with him, Truman—their great hope, their chronicler—to help them. Years in which all he could do was talk about this great opus, not finish it, even while he had to watch Nelle Harper Lee win all the prizes for her story about *their* childhood, *To Kill a Mockingbird*. Oh, Christ, the pain of watching that happen to Nelle, of all people! Clumsy, inarticulate Nelle! And the fear—shocking, jolting him awake at night so that his heart raced, his body swam in clammy sweat—that people would lose interest in the story—and him. And then he would be just another writer. And not the greatest of all time.

But finally, there were no more stays, no more last-minute calls from the governor, and the executions—oh, God, oh, Jesus, oh, Mama. They'd shamed him into being there, Dick and Perry and, yes, Nelle, who'd helped him research it, and William Shawn, who expected blood, no less, for what he was paying Truman. So he'd gone to see Perry and Dick only an hour before their execution. They were white as sheets, were still trying to be brave, flippant, but obviously terrified, poor boys! What had Truman felt, talking to them this last time? He hadn't processed it all; he wasn't brave enough for that. Truman knew he was a coward in many ways; it was, he believed, one of the most charming things about him. That night—it was near midnight, dark, raining, a horrible, bone-chilling nightmare that he knew had seeped into his very being, and that he would carry with him forever—his cowardice and bravery, both, astonished him. The cowardice that had kept him from going to Dick and Perry despite their pleas, until the very last moment when there would be no time for them to say what he knew they would, that he had deserted them, given up on them—*used* them. But he had come, after all, and his bravery overwhelmed him; the courage to stay when the two murderers asked him to witness their final moments—the barbaric ritual, the last words, the hoods over the heads, the knees buckling, the tortured writhing at the end of the noose, and then, finally, the eerie stillness, the absence of breathing, the one less person in the cavernous barn despite the fact that there were still the same number of bodies. The subtraction of a soul. The tragic waste of lives not unlike his own, if he was being honest—lives of men abandoned by their parents, treated like crap, like dirt, like fungus, all their lives. Men who had taken one turn while he had taken another, and that simple act of a change in direction, in wind, in air, of one foot in front of another, was all that separated the two of them, killer and artist.

But a killer could be an artist, he discovered. And an artist a killer.

The soul-searching, the exhaustion of reality, of bearing witness, of coming to the aid of a fellow man, even a killer—he must hold it all at bay. He could not examine it, for fear of what it would do to the work, which was the most important thing. This masterpiece he had crafted, astonishing himself with every perfect word, every exquisitely crafted paragraph. The book was all. He must write it, and he did, that last chapter coming quickly for a change, as usually he agonized over endings.

And the book was all he had dreamed it would be, all he had told everyone—his swans, his literary rivals, the doorman to his apartment building, the grocer on the corner, his crazy family back in Alabama, even his sniveling deadbeat of an attention-hog father. *In*

Cold Blood was a masterpiece, and this time the critics all agreed. And now that he was at the top of the heap—had *become* that spire in the great city beckoning others from lesser lands—he must rejoice in his success. For enjoying the fruits of his labor was just as serious as the writing itself.

So now he was throwing a party. The most swellegant, elegant party evah.

In Honor of Mrs. Katharine Graham:

MR. TRUMAN CAPOTE

REQUESTS THE PLEASURE OF YOUR COMPANY

AT A BLACK AND WHITE DANCE

ON MONDAY THE TWENTY-EIGHTH OF NOVEMBER

AT TEN O'CLOCK

GRAND BALLROOM, THE PLAZA

LATER, TRUMAN SAID THAT the morning the invitations went out, he made five hundred friends and fifteen hundred enemies.

Only one of these was an exaggeration.

. . . . .

A SUMMIT. A COUNSEL. OF UTTER FABULOUSNESS.
The day before Truman's party, Betsey Cushing Roosevelt
Whitney, accompanied by her sisters, Minnie Cushing Astor Fosburgh and Barbara Cushing Mortimer Paley, sailed into the Palm
Court at the Plaza. Her head held high, she didn't slow down, only
barely nodded at a maître d' who scurried ahead of her to pull out a
chair just as she sat down at an intimate table, one of her own choosing. Betsey Cushing Roosevelt Whitney did not wait to be told
where to sit, not even at the Plaza.

It was afternoon tea; all around them were adorable little girls
dressed in pink dresses with matching hair ribbons, white gloves,
patent-leather shoes, accompanied by indulgent parents or grand-
parents. There were other—lesser—socialites present, too, and
out-of-towners who couldn't help but gape at the trio of fabulously
dressed women, all with cheekbones as prominent as their good
breeding, but the triumvirate paid the tourists no attention. This
was a sister meeting, a ritual from their childhood. Long ago, their
tribunals had centered around who could borrow whose hair rib-

bon, or what birthday present should they pool their money for and purchase for their mother. But as they grew up and into the beauty and elegance laid out for them, like their school uniforms, by their mother, the conferences had turned to more serious matters, usually presided over by Gogs. Minnie's long affair with Vincent Astor, for instance, had been discussed and dissected and determined to have run long enough at one of their summits; Vincent found himself proposing soon after. And Babe's miserable marriage to Stanley Mortimer had come to a merciful end after one of their conclaves; Gogs and her daughters had weighed the pros and cons and finally determined that Babe could remove herself with her reputation intact. And so, she did.

There had been no summit, however, when Babe decided to marry Bill.

Tea, too, was a constant from the sisters' youth; back in the big Cushing house in Brookline, their mother, Gogs, had introduced the ritual of afternoon tea, ostensibly for the family, but before long it became a salon of a sort, a place where the best and most socially desirable of the medical and academic communities could "drop in." Every afternoon, a tempting assortment of tea and punch and finger sandwiches and pastries would be spread in the drawing room and a crush of people would arrive; the Cushing sisters grew up watching their mother preside over the tea table and flit among her guests, seeing to their every wish and comfort. Their father, however, rarely attended; he was always in surgery.

The girls watched—and it wasn't for amusement; Gogs insisted on their being involved in the preparations long before they were old enough to take part in these elegant soirees. They observed their mother see to every detail, no matter how small: the spotlessness of the aprons worn by the Irish servant girls, the ritualistic polishing of the silver, the placement of the cherries atop the pink-iced tea cakes.

There would often be music, a harpist or a pianist, some Cambridge student hired for the day. Other homes, even in Boston during those playful years of the 1920s, early '30s, might have also served cocktails in silver shakers accompanied by cheese biscuits, but not Gogs. She stuck to tradition: to bone china, English tea, lemon and sugar, clotted cream for the scones.

Betsey Whitney, Minnie Fosburgh, and Babe Paley, then, were more than capable of hosting elaborate spreads in their own homes, and they often did, but why hide themselves away all the time? It was time for a sister summit, so naturally, they went to the Plaza, for their mother had raised them to be seen and admired.

"I don't believe Mother ever had tea outside her own drawing room, did she?" Betsey, who was not the eldest but acted it, inquired as she removed her gloves. She was a shorter version of Babe, with the same cheekbones, but her coloring was less vivid; her hair a lighter shade, her eyes not quite as dark, her skin not quite as creamy. But Betsey had the more regal air; she could manage to look down her nose at anyone, even if she were the smallest person in the room.

Minnie, the eldest—and kindest, Babe always insisted—sister, shook her head. Minnie was the tallest, the most down-to-earth; she didn't have Betsey's imperiousness nor Babe's uncertainty. She didn't have their deep-set brown eyes, either, although she was the thinnest. She would have been gawky had she been anyone else's daughter but Gogs's.

Babe smiled fondly. "No, Mama never did like to dine in public, did she? She always felt the best hospitality could be found at home."

A waiter handed Betsey—how did he know she was the leader? He simply did—a beautifully lettered menu, but she waved it away. "Champagne, and Darjeeling. An assortment of sandwiches and pastries, but no sponge cake—I can't abide sponge cake. No onions on the sandwiches." Then she turned back to her sisters as the waiter bowed and hurried away.

"I like onions," Minnie protested. Her cheeks flamed as she resumed an argument that had begun when she was ten and Betsey eight. "Just because you don't doesn't mean that I shouldn't have them."

"Onions aren't proper for ladies. Do you want your breath to offend? Didn't Mama teach you anything?" Betsey shook her head and turned to Babe for backup.

Babe wrinkled her nose. "I don't like them, personally, but I don't see why Minnie can't have onions if she wants them."

"I didn't see why Minnie had to divorce Vincent, either, but she did." Betsey didn't even look at her elder sister; it was as if she weren't there.

"Betsey, don't start. I never wanted to marry Vincent in the first place. I don't think he wanted to marry me. Gogs wanted it, and so, of course, it came off. I put up with him as long as I could, then I found him Brooke, who needed his money and name more than I did. And then he died, and so what? Who cares? Why did you divorce James, if we're playing that game? Wasn't a Roosevelt good enough for you?"

"James didn't want to be a father to his daughters. I was looking out for my girls, just as Mama always looked out for us. I'm a good mother, Minnie. Not that you'd know anything about that." Betsey narrowed her eyes at her sister.

"Oh, please!" Babe anxiously looked from sister to sister. "Girls, please! Not here! Mama would be distraught!"

"Babe, we're not making a scene," Betsey scolded her little sister. "Our voices are perfectly normal. You worry too much, as usual. But let's do change the subject. Tomorrow's Truman's party. Of course, we all know what we're going to wear?"

It was another rhetorical question; Betsey was fond of asking them. The sisters had coordinated their wardrobes weeks ago, just as they always did prior to a party. From their childhood friends' birthday parties to Truman's fabulous Black and White Ball—the divine Cushing sisters knew how to dress for maximum trio advantage. Babe always got the first pick, which Betsey had always begrudged but had never been able to change; the one thing, perhaps, in her life that she had not been able to bend to her will. After Babe made her selection, the other two had to somehow dress in a complementary yet unique fashion, with certain colors deemed special to one or the other. Babe was an angel in blue; that was a truth universally acknowledged. Actually, all jewel tones were hers. Betsey was often in black. Minnie didn't care and, in fact, often simply asked Babe to find something for her to wear, which was a task Babe took great pride in, happy to be of help.

When it came to jewelry, however, it was every sister for herself; Betsey had Whitney money, Minnie had Astor heirlooms. Babe had the most modern jewelry, custom-designed by newer artistes: Fulco di Verdura, Jean Schlumberger.

"Well, we're all in white, this time—so there's no coordinating to do," Minnie said with obvious relief. "Designers?"

"I'm in a Castillo," Babe offered, even though Betsey knew very well who she was wearing.

"Dior," Betsey replied.

"Balmain," Minnie offered as all three sisters nodded in approval of their choices.

"Masks? I asked Halston to do mine," said Betsey.

"Same here." Minnie pointed to herself.

"I asked Adolfo—actually, I asked him to make three different versions, just in case," Babe admitted, lowering her eyes modestly. "I provided him with some paste versions of my jewels, and he made up three different designs, and then I picked the one I liked best, and he added the real stones."

"Oh, Babe!" Minnie was so open in her admiration, her thin face glowed. "Oh, that's just like you, darling!"

"Yes, that was very smart of you," Betsey admitted through gritted teeth.

"You know me." Babe shrugged, even as she was enjoying Betsey's obvious jealousy. "I don't like to leave much to chance. Mama taught me that, anyway." There was a lull while the waiter rolled a trolley up to their table filled with delicate sandwiches the size of silver dollars, luscious sugared cookies, and iced cakes. Each sister smiled in approval, allowed her tea to be poured in her cup, but when the waiter was gone, not one sandwich, cookie, or cake was selected. The onion argument had been moot, after all.

"What about Truman?" Betsey asked, moving the agenda along. "Are we certain he's done everything right? Babe?"

Babe stirred her tea slowly. "This is Truman's party, Betsey, dear. Not ours. I do think you might have forgotten that."

"Yes, yes, but, well—*Truman*! He didn't have the upbringing we did. And he's relied on us, all three of us, so much in matters of taste. That new apartment, for instance—you and Minnie practically decorated it for him, didn't you?"

"We did advise," Minnie said, uncrossing then crossing her

long legs, clad in silk hosiery, although she wore unbecomingly flat, rather plain shoes, something Betsey never did approve of. Even if Minnie was self-conscious about her height, couldn't she at least wear something stylish, like Babe? "It was quite fun, wasn't it, Babe, darling? But I do wonder at all the rattlesnakes he chose—so many stuffed specimens. Too much like the Museum of Natural History." Minnie shuddered.

"I would say that's an apt metaphor." Betsey pursed her lips.

"What do you mean by that?" Babe shot back.

"Babe, dear, I simply mean that little Truman has a bit of a sting to him, don't you think? Somewhat of a barbed way of looking at the world. Heaven knows he's been divine to you, to all of us. But he's not always that way to others. This whole party, really—I can't help but think that he could have managed it better. Without quite so much publicity. Why, the *Herald* leaked the guest list. Leaked? How? Who gave it to them? And now everyone who wasn't invited can't claim that they were and turned it down. The world knows who was invited and, more important, who was not. That's rather—bourgeois, don't you think?"

"Truman has a secretary, who sent the invitations out," Babe said primly. "He wasn't the only one with access to it."

"Babe, dear, your loyalty, as always, is touching." Betsey's lips curled up. "Let's hope tomorrow night isn't a disaster, because of course, people will assume we all had something to do with it, even if we didn't. Especially you, Babe, as close as the two of you are."

"I don't think we have to worry. He'll pull it off brilliantly, I know." Babe felt her cheeks flush, heard her voice rising ever so little, and so she sipped some tea and smoothed the skirt of her Chanel day suit. "I can't wait to see what you're wearing, Betsey, dear." Babe smiled serenely at her older sister. "I know you described it to me, but I can't wait to see you in person. Is Jock wearing a mask? I can't get Bill to wear one!"

"No, Jock won't, either."

"Jim is!" Minnie beamed. "He's spent weeks designing it himself!"

"Naturally," Betsey murmured with a significant look at Babe. "I'm not at all surprised, dear, to hear that."

"What do you think Gogs would say about the party?" Minnie mused. She had been her mother's "problem" daughter; the two had clashed often in private, although in public Minnie generally conformed to her mother's ideals. Betsey was so exactly like her mother that they had always been in agreement. Babe was too insecure ever to question her mother's decrees, except for when she married Bill—that had been quite the time! Minnie grinned, remembering her mother's utter disbelief that Babe, of all her daughters, would marry a Jew! "I often wonder how Mama'd feel about Truman," Minnie wondered.

"I hope she'd like him as much as we do," Babe said quietly.

"No, she wouldn't," pronounced Betsey the wise. "She wouldn't have trusted him one bit. I can't say that I'd blame her, either. But he is quite amusing. In small doses."

"Well, I do know that Mama would never have approved of all this publicity—photographers at a party! She must be writhing in her grave!—but secretly, she'd cut out all our photos and paste them in a scrapbook. And she'd demand to be shown our gowns beforehand; heavens, the idea of us dressing ourselves, at our age!" Minnie laughed fondly; she did miss the force of nature that had been her mother. Gogs, for all her prickliness, still had been the compass, the rudder, the sail; the very wind driving her girls toward the safe harbor of wealth and privilege. And it was safe, Minnie had to admit with a sigh. And she was a coward; she knew she'd never have made a good poor man's wife. None of them would have. Well, maybe Babe.

The pop of a champagne cork caused all three sisters to shift expectantly in their seats; Cristal was poured into their glasses, and Betsey raised hers first, to give the customary toast.

"To Gogs!"

"To Gogs," her sisters repeated, and the glasses clinked, causing everyone in the palm-filled room to look, and gape, once more.

Three beautiful women—the three fabulous Cushing sisters. Gracing the Plaza with their presence; granting their subjects a glimpse, laughing together, careless, privileged, so exquisite that it was impossible even to envy them. They were simply unattainable.

Then the sisters drifted away, blowing air kisses, bestowing smiles of recognition to a chosen few as they made their way to their waiting limousines.

After all, they must see to their gowns; they must try them on one last time, in case there were any unexpected tears or loose sequins. They must remember the code to the vault, so that they could retrieve their jewels. They must make sure their husbands had a good dinner, a perfect cigar, so that they were in such good moods, they might actually be persuaded to dance tomorrow night—or at least not mind if the sisters danced with other men. And then, of course, the sisters must also go to bed early, with cucumber slices on their eyes, special facial masks hydrating their skin.

For hadn't their mother told them always to get a good ten hours' sleep the night before a party?

. . . . .

THE MORNING OF THE PARTY, KAY GRAHAM WENT TO HAVE her hair done. Normally she just had a plain shampoo and set, but she was growing worried. Truman had told her of the elaborate preparations being undertaken by some of his friends, the really elegant ones, the swans, he called them—Marella Agnelli, Slim Keith, Gloria Guinness, Babe Paley. Kay had met them all—in fact, had been introduced to Truman by Babe, who was so elegant, so perfect, that Kay always felt dowdy next to her, no matter how nice a dress she was wearing. But Kay was simply missing that elegant, stylish gene, and she knew it, and besides, in Washington that didn't matter so much.

But in New York, it did, and tonight she was going to be on display—"Darling, you must look divine! All the newspapers will be sending photographers! Television networks, too! All eyes will be on you, my darling, precious Kay!"

Truman meant to be kind, she knew. He was excited for her. But his words filled Kay with despair, that familiar self-doubt. Frankly, she wished she could just stay in her hotel suite at the Plaza and watch television or read a book.

But she couldn't, and so, taking a deep breath, she grabbed her purse and ran out of the Plaza in her plain clothes—a cotton dress, low-heeled pumps. She hadn't put any makeup on, as she normally didn't wear any. She did plan to wear something—mascara, lipstick—tonight.

Grabbing a cab, she repeated the address given to her by Truman himself; in fact, he had set the appointment for her. "Kay, gorgeous lady, you have to see Kenneth. He's the one, the only one."

And certainly Kay had heard of Kenneth; after all, she knew the Kennedys when they were in the White House, and Kenneth styled Jackie's hair. So, of course, Kay guessed that Kenneth's might be a little busy today, the day of her party.

But nothing prepared her for the crush in front of the place. Nothing prepared her for the place at all, really; her salon in Washington was small, utilitarian, on the top floor of a retail building.

"Is this it?" Kay asked the cabbie, who shrugged and thrust out his hand for the fare. She paid it, got out of the cab, and couldn't prevent herself from simply stopping, and gaping, like the tourist she was.

For in front of an enormous limestone townhouse, a stunning building with columns and pediments and majestic windows and a festive yellow-and-black awning in front, was a line of limousines, Town Cars, and cabs. She wondered if the president himself might be here, for in Washington, the only time you saw a crush like this was when the president or vice president was out and about, trailed by the Secret Service.

There wasn't a lot of honking; the drivers seemed patient

enough, willing to wait. And emerging from the awning, popping out like BBs from a toy gun, were women. Gorgeous, stylish women far better dressed than she was, in designer dresses and furs; Kay immediately folded her arms across her chest, ashamed of her plain shift dress and cloth coat, acutely aware of her lack of jewelry and makeup. And on the heads of these women were concoctions worthy of Marie Antoinette: piles and piles of hair, most of it fake, bedecked with ribbons or feathers or jewels or sometimes all three. Walking with their necks stiff, their coiffures somewhat protected from the wind and drizzle of a late-autumn morning by loose-fitting plastic scarves and hoods, nevertheless each woman hurried to her waiting car, and the parade moved on. And on, and on; the line of black cars was endless.

Kay ducked her head and ran across the street, under the awning, and made her way through giant wrought-iron doors. Inside, she had to stop once more and take it all in, for she wasn't in a hair salon at all and wondered if she'd gotten the address wrong. She was in a mansion; a candy fantasy of a mansion with a grand staircase, polished floors from another, more opulent era—but the walls were papered in bright contemporary patterns of flowers and trellis, and around every corner Kay could spy cozy little nooks with ornately tented ceilings providing privacy, Turkish stools on which little manicurists perched, antique chairs, chandeliers, endless halls and rooms.

Climbing the stairs slowly, her hand on the railing, Kay tried not to be run over by manicurists and stylists charging up and down, their faces tense, perspiration on their brows, scissors and nail files bristling in their pockets. When she got to the top of the stairs, she gave her name to a frazzled-looking receptionist, who paged rapidly through a thick book.

"Graham? Graham?"

"Yes, Mrs. Katharine Graham."

"Right. We have you with Marco, one of our new stylists. May I take your coat?" And the young woman frowned at Kay's worn tweed coat.

"Thank you." Kay handed it to her, and once again felt ashamed of her plainness. For even the receptionist was dressed better than she was, in a gorgeous pink dress, her hair done up in the new fashionable bubble style, pin curls tickling her etched cheekbones.

"Come this way, please, Mrs. Graham." Another, equally stylish young woman, with false eyelashes as thick as caterpillars, was beckoning Kay up another flight of stairs. "Are you going to the party tonight? Truman's party? We're so busy!"

"Well, yes, I am. Actually, I'm—I'm the guest of honor." Kay felt rather silly saying this out loud; she didn't really know why she did. She guessed that she was a bit proud of the fact, after all.

"What?" The young lady stopped dead in her tracks, causing Kay to bump into her, and another woman, dressed in a wild Pucci print dress, to run into Kay. "You're the guest of honor? For Truman's party?"

Kay felt her cheeks burn, and she ducked her head again, feeling stares upon stares on her plain, unstylish figure. "Yes."

"Oh, no!"

Kay raised her head and wondered what she'd done wrong. "I'm sorry?"

"Oh, no, this will never do! You can't be seen by Marco! Come, come, Kenneth will see to you himself."

"But I don't want to be a bother; it doesn't really matter who does my hair—"

The young woman gasped. So did the Pucci-clad lady behind

Kay who, upon further examination, turned out to be Kitty Carlisle Hart.

"Of course it matters! Kenneth would be crushed if he wasn't allowed to do your hair for the ball!"

And so Kay had no choice but to follow the young woman up still another flight of grand stairs, to a bright yellow room with the golden glow of an inner sanctum. And before she knew it, she found herself—plain dress somehow removed, so that she was now clad in a beautiful orange-and-pink poncho—in a black patent-leather chair that resembled a throne, with a young, puckish man with thinning hair, in a dark suit and tie, like a banker, hovering over her with his hands full of combs and brushes and enormous hair clips. On her right sat a very young woman clad in a similar poncho, probably a model, for her face looked familiar. On her left sat a woman with her hair half covered in elaborate ringlets, powdered white; the other half of her head was dyed jet black and hung limply, obviously not yet done.

Rose Kennedy, her hair freshly dyed and hanging straight, obviously waiting to be set, sat opposite, waving gaily, and Kay waved back, thankful to see a familiar face. Yet even as she waved to Mrs. Kennedy, Kay felt as if she had stepped through the looking glass. She wasn't used to pampering herself on the scale of a Kennedy!

"Mrs. Graham!" Kenneth—Kenneth himself! The creator of Jackie Kennedy's bouffant hairdo and Marilyn Monroe's flip—put his combs and brushes down and clapped his hands, causing Kay to gasp. "It's an honor to do your hair. What kind of mask are you wearing? Did you bring it? And your dress?"

"Oh, no, I didn't think of that—"

"Never mind," Kenneth said kindly, with a sympathetic twinkle in his impish eyes. "Describe them to me."

"Well, they're quite simple, really, just a white dress, in a robe style, with long sleeves, with these crystals—hematites, gray—around the neck and sleeves, and on the mask, too. It's white."

"I think, then, something classic and chic. We'll set it, but then brush it up, from the face, secure it in the back very plainly and let the sides be, very sleek, very nice."

"Oh, yes! Thank you!" And Kay Graham could have burst into tears; Kenneth seemed to know exactly what she had in mind. Not for her the elaborate coiffures, curls upon curls, fake pieces, odd dyes that she'd seen.

"I think that sounds lovely, dear," Rose called to her in her brittle Boston accent, and Kay nodded enthusiastically. Then she allowed herself to relax and be pampered; someone brought her a tray, on which were tiny little tea sandwiches, a flute of champagne, a cup of broth. She nibbled, had her nails done, sat with her hair in rollers under the quietest dryer she'd ever experienced, watched as Kenneth created miracles on other women's heads, closed her eyes as he did the same to hers, once she came out of the dryer, and then—

"*Voilà!*"

Kay opened her eyes. She felt her face stretch into a smile so broad, so purely delighted, that she almost didn't recognize it, for it had been a long time, truly, since she'd smiled like that—beamed, actually.

But she looked wonderful! Oh, simply wonderful, and what a shame it was that Phil wasn't here to see her—but no, she wouldn't cry; she blinked away the few tears that sprang to her eyes. But he had been so handsome, and she so plain, and she always felt the difference even though he, when he was himself, never did. When he wasn't himself—

Well, that was it. He wasn't himself.

But now she looked so pretty! So young, her hair sleek and simple, but she would never be able to replicate it at home. It took someone as talented as Kenneth to make her more herself than she'd ever been.

Kenneth didn't have to ask how she liked it; he saw the tears in her eyes. He blinked his own away and sighed the satisfied sigh of an artist at the end of a good day's work.

Then he turned to do the same thing, all over again, to the next beautiful woman walking into his studio. Marisa Berenson. What a vision.

Kay Graham slipped away, careful not to muss her hair as she changed back into her dress, thankful that it had stopped raining as she walked outside, so afraid of disturbing her hair that she didn't even turn her head. But she had to hurry back to the Plaza to change, to have her daughter, Lally, make up her face (for Kay truly didn't know how), and to wait for Truman—dear Truman, kind, thoughtful Truman!—to knock on her door and escort her, Cinderella, to the ball.

Until this moment, Kay really hadn't been looking forward to it. But now she couldn't wait.

SLIM, TOO, WAS AT Kenneth's that afternoon, although she missed Kay Graham. She also—due to the brilliance of Kenneth's staff— missed Pamela Churchill Hayward, thank Christ! But she couldn't very well miss her this evening, and so Slim put herself into Kenneth's hands, knowing he would make her look beautiful.

She was looking forward to the party, even though she would see more ex-husbands and ex-lovers than she wanted to. But a party was a party, and maybe a good brawl would break out at this one—Truman once told her that was the sign of a really great party.

Although somehow she sensed that he wouldn't really think so, if it happened tonight.

TRUMAN WAS ALL AFLUTTER. He was simply exhausted by the phone ringing all afternoon in his suite at the Plaza; the Kansas group, the plain, darling people he'd met while researching *In Cold Blood*, kept calling him, keeping him abreast of their adventures (they'd had their hair done at the Plaza salon, their masks were all delivered, their gowns pressed). They were ecstatic at being invited to his party, and their enthusiasm touched him—really, it was nothing to have invited them, to have given their dreary lives a little color!—even if he didn't have time for it right now. The management of the Plaza had a flurry of last-minute questions about floral arrangements and details about the orchestra and did he want the buffet served at midnight or later? And about the security . . . that was a headache! They assured him his guests would appreciate a separate entrance, not through the main doors on Grand Army Plaza, so that some of them could avoid the inevitable cameras and onlookers.

Truman agreed—shuddering at the cost—even as he rolled his eyes. If he knew his guests, and he did, none of them would take advantage of this hidden entrance.

And then Kay kept calling, offering to help, and, sweet, kind soul that she was, it annoyed him to the point where he finally asked her to arrange for a light supper in her room for just the two of them, something they could enjoy before heading down to greet their guests. Even though they were dining at the Paleys', who were hosting the premier pre-party dinner. Still, they planned only to stop by for a drink before going back to the Plaza, as they had to be the very first ones there to receive their guests.

Anyway. Truman glanced at the stacks and stacks of newspapers surrounding him, all with some mention of the party. His party! The party of the year! The decade! The century!

Now it was time to dress, and he wondered for a moment if Jack was doing the same; dear, gruff, maddening Jack, who thought the whole thing a silly excuse, a ridiculous excess, oh, all the dreary things other people—people who weren't invited—were saying. "What a waste of time, Truman," Jack had tsk-tsked. "You have a literary reputation to uphold now. A *serious* literary reputation." But he'd promised he'd come anyway, and Truman simply adored him for that, and hoped against hope he would. He did love to show Jack off—when he was behaving.

Almost seven o'clock. Time to go down and fetch Kay. Poor, plain little Kay! God, he hoped Kenneth had done something marvelous to her; if anyone could, it was Kenneth. And he did hope she'd have a wonderful time tonight, the dear thing. Phil Graham's suicide had been tragic, coming after a lifetime of schizophrenia. Poor Kay deserved a treat.

With one last glance in the mirror at his tuxedo, he patted his pocket where his dime-store mask—shades of Holly Golightly!—resided. Truman decided he looked wonderful—no longer the lithe young fawn of his youth, perhaps; he was settled now, settled into his legacy, into posterity. Maybe a little heavier than he'd like, true. His hair, absolutely thinning but he had invested in a hair transplant a few months back, and so the battle line was being held, for now. But his eyes were clear and bright, and he was reminded of the last time he gave a great party, a really terrific party. It was back in

Monroeville when he was twelve and about to leave for New York, finally summoned by his mother. He'd thrown a farewell party for himself and invited a couple of local niggers, and the Klan had shown up and made a fuss, and it was *the* scandal of Monroeville for simply years and years.

Oh, he did hope tonight would be like that!

BABE STOOD IN THE DINING ROOM of her apartment, so filled with white, old-fashioned flowers, it looked like an English garden.

Babe had not had her hair done at Kenneth's, as she knew it would be a madhouse, and according to Betsey, who'd telephoned earlier, it was. So she'd had a stylist come to her, and was very satisfied with the result; she looked stunning, actually, in a white Castillo, a long chiffon column of a dress, but sleeveless, showing off her lovely arms, bracelets, and rings. Her hair was perfect for the mask she would wear, white satin, framing her eyes. She had made sure she looked perfect from every angle, posing sideways in the three-way mirror in her dressing room, turning this way and that. Every image was reassuring, despite her worries; the dress looked divine, the mask complemented it beautifully and did not obscure her eyes, which she had accented with darker liner than usual, and with false eyelashes.

She'd helped Truman in the weeks leading up to the party, relieved to the point of tears, actually, to have been asked. This was his party, but somehow she wanted it to be hers, as well, and she was shocked and ashamed of herself. He must have understood, for he did seek her advice when it came to picking the decorations for the Grand Ballroom at the Plaza; he'd wanted to drape the walls in red, but she'd convinced him that would be too claustrophobic, and he'd agreed. So they decided on massive red floral arrangements on every table instead, leaving the ballroom more or less in its own glorious state, with the gilded mirrored walls unadorned, the chandeliers unobscured. "Let your guests be the décor," she'd suggested, and he'd hugged her, one of his impulsive, childlike hugs. And for that moment, anyway, she felt their old kinship; she felt "his." And knew that he was "hers."

But other than that one instance, Truman had arranged everything himself, obviously reveling in his role as host. He so rarely was, at least on this scale—although he was simply brilliant at putting together casual, intimate little last-minute dinners—and she knew it meant so much to him, to be able to do this. "I'm paying you back, my love," he whispered. "I'm paying you all back. For all the generosity you've shown me."

Who could fail to be touched by that? By that innocent, impulsive generosity? Who could fail to be proud of him, Truman Capote, achieving such heights, basking in the glow of well-deserved success?

Yet . . .

Babe felt a little shaky, at that, as she put the final touches on the dining room, adjusting a knife here, a crystal glass there, picking up a few fallen flower petals. She felt a little shaky a lot these days; she never seemed to have enough air in her lungs. She was out of breath no matter what she was doing, shopping or talking to the help or even simply lying in bed reading. Her stomach, too, always sensitive, acted up far too often.

Change. Change was in the air, that's what it was. Bill was the same, she supposed; taking her for granted, trotting her out for shareholders' meetings, showering her with the best jewels and clothing, not because she desired or even asked for it, but to reflect well on him and his taste. Screwing around, discreetly enough.

But her children were grown now; poor Kate and her nervous condition at boarding school, same as Bill Junior. Her eldest daughter, Amanda, was married to a young up-and-coming politician named Carter Burden and suddenly, to Babe's astonishment, the Burdens were the "It" couple of the younger set.

Was Babe jealous of her own daughter? She asked herself this in times of honesty, and had to answer in the affirmative. After all, youth and beauty were fleeting and she was at the upper end of her prime, she knew it, faced it head-on—unflinchingly staring at herself in the mirror every morning and night, assessing, taking notes. She did everything she could to make the most of her assets while she had them; her hair was still thick and luxurious, although mostly gray now, defiantly so—another Babe Paley trend. Her skin was still firm, tight, due to repeated trips to spas and salons, daily facials, massages, electric treatments.

And, yes, perhaps a discreet tightening up, under the scalpel. She could admit this—to herself, anyway.

Her figure was still lean; no middle-aged pooch or hump for her, due to her devotion to a new form of exercise called Pilates—a torturous regimen of pushing and pulling and stretching. And of course she wore the best clothes, the most fabulous jewels—tastefully.

But the sixties weren't about taste, were they? She wasn't sure she would be able to accommodate these new times; Babe understood her style, had never given in to trends, but that didn't seem to be enough anymore. And if she wasn't the most stylish, the most perfect of them all, then—who was she?

Truman was the one who could answer that; he always had been able to. And despite her fears when *In Cold Blood* came out, he'd not really abandoned her or her friends; if anything, he'd thrown himself more fully into their midst, laughing louder, telling even more outrageous stories—"Oh, Babe, darling Babe, do you know what that awful Gore Vidal said about me this time? Of course, I drank him for lunch, so it doesn't matter now"—dancing even more desperately (gyrating, shaking all over, his eyes closed, his face beet red, wispy hair plastered to his head), indulging himself in every way. But it wasn't quite the same, at that; the moments when it was just the two of them were more precious, because they were more rare.

Truman was also drinking too much, and Babe had yet to mention this to him, although she felt she must, sometime. But lately, one martini at lunch was not enough; it had to be two, three, followed by brandy, and then on to the cocktail hour.

She must, mustn't she? Mention this to him? If she loved him, as she most certainly did? They'd always told each other the truth. But the truth wasn't always pleasant.

Babe bit her lip, glided back to her fabulous bedroom in her fabulous apartment on Fifth Avenue, twenty rooms, the penthouse, decorated fabulously by Billy Baldwin and Sister Parish with the usual fabric-covered walls, tented ceilings, priceless antiques and paintings—and Bill's prized Picasso, *Boy Leading Horse*, taking pride of place in the entranceway so it was the first thing you saw when you stepped off the private elevator. It was a glorious apartment and Babe was proud of it, the same way she was proud of her figure and her face and her clothes and her jewels. It was all for show, it was all for prestige; figure, face, and apartment all equally photographed and coveted.

But outside the tasteful walls, it was all changing; already Babe felt as much a relic as the gorgeous Louis XVI commode in the hallway. Prized and coveted—by a certain person, anyway. A person who looked back on the past, instead of forward to the future.

Oh, Babe! What a load of crap—she almost laughed out loud, so surprised was she by the little voice that called her out, shook her from her morbid musings. *Look at you! You're dressed gorgeously, about to go to the party of the year, see all your friends, be part of Truman's big night. What on earth is wrong with you?*

And then she heard the buzzer, footsteps as Bill left his room, the butler open the front door, and Truman's cry of, "Oh, it's gorgeous! So perfect! Babe! Babe, come here this minute and let me feast my eyes on you, you glorious creature!"

And Babe was happy again. She adjusted a shoulder strap, straightened the diamond-and-ruby floral burst of a necklace at her throat, and sailed out of her bedroom to greet her friend. Confident, serene, her stomach fluttering in anticipation of being the most beautiful, the most photographed.

The most loved by the only one who mattered.

THE DEWEYS WERE HAVING a ball. No pun intended.

From the moment Truman arrived in Kansas all those years ago, such a strange creature with his velvet jackets, long trailing scarves, and Gucci loafers, their world had been turned upside down. Of course, at first it was because of the terrible tragedy of the Clutter family, whom they had known very well, all four of them; that November of 1959 was just an awful month, what with the uncertainty, fear, and Alvin's around-the-clock pursuit of the killers in his role as detective for the Kansas Bureau of Investigation. Truman had been annoying at first, this New York outsider whom nobody trusted because obviously he was only there to make a buck, write a story about them, make fun of them, probably; the first time he asked to interview Alvin he stated blithely, "It doesn't mean anything to me if you ever catch who did this, it doesn't matter one way or another," and Alvin had had to forcibly restrain himself from punching the little fairy in the face. It meant a lot to *him;* he had to catch the killers, he had to close the case and bring justice and peace to his neighbors once more. That was his *job.*

But over time Truman charmed them and the other citizens of Holcomb and Garden City, Kansas, he and his friend Nelle Harper Lee; and even after it was all over and he went back to New York and he never really had to see them again, he'd stayed in touch. He seemed to need them, in a strange way; he was both fascinated by their midwestern plainness and envious of something about them, too. Marie preferred to think of it as their solid values, God-fearing trust in the land and in their fellow man. Alvin thought it was more like they were simply collectibles for Capote; strange, plain, twangy people to dust off and put on his shelf next to all those socialites, where they couldn't help but stand out.

But Truman was so generous, he overcame any doubts or fears the Deweys might have had about his devotion. He paid for them to go to Hollywood, where they'd been feted by movie stars— Natalie Wood had danced with Alvin at a party thrown by Dominick Dunne! Steve McQueen had sat at Marie's feet, asking her for recipes. And Truman brought them to New York regularly, got them tickets to Broadway shows, asked people like the Paleys to throw parties for them. He made them stay with him in his new apartment, that magnificent modern structure by the United Nations.

And now he had invited them to his party! They'd never been to the Plaza before and couldn't help but gape; it was nothing like the Muehlebach in Kansas City, the fanciest hotel in their previous experience. No, this was a palace, and the ballroom was fit for a fairy tale, with crystal chandeliers, masses of flowers, parquet dance floor, and gilded mirrors on the wall. There was a small orchestra—Truman had whispered, "It's Peter Duchin!" earlier, but the name didn't really mean anything to them. And the people—the people! Well, Marie simply had to sit and stare at the beautiful gowns. She was quite pleased with hers, bought from Bergdorf Goodman—oh, she'd never, ever tell Alvin how much it cost! She was going to save the box forever. But the entire effect of gorgeous black tuxedos and white gowns swirling about the ballroom, the jewels that were real, not fake, reflecting the chandeliers, the feathered and sequined masks—it really was like being in a movie.

And everywhere you looked, there was somebody famous! Lauren Bacall! Joan Fontaine, so big on the movie screen but so tiny in person! Margaret Truman and Alice Roosevelt Longworth and Lynda Bird Johnson, swapping confidences about what it was like to live in the White House!

Of course there were so many Vanderbilts and Astors and Whitneys that the Deweys simply couldn't keep them straight, so they didn't try. And Truman's friends, who were always so kind—the Paleys and the Guinnesses and the Agnellis, all complimenting Marie on her gown, her hair. They'd dined at the Paleys' before the party and had been stunned by their apartment in one of those fancy buildings overlooking Central Park. It had a real doorman, and a private elevator, and an honest-to-God Picasso hanging in the hallway! It was like a museum, really, but Babe's kindness had put them at ease. She and Bill made such an elegant couple! They were both so tall and glamorous, and they seemed deeply devoted to each other, but . . . well, Marie couldn't quite believe it, what Truman had told her about them.

Truman loved to shock her, that was true; he loved to tell her somewhat salacious tidbits about these rich and famous people who were his friends. So Marie wasn't sure if she should believe what he'd told her about the Paleys, how they didn't sleep together, and Bill had many affairs, and Babe had wanted to leave him more than once. Oh, Marie did love hearing the gossip from Truman; he had a way of making her feel like she was his very best friend, part of his world, too. And he was so funny about it, arching his eyebrows and making a great show of whispering while he told her simply awful things! So maybe it was true about the Paleys. But she did hope it wasn't; why, Babe had lent her a necklace to wear tonight! And Bill had been so nice in introducing them to the CBS cameras outside the Plaza, and Bill and Babe had drawn them in so that Alvin and Marie could have their pictures taken, too, in all the crush; the photographers' flashbulbs had practically blinded her! They'd fallen on Truman and Mrs. Graham in the receiving line, laughing, hanging on to them for dear life until Babe ushered Marie into a dressing room, where they could adjust their masks, fix their hair, before meeting up with the men and entering the Grand Ballroom, ablaze with light.

And while Alvin was content to sit and watch all night, Marie now wanted to dance. She gazed longingly at the dance floor; Truman was circulating, shaking hands. Most of the masks were off now—although at first it had been stunning, just stunning, to gape at the creations—someone named Billy had on a mask and headpiece that looked just like a white unicorn! But soon people discarded them, so that the tables looked as if they were littered with the corpses of a glittering zoo. And now the dancing was in earnest, and Marie's toe tapped, her hips shimmied, and she met Alvin's disapproving gaze with a defiant smirk.

"I don't care, Alvin Dewey! I want to dance. This is a ball, isn't it?"

Some young man passing by heard her, turned on his heel, held out his hand, and before she knew it, she was being whirled about in a fox-trot while the orchestra played "The Way You Look Tonight," spun around and around until she felt her head snap back, and there were many eyes on the two of them, this intense-looking, dark young man with mischievous eyes and herself, plain little Marie Dewey of Kansas, all dressed up and twirling around in the Grand Ballroom of the Plaza Hotel!

When the dance was over, everyone clapped, and the young man extended his hand toward her, and Marie bowed, giggling, and then she sat down and took a big gulp of champagne while Alvin glowered next to her, tugging at his tie, grumbling about some people making spectacles of themselves.

The next morning, Marie Dewey found out that the young man who'd spun her about so expertly was Rudolf Nureyev.

GLORIA GUINNESS'S NECK ACHED. Her head, too. For she was wearing such a heavy diamond necklace—the jewels the size of small eggs—that she knew, she told her friends solemnly, that she'd have to stay in bed all day tomorrow, to recover.

Truman found this hilarious for some reason. He laughed and laughed, and rushed off to tell everyone else what Gloria had said.

She narrowed her eyes, took a drag on her cigarette, and smiled at Bill and Babe, Slim, Gianni and Marella. Coolly, she surveyed her friends' gowns and found hers to be the most elegant, a simple silk column with jeweled sleeves, not too fussy. Babe—who had also chosen a Castillo gown, knowing full well that he was designing Gloria's—had gone a little too far, she decided, with her hairstyle and her mask. Supposedly she'd had three masks made, just in case. That sounded like Babe.

Gloria had removed her mask almost immediately; why hide her gorgeous face? Babe, she noticed, had clung to hers far longer, out of loyalty to Truman's wishes, but finally she had removed hers, too. As had most of the guests. Despite the fortunes spent on the masks—every milliner in town had been overworked—no one wanted to hide their famous faces.

Gloria found herself watching the young women, those glorious, ethereal creatures who were not adorned with gigantic jewels but who seemed to be the photographers' darlings, nonetheless. Ronald Tree's daughter, Penelope, was dressed as if for a burlesque Halloween party in black shorts and see-through tights. The black tunic over it was cut out so that her entire midriff was showing. Her hair was a travesty. That limp, ironed style simply hung on her shoulders like seaweed. She had pasted black triangles around her eyes. She looked like a ghoul.

But Dick Avedon was prancing about her, practically clapping his hands. So was Cecil Beaton. The whispers were that Penelope Tree was the sensation of the ball, the new face of fashion.

Gloria looked down at her hands; they were veiny now. No amount of gold or diamond rings could mask that, although her fingers were weighed down in jewels, anyway. She was still slim, could wear the youthful fashions like the miniskirts and the baby-doll dresses, if she wanted to. But it was hard work now. Gone were the days when she could—and did, back when she first arrived in

Paris—find a good remnant of jersey, cut a few holes in it, stitch the hem, tie a belt around it, and look fabulous.

No, now it took work, discipline, days and weeks of dedicated effort, to look as fabulous as she did. She hadn't eaten in a week, so that she could be a wisp in her gown. She'd stayed in bed for two days, resting up. She had a facial peel two weeks before, and had slept with cucumbers on her eyes the last three nights. She'd had a long massage earlier in the day, and then sat under Kenneth's hot dryer for an hour this afternoon.

She looked fabulous. For a fifty-four-year-old. But Penelope Tree had probably stayed up all night, thrown her outfit together at the last moment, and still, she was the belle of the ball.

Growing old was simply hell.

She was getting too tired for this, Gloria thought darkly. She'd spent her life reinventing herself, from Mexican dance hall girl to stylish waif to mistress of famous men, several staircase marriages— each more wealthy than the other—until, finally, she'd bagged the big fish, the fabulously wealthy heir to a British fortune. Through it all she'd been known for her looks, her style, her grace. She'd slept with Nazis to make it through the war unscathed; she'd even passed on a message or two from sympathizers. That's how she'd met Loel Guinness in the first place.

She'd done what she had to, to survive, but, upon surviving, had realized it wasn't enough. She wanted a greater reward for climbing out of the heap. And she'd claimed it, sitting atop a pile of cash and houses and yachts and cars and planes and Balenciaga dresses and jewelry so impressive, it ought to have been in a museum and probably was, at one time. Or would be, later.

But she'd claimed it, earned it, because of her drive, yes, but mostly because of her looks and youth. What the hell was she going to do, once they were gone? Once the Penelope Trees, the Jean Shrimptons, the Twiggys of the world took over? What use would she be then?

Gloria smiled as Babe murmured something in her ear; she really wasn't listening. But she reached out to her friend for a moment and the two women exchanged a look full of sympathy and understanding, of regret and longing and resignation and so much sadness, Gloria felt her heart constrict, her head ache even more.

Then she turned away and looked back out at the dance floor, now full of young people bouncing up and down to some loud music with a heavy beat.

She didn't recognize anyone at all.

JACK DUNPHY WAS DETERMINED not to have any fun.

He despised this thing that Truman had done, this frivolous, flimsy charade he'd spent so much time creating when he should be writing. Jack loathed the idea of so much money spent, money that, well, yes, Truman had earned, and could spend however he wanted, but didn't Truman remember how recently he hadn't had any money at all? The money should have been saved.

But more than anything, Jack hated the people that Truman had gathered, the glittering, chattering—God, his ears throbbed from the noise, the orchestra and the mad laughter and the screeches of recognition—sycophants that Truman collected as he collected those damn antique paperweights of his that cluttered every surface. Well, Truman had his own apartment now, which Jack did not visit as much as Truman would have liked. So the paperweights, like the people, filled the space that Jack himself had once filled.

He still loved Truman. He always would. He loved his drive and ambition and his touching, thoughtful little gestures. He loved his wit. His morbid fascinations, which few people knew about—his dark broodings, which he allowed only Jack to see. Well, he supposed Truman let Babe see that side of him, too, but that didn't matter because Babe was a woman. And Jack liked Babe, too; he liked her warmth, her kindness, that sense of grave uncertainty behind the beautiful façade.

But Truman wasn't the same Truman Jack had met back in the early fifties when they were both young and poor and ambitious. Truman was successful now. Jack hated to acknowledge that Truman was the kind of person who was fucked up by success, but he suspected it was true. He'd always been a strange little combination of intense focus while he was writing and impulsive, scatterbrained gadfly when he wasn't. The gadfly was winning out, sadly.

Jack took a drink—rare, for he didn't drink much these days—and sat alone at a table, studying the party. Truman had boasted of the guest list, declared it a masterpiece of curation, a brilliant mix of people and types—Society, Hollywood, Broadway, the literary world, artists and dancers, plain folks such as the Deweys. But Jack had to laugh; no one was mingling. The Hollywood types sat together, so did the Broadway types—Alan Jay Lerner, that prick, was holding forth with Stephen Sondheim while Hal Prince looked on—and of course, Truman's swans all swam together in their tight, prissy little formation, turning their jeweled backs to everyone who didn't have several million in ready cash.

And Truman—look at him! Jack was ashamed, really; he was sickened, his stomach tightened, and it wasn't just the bourbon. It was the waste, the shameful waste, and Jack knew, even if Truman didn't, that there was no turning back from this night. It marked the end of Truman Capote, the serious writer, and it made Jack want to puke. Jack worked and worked, just as hard as Truman, and his novels were never successful, despite Truman's loyal support. And Truman, having written what Jack thought really was a great book, was straying down a different path now, and Jack knew that Truman wouldn't have the fortitude to turn back to the grind, the reality, of actual writing.

Truman wanted to be loved, and now he was—so he thought—by about five hundred of the most famous people in the world, and he'd written the book he'd said he was destined to write, and so what more did he have to work for?

Jack knew Truman too well. And he was sick for him, and for what it meant for the two of them, because they would never be the same together, content to spend their days isolated, writing, cooking, reading aloud to each other. Those days were gone now. This damn ball marked the end of the two of them, Jack and Truman, Truman and Jack.

Jack set down his glass. He got up, stretched, knowing that he looked damn good in a tux, even as he loathed the thing—Truman had quivered in fear of Jack turning up in dungarees and an old fishing shirt. "Please, Jack, do come. It won't be the same without you, and I want to show you off. But please, dear, don't embarrass me!"

As he heard the music change—Peter Duchin was very good at anticipating the mood of the room, sliding smoothly from more current music to the classics, some of which had been written by some of the distinguished guests—Jack bent down, touched his toes, lengthened his calves, those former dancer's calves.

Then he spied Betty Bacall at a table; the actress had been out there cutting quite a rug earlier with Jerome Robbins, that mean bastard. Jack had never danced for Robbins—he had for de Mille, in the original production of *Oklahoma!*—but he'd heard stories of him, how he was such a stingy, tyrannical son of a bitch. Which didn't predispose Jack to like him, or even be civil to him.

Jack approached Betty, reached out his hand; she smiled that cat's smile, narrowed those knowing eyes, and joined him on the dance floor.

She followed his lead expertly, improvised when he did as they glided gracefully to the tune of "The Days of Wine and Roses," conducted by Henry Mancini himself, whom Peter Duchin had coaxed up to take the baton to his own composition. The two of them were a tall, lean, elegant pair; it was as if their bodies were built for each other, this dance, this party, this moment of simple elegance.

After the song was done, Jack felt a familiar gaze fall, warm as a caress, upon the back of his neck. He turned and locked eyes with Truman, who was standing on the other side of the dance floor; both their eyes filled with tears.

Jack gave him a gallant little bow, and Truman placed his hand upon his heart.

Then Jack escorted Betty Bacall back to her table, kissed her hand, and walked away.

Already, he was missing Truman.

FRANK SINATRA WAS PISSED.

Why the fuck he'd come to this fairy's ball, he had no idea. Well, yeah, he had. Mia. Mia wanted to go, she said it would be fun, there'd be lots of people there he knew, it was *the* place to be. So he'd put up with it—wore a fucking mask, at least for about five seconds, before he ripped it off after some little dick in the crowd outside the hotel had called out, "Hey, Frankie Batman!" He'd rounded up a few acceptable people, like Leland and Pam Hayward, the Bennett Cerfs, Claudette Colbert, that classy old dame, and commandeered a table, handed a waiter a hundred bucks and asked for three bottles of Wild Turkey, and watched as Mia happily danced with some of the younger crowd.

Frank Sinatra, it need not be said, did not dance. Except, on a few memorable occasions, when he was much younger and hungrier, in the movies.

He stayed clear of Betty Bacall; that was an affair that had gone sour. Likewise Slim Hawks Hayward Keith, Leland's ex. This wasn't his scene, not all this fancy fag shit like the gilded mirrors and the fucking stupid masks. The room was too big, too crowded, too hot, too full of people he didn't give a shit about, and who didn't give a shit about him, and that was something that Frank Sinatra did not put up with, not at all.

But Mia. Mia wanted to come, because she was young and starry-eyed, and look at her now, out on the dance floor dancing the fucking frug or whatever it was, that thing where you threw your arms up in the air like you were having an epileptic seizure, gyrated your whole body, the whole damn thing. That wasn't dancing. Not in his book. What the fuck was he thinking, marrying a kid like that? But even now, he could hardly take his eyes off her.

He looked at his watch. Two A.M. Not too late to be up but far too late to still be at this silly kid's costume party. Who dressed up like this anymore? Not him, that was for damn sure. Next time Mia wanted to go to something like this she could—hell. Next time Mia wanted to go to something like this he would just say no. Forget it, kid.

"C'mon," he said, rounding up the Cerfs and the Haywards.

Claudette shook her head, stifled a yawn, and gathered her purse and her gloves. "Let's leave this joint and go to Jilly's."

Jilly's was his scene; a dark, narrow, smoky piano bar with a quiet back room where he had his own special chair—no one else was allowed to sit in it—at his special table where he could hold forth, be entertained, worshipped, especially by Jilly Rizzo himself. Where all eyes would be on him, and not some swishy little fruit with a lisp.

Frank didn't even have to call ahead. He knew Jilly's would be open for him. It always was. It was his place.

"Oh, Francis, no, you're not going!" Truman was in front of him, wringing his limp little hands. "Stay, stay, do. You know how these things are, once someone like you leaves, the whole party is over. Don't do that to me!"

"Sorry, Truman. Nice evening. But I'm out of here." Frank snapped his fingers, Mia skipped over to him and took his arm, somebody gathered up their coats, and he strode out of the ballroom. Behind him, Truman still pleaded.

No dice. Frank Sinatra had been bored, and so he snapped his fingers and left.

And just like that, the party was over.

TRUMAN HID HIS DISAPPOINTMENT, fluttered from group to group as they prepared to leave, accepted the gushing compliments, squealed his own, asking everyone, "Wasn't it grand? Wasn't it a divine party?"

And they all said yes, yes, of course, it was. You are wonderful, Truman. You are the tops. This was the grandest night ever, the party everyone will be talking about tomorrow and tomorrow and tomorrow.

And when at last he escorted Kay, exhausted but quietly happy, back to her room, tiptoed up to kiss her on the cheek and admonish her, "Now, sleep tight, baby doll, and dream of the headlines in the morning!" he went to his own suite, unlocked the door with the heavy gold key, and threw himself on the turned-down bed with a loud sigh.

And it left him, just like that. The good feeling, the triumph, the accomplishment. It left just like Sinatra had, through the door without a backward glance. He felt empty, deflated, defeated. Alone.

Unloved.

What, who, would ever make this feeling go away? He reached for the phone to call Babe, but his hand touched a bottle of vodka on the nightstand instead.

He grabbed it, rejoiced in the cold bottle against his sweaty hand that trembled now as he poured himself a nice glass, tipped his head back, savored the liquid for a moment in his mouth, delaying the pleasure for as long as he could before he swallowed, the sting, the slap of it down his throat, more and more until he was foggy, until he saw the ball again, saw it as he'd dreamed it, and he giggled, remembering Billy Baldwin's glorious unicorn mask, Penelope Tree's bizarre getup that would surely get a huge mention in tomorrow's papers, Gloria's precious remark about her jewels being too heavy, Marie Dewey's breathless exclamation that she was going to paste every newspaper mention of it in a scrapbook just for him. Kay's tearful thank-you as she laid a hand on his shoulder when they said good night; her murmured, "I didn't deserve anything half this lovely."

Babe's proud smile the moment she stepped into the ballroom, her dark, grave eyes seeking him out, approving, loving, always loving.

He wasn't crying now. He took another drink, leaned back, closed his eyes, kicked off his shoes.

"Tell me a story," he whispered, his eyes heavy, his skin hot, his clothes too tight, his heart beating too loudly, as he could hear it in his ears. The room spun behind his closed eyes, but it was a gentle spin now, a carousel, not a hurricane. "Mama, tell me a story."

He fell asleep before he could remember that Mama wasn't there.

. . . . .

My God, it was the most divine party! Oh, what a night it was, I tell you!

Everyone was there, absolutely everyone. My God, the people—movie stars and politicians and everyone who was anyone. They all came out that night.

The music was divine. The food, perfect. The dancing, oh, the dancing! To see those glorious people dancing the Twist! Gliding about like Fred and Ginger to a waltz!

And my dear, what people are saying about it now. I've been inundated with phone calls! Everyone wants a quote. And that Penelope Tree, what a goddess. I'm going to put her on the cover of Vogue someday.

And you! You, you were absolutely marvelous. Well, everyone is saying so. No one can imagine a better party, ever. Anyone else who was even thinking of throwing one—well, they've all given up now, I should think so! Thrown up their hands and retreated. "Why even bother now?" they're all saying.

It was simply the most magical evening ever. I wouldn't have missed it for the world, you know. You are absolutely the toast of the town, the king of the world.

"I am, aren't I?" Truman opened his eyes; Diana Vreeland was grinning at him, waving her red talons, holding up newspaper after newspaper filled with coverage, pictures of him and his famous friends.

"Yes, you are. Truman, you've done it."

"I'm so glad you were there, really! The night would have been a complete failure without my darling dragon lady, the divine Mrs. Vreeland!"

"As I said, I wouldn't have missed it for the world."

Truman rose, they exchanged kisses, and he tripped out of her office at *Vogue,* waving his hand airily at one and all, as if he were royalty.

Diana smiled for a moment, then sat back down.

Thank God he hadn't realized she hadn't been there. She'd just lost her husband, Reed—why on earth did Truman think she'd want to go to a party? So she'd shown up for dinner at the Paleys', as invited. But when the time came to leave, she got in a taxi that took her straight home, not to the Plaza.

And Truman was none the wiser.

"NORMAN MAILER WENT AROUND trying to start a fight. All night long! First with McGeorge Bundy, then with George Plimpton, then with anyone named George, then finally just anyone."

"Oh, how divine! I saw him, and I thought, *Norman, you've made my party!* Although he wore that dirty raincoat the entire time—I doubt he even bathes, do you?"

"Only in the tears of his envy over you, True Heart. Now, tell me the truth." Slim arched an eyebrow, leaned back on the sofa of her hotel suite. "Didn't Pamela look hideous?"

"Absolutely. Completely stuffed, like a goose, if you know what I mean. You looked fabulous, my pet. Simply fabulous. What a shame Kenneth couldn't come."

"What do you mean? I would have been bored to tears if my husband had been there. As it was, I had a wonderful time."

"I thought Gloria looked a little tight. Did she have some work done recently?"

"No," Slim said, while nodding. "Of course not."

Truman cackled. "Big Mama, you're an absolute treasure!"

"Babe looked wonderful, of course."

"As always. You know what I always say. Babe Paley has only one fault—she's perfect. Other than that, she's perfect."

"Isn't that the truth? But I love her, of course."

"So do I, more than anyone in the world—except for you, Big Mama! But wasn't it a fabulous party?"

"It was a great party, True Heart. Really great. Have you seen the newspapers?"

"Oh, those old things." Truman waved his hand dismissively, but his eyes gleamed. He looked a little puffy and tired this morning, Slim thought—but then, who didn't? She wouldn't even look in a mirror yet, herself. But this morning, puffy and tired were badges of honor; only those who had danced all night at Truman's party—and looked it—were *in*.

"Did Kay have a good time?"

"The best. Tell me again, what was your favorite part?"

"When Tallulah Bankhead flashed her bush at Cecil Beaton. I thought poor Cecil was going to faint dead away."

"Oh, that's precious! Too precious! I didn't see that! But it was grand, wasn't it, my dearest Big Mama?"

"So grand. The grandest!"

Truman kissed her and went on his way. Slim picked up the papers. She'd hidden the ones that were not so complimentary; the ones that more than hinted it was just a little appalling that Truman had been able to give such a fabulous party because of the slaughter of a Kansas family.

The ones that wondered if, now that he was such a social success, Truman would ever write anything good, ever again.

TRUMAN HAD SAVED the best for last.

He walked into the apartment, past the Picasso, and into Babe's open arms. She looked gorgeous, fresh, completely made up, and he marveled again at her discipline, her devotion to her best creation, her exquisite self.

"Bobolink! My most precious person ever! Tell me, tell me all!"

"Oh, Truman, it was wonderful." And Babe said it quietly, seriously, with none of the exaggerated after-party brightness of the others, and maybe Truman registered that, and maybe he didn't.

"It was, wasn't it?" He sighed, kicked off his shoes and they both settled into a sofa, his head in her lap, his feet tickling a velvet pillow. She had tea waiting, and a special vase of lilies of the valley just for him—she'd known, hadn't she, that perfect creature, that simply everyone in the world would send him flowers this morning, flowers and gifts and thank-you notes and telegrams. So she'd saved her flowers—*their* flowers, the ones they sent to each other each time they suspected the other was a little blue—to give him in person. Babe was the most thoughtful person he knew.

"Truman, I mean it. I haven't been to anything like it. You did it, you were marvelous, and I'm privileged to have been there."

"You stood out, of course, the envy of all. Slim and I were just talking about you—were your ears burning? You, my dearest, were a rare flower, in a sea of garishness. Not that everyone wasn't beautiful—they were—although Slim, poor thing. What are we going to do with her? She has lost all her style. Simply lost it."

"I thought she looked lovely, Truman," Babe said, quietly admonishing. "I heard you tell her so, yourself."

"Well, of course I did! It was the charitable thing to do! But you, my darling Babe, were singular. You always are."

"You are sweet to say so." But Babe flushed, and she ducked her head, and Truman squeezed her hand. Dozens of people a day told Babe Paley how beautiful she was. But she really believed it only when Truman did.

"Now tell me—tell me everything. Everything wonderful about last night. Tell me a story, Mama." Truman closed his eyes, nestled deeper into her lap, and smiled in anticipation.

And Babe, who had never read a good-night story to her children when they were young, for she was always getting ready to go out or down to dinner when they were put to bed, and that took time, of course, time to array herself to perfection so that Bill might notice her, so that at least he would be proud to have her on his arm, took a deep breath and began,

"Once upon a time, there was a wonderful party, a beautiful fairyland of light and flowers and people, and one in particular, the most wonderful, the host. . . ."

And soon Truman was asleep. And Babe was content, that aching pit in her belly filled with gratitude and purpose, and still she talked on and on in her low, soothing voice, spinning him a tale that weaved back and forth through time, from a chance meeting on an airplane long ago, vacations together, shared intimacies, secrets, fears and hopes and dreams, until last night, and this morning, and the future, and the two of them together, always, trusting, loving, for they only had each other, didn't they? Children grew up, grew beautiful, grew successful in their own right. But Truman— Truman would remain the same.

He would love her. And allow her to love him.

And so she told him other stories, stories she'd never told anyone else, all of them true because Babe did not know how to lie. *"I had an affair,"* she whispered, "but you knew that, didn't you? You guessed it, long ago. It was only the once, because I couldn't stomach it. Yet Bill still sleeps with everyone but me, and I've told you that so many times before, it's a broken record, but in its way it's the truest thing of my life, the one thing I can count on and can you believe it, I've grown to rely on it? I'm getting old, older, and so is Bill, so I don't think of leaving him anymore, because who would have me now? Where would I go? Who would have him? Getting older means having fewer choices, I've discovered. Not that I had that many when I was younger. But when I was younger, I knew my face. Now, when I look in a mirror—but when I look in your eyes, I still see myself. And that's what love is, isn't it? Truman?"

She looked down at him; his mouth was open, his pink cheeks slack as he snored softly. So she whispered, "And, Truman? Bill can't hurt me anymore. My children can't, either. But you—you could. You're the only person in my life with that power. I don't know how you could, but it's true. And I'm afraid of that. Only a little. I'm also happy, because it means I do love you, truly." And she smiled, because to have Truman fall asleep on her lap was a gift, a precious gift; no one else could claim him like this. Babe knew he had made the rounds before coming to her; she knew it was his nature. Her approval wasn't enough, it would never be enough; one person's love never would be enough for him. And that was the difference between them, because she needed only Truman's love, and he needed the world's.

But still, hers was the lap he sought; her embrace was where he fell asleep, and she cherished his trust, his childlike repose. For once in her life, Babe felt peaceful, unhurried. Bill's dinner could go unordered, the dressmaker who was supposed to mend her dress from last night uncalled, the masseuse who was scheduled ignored. Truman's party receded into the realm of make-believe. This, this moment, was real, but more precious, more golden, than any fairy tale.

And outside, the world spun and spun, the elegant carousel of the 1950s and Camelot speeding up, wobbling on its machinery, threatening to become a psychedelic hurricane of change. But it didn't wake Truman up. Nothing could stir him from his dream. *Shhh, be quiet. Mama's here. Mama's back.*

Mama loves me best.

La Côte Basque,
October 17, 1975

. . . . .

"THE SUN," SAID SLIM, NIBBLING AT AN OLIVE, "IS OVER the yardarm. Let's have a drink."

"The sun has almost set," Gloria retorted, "and we've been drinking all day. What the hell is a yardarm, anyway?"

Slim laughed, noiselessly, her shoulders shaking, her glasses askew.

"What?" Gloria scowled.

Pam was quiet. Too quiet. Pickled, Slim decided, squinting, trying to get her into focus. Marella was mumbling to herself in Italian.

"You—you have a yacht!" Slim pointed at Gloria, gasping for air.

"So?"

"A yardarm is part of a boat, the beam or whatever at the bottom of the sail. You don't know that!"

"I employ people who do," Gloria retorted icily, in an exaggeratedly British accent. Then she muttered under her breath, *"Besa mi culo, puta!"*

"What?"

"Nothing."

"Papa used to say that," Slim mused dreamily. "It was one of his favorite sayings. 'The sun is over the yardarm.' It meant it was time to drink."

"Oh, for God's sake, Slim. Yes, we get it. You were Hemingway's muse. Papa's obsession. Papa's unfulfilled love. And C.Z. was Rivera's muse, and Babe was Truman's. Well, who the hell's muse was I?" Gloria threw a napkin ring down on her plate, hard, and everyone held her breath to see if the plate would shatter. It didn't.

"Jesus Christ, Gloria! Calm down! We don't want the Gestapo to arrive!"

"Oh, you would bring that up, wouldn't you? Wouldn't you?" Gloria almost spat at Slim; she reared her lovely head back, tasted the saliva in her mouth, felt the Mexican blood finally fire up in her veins, pushing her to do what she'd spent a lifetime suppressing— act, feel, love, live, hate—spit, *Dios mío! Spit at the puta's feet!*

She felt Marella's hand on her arm, settling her down, being the princess that she was, calming her court.

"Shhh, Gloria, shhh. We're not mad at each other," Marella whispered, maddeningly reasonable. "We're mad at Truman, remember?"

"Bastardo. Pendejo. Puto." Somewhat mollified, Gloria swallowed, drank the brandy stinger Slim was handing her—where did it come from? She hadn't ordered it—and lit another cigarette.

The smoky haze over their table was epic, even for La Côte Basque. It was like the smog of Los Angeles these days. The smoke from a forest fire. A monster from a horror film.

But no one seemed to care; they all simply coughed, waved, and lit up again. And again. And again.

"The ball, it was grand, though," Pam mused softly. "Really, wasn't it? One of the last times, the last elegant times."

"It was," Marella agreed.

"It all went to hell after that, didn't it?" Gloria asked. Rhetorically.

Each now-slightly-tattered—lipstick was smeared, eyeliner runny, hairstyles melted, like ice cream on a summer day—swan nodded.

"What happened? What happened to the world? To Truman? To us?"

"Nixon. Nixon happened," Slim answered Gloria's question.

"Vietnam. Then Nixon," Marella corrected.

"Whatever. Things changed. Our daughters became us, the beautiful ones, the socialites. Only they didn't want to be us, did they?" Slim's voice was hoarse.

"Just like we did not want to be our mothers," Marella pointed out.

"But why not? We were better than our mothers! We were—we are—magnificent!" Gloria's voice was a cry, a cry of anguish, of loss, regret. Slim patted her hand and signaled for another brandy stinger.

"We're old," Slim mumbled wearily. "Goddamn old. Truman made us feel younger, though, didn't he? For a while. Then he—left us. Went off with that Studio Fifty-four crowd, Liza and all. Started bringing around those terrible men—remember the air-conditioning man?"

"Oh, Christ. I'd forgotten about him. Or I've tried to, anyway," Gloria cackled. "What was his name again?"

"Danny. Danny something. I've never understood that obsession Truman had for him—he was so stupid, that one. Muscular, but dumb as a rock, out of his league. Remember when Truman brought him to Europe, took him to the best restaurants, and the poor slob was miserable, pining for hamburgers and baked potatoes? Yet Truman insisted this lug was the love of his life. He was just besotted, and heartbroken when the lug finally had enough. That's when I just started not feeling—right—about Truman. I tried, I tried to be the same friend, but something was off with Truman then, don't you think? And it all started after the ball." Slim handed Gloria her stinger.

"I've even felt sorry for him, lately, with all his heartbreak, all these stupid men who keep taking from him and then leaving." Gloria nodded. "Until now, that is."

"Yes. There were times he tore my heart—I know he wrenched Babe's. But he's crossed a line."

"Crossed a line?" Gloria gaped at Slim. "He *murdered* that woman. He as good as put those pills in her hand!"

"And he aired the Paleys' dirty laundry," Pam reminded them all. "And one doesn't do that, if one wants to remain, shall we say—intact?"

"He aired Bill Paley's *stained* dirty laundry, if you want to get right down to it," Gloria mused. "Stained, bloody laundry, according to that story. How explicit Truman has gotten in his writing! He never used to be so vulgar."

The other women nodded. Pam's cleavage was so exposed, Slim leaned over and tucked a napkin into it. "For the sake of the children, dear."

"Yet, of course, it was Bill who betrayed Babe in the first place. And who apparently told Truman all about it. Just like a man. A foolish, vain man. Oh, why do we do it?" Gloria wailed. "Why do we put up with it, with these men? These men we married when we were young and beautiful and desirable, even though *they* weren't?"

"Money," Marella and Slim answered simultaneously. Pam

wrinkled her freckled nose; talking of money was so crass, but so American. Yet, of course, they were right.

"Why do you even ask?" Slim added.

"Because—oh, shit." Gloria shrugged. This was the reward, then? Married to an ugly old fart who gave her things, yes—but kept the really good jewels locked up, doling them out to her on occasions he deemed appropriate. The Guinnesses had houses, yachts, servants, the best clothes, but now nobody cared, nobody looked at her twice in her Givenchy gowns, her Balenciaga suits. Because she was goddamn old, and she was stuck with a man who farted in bed, and she'd never get anyone else, there was no trading up, not anymore, and all she could look forward to was losing her teeth, more face-lifts, orthopedic shoes instead of Ferragamos, the constant battle of the dye bottle (*Dios mío*, she couldn't go a week before the gray started to show now, at her hairline), and all the money in the world couldn't stop any of that, couldn't stop the ravages of time and regret.

And that was the secret, the wonder of Truman, she realized suddenly. Truman had made them forget all that. He had amused them. Their husbands didn't want to talk to them. They grew bored talking to one another, these glorious creatures, for they were all the same. Blond, brunette, tall, short, European or Californian, they were still the same; only the exteriors were different. And they devoted their lives to maintaining this difference, striving to shine, be the one jewel who stood out. Yet at night, they took off the diamonds and gowns and went to empty beds resigned to the fact that they were just women, after all. Women with a shelf life.

And then Truman leapt into their midst, and suddenly the gossip was more delicious, the amusements more diverse. He had sat on the beds of every one of his swans and whispered how beautiful she was, how precious, how devoted he was to her and her alone, and even though they all knew he was saying the same thing to each one of them, they didn't mind. Because, beneath the beauty, they were all so goddamned lonely.

And the ball, that glorious Black and White Ball when they were so exquisite, so rare and coveted, that was their summit. Everyone's summit—New York's summit.

"Nobody dresses for lunch anymore," Gloria complained, looking around the room. Yes, ladies of a certain age, like them, still clung to dresses, hats, gloves, polished shoes. But women in pantsuits were now allowed to dine at La Côte Basque, the Colony, the Plaza. In less rarefied places, men and women both now regularly wore jeans, sometimes torn, and tennis shoes, and athletic shirts. In public.

"You know, the funny thing is that Danny, the air-conditioning man, wouldn't have been invited to Truman's ball, back then," mused Slim. "God, we were all so beautiful, weren't we? The gowns, the masks. It seemed fun at the time, just another day at the office, but now, I don't know—it seems like a lost dream, doesn't it?"

"It's all lost. Truman giveth, and Truman taketh away," muttered Gloria. "And now he'll get away with murder."

"No. *We* taketh away. I'll bet anything the little shrimp has been phoning us all day long. Well, I gave my maid instructions to tell Mr. Capote that Lady Keith was unavailable. Indefinitely."

"Yes, I did the same thing." Gloria nodded. So did Marella.

"I wonder what he'll do, without us—without *her,* especially? He didn't know it, but he needed us. More than we needed him."

"Slim!" Gloria raised her glass in a toast. "That may be the most insightful thing I've heard from you all day. You're damn right.

Come." Gloria set the glass down, signaled for the bill. "Let's do something truly cruel. Let's go home and rest up, then dress, and all of us go out on the town together, as if there's nothing at all wrong. As if the bastard simply doesn't exist. I'll have my secretary call Suzy Knickerbocker and Liz Smith and let them know; of course, they'll tell Truman."

"That is one hell of an idea, Gloria." Slim reached for her purse. "Except—well, it doesn't feel quite right, without her." And once again, they all looked at the empty chair.

"Oh, it's not fair, not her. We're all shits, all of us at this table. We've all done mean things to each other, we've all had our moments." Slim slumped back down. "But Babe never did. She never said a bad thing about anyone, or did anything cruel or catty."

"Life isn't fair," Gloria reminded her briskly. "We all know that. If life was fair, we'd be the ones with the fortunes and our husbands would look like Paul Newman. Come on, we're doing this. I insist. We need some cheering up. And more importantly, we need to show that little shit we could give a fuck what he says or does—or *writes*. Babe would understand."

"Yes, *mamacita*." Slim drew herself up, stifled a burp. "Oh, I wish Papa were still here! We could take your plane and fly to Cuba, wouldn't that be grand?"

"For God's sake, stop it with the Hemingway crap. I'm not Truman. I'm not that easily impressed," Gloria snapped, handing several hundred-dollar bills to the waiter.

"I think that's what I'll miss the most about him," Slim said as the four ladies rose, unsteadily, to their feet.

"What?"

"Truman. I'll miss having someone to tell my stories to. Say what you want about him, Truman was a very good listener."

"And a very good thief, remember? If it wasn't for us, he'd have nothing to write about. He stole our stories. He's a thief. And a murderer, in case you've forgotten."

"He's a storyteller." Slim shook her head. "Just like Papa—"

Gloria cut her short with one flash of her dark eyes. The others followed, their heads held high, smiling at one and all. Stopping in the ladies' room to repair the damage of alcohol and time, as best they could; elbows out, powder flying, lipsticks wielded like daggers. Just in case there were photographers outside.

There were. The familiar, loving click; the adored flash of bulbs, more intimate, more caressing than any kiss. The reverent "Mrs. Guinness! Look this way!" "Lady Keith, give us a smile!"

But then—a cold breeze blew past. Another door opened. A couple—the woman in a floppy hat, wide-legged trousers, the skinny man clad in a fur vest and striped pants—emerged, standing uncertainly on the sidewalk a few feet down. The photographers rushed away.

"Bianca! Mick! Mick Jagger!"

The Swans were forgotten.

Long live the king.

. . . . .

IT WAS THE BEST OF TIMES, IT WAS THE WORST OF TIMES. . . .

The Manhattan of the late sixties, early seventies.

Well, actually, it was just the worst of times.

After the ball is over, after the break of day . . .

Did they know, the morning after Truman's party, that nothing would ever be the same again? No, they did not. Some claimed, later, that they did know it; that even as they were dancing, they felt a bit like Nero fiddling while Rome was burning. And some newspapers and magazines, in the days and weeks following the bash, did question the whole endeavor, likening it to Marie Antoinette during the Revolution.

But in truth, when the glittering and gay left the ball, removed their dancing shoes, sent out their finery to be cleaned and repaired (or returned, if they'd been gauche enough to have to borrow it), they simply reflected on what a grand time they'd had. And looked forward to more.

But Manhattan, in the sixties and seventies, said, "No. No dice. I'm turnin' on you, kid."

Strikes—transit strikes (which Truman and his swans did not notice), garbage strikes (which they did; goodness, even on Fifth Avenue, the garbage piled and piled, up to the sky; the air was fetid with filth and when the winds swirled, garbage took to the skies like soiled, stinking confetti from a macabre ticker tape parade; no one could even go out on the streets without a perfumed handkerchief pressed to her face). Riots—after Martin Luther King Jr. was killed (what a nice man, really; a few had met him in Washington. Kay Graham was really upset by his death), Harlem erupted, not that Babe or Gloria or Slim or Marella or Pam ever went to Harlem, mind you. But still, they could hear the sirens all night long, nobody left her penthouse for fear of—something. Then Bobby Kennedy, and Truman cried and cried; Bobby had been a neighbor of his in the UN Plaza, and they'd had a couple drinks together, although he'd always felt Bobby thought he was performing some kind of civic duty in befriending a homosexual. Still, he'd cried at his death, written poor Rose Kennedy a magnificent letter of solace, which he knew she would treasure forever, if he did say so himself—and to anybody who would listen.

Then Stonewall, and the Village was suddenly crawling with drag queens and homosexuals, and surprisingly Truman had little opinion about all this, even though Babe and Gloria and Slim and Marella and Pam all looked at him with great sympathy in those few days. But Truman went on as normal, didn't feel compelled to go down and march with any of the other homosexuals, or engage in kick lines in front of the police. And when they all asked him if he'd ever been to the Stonewall Inn, he wrinkled his nose and exclaimed, "God, no—*that* place?"

And crime. Crime and dirt and filth, the hallmarks of Manhattan in the sixties and seventies. Of course, the swans and their consorts could flee, and they did, whenever possible. But still, they had to be in New York sometimes, carry on the banner of good taste and social responsibility; there were still opening nights, benefits, galas to attend. But crime was right outside their door; Central Park was no longer safe at night, not with all the muggings and beatings and knifings. Times Square—oh, Times Square! For Slim, in particular, who had been part of Broadway's golden age, it was heartbreaking now to see the empty storefronts, hookers perched on stools on every corner, drug dealers lounging in doorways, cops on the beat, dirty, cheap stores that sold sex toys, inflatable dolls, plastic-looking lingerie.

The people changed, too. No one had manners any longer. No one dressed. Those hippie young men did not hold the door open for ladies. Highballs were no longer the drug of choice; pot and coke and LSD were the new amusements.

A few of them did try LSD, at their therapists' urging. For a while it was the thing to do—go to a party, drop some acid, lie on velvet pillows staring at the ceiling, waiting to be told the secrets of the universe. But the next morning was always hell, and the ladies didn't like what it was doing to their skin, so they stopped.

Truman didn't, however. Truman, in the years after *In Cold Blood*, the fabulous ball, the apex of his fame, grew puffier, less disciplined. Slept later, roamed pockets of the city he'd never roamed before, brought home men he'd never have looked at before. None of his swans ever figured out exactly what happened between him and Jack. They only knew that the relationship no longer involved sex—Truman was more than happy to let them know that, anyway! And they all found, to their surprise, that they missed Jack, that gruff, humorless, rude-to-the-point-of-insanity man (after all, he'd once told Loel Guinness that he was a Nazi, and while everyone knew this to be true of both Guinnesses, no one had ever said it to their faces!). But they all recognized the steady, no-nonsense influence Jack had had on Truman; he was the ballast to Truman's airy sails. While they were still somehow in each other's lives—they still took vacations together, to Verbier, Switzerland, to their twin houses on Long Island—it wasn't the same as before. Truman was different, because of it. More unstable; some said untrustworthy, at least when they were outside of Babe's hearing.

But Gloria and Babe and Marella and Slim and Pam weren't any different. They held on—clung—to their disciplined lives, their shared belief that sophistication and elegance counted for something; counted for everything, in their world. Their clothes might have changed some; Gloria was one of the first to introduce the Pucci pantsuit into society, and Babe's skirts grew imperceptibly shorter. They all flocked to Halston, their former millinery magician at Bergdorf's, when he opened his own salon and introduced long, flowing, caftanlike dresses made of jersey, sometimes one-shouldered, sometimes halter-backed. Still tasteful, but smacking, slightly, of the younger fashions.

They clung to their former hairstyles with strange devotion; if their skirts were looser, no longer requiring girdles (although of course, they still wore them), then their hair remained rigid, unyielding. Not for them the long, stringy styles of the flower children or the precision boy cuts introduced by Vidal Sassoon. They still looked forward to their twice-weekly visits to Kenneth's, depended on them, really; found refuge in the soothing music, teacups, champagne flutes, stylists still clad in the suits and ties that Kenneth himself wore. They were pampered, but, more important, they were prized, still. In the reliable townhouse in which few young women would be seen, the Babes and Marellas and Glorias of Manhattan still found themselves desired, and desirable. And so they retained the kind of hairstyles that required setting, hairspray, sleeping in a hair net or curlers every night. Hairstyles that, unlike the rest of Manhattan, were impervious to the winds of change.

But Truman, oh, Truman. How he changed! How he adopted the fashions, tragically, of the youth movement (he never wore love beads, but, good God, those caftanlike suits he wore! The Nehru jackets!). The feuds he got into! Of course, he and Gore Vidal had never liked each other, but now they were actually engaged in a lawsuit (Truman repeating a story he insisted that Gore had told him, of Bobby Kennedy decking Gore in the White House; Gore was suing for libel). And he'd always had a love/hate relationship with Norman Mailer, which devolved into hatred, pure and true, when Mailer won the Pulitzer Prize and the National Book Award for *The Armies of the Night*—awards that Truman hadn't won for *In Cold Blood*. So Truman accused Mailer of ripping him off, of doing what Capote had done first, and more brilliantly; of writing another "nonfiction novel."

And the things he'd said about Jackie Susann! That the *Valley of the Dolls* author was a truck driver in drag—even if he had a point, it was a vicious thing to say. Especially on *The Tonight Show*.

Truman. On *The Tonight Show*. Talking to Johnny Carson on the West Coast, Dick Cavett on the East. Truman had gone Hollywood, of all things. Truman had gone global; he was everywhere and nowhere, peripatetic. He was in Rome, he was in Switzerland, he was in Palm Springs, he was in Venice. He was on the cover of *Time,* he was writing articles for *Rolling Stone*. He was dropping acid with The Who.

What he wasn't doing, as far as anyone could tell, was writing his next book.

"So what are you writing next?" asked Johnny, asked Dick, asked the world.

"It's brilliant. My masterpiece, called *Answered Prayers,* after that saying by Saint Teresa of Avila— *'There are more tears shed over answered prayers than unanswered ones.'* Isn't that brilliant! It's going to be a darkly comic observation of society, real society. I've had a first-class seat to it all, and darlings, the things I've seen! I'm a modern-day Proust."

"When will you be done?"

"Oh, soon, soon! It's all up here." Truman tapped his now-bald head, wrung his fat little hands dripping with rings, twisted up his baby-soft lips in a smirk, shifted his caftan-clad lard about in the chair. "I've spent years observing this world. Years!"

Curled up in an overstuffed armchair, an empty ebony cigarette holder in her hand, Babe eyed Truman on the television screen. Her hands itched to fill the holder with a cigarette and light up, but she swallowed, breathed as deeply as she could, and took a sip of water, chewing resolutely on an ice cube instead.

When she set the crystal glass back down on its coaster, however, she missed; the glass hit the tabletop with a loud crack, and water spilled everywhere. Babe gasped, and let out a small cry.

"What? What is it, Babe?" Instantly Bill was by her side, kneeling on the floor, looking up into her face. She grimaced, and laughed.

"Nothing, I just made a little mess, that's all."

"Oh." Bill looked relieved; he ran his hand through his very thin, very silver hair, and exhaled. "I thought—I thought, well, never mind. I'll get a towel." He turned to see what was on the television. "Truman? What's he up to tonight?"

"Oh, the same thing, I'm afraid. He's wasting his talent, still talking about that book of his. Bill, do you think he's written a single word of it?"

"No, I don't. He talks a good game, but he lacks discipline. He didn't used to. It's really a damn shame."

"Yes, it is." Babe turned back to gaze at the television screen; now Truman was repeating an oft-told story, one that she'd laughed at many times, along with all her friends. "Well," he drawled, his voice even higher, more exaggeratedly fey; she'd noticed this lately, how he seemed intent on becoming a caricature comprised of his most studiously affected elements, the lisp, the drawl, the limp wrists. Back when she first met him, these had simply been part of a more sharply etched, richly detailed picture. Now he was a walking—mincing—Hirschfeld cartoon.

"Well," he continued, shifting in his chair on the garishly loud *Tonight Show* set, looking up at the ceiling, as he always did whenever he was about to "tell a whopper," as he so endearingly put it. "I was at this restaurant, minding my own business, when a woman came over and asked me for my autograph. I said of course, but what did she want me to sign? She proceeded to expose her breasts—" And here Truman paused, rolled his eyes, and allowed Johnny Carson to lead the audience in knowing laughter.

"I know! Anyway, I signed it. I mean, why not?" More laughter. "But then her husband, who was fuming, came over, and he, well—he whipped out his *thing*, and said, 'Sign *this*!' And I looked down, and said, 'Well, I don't see how, but maybe I can *initial* it.'"

The audience was rolling in the aisles, Johnny Carson was beet red, laughing so hard there were tears in his eyes.

Babe and Bill exchanged a look.

"He told it better the first time I heard it," Bill said.

"It's so crude." Babe shook her head, switching off the television with the remote. "I don't know why he has to be so vulgar."

"He's always been, to a certain extent. Except around you."

"Yes, but there was a line he wouldn't cross. Lately, however—oh, those men!" Babe shuddered, thinking of the parade of truck drivers, bankers, and air-conditioning repairmen he brought to Kiluna, uninvited, just the way he used to bring Jack. But Jack, despite his gruffness, was a decent man, interesting, and so obviously in love with Truman. These men, this latest, particularly, John O'Shea—actually a banker! A middle-class banker who berated Truman, put him down, told anyone who would listen how lousy he was in bed—Babe simply didn't know what to think, what to do. She couldn't very well ask them to leave, so she did what she always did. She smiled, was polite, interested, fed them, made sure they were well taken care of under her roof. And then let Truman cry on her shoulder when they left, his heart broken every single day, every single minute, it seemed. Dan had been mean to him, called him a fag, left to go back to some horrid woman. Bob had told him he was awful in bed. John had told him he was a hack.

"I don't know what to do for him," she whispered. She glanced at the table next to her, cluttered with amber prescription bottles, and sighed. "If something happens to me, who will take care of Truman?"

"Nothing is going to happen to you," Bill said, too quickly. "You're getting the best care possible. The doctor said if you quit smoking, you'd live a long life, and I'm going to make sure you do."

Babe smiled. She adjusted her wig, for even now, she wouldn't let Bill see her at less than her best. But something had broken inside her, the day the doctor told her it was cancer, this thing that was squeezing the air from her lungs, taxing her energy, causing her feverish dreams, making every step seem as if she were climbing a mountain. Something had come tumbling down, releasing all the fetid ugliness she'd spent a lifetime stifling.

Babe could put into words feelings and emotions that she'd never been able to before. All the books Truman had made her read—none of that had given her the vocabulary the simple diagnosis of "malignancy" had.

"Let's get you into bed now," Bill said, reaching down to help her out of the chair.

"Leave me alone," Babe snapped. "I'm perfectly capable of that."

"Would you like me to sleep in here tonight, just in case you need anything?"

"Interesting that you offer this now, when I could give a shit about sex."

Bill bit his lip, accepted his wife's wrath. And watched her walk tremulously, but defiantly, into the bathroom, head held high; she closed the door in his face.

Something had broken inside William S. Paley, too, that terrible day at Mount Sinai, when the most famous cancer doctor in the world had sat the two of them down and given him his diagnosis.

Shock. Pure shock. That this could happen to him.

To Babe, that is. To Babe.

No, goddammit, to him.

He was older than Babe. A lot older; older than he told people. When she was diagnosed back in January of 1974, and a third of her lung removed, he was seventy-two to Babe's fifty-eight. Bill Paley, despite his lifetime hypochondria, had never been a man who thought about death—his own, anyway. Still, he'd never imagined he'd have to grow old alone. He'd never imagined that Babe would not be there to take care of everything, as she always had.

He'd never imagined that he'd have to start looking back on his past actions with regret, remorse—shame, even—because his beautiful wife might be dying.

When they left the doctor's office, they'd gone straight to their apartment on Fifth Avenue. Babe had gone to her room to rest. Truman was the first of her friends she called; she must have rung him before she lay down, because Bill, still in his study, his head in his hands, an untouched glass of Scotch in front of him, was stunned to see a pale Truman, tears streaming down his cheeks, standing next to him, putting his arms around him, comforting him like he'd never been comforted in his life.

"I had to come to you first," Truman whispered, rocking the bigger man back and forth, even though Bill wasn't crying. "I know Babe is strong. But you, my dear friend, you're the one who will have the hardest time figuring out what to do next."

And Bill had to admit that Truman was right; Babe was strong, she'd know how to handle this crisis—with the same grace and beauty and guarded privacy with which she'd handled everything else. But Bill absolutely didn't know what to do when faced with a foe that money couldn't vanquish. Or a life without someone to see to his every need; a life without Babe, whom he had wronged so many times.

"I'm such a bastard," he'd told Truman that afternoon, so eager to find absolution for his sins he spilled them all. "You don't know how big a bastard I am. I've screwed everyone. Right here in our apartment, in all our beds, in all our homes. I never thought about Babe at all. I wanted what I wanted, and I took it. God, one time— one time I was sure she'd find out, because the woman, well, she left a mess. Blood. You know, that time of the month. And Babe was due home, it was back when we had that place at the St. Regis, and I couldn't send the laundry out and get it back in time, so I scrubbed that stain, scrubbed it like I was Lady Fucking Macbeth. I didn't have any way to dry the sheets, so I baked them in the oven until I could put them on the bed, still wet, and then I fell asleep. And do you know, Babe never once disturbed me? I woke up to find she wasn't even there; she'd come home and found me asleep on the damp sheets, thought I had a fever or something, and left a note saying she'd gone on to Kiluna so she wouldn't bother me. I'm such a bastard. A lousy bastard, and now she's sick, and it's what I deserve. But it's not what she deserves."

"No, it's not." Truman's voice was hard, and Bill looked up into blue eyes that were not wide with obsequious approval, as they always had been. Now Truman's eyes were like chips of ice, and Bill actually shivered. "You are a goddamn bastard, Bill. I like you, I've always liked you, but I've never liked the way you treated Babe. But I'm not going to make this harder on you now. It looks like you're doing that yourself. And besides, you need to stop sniveling, and be there for her. She deserves that, at least."

"I know, I know." Bill shrugged Truman's arms off his shoulders, got up, and poured him a drink; his hands were shaking as he grabbed the tongs, filled the glass with ice. Both men relaxed at the blessed *clink, clink* of ice against glass; once the drink was in Truman's hands, they each exhaled.

"How is she?" Truman asked, after taking a greedy gulp.

"Quiet. She didn't say a word on the drive home. What did she say to you?"

"She said, 'Please come. It's cancer.' That's all."

"So go. Go to her. I know she needs you, you're better for her than I am, you always have been, and God knows if I understand why, but I don't care right now."

Truman finished his drink, set the glass down on a mahogany table.

"I'm better for her because I love her."

"So do I," Bill whispered. "Funny how it takes something like this to remind you."

"Funny how it shouldn't." And Truman left Bill, strode through the fabulous duplex, for once not pausing to gape and admire the magnificent furniture, the crystal chandeliers, the precious *objets* grouped like still lifes on the polished furniture. What did any of it matter to the Paleys now? Except to provide Babe with a fabulous setting in which to be sick, perhaps die?

Truman knocked on Babe's door that awful afternoon; softly, for the first time ever not sure of his reception. And he was terrified, he was ashamed to admit; terrified of what—who—she might become. Would this ruin her beauty, this awful thing that was eating away inside? And then he hated himself for thinking that, but he was honest enough to admit that that was Babe's greatest appeal, even now, after decades of friendship and intimacy and confession. She was simply so lovely, so restful, to look at. And Truman did love beauty so.

"Come in," she said, sounding like herself, and so he did.

Babe was pacing around her fabulous room—all vivid Oriental fabric on the walls, the curtains, the spread. Priceless paintings hung on her walls, yet this was the room in the house that felt the least like a museum; she had made it personal with framed photos—so many of just the two of them, Truman and Babe in happier times!—silly little knickknacks from dime stores mixed with exquisite antiques from Third Avenue. That old white paper flower, now encased in glass as if it were from Tiffany's and not a market in Jamaica. Truman recognized it and tears scalded his eyes; tears he hastily blinked away, before Babe could see.

"Well, it's cancer," Babe said bluntly, no self-pity in her husky voice. "Cancer. They're going to remove part of my lung."

"Oh, Bobolink!"

"I have to stop smoking." But her hands were reaching to light one up even as she spoke. She did so, taking a defiant drag. Then she stabbed it out viciously after only one puff. "My last one." She opened a gold filigree casket full of her L&M brand cigarettes, raised a window—letting in the city sounds of cars honking, brakes squealing, the far-off wail of a police siren—and dumped the contents out. Cigarettes spun through the air. Then she slammed the window shut.

"Oh," she said, looking suddenly stricken. "I should have saved those for the help. That was wasteful."

"Babe!" Truman held out his arms, walking to her, but she refused to run into them. She was paler than usual, but other than that, she looked like herself, only livelier, more vivid; as if the painting had finally come to life.

"No, no, I'm fine. Really. I'm not afraid. I'm just angry. Angry at myself for somehow allowing this to happen. Angry at the damn cigarettes. Angry at Bill, to tell the truth, although I really don't know why."

"Yes, you do."

"Yes, I do. Of course. You know that. How is he? I assume you saw him just now?"

"He's a mess. Very remorseful, if you want to know. Very afraid for you."

"I doubt that will keep his dick in his pants." Babe's hand flew to her mouth; her eyes grew wide. And then she giggled.

So did Truman. And then the two of them were seated in a chaise longue, entwined, her head on his chest. Strange, she thought, as she appreciated his surprisingly strong arms about her, how it always was the other way around. Except for that one night, that precious night when she'd bared herself to him, she was always the comforter, even as he was always her confessor.

"You'll be fine," Truman soothed.

"I might not be."

"No, you might not, but still, you don't know that. You don't know anything right now."

"Do you know what I keep thinking? I keep thinking that I'll only be remembered as the woman who tied a goddamned scarf around her handbag one day, and sparked a national trend."

Truman laughed; he remembered that day, how, after walking out of one of their favorite restaurants, Babe found the day had turned sultry, so she removed the colorful scarf she'd tied around her neck, and wrapped it around the handle of her Hermès bag, tying it in a jaunty bow.

Some photographer—there were always photographers waiting for her, for them, for the two of them together—snapped a shot, some magazine ran it, and soon every woman from Manhattan, New York, to Manhattan, Kansas, was tying her scarf around the handle of her purse.

"You'll be remembered for much, much more than that," Truman assured her.

"I doubt it. I'll only be remembered for the way I look, the way I dress. That's always been enough—it was what I wanted, when I was younger. I worked hard at it, cultivated the photographers, begged the designers for the clothes I wore when I couldn't afford them. It was both a way to be remembered and a way to bag a man. A wealthy man. The two grand lessons my mother taught me in life." And for the first time, Truman detected a real bitterness in her tone as she talked about her mother. "Mission accomplished, but now, now that I'm at the—that I'm facing *this,* I'm appalled. I've wasted my life. And that's why I'm angry."

"And I'm angry that you think that. Babe, the way you live, the way you cultivate yourself, your homes, it's not a waste. Beauty, graciousness—these things are necessary. For the soul—for my soul, anyway. I know there's so much more to you, but don't discount these things."

"Tell me," Babe demanded. "Tell me, would you have wanted to know me if I'd not looked the way I do?"

"No."

Babe winced; he hadn't even hesitated. But then she was grateful. Truman was the one person who told her the truth. Always.

"But," Truman said, stirring a little, stretching his legs, although they did not lengthen to match hers, "what's wrong with beauty being noticed? What's wrong with attraction based on appearance, if it leads to so much more, as it has done with us? Would you have wanted to know me if I'd not been famous? If I'd not looked interesting? Different?"

"I don't know," Babe replied, shrugging. "I suppose not."

"And see what we would have missed out on?"

Babe nodded. Then she closed her eyes, for the first time, it seemed to her, since the doctor had said "cancer." Now she did feel herself letting go, falling, falling into a spiral of fear, of uncertainty, of nausea, a cold, metallic taste in her mouth, the beautiful room spinning behind her closed eyelids. "You'll be here, won't you? When I have my surgery, the treatments? You won't forget me?"

"Of course not! I'll be here, every step of the way, beside you."

"Good." And Babe had allowed herself, then, to relax, even to nap; she'd awoken later, alone, but joined Bill and Truman in the drawing room, where they had a cozy dinner in front of the fireplace, just the three of them. And she could almost convince herself everything was as it had been, before.

But Truman had not been with her every step of the way. He had resumed his life, his ruinous loves; he'd continued to cultivate his celebrity, always calling, sending her bouquets of lilies of the valley and thoughtful, scathingly witty notes.

But for the first time in their friendship, he wasn't there when she needed him.

To her friends, to society as a whole, Babe presented her usual calm, perfectly made-up face. After the surgery and the radiation treatments, during which she lost her hair, but Monsieur Marc, her devoted stylist (she'd stopped going to Kenneth years ago, simply because Monsieur Marc made house calls and Kenneth didn't), made her fabulous Babe Paley wigs, she resumed her normal life. She entertained as usual, sat on her charitable committees, went out to lunch. Slim and Gloria and Marella and C.Z. and even Pam were kind, and they never once made mention of her illness, for which she was grateful. Yet it was there, of course. This repulsive, distasteful thing that shouldn't be mentioned, should only be endured in private, yet it stained everything, the table at Le Grenouille, the flowers at Kiluna, the jewelry at Van Cleef, the shoes at Bergdorf's, with an ugly coating of disquiet. People would sometimes catch themselves in conversation, in her presence—"Yesterday I was thinking, will we really need our yacht five years from now"—and there would be a guilty swallow, an averting of the eyes by the healthy, for having the tactlessness to think five years ahead. When she, Babe, might not have that luxury.

Or her fitter at Bergdorf's might remark about how thin she was, then catch her breath, stuff some pins in her mouth, and hurry away with tears in her eyes, and Babe would think, *How funny. Being thin when one is healthy is an accomplishment. But when one is sick, it's something else altogether.*

And how solicitous everyone was! How extremely interested they were in her comfort, simply begging to adjust the thermostat if she was too cold, kicking at furniture in disgust if she gave any indication that a cushion was too hard, or too soft.

She often caught herself in the mirror and marveled at what she saw; her same self, beautifully composed, clad in her usual tailored clothes, tastefully ostentatious jewelry. Because she didn't feel like herself at all; she felt as if she was constantly holding everything in, walking around like an egg that had been glued back together, walking rigidly, turning her head slowly. She *was* an egg; a Fabergé egg, perhaps, but her scar—a gaping purple slash across her chest—never felt healed enough to hold everything in. She wondered, every time she moved abruptly, if some part of her, some necessary essence, was oozing out.

And always, the wonder, the terror: Was the cancer truly gone? Or was it merely lying in wait, gathering forces, hungry to assault her again?

The answer came a year later, this past January of 1975. Another tumor, in the other lung. And now her friends couldn't hide their distress; they burst into tears every time they saw her. Bill wouldn't leave her alone for a minute, and instead of being grateful or touched by his devotion—finally, after all these years!—she was irritated by it, saw it for what it was: Appreciation, too late, for all she'd done for him. Appreciation fueled by guilt. And fear. Selfish fear. For himself.

And Truman. Her Truman. Spinning out of control.

What would happen to Truman when she was gone? Because it might not be too long now. Babe had a secret. She had stashed some pills away, in a tiny Moroccan pillbox on her dresser. And if the pain ever got too bad, and there was really no relief left to her, she would take them. And spare herself, and those she loved, the ugliness of a drawn-out, protracted death.

But for now, the doctors were still talking about a cure; they were still careful to couch her prognosis in optimistic euphemisms. "There's every reason to believe you'll be around for a long, long time." "We're getting closer to a cure every day, and you have a lot of days ahead of you, Mrs. Paley." "I wouldn't worry if I were you; the chances are greater of being hit by a truck than of dying of this."

Babe came out of the bathroom. Bill was gone, thank God. She locked her bedroom door so she could finally remove her makeup, take out her damned teeth, which were even more ill-fitting than usual due to her weight loss, and remove her wig, which felt like a leaden, furry animal on her head, suffocating her pores. It was hell on hot days, but she would not give in to a turban. Not yet.

Babe stared at herself in her vanity mirror; without the makeup, her skin still looked surprisingly smooth and youthful, if a bit waxy, and she wondered if there was something in the treatments that made it so. She cackled. "Babe Paley discovers magic new treatment for skin!" She could just imagine the headlines, the hordes of women all lining up to have radiation treatments so that they could look just like her.

Her scars were still there, those scars that only Truman had seen; she ran her fingers across the one on her left jaw, felt the rough skin there.

Then she ran her fingers across her skull. Her bare skull, only a few wisps of hair at the base, wisps she couldn't bring herself to cut or shave. They were fine, like a baby's hair. Faded, though; thoroughly white.

She stared at herself for a very long time; the skeletal face, sunken cheeks, startled brown eyes, hairless head. She didn't even have eyebrows now. Strange, she mused, transfixed by the ghastly, yet oddly innocently compelling, visage gazing back. You come into this world alone, toothless, hairless. And that's how you leave this world.

Alone.

But Babe Paley did not weep. She only wished, for one terrible, vindictive moment, that her mother could see her face now.

. . . . .

TRUMAN RECLINED ON A DAYBED, A WRITING PAD PERCHED
on his protruding belly, pen in hand. The pad was full of pages and
pages of paragraphs, jotted notes, words crossed out, scribbles in
the margin—*A severe injury to the brain . . . Kate McCloud—Mona
Williams? . . . And Audrey Wilder sang . . . Gloria . . . Carol . . . La
Côte Basque.*

At the top of the page, underlined, *Answered Prayers.*

Bennett Cerf once said that none of his authors was as good at
stirring up publicity as Truman was; the publisher adored the way
Truman started talking up a book long before it was finished. He
had none of the usual guarded secrecy concerning his work in
progress that most authors possessed. Talking about something
made it real in his mind, even if he didn't have a word on the page,
and so he chattered away happily, dropping hints and tidbits.

He'd been doing this, concerning *Answered Prayers,* for years
now. And he'd almost convinced even himself he'd written the
damn thing.

Earlier in his career, he'd always started at the beginning and written in chronological order. But this time, he told himself he was crafting a quilt, a beautiful, terrible quilt composed of brilliant insight, scathing commentary, memorable characters. How he would stitch it all together remained to be seen, of course, but Truman had no fear; he knew he would make it work.

Well, maybe. Perhaps.

Truman reached for a glass, full of vodka even though it was ten in the morning. Life was so ugly lately; he felt his eyes well up in tears as he sipped the alcohol, knowing it would have no effect on him, not yet; that's why he had to start so early, because it took too many drinks these days to make him feel happy, and the world was just so terrible, he couldn't bear to look at it sober.

But it had been so beautiful! Not that long ago, either, at his gorgeous, wonderful party, when everyone was perfect and magical and the air was filled with music and the smell of flowers and the heady mix of a thousand perfumes, and he was happy, loved, triumphant.

Now the world stank, was a shithole, and he was a star, still, a celebrity, but he sometimes shuddered at his own ugliness, the way he looked on camera, so bloated, so stoned, and the stories he told that, while funny and outrageous, were revolting, too, and he knew it, but dear God, he loved the fame and the publicity that followed him like the tail end of one of his silk scarves; he needed it, because it sheltered him from the sleaziness that was there, always, whenever he let his guard down. Or forgot to take a drink.

What had happened with the world?

Vietnam, of course. God, what a mess. The breakdown of barriers, racial, sexual, social: these things in which he should have rejoiced, but he didn't, he couldn't find any beauty in it. When the barriers came down there was only chaos and excess and foul smells and tattered fabric, unraveling, uncared for.

The ugliness had always been there, he knew; didn't he know it better than anyone? The stories behind the stories; the bargains and sacrifices he had made, that his swans had made, all of them, throughout their lives. The sordidness they were so determined to hide from the world; he remembered that one holiday in Italy, when it was just him and Babe and Bill having a wonderful time; a bright, shiny Christmas star of a time, enveloped in their wealth and privilege, staying at the finest hotels, being feted and adored. Bill bought and bought and bought; they were furnishing the apartment on Fifth then, and Bill was in one of his hungry moods. There was a hole inside him that couldn't be filled but he would die trying to, and so he threw money everywhere, bought gilded this and antique that, Renaissance draperies, Florentine carpets. They had the most magnificent meals and wines, and Truman gazed at Babe, and gazed at Bill, and felt life couldn't get any better than this, especially after Babe took him shopping and outfitted him with the finest Italian loafers and silk scarves and straw hats. . . .

Then, one night, they were invited to some minor prince's house, and Babe and the prince danced for hours; Truman was too tired, and Bill never did dance. Like so many successful men, he avoided anything that might make him look frivolous. When the trio returned to their hotel suite—for of course they always booked a suite, three bedrooms, so they could all be together, every single minute of every day—Bill, his divine Mr. Paley, turned grotesque. He threw things—first his shoes, then his belt, then anything he could find—and spat out horrible accusations about Babe and the prince, and even when Babe pointed out the prince was gay, and

Truman backed her up, he didn't care, he only yelled, "I know that type, I know the type who will say that, pretend to be a pansy and then mess around with your wife," and continued to shout and rampage until Babe and Truman locked themselves in another room, their hearts racing, but still it was so ridiculous, so hilarious, that they giggled, trying to stifle the sound because a furious man does not want to be thought a fool; it's like throwing kerosene on a flame. Finally they relaxed, lay together on the bed and waited him out; Truman had fallen asleep, in fact, waiting. When it was all over, when there was only ominous quiet outside, Babe awakened him gently with a kiss, but even so, Truman woke up with a jolt of panic, sweat on his brow. The locked door reminded him of all the times that his mother had jailed him in a hotel room, any hotel room, and went out with her friends, leaving him alone. All alone.

Except, of course, this time he had Babe. And when they all emerged from their adjoining rooms in the morning, washed and beautifully clothed, and went out again, the envy of all who saw them, this happy, shiny, privileged trio, only they knew the repulsiveness they had left behind in the hotel, for the chambermaids to clear away.

It paid, he thought sourly, to tip big. That was one thing the Paleys taught him.

But Babe was ill now, so ill she couldn't make everything better through the sheer power of her beauty, her kindness, her understanding. She was frail and snappish and sick, sick, sick, and it tore his heart, made him want to vomit, just as he had the night poor Perry and Dick were hung, God, those boys, those poor boys with their imploring, accusing eyes—but there wasn't anything he could do for them! He'd tried, he really had! And there really wasn't anything he could do for Babe, was there? Other than call her, send her flowers, cards, and try to make her laugh.

And Bennett was dead. God, he'd almost forgotten. Bennett Cerf was dead, and Random House was breathing down his neck for this fucking book that he'd promised years ago. They never would have done that, before; they never would have insisted on him meeting a deadline, given his genius. Bennett had protected him. Just like Babe had. But no one wanted to protect him now.

And the world was repellent, the beauty was fading, and it wasn't only the years advancing. Was it? The talent was receding from his fingertips; he could feel it seeping from him, and the panic it induced was like a sickness, a Saint Vitus' dance, so that he had to go out there and talk and talk and sparkle and recount and sing, sing, sing for his supper in the only way that had never really let him down, not the writing, but the entertaining. Dance, monkey, dance in your caftan, your tight black Rolling Stones T-shirt tucked into your leather pants, tell the stories, tell all the stories, because that's what they crave, isn't it? To hear the tawdriness, to sniff the seediness that even Holly Golightly in her Meanest, Reddest state would find repulsive.

And face it, Truman, baby doll. Telling all the stories—all those delicious, decadent secrets—is what you enjoy the most, anyway. It's what you're the best at.

It's who you are. The snake in the grass . . . why else do you collect snakes? That story about the cottonmouth biting him— God, he hadn't told that story in years, but they'd all fallen for it, hadn't they?

What they didn't know was that he had bit the cottonmouth first.

Still, he had to *write* something, because that was who he was, too. He was a literary genius. Not a thieving shit like Mailer, who couldn't write an original book if his sorry life depended on it— Truman poured himself more vodka, in the plain water glass. He didn't even take time for the niceties anymore, the twist of lime, the chilled highball glass.

He was just as bad as everyone. Worse.

But he had been writing, some. Little sketches, picking away at this idea he'd had for more than a decade, his Proustian epic about society. Some of it was good; some of it was crap. Oh, maybe all of it was crap; Truman couldn't really decide, anymore. Truth was, he was terrified of publishing again, because of the glorious success of *In Cold Blood*.

The knives were out; the knives were always out. But *Esquire* had just made him a lavish offer to publish a story. One story, that was all. And if it did well, maybe others. He could do that; he'd begun his career publishing stories, not novels, epics, opuses. Rivals to Proust.

Baby steps, baby. Baby steps.

He picked up his pen, turned a page, and began to scribble some of the best stories he knew; stories that were not his, but that just made them even juicier. He could tell them better than their owners could, and why else had they been told to him, if not for him to use them? Oh, those swans of his might be coy and say, "Now, True Heart, don't you dare repeat this!" before telling him something particularly divine, and he might cross his heart and hope to die if he ever did.

But neither of them meant it. They couldn't have. Or they wouldn't have told the stories to him in the first place.

They wouldn't have let him *in*.

———

THE FIRST STORY APPEARED in *Esquire* in June of 1975. "Mojave" by Truman Capote—an excerpt took up the entire cover, followed by "continued on page 38."

Tennessee Williams declared it Truman's best writing since the short story that had launched his career back in 1945, "Miriam." All the critics loved it; it was received with rapture, cries of "He's back!" and pleas of "More, more, more!"

"Well," Truman drawled to one and all. "So you liked this? Maybe next I'll give you a taste of my novel! It's going to be grand, you know, my best yet! Maybe I'll give you a little taste."

Did anyone in Manhattan that summer of 1975 recognize the players in this work of fiction? Sarah Whitelaw, the devoted, almost geishalike wife of George, who narrates the bulk of the piece, the story within the story? Did anyone take note of the fact that Sarah massages George's feet while he talks, that this outwardly perfect domestic scene is, in fact, completely loveless, just an arrangement? That Sarah looked an awful lot like Babe Paley, with her "tobacco-colored" hair?

If anyone did take note of this, they didn't say a word. The story itself was too good, perhaps; they were only dazzled with Truman's writing. And nobody ever accused Bill Paley of being as introspective as the George Whitelaw of the story.

Babe read the story, along with Slim and Marella and Gloria and C.Z. and Pam; they all sent Truman telegrams of congratulations and exhaled. Perhaps Truman wasn't so far gone as they'd all feared. After all, he was writing again! And despite the explicitness of the story—the language! the sex!—the story was good. Or so the critics said.

Still, Babe did fold the magazine in half when she was done, a small rumble of discomfort worrying her. But it was only a tremor, so easily obscured by the greater earthquake of her failing health, more surgeries, barbaric procedures that poked and probed and irradiated and otherwise treated her previously admired, couture-clad body like a science project; medicines that gave her headaches, medicines to relieve the headaches, medicines that took away her appetite. She conserved herself now; she remained in bed for long periods at a time so that she could emerge and carefully, oh, so painstakingly, apply her makeup—an entirely different prospect now, not just to conceal and enhance but to turn her into an entirely different person. She felt like Lon Chaney, rather: the man of a thousand faces. She was an expert at turning a sick old woman into a reasonably vibrant middle-aged one.

She would emerge, makeup perfected, wig in place, wearing a superbly styled outfit, the accessories just right, the jewelry carefully chosen so as not to call attention to her emaciated wrists, neck, fingers—she wore a lot of whimsical brooches these days, like her favorite bumblebee brooch designed by Verdura with a fat coral body and glittering diamond wings—and go to lunch with her friends, and smile breezily at the cameras, and assure the world, her world, that Mrs. Paley was just fine, thank you so very much for asking.

Because to let the world know otherwise simply wasn't an option. It never had been. She had an image to uphold. She and Bill. Mr. and Mrs.

So no, Babe didn't trouble herself too much with "Mojave," other than to be grateful that her friend—for he was still her friend, despite the distance, the distractions, her illness—was working again.

But were she and Truman as close as before?

Babe would have answered *yes,* unhesitatingly. Truman would have declared, "Of course we are, I love Babe more than anyone in the world, she's my dearest, *dearest* friend!" But it was an affirmation based on the past, not the present. The present wasn't recognizable or palatable to either of them; she was too ill, he was too self-destructive. Like so many, they chose not to recognize themselves in the mirror, but in old photographs, scrapbooks, shared memories.

That summer of 1975 was one of relative peace. Saigon had fallen in April, so the war was over. Nixon had been gone almost a year. Already people were talking about the Bicentennial; the swans were on numerous committees charged with planning the upcoming galas.

Slim had divorced her dull English lord, had absolutely no money, but still managed to enjoy life, peering at it through her ridiculous, outsized glasses, living in hotels and at friends' country homes and yachts. All her friends were sympathetic, although one time Babe shocked Truman by saying, "Slim really never made it, did she?" And Truman knew exactly what she meant; Slim had wasted her assets, never really married well—or, rather, wasn't quite able to *stay* married well—and now she was in her sixties, firmly in the "kooky aunt" category, sad to say.

Marella and Gianni were still married; Marella had pulled away from Truman, ever so slightly, in recent years, cloaking herself in her princess robes, no longer inviting him to stay or dine. So, of course, he told anyone who would listen all about Gianni's affairs with Italian starlets. He didn't even bother to see if this was true or not; he just told everyone it was. And people simply lapped it up! Same way they lapped up what he'd started saying about Ann

Woodward, that sow, who still hung around at the tattered edges of his world, popping up, soused to the gills, at parties now and then. He'd started telling people that she'd been married before Billy, poor dead Billy, and so she was a bigamist as well as a murderess.

Well, it might have been true! And it just made the whole thing more interesting—really, nobody cared any longer that the woman had gotten away with murder—and served Ann right; he'd never forgiven her for calling him a "garden-variety fag" all those years ago.

Gloria and Loel still did enjoy their Truman, when he wasn't drunk or stoned or carting around some dock boy. Which meant— they really didn't enjoy him at all, but then, neither did he enjoy them. God, they were becoming tedious, Loel looked like he'd been pickled in brine, and Gloria was so obsessed with her fading looks that she wouldn't even come out of her bedroom before three in the afternoon, when the light was best.

C.Z. was as ever: irreverent, yet surprisingly prissy at times un- less Truman called her on it—"Oh, dear, it's Miss Boston Brahmin again. Or has she forgotten she has a nude Diego Rivera of herself hanging over the basement bar?" She—like Babe—professed to worry about him, but then she'd forget about him as soon as he left; she'd go off and write another gardening book or smell a horse, and put him completely out of her mind. But she always welcomed him with her sunny smile the next time they met.

Lady Pamela Digby Churchill Hayward was now Mrs. Averell Harriman—Christ on a cracker, Harriman was old, older than Me- thuselah, but he had so much money!—and had reinvented herself once more. Now she was a Washington hostess, the queen Demo- crat with Republican tastes. She claimed she did not own a "televi- sion machine," and so she regretfully missed a lot of Truman's more delightful appearances. Although she was still happy to include Truman in her fund-raising dinners and parties, if he promised to behave himself. Sometimes he did.

Old habits die hard. Particularly among the wealthy.

And the storytellers, gossips, and snakes.

After "Mojave" was published, *Esquire* begged Truman for more. And more was what they got.

"What do you think of this? Isn't it just delicious? Brilliant in every way?" And Truman handed the piece to Jack. Dear, unsuccessful, bitter Jack; he still loved him, always would, even if Jack could barely stand to look at him these days when he was foggy and bloated with drink from ten in the morning on. But still, the two of them could never really sever the tie. And they still trusted each other's opinion.

"Truman," Jack had said, aghast, after he'd read the story. "Are you sure about this?"

"What do you mean? Isn't it good?" Truman, reclining on a rubber raft in a pool, dabbled a pudgy red hand in the cool water. He was on his fifth "glass of sunshine"—a tumbler of vodka with a splash of orange juice.

"To be frank, no, it's not. Not your best work, my boy."

"I know someone who's j-e-a-l-o-u-s," Truman sang, splashing the water after each letter.

"You know that's not true. No, it is. It is true. I've always been jealous." Jack met Truman's triumphant gaze head-on, not flinching. "And you know that. You also know that I've never let my jealousy cloud my professional admiration of your work."

Truman pursed his mouth, took another sip of vodka. "I know," was all he said.

"But this isn't very good. And that's not even the most disturbing thing. Truman, don't you think they'll all be upset? All your goddamned swans? The Paleys, especially? Won't they be furious?"

"Nah." Truman closed his eyes again and tilted his face toward the sky, not caring if he got sunburned. "They're all too stupid. They'll never recognize themselves. Besides, I'm very clever; I did use a few specific names, just to throw the others off the scent."

"If you say so," Jack replied. "But I'd think twice."

"I don't have to. Anyway, even if they do recognize themselves, what do they expect? They're the ones who told me everything in the first place. Even after *In Cold Blood*. Even after I told them, the dumb bunnies, that I was writing a book about society."

"What about Babe?"

Truman put his sunglasses on and splashed away on his raft.

"Just think twice, Truman, okay? Promise me you'll do that?"

What he couldn't tell Jack was that he couldn't afford to think twice. He'd promised *Esquire* a second story, and this was all he had, because he couldn't write, not really, the pages paralyzed him, his thoughts couldn't be corralled, and he couldn't let Jack, of all people, see. Jack, who had fallen in love with him because he was a writer; that was how they met, two serious artists who, on those first cozy mornings in bed together when they were intoxicated by discovery, like conquistadors conquering Mexico, planting flags and staking claim, jokingly argued about who was the Virginia and who the Leonard Woolf of their relationship.

No, he couldn't let Jack see. And so he sent the story off, the first installment (only?), he told the editor, of his new book, *Answered Prayers*.

"La Côte Basque 1965," the story was called.

CHAPTER

18

. . . . .

ANN WOODWARD WOKE UP THAT MORNING FEELING
like hell.

She always felt like hell, but that morning of October 9, 1975,
the sky appeared grayer, the air colder, her breath more of a waste
than it had seemed the day before. She had a headache; she'd had a
headache for so long, she knew she'd feel worse without one. It
was a companion. One of the few she could claim.

The headache, the ostracism, the entrapment—for she really
was an animal in a cage, a gilded cage, but the bars were well con-
structed by her mother-in-law, Elsie. The food doled out grudg-
ingly. The few glimpses of sunshine rationed. Her life was a prison.

Her sons, removed from her, raised by Elsie, and really, who
could blame her? It wasn't as if Ann was a good mother, she knew
she wasn't, but still it stung to have them taken from her like that.
Her sons were now two more things she couldn't call her own anymore.

So Ann rose, took a pill or two—because why not? She didn't
even know, for sure, what they did for her anymore—went to get

the mail, and found, in a manila envelope, a copy of the upcoming *Esquire,* with a photo of Rich Little in a rumpled raincoat on its cover. One of the headlines trumpeted, *"At last, Truman Capote's new novel,* Answered Prayers, *a first look."* And that headline was circled, with a handwritten suggestion that *"You might want to take a look at this."*

Ann's first reaction was to laugh and toss it in the trash. Why the hell would she want to read Truman's new book? She despised Truman; he despised her. She really didn't know why, except that he told someone, who told her, that once she'd called him a fag. Apparently, he took offense at that, which was odd. Lots of people called him a fag, and he was a fag, wasn't he? So why would she want to read his pathetic little story?

But then Ann thought of the day ahead; of the endless, yawning nothingness, perhaps a pained visit from Elsie, the old cow, or if not a visit then a phone call, just so Elsie could tell one and all that they were still close, of course, why wouldn't they be?

Well, for starters, Ann always longed to tell her, *I killed your son.*

That was true. That was fact. Ann had killed Elsie's son, Ann's husband, Billy. Billy Woodward.

Sometimes it sounded so strange to say his name. It was like the name of a stranger to her now, he'd been gone so long. Dead, dead, dead . . . from a bullet that came from a gun held by her. Ann had never tried to claim otherwise.

As far as the accident part, though . . .

Yes, it was an accident. She hadn't meant to kill him, not really. No, it wasn't an accident. She sure as hell intended to scare him, or wound him, or do something that would release her from him, cause him to divorce her, give her a good settlement. Billy was a fag, too. He was. Nobody knew that about him, except Ann. She'd tried to use this as leverage, but he'd not risen to the bait. "No one will believe you," the bastard told her that night, after yet another fight, a knockdown, drag-out brawl in the bedroom hall, even as their sons were asleep at the other end of the house.

So Ann went to sleep with a gun beside her. Who didn't? Well, Billy did, too. Or at least, that's what she told the police when they came, later. And indeed, when they went to Billy's room to see, they found a revolver next to his bed.

She'd heard a prowler. Everyone knew about the prowlers! She'd heard steps on the roof, the dog barking, and when she went to her bedroom door, she saw a figure in the hallway. She blasted away at it, thinking only of her sons, her precious boys, whom she had to protect, didn't she?

It wasn't her fault that Billy had gotten up to pee.

That's what she told the police. Upon her lawyer's advice. Elsie's, too.

And so began a lifetime in hell, a hell even more scorching than her miserable marriage had been. Elsie swooped down on her, paid everyone off, locked Ann up only to take her out occasionally, telling one and all that it was a terrible, terrible accident, pure and simple. Of course she believed her daughter-in-law! Of course the two of them were grieving together, finding solace in memories of dear Billy.

When the two of them were alone, though, Elsie was anything but the gracious society lady; she spewed forth a lifetime of pent-up venom against "the other woman," who just happened to be her daughter-in-law. Did Elsie truly mourn her son? Ann never really knew. She had to sit through streams of invective followed by the cold shoulder, then a car would pick up her and deposit her back into her apartment, until the next time Elsie wanted to trot her out for "appearance's sake."

Then even Elsie ran out of hateful things to say, in her crisp, modulated voice, and sent Ann away to Europe with instructions to stay put or else. Well, Ann did, for a while, but Europe was so damn old and boring and nobody there wanted anything to do with her, either, so she came home. Elsie then locked her back in this cage, not even bothering to trot her out to ease the gossip, but it didn't matter. Everybody had forgotten about the whole thing, anyway. Society had a very short memory. But still, nobody wanted to see her. The phone didn't ring. Invitations didn't appear in the mail.

All she'd ever wanted was to have a little fun, ya know? Back in Kansas, where she was born, where she had first married for kicks, then ran away from the louse, then to New York, where she got in the shows, had the stage-door Johnnies eating out of her hands, then bagged a big fish, ol' Bill Woodward, who then passed her on to Billy. Who married her. And took all the fun away.

Because being rich, she'd found out, wasn't really that much fun. In order to be rich, she was supposed to act differently; the money, the position came with so many gilded strings attached. She must dress a certain way, behave a certain way—decorum, Elsie was always harping. Taste, dear, taste. That's the thing.

The other dames could do it—look at Babe Paley, with her quiet voice, her regal posture, her graceful movement, unhurried, focused. But Babe wasn't much fun at all; Ann had never seen her really cut a rug in public, or laugh with abandon, or drink too much, or smile too broadly. What good was money, without fun? Ann really couldn't play the game, when all was said and done.

You know who else couldn't play the game? Capote. That mincing little creep. He might give himself airs, throw that goddamn party to which she hadn't been invited, not that she ever expected it, but still. *Elsie* had been invited.

But Capote wasn't any better at being rich than Ann was; he couldn't hide his stripes any more than she could. The two of them were trash, scum, or maybe even worse.

The only difference was the Babe Paleys of the world didn't know it about *him*, because he hadn't pulled that goddamn trigger.

Not yet, anyway.

Goddamn, the day was shaping up to be another winner. Ann fingered the torn lace on her negligee and whimpered. She'd have to beg Elsie for another, and the thought of scraping through the rest of her life on her knees, begging for handouts, all for the sake of *appearances*—

Wasn't it time for a drink yet? Or more pills?

Ann poured herself a good one—a tumbler of bourbon, no ice—and settled in an armchair with the magazine.

She might as well read what the faggot had written. It couldn't be any worse than the stories she told herself, every single worthless, endless day of this worthless, endless life she was barely living.

WHEN THEY FOUND HER the next day, the tumbler was empty. And the magazine was still clutched in her cold, stiff fingers.

. . . . .

OCTOBER 17, 1975,
LOS ANGELES

Truman was on top of the world. He, Truman Streck-fus Persons Capote, Mama's Little Disappointment, was starring in a movie! Finally, after years and years, ever since he was a little boy watching Shirley Temple wiggle and flirt and tap her way to fame—oh, my, remember that time he dressed up in one of Sook's old dresses and tapped for his mama in the kitchen of the house in Monroeville? It was during one of Mama's rare visits. Sook loved to let him dress up in her old gowns, so this time, they rigged him up in a yellow silk dress with torn lace flounces; Sook pinned it up so he wouldn't trip over it, and then she turned on the phonograph and he tapped and lisped around like Shirley herself, giving the performance of his life. Mama, it need not be said, was not amused; she ran to the outhouse, actually, and he heard her retching from inside the kitchen.

Well, look at me now, Mama! I'm a movie star!

Neil Simon had asked—begged! implored!—him to play the part of the villain in his latest movie, *Murder by Death*. "What Billie Holiday is to jazz, what Mae West is to tits . . . Truman Capote is to the great god Thespis!" Truman crowed to one and all.

And it was true! Maybe.

If he was being honest with himself—which he was not in the habit of being, but sometimes one did slip a little—making a movie was not easy, even if he was basically playing Truman Capote, as he'd been instructed to do. But he had to speak other people's words, not his own; Neil Simon had not taken kindly to the suggestion that Truman rewrite his part, even after Truman reminded him he had written very good screenplays in the past. So Truman did, sometimes, stumble over the dialogue—when he could remember it. And, yes, perhaps he did keep looking down at those marks that he was told, repeatedly, that he *had* to hit or else he'd be out of camera range; how on earth was he supposed to hit them without looking at them, while remembering someone else's words to say? But the director didn't seem to understand this predicament.

And the hours were ungodly! Strange, he didn't remember having to get up at the crack of dawn when he was working on *Beat the Devil*, with Bogie and Huston, true cinematic geniuses, not like this hack director. But he had to report to the studio every morning he was on call at six A.M., even if all he did during the day was sit around in his costume, just biding his time. And the lights were hotter than Hades, and the other actors—Maggie Smith and David Niven among them—didn't seem as amused by his stories as Bogie had been, back in the day.

But now the phone was ringing, and it was Liz Smith, calling him from New York. New York! Oh, how he missed it! He squealed into the phone, happy to hear a familiar voice.

"Liz! My angel, my rescuer! I'm so glad to hear from you! Do you have any idea what that amateur Maggie Smith said to me the other day? Now, this is strictly off the record, of course—unless you think it should be otherwise—but—"

"Truman, do you have any idea what's going on here?" Liz, in her laconic Texas drawl, interrupted him.

"No, what do you mean?"

"Well, *Esquire* came out today."

"Of course! I'd nearly forgotten! Tell me, tell me—is it brilliant? Wonderful? The most astonishing thing you've ever read?"

"Well, it's astonishing, all right. Did you hear about Ann Woodward?"

"No, what about her? What did Miss Bang Bang do now?"

"She killed herself, Truman."

"No!" Truman sat down; oh, this was good! He hadn't heard half so good in ages.

"And, Truman, the rumor is she had a copy of *Esquire* in her hands. And the pages were open to your story, 'La Côte Basque 1965.'"

"NO!!!" Truman didn't try to stifle a squeal; think of the publicity! *Oh, thank you, Ann Woodward, you fag-hating murdering bitch!* "Oh, Liz, really? You're not making that up, are you, my darling girl?"

"Truman," Liz said slowly, "I don't think you quite understand."

And then Liz proceeded to inform him that all hell was breaking loose in Manhattan; screams and hysterics were being witnessed in penthouses, restaurants, 21, Bergdorf's. His name was on everyone's tongues—for his friends, his swans, were not so dumb as he'd assumed them to be; they'd recognized themselves and their stories, after all. *Everyone* had. And were happy to tell Miss Smith that never again would Truman Capote darken their marble doorsteps.

"How delicious!" Truman kept screaming throughout. "How delightful! What a dream come true!"

"Slim, Gloria, Marella—they've all vowed that you'll never be accepted again. Jackie O, apparently, has taken to her room with her salts. Gloria Vanderbilt is seething, possibly suing."

"Oh, they're just saying that! Their plastic noses are out of joint, that's all. They'll change their minds in a few days—they always do. I'm simply too famous and fun for them to give me up! But, Liz, really, my darling—is it truly a scandal? A divine, delicious literary scandal, just like in the good old days of Hemingway and Fitzgerald?"

"At the very least," Liz affirmed. "Truman, everyone is furious, even those who aren't in the story! And Ann—well, you've managed to get everyone all misty-eyed about someone they all simply hated before your story. That's quite an accomplishment."

"How did she die?"

"Cyanide pill."

"Well, darling, I didn't go out and buy the pill for her, so why blame me?"

"Because of the *story*, Truman. The part about Ann—you really dredged it all up, and then some, saying that she'd never divorced her first husband. Is that true?"

"It might be."

"Well, everyone thinks it was vile and unnecessary, at the very least. But the stuff about the Paleys—well, that's the capper. The nail in your coffin."

"There's nothing about the Paleys in my story," Truman said primly.

"Truman, cut the crap. A Jewish media mogul with a fabulous, kind, beautiful wife, and who can't keep his pecker in his pants?"

"Darling, read it however you want. That's what great literature does—it allows people to interpret it in different ways."

"Great literature?" Truman heard the wry doubt in Liz's voice.

"Yes, darling, my gossip queen." And Liz heard the acid condescension in his.

"Well, I can't reach the Paleys—they're the only ones who won't talk to me. Slim, however, is absolutely livid. She's threatening to sue."

"Oh, my dearest Big Mama—she never will! Slim's a smart girl. She knows better—they all know better. What did they expect, anyway? Who did they think I was? I'm a writer! This will all be over soon. But not too soon, I hope!"

"Well, I'm going to write an article about the whole thing for *New York* magazine."

"Oh, wonderful! Tremendous! How can I help?"

"I'll be in touch."

Truman hung up the phone and clapped his hands with glee. Oh, goody, goody, goody! Maybe Hollywood didn't know what to do with him—he knew the film was going to be a turkey and he wasn't going to exactly set the screen on fire. But New York certainly did! He imagined he could hear, from across the continent, all the millions of voices shouting his name—*Truman, Truman, Truman!*

He looked down at his knees; they were knocking, hitting each other, and he thought, *How odd*. Then he plopped down on a chair, licked his lips, and reached for the ever-present vodka.

Then he bit his lip. He rubbed his forehead, which had begun to throb. He picked up the telephone. He began to dial. And dial. And dial.

"I'm sorry, Mrs. Agnelli is out."

"I'm sorry, Lady Keith is unavailable."

"I'm sorry, Mrs. Guinness is away."

"I'm afraid Mrs. Harriman isn't in."

"I'm sorry, Mrs. Paley is resting."

He hung up, drank more, watched the clock; concentrated on the second hand, ticking away steadily, and he decided to take a small sip of vodka with every tick, until he grew dizzy and gave it up. But an hour had gone by, and so he dialed again.

"No, Mrs. Agnelli is still away."

"No, Lady Keith is not available."

"No, Mrs. Guinness is still out."

"No, Mrs. Harriman isn't in yet."

"No, Mrs. Paley is still resting."

Two more hours; two more tumblers of vodka, no ice, and Truman was now shaking from head to toe, his chest constricting, tightening, so that he felt his face growing more and more purple, he knew it, even if he didn't look in a mirror. He imagined himself this violet, pulsating monster, and then he took another drink and dialed again.

"Mrs. Agnelli asks that you please stop calling."

"Lady Keith says to tell you to go to hell."

"Mrs. Guinness has requested that you no longer call."

"Mrs. Harriman would like you to stop phoning."

"Mrs. Paley is—is no longer taking your calls."

And that's when Truman began to cry; he rolled off the chair, threw himself on the carpet, threw himself a tantrum that splashed over him like a hallucination from his childhood, drowning him with its force, and he was alone again, all alone in the dark, and the door was locked and Mama was gone, and when would she be coming back? What if she never came back? What if he died here, alone?

And then he vomited into the thick shag carpet of the tacky Beverly Hills apartment he had rented; his stomach spasmed, his throat burned as he puked vile, pink-tinged liquid all over the white carpet, and soon his face was covered in his bile, and he started to roll around in it, slathering himself with shame.

And then he passed out.

OCTOBER 17, 1975,
NEW YORK

E ARLIER THAT MORNING, BABE PUT THE MAGAZINE DOWN. Or, rather, it slipped from her trembling fingers, falling to the carpeted floor.

Her mouth was dry, her body shaking. She had the curious feeling of falling, even though she was sitting up, straight-backed in an armchair. She gazed down at her feet; they were solidly on the ground. But still the room seemed to loom up at her, and she felt herself being weighed down by gravity so palpable she could see its mist.

When she'd heard the whispers about Ann last week—that she'd swallowed cyanide pills—she hadn't believed them. Even when Elsie told Slim, at the wake, "Well, Ann killed Billy, and now Truman killed Ann. So I guess that's that"—still, Babe hadn't believed it.

That a woman, even tattered, self-destructive Ann Woodward, would kill herself simply because of a story? A story written by Truman? Babe couldn't comprehend it. For Truman wrote fiction, or serious nonfiction, like *In Cold Blood*. Why on earth would Ann Woodward kill herself over something he'd written?

Babe understood now. She understood humiliation and betrayal, as well, but these were familiar to her.

What was unfamiliar—unbelievable—was that Truman could be the one to humiliate and betray.

She sat for a long while, her ears ringing with the whispers of all New York outside her window. Finally she sipped some water, until she felt she could speak in a normal tone. She would not allow her voice to quaver; she would not dissolve into tears. She was Barbara Cushing Mortimer Paley—her mother's daughter, after all. When she finally felt composure settle over her like a silk shawl, she picked up the phone.

"Slim? Slim, have you read the new issue of *Esquire*? And Truman's story?"

"No." Slim sounded sleepy, and Babe realized it was rather early in the day. But first thing this morning, after another restless, sleepless night, she'd had an urgent need to read the story, and so she'd asked her maid to go out and buy an issue, hot off the newsstand.

Odd, she had thought at the time, that Truman hadn't sent a copy himself, as he always did. But then, he was away in California, preparing to make a cameo in a movie. Absurd, to think of it— Truman in a movie! But then so many things were absurd these days.

"Slim, go out right now and buy it. Then read it and call me. Call me right away."

"Babe, are you all right?"

"Just do as I said."

Babe hung up the phone, bit her lip, reached down for the magazine, and read the thing again. It was not easy to read; she grimaced through it as she'd never grimaced through the carnage of *In Cold Blood*. The Clutter family's gruesome wounds had nothing on what was dripping from the pages of Truman's latest—story.

And the thing was—oh, the damnable thing was—Babe could hear Truman's voice in every word. Absolutely in every word, phrase, inflection. As if he were seated at her dinner table, or they were gathered around the terrace of Round Hill, or the two of them were curled up with Slim in a private cove in the garden at Kiluna with a thermos of martinis snuck out of the house, laughing like naughty schoolchildren. Always listening to Truman talk and talk and talk, outrageous, hysterical, but just to them. Only to *them*.

Not to the world.

Babe skimmed through the first part of the "story"—it wasn't that, not really. It was a poisoned pen letter, a grievance, a mockery. She skimmed through it, sucking in her breath as she read about a typical lunch at La Côte Basque, narrated by Lady Ina Coolbirth, gossipy, catty—and sounding and acting an awful lot like Slim Keith, "a big, breezy, peppy broad" who happened to be married to a dull English lord. And who grew louder and drunker as the story progressed.

In the story, Lady Ina gossiped and catted about a parade of the rich and famous—Jackie Kennedy looking like an exaggerated version of herself, Princess Margaret so boring she made people fall asleep, Gloria Vanderbilt so ditzy she didn't recognize her first husband.

And then who should enter but "Ann Hopkins," and the entire lurid Woodward tale was laid out, by Truman's pen, for everyone in Keokuk, Iowa—people who had no business knowing about it in the first place—to salivate over. Babe winced as she read how Lady Ina wondered about Ann and her mother-in-law, "What do they have to talk about, when they're alone?" For Slim had asked that exact same question once, long ago. In front of Truman.

But it was when Truman—or rather, Lady Ina—started to tell the tale of Sidney Dillon that Babe felt nauseated. She had to go to the bathroom, press a cool cloth against her head, take another drink of water, before she could read the tale again.

The tale of a man, a "conglomateur, adviser to presidents." A Jew, the story emphasized; a man forever on the outside looking in. A man with a wife named Cleo, "the most beautiful creature alive." A man who had many affairs.

One in particular: a slovenly mess of a one-night stand involving bloodstains, sheets, a cool, collected blond shiksa whom he desired for the sole purpose, evidently, of making up for his Jewishness, for seeking revenge upon the Protestant world that wouldn't have him in their clubs. Seeking revenge in the most disgusting, sordid way.

Babe set the magazine down once more, just as the phone rang.

"Babe?" It was Slim, breathless, cautious.

"Yes."

"I read it. I'm—I'm horrified. Beside myself. That little twerp! How dare he put such bitchy words in my mouth? How dare he make me the centerpiece—'Lady Ina,' my ass. It might as well say 'Lady Keith'!"

"Did you read the part about the man? Sidney Dillon?"

There was a silence, and Slim finally whispered, "Yes."

"Who do you think it is?"

"I really don't know."

"You don't?"

"I have no idea, Babe."

"I'm not sure who the woman in the story, the mistress, is sup-posed to be. But I think I know who the man could be."

Slim didn't answer for a moment. Then she began to sputter anew. "I'm so furious, I'll kill that bastard, absolutely kill him, just wait until everyone reads this—and Ann Woodward! Poor Ann Woodward! He murdered her, Babe, that's what happened. You know she was found with the magazine in her hands? He drove a woman to suicide, Babe! And he used *me* to do it!"

"Oh, Ann!" Babe's gut took another punch; she was appalled that she'd forgotten about poor Ann, and those motherless boys— orphaned boys now. "I—I don't know anymore, Slim. I don't know how he could have done this—why? I'm so sorry, dear, that you've been used in that way. That we all have been—used. I—I have to go now. I'm sorry."

"Babe? Are you all right? Do you need me to come over?"

"No, I'm not all right. But I prefer to be alone now."

Babe hung up the phone, and she had never craved a cigarette in her life as she did right now. And she would have had one, too— hang the doctors and their ridiculous worries! She was going to die. So what did it matter if she smoked once in a while? But she had thrown them all out, forbidden the household staff to smoke. And she wouldn't send anyone out to buy more, that was too desperate.

Then she glanced over at the little red Moroccan pillbox. And she buried her face in her hands, remembering how Bill had found the pills, how white with fear and rage he had been when he heard her plan—so rational, she'd thought at the time. But now, now that poor Ann had done the same thing, and the way people were talking—Babe shuddered. Bill was right to have taken them from her, doling out her medicine now himself. She must spare her children—and her husband—that humiliation, anyway. She mustn't let them be the talk of the town, like poor Ann's boys were now.

But Truman hadn't been that kind, had he? And Bill—she snatched up the magazine and strode into Bill's room; he was at work, of course. She laid it on the bed, where he couldn't help but see it. Then she went back to her room, lay down on her bed, sprawled on it, ungainly, her face pressed deep into the pillow, and she knew her makeup would stain it beyond repair, but she didn't care. She didn't care about anything anymore.

There was an ache in her chest, a hole, and for once it wasn't the memory of what had been taken from her physically—her lungs, her future; now it was the memory of what had been excised from her even more precisely than the surgeon's scalpel. The one relationship she thought she could count on for however much time she had left.

The memories she carried with her of golden days, of communion, of a filigreed cocoon built for two; that cozy, intimate table big enough, and small enough, just for them. Truman. And Babe.

He hadn't loved her, after all; he'd used her, just as he used the others. She was important to him only for material—oh, it wasn't true, it couldn't be true! The one person in her life whom she had trusted enough to expose herself, scars and all—her Truman.

And now it was gone. All gone. Only her emptiness remained.

After all the time together, all the confidences shared, the fears revealed, how had he not understood her at all? He alone saw how desperately she worked to hide the unpleasantness in her life, in herself—and in her husband; to live up to the expectations bestowed upon her from birth. Truman, alone, knew how terrified she was of anyone seeing the truth.

Anyone but him.

So how could he not understand that in publicly exposing Bill's true nature, he was exposing Babe, as well? He'd humiliated her beyond reason, beyond anything Bill could ever do. Because Bill, for all his faults, was not a storyteller. Bill did not know how to use words to wound and expose. Now every housewife from Maine to California would read about her, Babe Paley—the woman in the fashion magazines, the epitome of all they desired to become—and see her, defective, ugly, out of control; all the flaws she battled, all her life, so that she could be a good girl, the perfect girl, Beautiful Babe.

Daddy's perfect little girl; Mama's great hope.

Babe rolled over on her side, wrapping her arms around herself for comfort, and began to rock back and forth. She heard the phone ring, and she knew who it was, but she did not leap to get it, as she always had, and knew, finally, that she never would again. Hot tears oozed out of her eyes, and she began to sob, mourning, keening, the loss of something so profound she marveled that the world outside her window still seemed to continue on, untouched.

The loss of trust, the loss of joy; the loss of herself.

The loss of her true heart.

WHEN BILL JOINED HER for a quiet dinner in her room—she took many of her meals now on a tray, barely able to eat although she still did her best to see that Bill's palate was continually delighted—he didn't say anything at first. Babe folded her arms and glared at him, steadily, all the while he was peppering his steak. Finally he looked at her.

"I read it," he said.

"And?"

"If I ever see that fat little fag again, I'll kick him all the way back to Dixie."

"And?"

"I'm sorry." Bill put the pepper grinder down with a weary sigh. "I'm sorry, Babe. I'm sorry for everything. I'm sorry you're ill. I'm sorry I'm such a bastard. I'm sorry that our friend did this to you— and to me. I'm sorry I ever saw Truman Capote, allowed him on my plane that evening. I'm just sorry, all the time, every minute of the day."

"All right."

That's all Babe said, that's all Bill said, about the matter. They ate their dinner in silence. And they never spoke to each other of ugliness, betrayal, mistakes—or Truman Capote. Ever again.

The end.

. . . . .

THE NEXT MORNING, TRUMAN WENT TO THE SET WITH A mouth so dry he could barely whisper his god-awful lines, but nobody seemed to notice; in fact, the director had already given up on him and this picture. The man simply threw up his hands and filmed what he could, which wasn't much. Truman was excused from the set and spent the rest of the afternoon composing witty telegrams and sending them off.

His phone rang, all the time, and he answered, with a practiced smirk, "Truman Capote, literary assassinator," which never failed to elicit a laugh. It rang and rang with the calls of gossip columnists, the booking agents for Johnny and Dick, old "friends," such as Mailer, asking, with fake concern, how he was holding up; it rang with the calls from the editor of *Esquire,* who gloated over the number of copies flying off the stands—"You'll give us another story, won't you, Truman? As soon as possible?"

But Babe didn't call. Neither did Slim nor Marella nor Gloria nor Pam; he had no one with whom to gush and preen and tell him he was simply the tops, True Heart, really; how on earth do you do it? He had reached C.Z. late yesterday, and burst into tears, so relieved to have someone—*important,* familiar, and dear—answer the phone that he could scarcely articulate his joy, his appreciation at being invited down to Palm Beach to commiserate—no, of course, he meant *celebrate*—on her golden shoulder.

Then he glanced at the clock; it was nine o'clock in the evening back in New York. Well, why not give it one more try?

He dialed the Paleys, and at the last minute had the brilliant idea to ask for Bill, instead of Babe. And joy of joys! He was put right through! His heart pounded so loudly in his ears, he was afraid he wouldn't be able to hear a thing. But then Bill's voice said "Hello," and he sounded perfectly dry and calm. Normal.

"Bill! It's me, Truman, darling!"

"Yes?"

"Well, did you read it?"

"What?"

"My article, my story in *Esquire*! What did you think? I'm dying to know, of course—everyone is being so coy!"

"I started it, Truman, but then I fell asleep. And then someone threw the magazine away while I slept."

"I can get you another one, you know—"

"No, it's fine. I don't have time for that right now. My wife is very sick."

And then Bill hung up.

His wife! Not Babe, not their shared dream, not his dearest friend in the world. But simply "my wife." As if Truman didn't know her at all.

Oh, the bitches! Bitches, all! And he was glad, glad, glad that he'd stung them so. Look what it was doing to his career! Look at how many more people recognized him on the street!

"I simply don't understand," Truman said, with a sorrowful, superior sigh, to Jack, to Liz Smith, to C.Z., to anyone who would take his call these days, who were never the people he wanted, after all. "They knew I was a writer. They knew I'd remember everything. What did they expect? And Babe! I really thought she was smarter than that. More sophisticated. Doesn't she get it, that I love her so, even if Bill never did? And now the world knows what a bastard he is. I did it for her! Doesn't she understand that?"

"You did it for yourself, Truman," was all Jack replied. He never, not once, said, "I told you so."

"Well, so what? So what if I did? I have to look out for myself, don't I? Nobody else ever has."

And so he girded himself; he booked a facial, a manicure, he bought some new clothes and took a flight back to the East Coast, descending upon Manhattan like a potentate. Grandly, he granted interviews, cooperated with Liz Smith in her article—"Truman Capote in Hot Water"—and fanned the fires of scandal, dancing ever faster as the flames leapt ever higher. He lunched at La Côte Basque, accompanied by photographers; he grinned devilishly up at the camera as he brandished a knife and fork. When *Esquire* ran another story, Truman gleefully posed for the cover dressed in black, pretending to file his fingernail with a stiletto.

Truman Strikes Back! Another Excerpt from Answered Prayers!

And that was it for *Answered Prayers*. He didn't have much of anything else written, and he knew, now, he never would. But he didn't tell anyone, not even Jack.

His phone rang; it rang off the hook. Mostly it was people eager to tell him just whose party he hadn't been invited to.

"Never mind," he told one and all. "I've been thinking of giving another party myself, you know, even better than my famous Black

and White Ball! And this time, I won't invite any of those old dino-
saurs, those ancient swans. This time, baby, it's only the *fabulous*
people!"

But he didn't give another ball. For some reason, all he could
picture was an image of himself standing in an empty ballroom,
holding a lone balloon.

"Who needed the Plaza, anyway?" Truman told Johnny, told
Dick, told the world; the world that still listened to him, at any rate.
Why, disco was where it was at! What a thrilling, absolutely divine
time to live! Truman Capote and Studio 54—soon the names were
joined together, he was just as much a fixture as Halston and Liza
and Bianca. He danced until his eyes rolled back in his head while
the cameras flashed away; he had sweaty sex in the basement dun-
geons with anonymous young centaurs who didn't hide their disgust at his bloated, decaying body, but who could be bought with
handfuls of coke and a few dropped names. He told himself this was
where it was at, baby; he was there, here, in, not out; he was dancing, spinning, twirling—top of the world, Ma!

So he wasn't invited to spend an endless, pampered summer on
Gloria's yacht anymore, every whim catered to, Babe and Gloria
and Loel and Bill hanging on his every word, applauding, adoring?
So what?

So Mrs. Vreeland didn't include him in her elegant dinners any
longer, although she did at least have lunch with him in her office,
on occasion, when no one else was around. So what?

So he spent too many nights passed out on his velvet couch, the
television flickering ghostly images across his closed lids, dreaming
of Babe, of lying next to her in her bed, not touching, not possessing, but belonging so thoroughly that he woke up sobbing, terrified

he was in one of those locked hotel rooms of his childhood, his pulse racing, his skin clammy, his mouth so dry he couldn't cry out despite the despair clawing its way out of his belly, up his throat, pounding his brain?

So what?

He saw the other swans sometimes. They couldn't keep him from the Met Gala, even if they tried. He'd taken an excruciating elevator ride with Gloria at Bergdorf's one day; she hadn't seen him when she got in. "Hello, Truman," she said icily, and that was that; La Guinness turned so that all he could see was her exquisite profile, her delicately etched face perched on that glorious neck. Her eyes flashed darkly, every muscle in that neck was clenched, but she didn't say one more word. He got out on the very next floor and took another elevator back down, where he ran out on the street, flung himself on the edges of the Pulitzer Fountain outside the Plaza—the spray of the water splotched his linen suit—and he was unable to remember why he'd gone into Bergdorf's in the first place. Then he put on his dark sunglasses and swept through the lobby of the Plaza, all the way back to the Oak Room Bar, where he had six martinis and had to be poured into a cab.

Once he telegrammed Slim—*Big Mama, I've decided to forgive you.* Now, how could she resist that? Big Mama, with her sense of humor, her love for her True Heart?

But all he heard was silence. Everywhere he went in Manhattan—and he haunted the places he still held dear, Tiffany's and the Plaza and Bergdorf's and 21; to tell the truth, he loathed Studio 54. It was so hot and the music hurt his ears—all he encountered were icy stares. The time-honored social "cut" he himself had practiced so many times.

But never had Babe used it, he realized. No, Babe had been too kind ever to do that to anyone. He wondered how she was doing. He'd heard that she wasn't getting any better. He picked up the phone to call her, dozens of times a day. But he always put the phone back on the receiver before he could.

And then, one day, he saw her again.

. . . . .

*T*HERE ONCE WAS AN OLD WOMAN WHO LIVED IN A SHOE. . . .

No, this couldn't be her, the woman he saw at lunch one day at Quo Vadis. No, this couldn't possibly be his Bobolink, not this frail, terribly aged creature who was so thin the clothes, for the first time in her life, did not look fabulous. No amount of expensive tailoring could make this woman look as if she belonged in anything but a hospital gown.

But it was Babe, after all; her beauty still shone, gallantly, through the grim mask of pain. And Truman, who had been lunching alone—none of his new "friends" ever got up before three in the afternoon—felt his heart beat wildly at the sight of her. For the first time in months he felt whole, perfect, and beautiful. As beautiful as he once had been—with her.

"Hello, Babe." He rose, his napkin clutched in his sweaty hand.

Babe paused; she was with her sister Betsey, who looked down at Truman as if she might want to eat him. "Hello, Truman." Babe didn't look at him; she didn't break into the joyful, delighted smile that he had been used to seeing.

Once upon a time.

"I—Babe, I did it for you," he found himself blurting out, even if she didn't appear to want to know anything further about him other than what he was eating for lunch. "I only did it for you. I thought you should know."

Babe cast her glorious eyes downward; he saw her shoulders tremble before she gathered herself. When she raised her face to him, she was herself once more; *his*, his beautiful Babe. The only woman—hell, the only person—he realized with a jolt, that he had ever loved.

Even more than his mama.

Babe's eyes, for just that moment, were completely sympathetic, aware; full of knowledge. Knowledge he alone had imparted, a secret code between best friends. Her eyes were warm—and grateful.

"I know," she whispered, turning away from Betsey, her voice intended for only his ears. He had to lean in to hear. "I know. And thank you."

He wasn't sure he'd heard it right; he thought he had. He *wished* he had—*Dear God let this be true forever and ever Amen.*

But she was already gone, gliding away, pulled by her sister; elegant as always, although very slow, each step deliberate, a defiant act of living. Her back was straight, formidable; she never turned to look at him. And so he wasn't sure, after all.

"Babe?" he whispered, and it was like before; he was sure she would hear him above the din of people laughing and chatting, and stop, pick him out, come back for him, take him with her.

But she didn't. He turned around, blindly, and felt hot, disapproving stares burning into his flesh. His ears buzzed with hissing and sneers, taunting, dismissive.

Truman plopped back down, knocking over a water glass, sending cutlery falling softly to the plush carpet. His heart slowed, but now his lungs seemed to be working overtime; he was cold and clammy, listing to the right, then to the left, as helplessly as if he were on choppy water, unmoored. Unloved.

And to his astonishment he burst into tears, sloppy, messy tears, and whispered, a cry from the tattered heart that he hadn't understood he'd possessed until now, "Babe, Babe, Babe," and then the maître d' was grabbing his arm, holding him up and escorting him from the restaurant, trying to shield him from the stares. The proprietor mumbled something about taking care of the bill, but Truman didn't care.

He knew that he would never see her again.

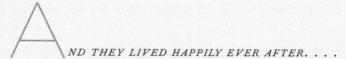

AND THEY LIVED HAPPILY EVER AFTER. . . .

Who did? Who the hell did? Babe wanted to know, on the days when she felt strong enough for outrage. Because she didn't. She sure as hell didn't. Life was no fairy tale, no matter what her mother had told her. She had no prince to kiss her, to wake her up from this nightmare.

She'd had a prince. Once.

It wasn't the tall man, stooped now, his shoulders hunched always with regret, with thinning silver hair, who sat by her bed and held her hand and sloppily cried on it. No, Bill wasn't her prince, and had he ever been? Maybe, once, when he promised her salvation in the form of riches, a fabulous partnership designed to be the envy of all. Maybe then. When riches and prestige were the only things that mattered to her; when she was still her mother's daughter.

But then she met another. A fair-haired prince, her true love. And they told each other all their secrets, bared to each other their souls, and were going to live happily ever after together. They'd even talked about it, how she'd most likely outlive Bill, and so the two of them would live together, become one of those touching older couples who still held hands, still danced in the evening when the shadows were long, while a scratchy phonograph played "The Tennessee Waltz."

That was the story they told each other, after the first story, the story of how they met, was no longer sufficient; when the future was closer than the past. But no less golden.

But now she was dying, and Bill was the one who would remain. And Truman could not be by her side, holding her hand, even though she longed for his touch, cried out for it, she feared, when she was not herself, when the medicine could not ease the pain, the terror of not being able to draw breath, of being suffocated. She wanted Truman in the same way she'd wanted her father when she was little, when she was scared, when she knew something ominous and terrifying was looming, and she was too small by herself.

But she couldn't have Truman, she wouldn't have Truman. Truman had betrayed her, betrayed Bill, betrayed the family they had created. "We stick together. We don't air our dirty laundry. Family is first, family is everything." Her mother's words still trumped all—all feeling, all impulse, all longing. All compassion.

Because deep in her heart, Babe knew something else, too.

"We betrayed him," she told Slim on one of her good days, when she was able to sit up against the pillows, wear one of her beautiful quilted satin bed jackets, have a visitor for a precious few minutes. One of the days when the medicine didn't dull her senses and put her under so deeply that she had no idea what day it was, even if it was day or night, if she was five or twenty-five or fifty-five, if she was Alice through the Looking-Glass or Tweedledum or Tweedledee; if she was healthy or ill.

"What on earth are you talking about, Babe?" Slim sat in a chair next to Babe's bed; her hands twitched, not sure what to do without the usual cigarette. Babe always insisted that her guests be treated as of old, but most were too polite to smoke in her presence.

So Slim examined her manicure instead and frowned at Babe. "What the hell do you mean, Babe?"

"I think—I think part of the whole thing was that he was testing us, testing us to make sure we loved him. Really loved him. Because true love means forgiving, no matter what. And we failed him. We didn't love him that way."

"Nonsense. You did."

"I did. But—maybe I didn't. Not enough. Maybe I never could love anyone, truly. Maybe I'm just not capable."

Babe's eyes were dry, her voice weak, but steady. She was not seeking sympathy, Slim understood. She was quietly stating a fact of her life, a fact that she must have suffered hell to conclude. Her friend had gone through the trials of Hades lately; maybe she'd gone through them all her life but never let on. Because, of course, she wouldn't. Babe Paley could never reveal that her life was anything but enviable.

"I think you're wrong, Babe. Don't make excuses for Truman. That bastard doesn't deserve it."

"Yes, he does. We all do, Slim. You'll understand, one day."

Babe leaned back and closed her eyes; Slim wondered if she should leave her.

"I have everything planned, you know," Babe murmured, opening her eyes, even more solemn and thoughtful now that they could see beyond the physical plane.

"What do you mean?"

"My funeral. The reception, after. The menu is already planned. The flowers, everything. I couldn't leave that for Bill, or my children. They shouldn't have to worry about all that. So I left everything with my secretary, but I wanted you to know, too. She has all the details. The caterers and florists have already been notified."

"Christ, Babe." Slim was shaking. Babe smiled and reached out her hand; Slim grasped it blindly.

"It's fine, Slim. I wanted to do it. It seemed—it seemed right. The best way. I'm a doctor's daughter, remember? I know what's happening, what will happen. I have no illusions about death. We do what we have to do, what's right and important, while we're living. Not after."

Slim inhaled, a big, sloppy, phlegm-soaked breath; she started coughing, a true fit, and had to have a glass of water. When finally the fit was over, and her chest hurt and her eyes were streaming, she saw that Babe was laughing, quietly.

"I'm the one who's supposed to do that," she teased, with that rare twinkle in her eye; the twinkle that Truman had so often brought out, to the surprise and delight of all. "Not you!"

"I'm going to miss you," Slim blurted out, then clasped her hand to her mouth, horrified for saying it.

"I know." Babe nodded, and seemed relieved to hear it. "But you'll be fine, Slim. That's one thing I know about you. You're a survivor."

Slim left Babe then, after a kiss to her smooth, moisturized, made-up cheek, and a whisper to "get some sleep, dear."

But as she went down the hall, stopping first to see Bill, who was slumped in an armchair outside Babe's room, kissing him, as well, embracing him as if the big, rangy man was a child, clutching him to her chest for a few moments while they both murmured soothing, nonsensical words, she wondered what Babe had meant by that.

"You're a survivor," Babe had said, and there was no emotion in her voice at all, none of the tears that Slim had shed upon hearing it.

What did she mean? Slim told herself she'd never know, even as she felt a tickle of fear race up and down her spine. She turned to Bill, thought about asking him, but knew that now was not the time. Bill was a broken man, crumbled by enough guilt to bring down the Empire State Building. No need to pile on. She would not be that woman; the kind of woman who made someone else's tragedy all about herself.

There would be plenty of time for wondering, once it was all over. Too much time. Too much time without Babe, without Truman, without kindness and elegance and oh, Christ, the laughter.

A dull, dismal lifetime.

BABE WOKE UP ONE MORNING knowing that she wouldn't wake up again; it had been too much effort to swim up from the darkness, and she didn't welcome consciousness and one more glimpse of the sun; one more day lying like a specimen, her family hovering over her, counting every single breath she managed to take.

So she gestured to a nurse, who understood; the nurse brought her a tray filled with her cosmetics, a small mirror on a stand, and Babe Paley did her makeup one last time, with the same calming sense of ritual she'd always had when she'd looked in the mirror, starting first with the foundation, applied with a sponge, so shakily now—the sponge weighed like a heavy stone in her translucent fingers although she couldn't really feel it, as her extremities were cold and numb. But she didn't flinch from the mirror, from the ravaged remnants of a person staring back; she knew she could conceal the damage, the flaws, and emerge beautiful, the butterfly from the chrysalis, one last time. She had to pause and take long gasps from the oxygen mask; she had to rest between applications, between the foundation and then the blush and then the concealer, and then the eye shadow, the intricately applied layers, and then the liner, which, with a grim determination, a gritting of her teeth, she managed to quiet her shaking hands long enough to apply flawlessly, the line straight and smooth, and she lay the liner brush down with a sigh, and felt as if she'd won a battle, the last battle. Now she was ready.

Now they could all come in, Bill and Tony and Amanda and Bill Junior, and Kate, the bald little girl whom her mother could barely look at, because her own flaws were on flagrant display in this child. Kate was now an angry young woman, and Babe sensed that she didn't want to be there because she still couldn't forgive her mother for her neglect, and Babe didn't blame her. Babe really didn't care who was standing vigil around her deathbed, but she knew that Kate would regret it forever if she hadn't been there. Babe remembered sitting by her mother's bed when Gogs passed away; she had felt so very detached and even resentful, but still.

It had been the right thing to do.

"Where's Truman?" She heard the words, and since she was too tired to speak them, they must have escaped from her heart. She was so very tired now, so weary, so done with it all. They were all there, but she had never felt so alone. Not since—before.

No one answered, and Babe had to wonder if anyone else had heard the question. She shouldn't have asked it; she didn't mean to. She shouldn't let them all see how much she needed him. This was their moment, her husband's, her children's. She saw them, through fluttering eyelids; their eyes were red, their expressions numb. She felt them pressing around her, holding her hands, touching her shoulder, but still they weren't enough, she was cold, she was drifting, she was alone, so alone.

And then she was nothing.

FOR HOURS, BILL SAT HOLDING his wife's hand; the children drifted in and out, but he remained. Bill Paley, titan of the boardroom, king of the airways. He sat holding his wife's chill, fragile hand, long after she had stopped breathing.

She still looked beautiful. Like a Modigliani, an Italian sculpture, etched in marble.

She'd died hating him, he knew. Hating him, but loving Truman.

But granting him the privilege of a grieving husband; one last time, covering for him, and his sins. Allowing the world to see him as who he wanted to be, and not who he was.

That was Babe, he thought. Graciously and thoughtfully arranging his life, to the very end.

. . . . .

TRUMAN READ OF HER DEATH IN THE *TIMES*. "BARBARA CUSH-
ing Paley Dies at 63; Style Pace-Setter in Three Decades; Symbol
of Taste."

When he read it, he had to smile; she would certainly be pleased.
For despite her protests, Bobolink had reveled in her image, had
worked hard at it, harder than he had ever worked on a book in his
life. Every minute of every hour of every day was spent cultivating
her style, perpetuating the myth, and he had always admired that
about her, even when Jack and others decried it as shallow and
pointless.

"You don't understand," he'd always said, defending her.
"She's an artist, like you, like me. She dedicates her life to creating
beauty. It just happens that the product is herself instead of a canvas
or a sculpture or a poem. What's wrong with that?"

They'd never understood, his artist friends, his fellow authors,
the ones he'd met back at the beginning at Yaddo, the dreary, serious souls who couldn't afford lunch at Quo Vadis unless their publishers were paying; his "contemporaries," as they insisted on being

called. But then, they never understood Truman, either. They were jealous, that's all. Envious. Green with it, absolutely emerald.

He knew Babe was dying; hadn't he resigned himself to the fact that they wouldn't reconcile? Hadn't he taken it like a good, stoic little boy? Hadn't he stopped calling, stopped telegraphing, letting her die in peace?

Hadn't he known he wouldn't be invited to the funeral, and had determined to spend that day in quiet reflection in his apartment, surrounded by the things she'd bought him over the years, the antique paperweights for his collection, a painting here, a bibelot there, the Oriental rug in the foyer, the ruby cuff links, the silly, thoughtful little things that amused him, like the scarf printed with tiny little Elvises holding guitars, because Truman had once rolled his eyes and growled, "That boy from Memphis really gets my motor running!"

But when the day arrived, he couldn't get out of bed. He felt crushed by a despair more enormous than his good intentions. He watched those intentions fly right out the window; weightless, fluttering, silly little things, chased away by the rhinoceros that settled on his chest.

So he reached for a drink; the vodka bottle was on the nightstand.

Soon, he'd had enough to enable him to shove that rhinoceros off the bed, throw on some clothes, cover himself in a black opera cloak—and in a corner of a drawer, a flash of color caught his eye. It was the orange flower he'd bought at the market in Jamaica that wonderful, glorious day with her, when the sky was azure, the sun was a luscious golden dream, and everyone was smiling, bright white teeth flashing, the air scented with jasmine and Babe's perfume—what was it again?

Oh, yes. Vent Vert, that grassy, crystalline fragrance.

Truman's hands shook as he picked up the flower, now faded, the edges frayed. He pinned it to the cloak with fat, fumbling fingers; he stuck his forefinger with the pin and sucked the droplet of blood. *Tasteless,* he thought, only mildly curious. *My blood has no taste. I have pickled it beyond its essence.*

Then he stumbled out the door, into the elevator, and into the arms of the doorman. He mumbled that he needed a taxi.

"Where to?" inquired the doorman.

"Manhasset."

"Long Island?"

"Where else?"

The doorman shrugged, picked up a phone, and in five minutes a taxi was at the door. Truman handed the man a wad of cash and croaked, "Christ Episcopal Church in Manhasset."

The driver pocketed the money and they drove off; once in a while, he looked in his rearview mirror, unsure if his passenger was or was not Truman Capote. The bloated, pink face, the outrageous black hat, black opera cloak, flaming flower—they sure looked like something a fag would wear. But the eyes were obscured by dark round glasses, so he didn't know for sure.

"Hey, are you Truman?" He couldn't stand it; he had to know.

"Yessss," Truman lisped, exaggeratedly, like a snake hissing. "Yesssss, I ssssure am."

"Thought so!" And the cabbie left him in silence the entire way, except for when Truman asked him to stop at a liquor store and he said, "Sure thing!" and waited while Truman lurched inside, only to emerge with a bottle of vodka.

"Proceed," Truman instructed. So they did.

"What's the traffic for?" the cabbie asked, when finally they drew near the church fronting a tree-lined street packed with limousines and Town Cars and cabs. "Is it a wedding?"

"No." Truman told the cab to stop and wait; then he got out, still grasping the bottle. He looked about, furtively; he seemed to tuck his head into his cloak, like a turtle, and he sank back into the embrace of a wisteria tree. The cabbie rolled down his window; it was hot this July of 1978, and he wondered how Truman could stand the heavy cloak.

Truman, safely hidden, watched as they gathered on the sidewalk in front of the church, embracing, air-kissing, dabbing eyes. There was Diana, the divine Mrs. V, in a fabulous long-sleeved embroidered dress with a dragon-red mandarin collar; there were Betty Bacall, Kay Graham, Kenneth himself, and, of course, all his swans, Slim and Marella and Gloria and Pam and C.Z. Those bitches. Those glorious creatures. Oh, what were they talking about? Were they mourning Babe?

Had they ever mourned him, as he mourned them?

And did they hate him, as he hated them? For being so stupid, so breathtakingly idiotic, as to not understand who he was, after all?

"I *made* you all," he whispered, the words as tart upon his tongue as his blood had been bland. "You were just *material*. And I fooled you. I fooled you all."

As he watched them air-kiss and shake their glorious heads—goodness, Gloria's turban was absolutely to die for, he could see the ostrich egg–sized jewel all the way over here!—it was like his ball, all over again, all the same players, only this time, everyone was wearing black. A black ball. And he was blackballed—Truman giggled, and drank more, and his stomach was like a vat of gurgling lava, everything bubbling up and over, and he belched, hiding it behind his hand even though he was across the street and in a bush, and nobody could see him.

And then he saw the casket come out, and Bill was following it, his hands clasped in front of him, his head bowed, and Truman studied him for a moment, silently applauding his performance. The man did look devastated, he'd give him that. He wondered if the bastard would pick up someone at the funeral reception?

But then Truman forgot Bill, and vowed that he never would again think of him, Big Bill, the Great White Father. Instead, he watched the casket, very small, covered in flowers, carried on the shoulders of men he couldn't identify from so far away, presumably Babe's nephews and cousins. The casket was his only focus, and inside it was the very best part of him and he knew it would be buried deep within the ground, and soon it would be autumn, then winter, and snow would fall upon it, covering all traces of the only good thing that had ever happened to him. He heard sounds coming from deep within himself, moans, songs of sadness, broken lullabies, as he rocked back and forth, registering, finally, the loss of love, the shattered romance of it, the tragic ending handed to him by fate and disease.

It wasn't his fault, it wasn't hers. It was simply the universe, deciding to tear them apart, like all great lovers. Romeo and Juliet. Tristan and Isolde.

Truman and Babe.

And it was hell now, knowing that he wasn't invited, wasn't asked to say good-bye, and it was the same old thing, the same well-worn record, played over and over and over, that he wasn't good enough, wasn't man enough, wasn't enough for her, after all. For anybody. Look at him, standing here, crying all by himself, pissing himself, choking on vodka and tears, all alone, again. Still. Forever.

Truman watched as the casket was loaded into the hearse; one of the pallbearers fumbled a bit, didn't let go, and almost found himself dragged into the hearse right along with it. Then the door was closed, the beautiful people slid into their cars—into the backseats, behind their drivers—and the procession left, and Truman still remained, freezing cold despite the sun, a terrifying emptiness in which something cold and brittle rattled around, maybe it was his heart, maybe it was just the glass shards of the last vodka bottle, and he didn't know what to do next; he was Vivien Leigh at the end of *Gone with the Wind*, a tearstained, remorseful bitch.

Oh, Rhett! Where shall I go? What shall I do?

"Rough day, huh, Truman?"

Truman blinked, squinted his eyes; the cabbie was in front of him.

"That's not the line, darlin'."

"Huh?"

"Never mind."

"Let's go home, huh, Truman? You don't look so good."

"Neither do you," Truman retorted, but it wasn't malicious; he hiccuped, shook with drink and loss and grief, and allowed the cabbie to fold him back into the car.

"Let's go home, chum."

As the yellow cab turned around in the now-empty street, Truman leaned back, dizzy and suddenly drenched in heat and sweat; he threw off the black cloak, crushing the flower beyond repair. He closed his eyes and slept.

An hour later, he opened them; they were on Fifth Avenue.

"Tell me," he cooed, rubbing his eyes, "are you single?"

The cabbie's eyes met his in the rearview mirror; there was a flicker of interest that Truman had seen all his life in men of the heterosexual persuasion who suddenly found themselves propositioned by a celebrity.

But then the cabbie flashed an apologetic grin and said, "Nah."

"Pity," Truman replied, closing his eyes, resigned to his loneliness now and forevermore.

And then he took another drink. Because that's what Mama would want him to do.

"I HALF EXPECTED TRUMAN to show up," Pamela whispered, and though everyone leaned in to hear, they were not accosted by her bosom, as she had covered it up with black Italian lace for the solemn occasion.

"If he had, Bill would have thrown him out himself." Gloria sipped the impeccable wine that Babe had chosen for the occasion, her favorite Pouilly-Fumé de Ladoucette.

They were at Kiluna, surrounded by Babe. In every flower, every white-jacketed waiter, every elegantly folded napkin, every soft note of music playing from the outdoor speakers, even the birds chirping, the scent of freesia, lilies, roses everywhere—she was there.

The women were seated together; their husbands surrounded Bill, a silent ring of wealthy and powerful bodyguards, protecting him from something, something none of them could recognize, but there was a threat, nonetheless; they sensed it.

And the threat was female, had they been able to think clearly; already there were anxious women circling, hovering, waiting to have a sympathetic word with the new widower, to assure him they were there for him, would be happy to console him in his grief with a quiet dinner, just the two of them, some evening when he was up to it.

"Babe wouldn't have minded, I don't think, if Truman had been there," Slim said, and the others gasped in shock. "No, really. Do you know what she said, before she died?"

"Nothing about him, at least not to me. You know, I saw her the day before," Gloria said icily.

"I saw her the evening before," Pamela pointed out.

"I was in Palm Beach," C.Z. said glumly. "But I telephoned that night."

"Anyway," Slim interrupted. "She told me that she had betrayed Truman, and not the other way around."

"No!" All four gasped.

"Yes. She said that he'd thought we loved him, and that if we really had, we'd forgive him anything. That he was trying to test us, to see if we did, after all. And so we failed him."

"I never said I loved him!" Gloria was aghast, she began to twitch all over. "How dare he? He was amusing, that's all. Amusing, for a while. Talented, yes, of course, once upon a time. But no longer. And—not to speak ill of the dead"—she crossed herself vehemently—"but Babe is—was—an idiot, a softhearted idiot, to think any differently. He betrayed us. *Finis!*"

"You know how I feel about it all," C.Z. drawled, and everyone else stiffened in preparation, for they did know. "You have only yourselves to blame, not Truman. I think he's a helluva lot of fun— well, not lately, but back then, although he did bring me to that Studio Fifty-four thing, which was exciting, but I wouldn't go back—but the point is, I never told him anything important. Not a thing. I kept it all fun and light with him, and so he had nothing to use. You all should have done the same."

Slim, observing Gloria's neck begin to tense, her fingers fumble with the cutlery, hissed a warning: "Remember what we're here for, girls. We're here for Babe. *For her.* I shouldn't have brought it up. Never mind."

Gloria rose from her chair, stretched a little, balancing on the tips of her toes. Something in her knee popped, though, so she sank back down.

"In a way, Babe was the lucky one," she said, staring into the water glass, sensing the clouds begin to gather, soon to crowd out the sun.

"Oh, Gloria! What could you possibly mean?" Marella shook her head.

"She was only sixty-three. She got out with her beauty still more or less intact." Gloria smiled ruefully. "She didn't have to grow old. Hellishly old."

No one said anything, although each glanced at her own hands, then the hands of her friends, and where they once silently compared rings and jewels and bracelets, now they compared veins and wrinkles and dark spots.

"How long do you think Bill will last, before remarrying?" C.Z. nodded toward Bill, surrounded by his friends, his children. He looked dazed; he was eating a plate of Babe's marvelous food, but methodically, not with his usual gusto.

"Not long," Gloria replied.

"I think he'll stay single," Slim said defiantly. "I think he'll be fine, on his own. He'll surprise us all."

"No." C.Z. shook her head. "If ever there was a man who couldn't be single, it's Bill Paley. I'm grateful my Winston died before me. He couldn't have been on his own, either. Men like that—men who are so focused on one thing, one great, big thing—can't."

"I wonder how long Truman will last now. No matter what we think of him, I'm positive he's devastated by this," Pam mused, shrugging at Slim's glare.

"Not long," C.Z. said with a sigh of true concern. "Have you seen him on television lately? He's killing himself, just killing himself. It's like he wants to die, with all the booze and the coke and the pills."

"Well, that's one way to go," Gloria retorted. "And not a bad one. If he's really intent on doing himself in. He committed social suicide, and he caused a real suicide—poor Ann!—so who gives a damn if it leads to his own? Sometimes you just have to know when it's time to leave. You have to understand when your time is over. Your time in the sun. Our time is over, you know. With Babe gone, now it's well and truly over. The world isn't the same."

Slim narrowed her eyes at Gloria; apparently, she *was* the type of person who made someone else's tragedy all about herself.

"Shut up, Gloria. You're just feeling morbid today. So is everyone. I don't know about you, but I intend to live forever." Slim lit up a cigarette, wincing at the fact that she didn't have to think of Babe anymore when she did. "As for Truman," Slim retorted, inhaling in pure ecstasy, her eyes closed. "He's like a snake—no, a cockroach. He'll outlive us all."

Then she opened her eyes; they were full of tears.

"But Christ, wasn't it fun, back then? Back when we were young?"

The swans nodded, each lost in her own thoughts. Primarily of Truman, to their surprise; on this day of Babe's funeral, it was Truman they were thinking of. Truman, back then. Truman, sitting like a little boy, lithe legs crossed, at their feet, his blue eyes big with wonder, his golden hair brushing his forehead; Truman, reading his short stories at the Ninety-second Street Y, their pocket pet suddenly all grown up, brilliant, electric, a new jewel in their collection.

Truman and Babe dancing in the shadows at Kiluna, that meltingly beautiful, blissful smile on Babe's face, a sparkle in her eyes that none had seen before as she twirled around with abandon, finally sliding into Truman's arms, the two of them so content with each other, so at peace, that everyone else felt like intruders to look at them. Yet no one could take their eyes off the pair.

That's what the swans remembered, as they drank Babe's wine and ate her food one last time. Truman and Babe. Darkness and light, elegance and impudence. Beauty and brains, heart and soul.

Together.

La Côte Basque, 1984

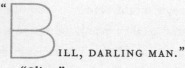

"**B**ILL, DARLING MAN."

"Slim."

They air-kissed, then allowed the maître d' to escort them to one of the front tables.

The restaurant hadn't changed much since Henri Soulé's death in 1966, the year of Truman's ball. The seaside murals on the walls were still there, the linens still the finest, the tables still groaned with fresh flowers, the bill for these rumored to be in the thousands per week. There was a new chef, but the food was still heavy French, with an emphasis on cream and butter.

Bill Paley and Slim Keith took their seats at an intimate table *à deux*. Instinctively, each sucked in his gut, sat up straight, scanned the room surreptitiously. But they were disappointed, it must be said.

For few of their contemporaries were present; the restaurant was mainly filled with businessmen on expense accounts. Bill, of course, knew some of these and nodded, while Slim relaxed, let out her breath, and lit a cigarette.

"Where the hell is everybody?" Slim asked, but it was a rhetorical question. She knew.

They'd gotten old, some had died. The Duke of Windsor had passed away even before Babe. Wallis was in France now, rumored to be mad as a hatter, locked away by servants.

Marella and Gianni still puttered around on their yachts but increasingly remained in Italy, at their palace, forgotten gods taking refuge on Mount Olympus. C.Z. still had her gardens, published many gardening books, and remained as unflappable as ever. Slim did still see her now and again when C.Z. was in Manhattan, serving on charity boards, her blond Boston beauty finely honed and weathered, so that she resembled that type of Brahmin matron she'd sworn she always loathed, but never tried too hard to prevent herself from becoming, at that. For all her fun, her breeziness, her memories of Diego Rivera, C.Z. had always dressed like a debutante. And now, like a figurehead with her pearls, cashmere, and tweed.

Then there was Gloria. La Guinness, as Truman had dubbed her.

Ah, Gloria.

"What do you think, Bill?" Slim turned to her companion, now very stooped, thinner than his rangy frame warranted. His hair was very sparse, and he had a hearing aid in one ear.

"What?" He turned up the aid.

"What do you think about Gloria? Do you think she really did it? Commit suicide?"

"It was a heart attack, wasn't it?" Like many men his age—eighty-three—his voice was querulous, high, and loud. Not the commanding bark it once had been.

"That's what Loel said, anyway. But one of her maids—well, it's just that she had been so despondent, so low, those last few years." Gloria had died in 1980; only two years after she'd envied Babe for checking out before growing too old.

"I don't believe that bunk." Bill signaled for the waiter, ordered some wine for the two of them. "Not Gloria. Why would anyone do that? Especially her?"

"Because she was beautiful," Slim replied quietly. "Once."

"So were you. Still are, to some." Bill grinned, and she glimpsed the man he had been, the man she'd known for more than fifty years; the man she first met, before he married Babe, on a fishing trip in Cuba with Papa. If she closed her eyes, she could visualize him then, brown all over, except for that blinding white smile. His hands, she remembered; that's what she first noticed about him. His hands, huge, always open, always grasping. Wanting more.

"Stop," Slim retorted, slapping away one of those hands now, as it grasped her knee. "We're too old for this."

"We didn't used to be. We could go up to the apartment, just like we used to." Bill grinned, and suddenly looked ten years younger. Maybe twenty.

And Slim relaxed; she allowed Bill to grasp her knee, she squeezed that huge hand, the fingers now knobby, arthritic, but the grasp still powerful. Sure of what he desired; certain that it could be attained.

Sex hadn't packed up and left, after all. She was surprised to feel that eager tingle between her thighs.

"I assume your wife is out of town, then?" Slim knew it was cruel, to remind him of their old game. But it slipped out.

Bill released her hand. They both picked up their menus.

"So, I imagine you heard about Truman?"

"Yeah." Bill sighed, then frowned, that old Bill Paley icy glare. "Well, I can't say I'm sad about it, Slim. Not at all. Not after what he did to Babe, to you, to me."

"Joanne Carson called me—you know, he'd been staying with

her, in that little room she had for him in Los Angeles. After we all banished him, that's where he ended up, in the back room of a TV star's ex-wife." Slim smiled grimly. "But she called me, after they took him away to the mortuary. She said that his last words were 'Beautiful Babe.' She wanted me to know that, for some reason." Slim choked a little, her eyes misting over with tears.

"Do you really believe that?"

"I'd like to. Wouldn't you?"

"No. I don't want to believe that little bastard was still in love with my wife. I don't want to believe his last words were about her. I don't want to believe anything other than Babe died peacefully, loving only me, and that Truman died painfully, alone. Call me cruel, if you want. But—"

"That's the story you want to tell yourself," Slim whispered. "I understand, Bill. Because I tell myself a lot of stories to help me sleep at night. Stories about how Babe was my dearest friend, and I never betrayed her. Stories about how you and I had a great love, not just an occasional roll in the hay whenever she was out of town. Stories about how wonderful life was back then, when none of us told each other the truth, but so what? It was all so beautiful, wasn't it? It was all so lovely and gracious. Not like it is now."

Neither spoke for a long time; they just gazed out at Fifty-fifth Street, full of tourists in their tourist clothes, sneakers and jeans, sweatshirts, windbreakers, those absurd Walkman headphones over their ears, blocking out the delicious sounds of the city. The St. Regis was just across the street, and still grand, but now rock stars stayed in the suites and nobody lived in hotels anymore. And it was owned by Sheraton. Astors and Vanderbilts and bears, oh, my; no one was afraid of any of them and their old money now. Not in the garish New York of the eighties and Donald Trump.

Bill Paley was still chairman of CBS, despite efforts over the last few years to oust him. Still, he was selling off stock, a little bit at a time; his days of acquisition were over. He'd already made plans to give his astounding collection of art to MoMA. Mostly, he played golf and swam and slept in his office between meetings at which he still made appearances, just to remind people who built the damn place, after all. To remind himself of that, as well.

"We do have a great love," Bill told Slim, told himself, as he told every woman he still took up to the apartment on Fifth, even now— why, hadn't he just been named one of *People* magazine's top ten eligible bachelors?

Although every time he brought some little cutie up there, he couldn't stop himself from giving a tour, a running narrative of Babe—Babe bought this, Babe put that there, Babe used to sit here, Babe felt that the dining room should be in this color . . . he'd never changed the apartment, had resisted efforts from his children to redecorate there, and at Kiluna. He couldn't bring himself to; they were the last things in the world he had of her, her essence, that gracious living that Slim was talking about. He knew everything she had picked out was now out of fashion, but he didn't care. He was too old to care.

"No, we don't have a great love, Bill. You were kind and very generous with money when I needed it; I was there for a diversion when you needed it, one of your blond shiksas. And I have to ask you a question, now that Truman's gone. Do you think Babe ever knew, Bill? Did Truman? Because the story—Truman's story in *Esquire,* about Sidney Dillon and the bloody stain—did you ever tell him about that? That one time with us?"

"No. Did you?"

"No."

Truth or consequences. That old familiar game. Neither really wanted to play it, after all.

"But Babe," Slim said after a pause, unable to let the subject drop as she knew she ought, "Babe said something before she died. She said I was a survivor. It seemed odd, at the time. Out of the blue. And then, you know, she didn't leave me much in her will, not like everyone else. God knows, I didn't care about that, except it did seem strange, considering how generous she was with everyone else, like Gloria and Marella and C.Z. I don't know. I just wonder."

"Babe didn't know. She couldn't. How? She could never have known that the woman in the story was you. Although she sure as hell knew the man was me." And Bill remembered how bitter Babe was those last couple of years; how free she was with her regrets, her suspicions. Her accusations.

"I hope she didn't know," Slim whispered, picking up a fork, weighing it in her hands, enjoying the cool heaviness of fine silver. "But I wonder . . ."

"Don't worry about it, Slim. It's over. They're both gone. And we're left."

"We're left with the memories. Not a great love, no, Bill, I don't think either of us was capable of that. But Truman and Babe, they were—well, Babe was, anyway, and I think that blinded her because in the end, Truman was Truman. But he did what we never could. He began to speak the truth. Not someone else's truth, not Perry Smith's or Holly Golightly's or even his own. No, he began to tell the truth about *us*. And the thing is, Bill, darling—the truth is ugly. Yours. Mine. Even Babe's."

Bill made a garbled, anguished sound; Slim saw his throat working, as if he was trying to swallow something, and she grasped his hand again, and placed it against her breasts, her saggy, deflated breasts, so that he could feel her, feel her heart, her femininity, her warm, solid self. She closed her eyes, enjoyed a man's hand upon her breasts for the first time in eons, and knew, right now, that she was alive, she was still here, not a memory, not a relic; not some old woman nobody looked at twice on the street. Not some forgotten name in a faded magazine, an answer to the question of "Where are they now?"

She opened her eyes. Bill was grinning at her with that ageless boy's leer, quite at odds with his watery, faded eyes, his visible hearing aid. But he had relaxed, his hand still upon her breasts, until she removed that hand and tucked it back on his own lap.

"So I still like to see you, my friend. I still like to sit in La Côte Basque and sip wine and eat fine food and indulge in our memories— the good ones, the ones we want to remember. So let's do that. That's the story we can tell ourselves, at night when we can't sleep. We can tell ourselves that there is one other person in the world who sees it in the same way, who remembers. Who remembers her. Babe. And Gloria. And even Truman, I guess, as he was, back then. Our fun, gossipy friend. Our entrée into a different world, for a time. An amusing, brief little time. A time before it was fashionable to tell the truth, and the world grew sordid from too much honesty."

Slim raised her glass; so did Bill.

"To Babe. To Truman. To Papa and all the other glittering, prevaricating ghosts of the past."

"To Babe," Bill echoed. And they clinked their glasses together in a toast, and spent the rest of the afternoon talking about their grandchildren.

———

IN THE END, AS in the beginning, all they had were the stories. The stories they told about one another, and the stories they told to themselves.

"I loved her, she was the great love of my life, my only regret," Truman breathed near the end, as he lay, exhausted from the world, from abuse, from himself, always himself.

"I loved him, he was the great love of my life," Babe whispered to herself as she closed her eyes and gave up the struggle, for it was ugly, and she'd never done an ugly thing in her life, and she wasn't about to start now.

"I'm alone," they each thought, and one was amused, the other appalled.

"Mama," Truman whispered, as a stranger held his hand, and called for an ambulance.

"Truman," Babe thought she said aloud, as she felt herself sinking, sinking, and then rising. But then she knew she didn't. And then she didn't know anything, ever again.

"Beautiful Babe," Truman said, and he knew he said it, he heard his own voice, very weak, strange to his ears. And then he heard no more.

Now there were no more stories to tell, to soothe, to comfort, to draw strangers close together; to link like hearts and minds.

To wound, to hurt. To destroy the one thing they each loved more than anything else—

Beauty. Beauty in all its glory, in all its iterations; the exquisite moment of perfect understanding between two lonely, damaged souls, sitting silently by a pool, or in the twilight, or lying in bed, vulnerable and naked in every way that mattered. The haunting glance of a woman who knew she was beautiful because of how she saw herself reflected in her friend's eyes.

The splendor of belonging, being included, prized, coveted.

The loveliness of a flower, lilies of the valley, teardrop blossoms snowy white against glossy green foliage. Made lovelier because of the friend's hand tenderly proffering the blossom, a present, a balm.

The beauty of understanding tears in an understanding face.

The beauty of a perfectly tailored shirt, crisp, blinding white, just out of the box.

The beauty of a swirl of taffeta, the tinkling of bells, diamonds, emeralds; a pristine paper flower.

Beauty.

THE SWANS SWAM AHEAD, always ahead, their bodies gliding so that none could see the effort of their feet beneath the surface, paddling, moving, propelling them forward, forward, to that beautiful spot far ahead, an incandescent curtain of light, a shower of moonbeams, a heavenly constellation of stars.

His body, however, was not like theirs; the effort always showed, and he panted and grunted, trying to keep up, sometimes managing to sprint ahead, but always his brow perspired, his chest heaved, his breathing was labored.

Sometimes the lead swan held out her hand, long and white and graceful, sometimes revealing rubies, sometimes emeralds; sometimes empty, waiting only for his hand to grasp it, and the two of them smiled their conspirators' smile and he felt himself no longer working so hard or falling behind, and it was effortless, the two of them together, pulling ahead of the others, sometimes turning to wink or grin.

But then, at the end; as the radiance began to descend upon them, *raining down diamonds and sea glass, something happened. He never knew what. Only that he faltered once, smiled, danced, turned his back or ran too far ahead, he never could quite understand which it was. But he closed his eyes, opened them, and found himself once more back on the shore, his feet caked in mud, rooted, left behind. Alone.*

And the swans swam on toward that shimmering waterfall of luminescence; they never looked back, no matter how much he cried, how he screamed until his throat was raw and his face was red; they glided forward, one by one disappearing into the slender shadows between the moonbeams, the lead swan allowing the others to go ahead; she stood guard, watching them. And finally, she turned to gaze at him once more with those grave, understanding eyes, and he screeched her name, begged her forgiveness, pleaded her favor, but she turned away to follow the others.

And she, too, vanished into the shadows between the light, and there was nothing left of any of them, only the faint ripples of their wake in the water, which he watched and watched with tears in his eyes, tears that turned into diamonds that turned into dust, the tremors of that wake widening, spreading, rippling into the crystal-dusted indigo of the pond that was the lake that was the ocean that was the dream of a forgotten world.

Until it, too, disappeared.

When I was a girl, I was one of those people who were drawn to New York.

I was born and raised in Indianapolis, Indiana. A lovely place, but I always had the sense that I didn't quite belong. Somehow— and I honestly don't remember how on earth this was possible— when I was fairly young, I got my hands on copies of *Vanity Fair* and *The New Yorker*. I suppose maybe they were carried in the local library, or perhaps the one bookstore at the mall stocked them. All I know is the first time I opened *The New Yorker*—not quite under- standing the cartoons, but pretending I did—I realized, finally, where I was meant to be.

And so I wished myself onto these magazines' sophisticated pages.

I read about—and imagined I knew intimately—people like Norman Mailer and Gore Vidal and Brooke Astor; I devoured de- scriptions of night life and openings and galas and vignettes about Central Park, Tiffany, Bergdorf Goodman, 21. Truman Capote was always featured in the pages of these magazines, and of course I knew about *him*. I saw him on television, a bloated, campy figure waving his hands, telling outrageous stories. I saw him in *Murder by Death,* which at age thirteen, I thought to be hilariously witty.

I knew that Truman Capote was the author of a book called *In Cold Blood,* a book my mother owned but wouldn't let me read. That was about all I knew about him from a literary perspective, however. He was simply one of those flamboyant 1970s characters, just like Liza Minnelli and Halston and the Village People.

In the pages of *Vanity Fair,* I also read, frequently, of a woman named Babe Paley. A fashion icon—that was always how she was described, along with other names like Gloria Guinness, Marella Agnelli, and Slim Keith. By the time I was aware of these women, they were already spoken of reverently, in the past, a past that was still longed for even in the late 1970s. They were ghostly, beautiful images to me, wearing clothes that were exquisite and unattainable. I didn't know anything about "fashion," of course; I got all my clothes at Sears and J.C. Penney. But I dreamed of fashion, just as I dreamed of New York, and the only thing I regret in my life is that I didn't get there. I was a child of the Midwest, of midwestern parents who, well-intentioned, instilled the fear of God and big cities in me, even as I visualized myself on gritty urban streets, fantasized about taking the subway, longed to be surrounded by skyscrapers and people who talked loudly and in interesting accents. But the fear won out, I'm sorry to say. For a very long time.

But these people, and these streets, have lived in my imagination ever since, and I've read everything there is about them. *Party of the Century* by Deborah Davis, about Truman Capote's famous Black and White Ball. *Capote* by Gerald Clarke. *Truman Capote* by George Plimpton. *Fifth Avenue, 5 A.M.* by Sam Wasson. *Slim,* the memoir of Slim Keith. And *The Sisters* by David Grafton, about Babe Paley and her sisters. I've seen *Breakfast at Tiffany's* more times than I can count. I continue to subscribe to both *Vanity Fair* and *The New Yorker.*

And of course, now I've read Capote's own work, and admired most of it—*Other Voices, Other Rooms; In Cold Blood;* his short stories; and *Breakfast at Tiffany's.* The only work of his that I didn't admire, and which was rather a shock to read, was *Answered Prayers,* which included the short story "La Côte Basque 1965." It didn't seem like his other writing, not at all. I tallied it up to an unfortunate mistake.

But then, one day, I decided to learn more about this unfinished novel. I had known, vaguely, that it resulted in a good old-fashioned literary scandal. I understood the basic details—Truman had divulged secrets that he shouldn't have. He'd tattled, and called it literature. His friends had shunned him. And then he turned into that grotesque figure I knew from my youth. And then he died.

But of course, there's more to the story than that. Isn't there always?

At the heart of everything written about Truman Capote and *Answered Prayers* is always the story of his friendship with Babe Paley. Babe is a sometimes aloof, if gorgeous creature. To me, she's always a bit heartbreaking. "The original trophy wife"—I've seen that phrase used to describe her, often.

Yet that friendship kept buzzing about my brain. That unusual friendship between the grotesque Truman and the exquisite Babe. How? Why? What did it really mean to the two of them? When I looked at photos, and I saw how physically stunning Truman was, back when this relationship was new, I was astonished. This was *not* the Truman Capote I had known growing up.

And that was the puzzle, to me. What had happened to him, to turn him into the caricature I remember, that we all remember when we hear the name "Truman Capote"? What had happened between him and Babe, who was purported, by so many who knew him, to be the one person he had ever loved?

What had happened to them all, these mythological creatures in their penthouses; what had happened to New York, to sophistication, to elegance, to fairy tales?

That's what I wanted to write about; that's the story I wanted to tell: What happened to Truman Capote. What happened to his swans. What happened to elegance. What truly was the price they paid, for the lives they lived. For there is always a price. Especially in fairy tales.

WITH EVERY BOOK I write, I am more aware that some readers are very curious to know what is fact and what is fiction. I have to say, this book has been the most fun to write by far, since all of its characters were incurable liars in life. This gave me quite a lot of leeway, and it was tremendously interesting to imagine myself into all of these wonderful storytellers' lives. But for those who are curious, here are some guidelines:

All conversations are imagined, although some—like the conversation between Truman Capote and Liz Smith near the end—are known to have occurred. But what exactly was said? That is what I fictionalize. The timeline is faithful. The fallout from *Answered Prayers* is true to life. The relationships are real; in other words, Truman and Babe and Bill Paley were that tight little trio. Slim was Babe's closest female friend. And the salient facts are from life: Ann Woodward was suspected of murdering her husband. She did commit suicide after reading "La Côte Basque 1965." Babe Paley did have cancer. Truman Capote did die in Joanne Carson's guest room. And so on. The biggest liberty I took concerns the rumored identity of the woman with whom the Bill Paley character had an affair in "La Côte Basque 1965." At the time, the gossip was that it was Happy Rockefeller, the wife of the governor. More likely, the woman in the story was an amalgamation of the many women with whom Paley had affairs—including, if the gossip was to be believed, Slim Keith. While Slim was definitely the model for Ina Coolbirth in the story, it is also a fact that Babe did not, in her will, leave her dear friend very much. Who told her, then, about Slim and Bill? Who, indeed?

As I always say, the emotions are what I imagine; the motivations and intent behind some of these documented acts. The facts are the bones upon which I stretch the fictionalized flesh. And I hope that you are inspired, after reading *The Swans of Fifth Avenue*, to learn more about these extraordinary, impossibly glamorous, yet ultimately tragic lives on your own. The books I mentioned earlier are excellent places to start, along with Sally Bedell Smith's *In All His Glory: The Life of William S. Paley* and *Conversations with Capote* by Lawrence Grobel.

I never did make it to New York to live. But I did make it to Chicago, which I love; finally, I'm a big city girl. And I visit New York a lot now. I see ghosts in the streets, everywhere I go. Once, in the Plaza, I thought I saw Babe Paley and Truman Capote sitting in a corner, having a glass of champagne.

But it was only a dream, after all.

A C K N O W L E D G M E N T S

ONE CAN WRITE A BOOK ALONE, BUT THAT BOOK WON'T
see the light of day without the help of a lot of very special people:

Thank you, as always, to the wondrous Kate Miciak, my editor;
we have climbed a lot of mountains together and I know there are
more to come. Also to Laura Langlie, my agent, who fights so many
battles on my behalf.

Much gratitude to Gina Centrello and her team of dedicated
professionals at Penguin Random House: Libby McGuire, Susan
Corcoran, Kim Hovey, Gina Wachtel, Sharon Propson, Quinne
Rogers, Leigh Marchant, Robbin Schiff, Allyson Pearl, Benjamin
Dreyer, Loren Noveck, and Julia Maguire. A special thank you to
Scott Shannon and his amazing digital team. Also to Bill Contardi,
to Caitlin McCaskey and Anastasia Whalen at the Penguin Ran-
dom House Speakers Bureau, and to the amazing Penguin Random
House sales reps.

Special thanks to Victoria Wasserman at Thornwillow Press,
and Courtney Scioscia and Slater Gillin at Meg Connolly Commu-
nications for allowing me to tour the St. Regis Hotel. Also many
thanks to the Research Division of the New York Public Library.

And as always, I would be nothing without the support of my
family, especially Dennis, Alec, and Ben.

The Swans

OF

Fifth Avenue

MELANIE BENJAMIN

A READER'S GUIDE

WHAT WOULD BABE DO?

Since the hardcover of *The Swans of Fifth Avenue* was published, I've been asked by many readers if there was any one particular Swan who has influenced me in my own life; if there's one I personally identify with.

I always answer that I think I identified the most with Slim Keith; her voice in the book is the most like my own. I loved her attitude, her ability to cut through the bullshit. I loved that she alone didn't really seem to take all the trappings of wealth seriously.

But as far as who's influenced me the most, I think I'd have to answer Babe. Because there have been several times, since writing the book, when I've found myself asking WWBD?

What Would Babe Do?

It came up when I was preparing for my book tour last winter. All of a sudden, my typical author wardrobe didn't seem up to snuff: How could I go out and talk about these fabulous women wearing my usual black upon black upon more black? So I asked myself, What Would Babe Do?

Babe would purchase an entire new wardrobe. She would build it meticulously, piece by piece. She would spend days trying each piece on, combining them in different ways, looking for maximum impact. Maximum fabulousness.

It was a little hard to convince my husband that my frequent outings to Bloomingdale's and Nordstrom were vital to my career, but ultimately, I stopped trying to convince him, asking myself once more—

What Would Babe Do?

She'd go shopping anyway. And so I did.

When it came time to pack this fabulous wardrobe for the tour, I wrestled with the usual dilemma. Do I bring everything or pack lightly? WWBD?

She'd bring everything. So into my brand new suitcase (another result of WWBD?) everything went.

Should I pack carry-on? Resign myself to a few tiny jars of the bare minimum of toiletries—a tube of all-purpose moisturizer, toothpaste, mouthwash—and hope for the best? Or should I bring along my dependable arsenal, my jars and tubes of unguents and potions: the toner and concealer and night cream and day cream and wrinkle cream and eye cream, the perfume, the liquid foundation, the shampoo and conditioner and styling product, the hairspray? The hand lotion that smells like lavender?

What Would Babe Do?

In the suitcase went everything; out the window went the convenience of not having to check the bag.

Now, I know authors who can breeze through a tour with one single backpack. I have never been one of those authors, but I've always felt terrible about that. I've always suspected that I'm way more high-maintenance than most of my peers, and that isn't a comfortable feeling. Or—it wasn't. Until I spent a lot of time with Babe Paley while researching and writing *The Swans of Fifth Avenue*. And I realized that depending upon a ritual, finding delight in the discipline of maintenance, of pampering, of making up and dressing well, isn't the frivolous time-waster I used to think it was.

Babe lived in a different era, an era when a hairdresser visited her every day to set, style, and spritz. A fabulous, glamorous time—a time I sometimes long for, to tell the truth, especially when I'm jammed into an airplane protected from my seatmate by only a thin layer of yoga pant, watching fellow passengers floss their teeth or trim their nails.

Every day, after hours spent perfecting herself, Babe emerged from her home looking rested, ready, and beautiful. Every single day, even if she was just walking the dog. And it was a treat to see her, according to every account. A feast for the eyes. And for the senses.

Isn't that lovely? That she cared enough to give that to the world? That she respected people enough to live up to their expectation of her?

I'm not saying I present such a picture, and even at my most vain, I don't spend hours on my hair. But I do appreciate the time and consideration that Babe gave to her appearance; it's a treat to look at all the photos of her, and marvel at such perfection, such an ornament of a different, more glamorous time.

I know I'll never look like Babe Paley. I also know I don't have to; I have a different canvas for my art—the page—whereas Babe's only creative outlet, her only canvas, was herself. I'm the lucky one, of course.

But I also no longer feel uncomfortable about my own somewhat high-maintenance schedule; I don't discount it as wasted time or vanity run amok. I no longer feel sheepish about not being able to travel with only a backpack and a toothbrush. Because at the end of the day, after I've unpacked all my unguents and potions and hung all my nice clothes and lined up all the shoes, I feel special. Cared for. By myself.

And isn't that a nice gift? To bestow attention upon yourself, to pamper yourself?

Isn't it a nice gift to give to everyone who happens to pass you on the street, or sit next to you on a plane, or show up at your book signing? The gift of your best, most polished self?

I think so. And that, more than anything else, is What Babe Paley Would Do.

QUESTIONS AND TOPICS
FOR DISCUSSION

1. The Swans have very complicated relationships with one another—perhaps most notably, Slim and Pamela were both married to the same man. What ties these women together, despite their differences and the sometimes competitive nature of their friendships?

2. Truman is embraced wholeheartedly by the Swans when he first appears on the New York social scene. What do you think draws them to him?

3. Discuss Babe's marriage to Bill. What are its strengths? What are its weaknesses?

4. What do you think of Truman's relationship with fame? At times, he seems willing to sacrifice almost anything (love, his health, and his friendships) in pursuit of the limelight. How does that serve him, ultimately?

5. Why do you think Truman published "La Cote Basque 1965"? What point was he making about (or to) the story's subjects?

6. Truman and Babe were both heavily influenced by their mothers. In what ways were their childhood experiences similar? In what ways were they different?

7. Babe and her sisters were raised for successful marriages. Did they live up to their mother's hopes?

8. Pick three words to describe Truman and Babe's friendship. (Or pick one word to describe Truman, one to describe Babe, and one to describe their friendship.)

9. Do you think Babe forgave Truman in the end?

10. A number of characters tell stories throughout the novel. What are some of the stories that you tell—about yourself or about others? In what ways do stories shape our experiences?

11. Who was your favorite character? Why?

12. Who surprised you the most? Why?

13. Aging is a prominent theme throughout the novel, as the opulent fifties come to an end and a new generation of socialites supplants the glamorous Swans. What did you think of that? How do you feel about getting older?

14. Discuss the significance of memory in this novel. In what ways do we distort our memories? What, if anything, is the significance of this?

15. If you have read any of Melanie Benjamin's previous books, compare and contrast this work with her earlier novels. Is this story a departure? If so, in what ways? If not, how is it in keeping with her other writing?

16. Babe always presents a very carefully composed face to the world. Only occasionally do we see that mask slip. Discuss those moments. Who is the real Babe, beneath the makeup and jewels?

17. How has the role of women in society shifted from the 1960s to today?

18. Can you think of a woman who is the modern equivalent of Babe Paley and her circle of friends?

If you enjoyed

The Swans of Fifth Avenue

. . . .

read on for a preview of

MELANIE BENJAMIN'S

next enthralling work
of historical fiction

. . . .

THE GIRLS
IN THE PICTURE

1969

LATELY, THE LINE BETWEEN REAL LIFE AND MOVIES HAD begun to blur.

There were times when I would be pounced upon by a memory—the cracked rearview mirror of the first car I ever owned, say, or the ghostly dance of a curtain in front of an open window when I was small and impressionable and plastered in bed with a fever. Or the teasing curve of a man's lips, a man whose kiss I must have known at some time in my life. And the longer I dwelt on the memory, the less certain I would be of its origin. Was the memory really mine?

Or was it borrowed from a movie I'd written? Was the curtain dancing because there was a fan off-camera, trained at precisely the right angle? Were the man's lips curving as they came near mine, or were they moving closer to the camera lens instead?

More and more, I couldn't always tell the difference. And I wasn't quite sure how I felt about that, to tell the truth. On the one hand, it might be easier to live the rest of my days believing all my memories, particularly the bad ones, were invented for someone else to experience on screen.

On the other hand, if I can't claim as my own the memory of Fred's head always ending up on my pillow during the night, as if he simply couldn't stand to be apart from me for even the span of his dreams, how on earth would I ever be able to fall asleep again?

And the number of people who might be able to place the memories firmly into either category—real or cinematic—was dwindling.

No, not "dwindling," Fran. That's a prissy word. Say what you mean. They were *dying*. Your friends, your colleagues, all the Hollywood relics like yourself—dying off. Like old war horses put out to pasture; like plants that have hung around far too long in the florist's window.

Even on those occasions when I knew that I was most certainly standing in front of a real house, one I had visited many times before, and that I was being cooled by an actual breeze and not studio fans, I couldn't help but touch the rough stucco on the wall, just to make sure I couldn't poke my finger through it. And so I did touch it. Then I rang the doorbell again.

"I'm sorry to have kept you waiting, Miss Marion." A liveried butler opened the door, catching me as I poked at the stucco once more. He squinted at me cautiously as if I really were the dotty old lady I must have seemed. "Miss Pickford is not receiving visitors today."

"You told her it was me? Frances? That I asked for her, for *Squeebee*, for God's sake?"

"Yes, Miss Marion. Miss Pickford still says she is not receiving visitors today."

"Is she ill?"

The butler looked down at his polished shoes, and declined to answer.

I glanced at my watch and considered my options: Leave, simply walk away and let the tragedy play itself out. After all, the last time I'd tried, I'd been insulted and thrown out of the house. That time, I'd vowed I'd never come back. Yet here I was. Trying to revise the tragedy one more time like a fool. A sentimental old fool.

Closing my eyes, I pictured my small apartment, the cool tiled floors, the plush embrace of my sofa, a nice tall glass of iced tea at hand, maybe dozing to the comforting chatter of *The Edge of Night* or another of my soap operas. Because I really was too ancient for this, this arduous, thankless business of *saving*.

And where had Mary been, when *I* needed saving, so long ago? Here, as a matter of fact. Hiding behind this very closed door. So why was I knocking on it now?

Shared memories; triumphs and tragedies; the heroine doing right in the end despite temptation—all the plots of all the movies I've written tangled together into one gigantic ball of yarn I couldn't begin to unravel. Finally, I tugged on the loosest, biggest thread.

Because time is running out.

I squared my shoulders, sucked in my stomach, and pushed past the startled butler until I was inside the cool front hall of Pickfair. "Where is Buddy—Mr. Rogers?"

"He's attending a luncheon and should be back momentarily."

"Let me go up to her. Do you know how many times I've been in this house? How many times I've held her hand and told her everything would be all right? No, of course you don't, you're too young, you're an embryo and I'm a dinosaur, I know. Well, young man, let me tell you—*plenty* of times!"

The young man, sporting the usual Hollywood tan, paled anyway. Sucking in his breath, he showed his enviable cheekbones to their best advantage, daring to give me a glimpse of a blindingly white, perfect smile. I nearly laughed out loud. Of course! The Pickfair butler was exactly like all the other poor undiscovered souls in Hollywood, biding time until his big break. Oh, how some things never changed.

"I know Sam Goldwyn, young man. He's a personal friend of mine. If you want . . ."

"Of course, Miss Marion, go right on up!"

I bit the inside of my cheek as I started across the hall. "And if you'd like," the young man called out in a suddenly rich, resonant baritone, "I'll give you my head shot when you leave!"

I had to chuckle. Poor boy. He had no idea that Sam Goldwyn was even older than I was, and mad as a hatter, at that.

Shifting my handbag to my other arm, I set off across the slick, polished floor of the front hall, certain that I would not slip or falter, even though I had seen many people do that in the past. Charlie Chaplin once tied some of Mary's monogrammed dinner napkins to his shoes and skated across this floor, re-enacting one of his scenes from *The Rink*.

Mary had looked on with an indulgent smile—the same tight, practiced smile she granted Chaplin in all the photographs and newsreels—but she'd been furious all the same. I could tell by the way my friend's chin seemed more determined than ever, as if someone had outlined it with black ink. Doug, of course, had not only egged Charlie on, but then had to top him by tying napkins to *his* shoes, lifting Chaplin onto his shoulders, and twirling him around and around, finally throwing the smaller man into the air and catching him, to the delight of the assembled guests.

The Duke of Alba had been there that night. Along with Gloria Swanson, Rudolph Valentino, Vilma Banky, and Aimee Semple McPherson. Just a typical evening at Pickfair, the royal manor of Hollywood, where Mary Pickford and Douglas Fairbanks reigned supreme, Charlie Chaplin their unofficial court jester.

Of course, I'd always attended when invited—or rather, *summoned*—but I wasn't fond of those formal evenings, when Mary and Doug sat side by side at an enormous table properly set with finger bowls and several different forks. Try as I might—and risking Doug's not-so-silent wrath—I never could hide my amusement at these actors and actresses elevated to deities simply because of their looks, troupers with whom I'd once shared cheese sandwiches and glasses of beer who suddenly wrinkled their elegant noses if a servant happened to spill a drop of champagne. *"The help,"* they'd whisper with raised eyebrows, these gods and goddesses who had once been maids or gardeners themselves, and we all knew that it was only because of a fluke, a genetic lottery won or a benevolent mogul slept with, that they now wore tiaras and aped the regal characters they played on the screen. The characters I wrote for them.

They took themselves so seriously back then, these newly christened *movie stars*, still too unsure if the fledgling industry in which they worked—that we all had actually created with pluck and luck—would endure to be able to mock it, and none more than Mary Pickford. Sometimes I would gaze at her, draped in diamonds, her golden curls piled upon her head so that her sapphire earrings could be more easily admired as she nodded regally and conversed with royalty, and I couldn't believe my eyes. How had this happened? How had a fatherless little Irish girl from Canada come to dine with kings and queens?

And how had a twice-divorced bohemian from San Francisco come to be one of the honored guests? I had to lump myself in with all the rest; my own journey had been no less fantastic. I went toe-to-toe with Louis B. Mayer and William Randolph Hearst. I was the highest paid screenwriter in the industry. And I, too, had "gone Hollywood."

At least, until Fred died. Then I came crashing down to earth, and the tiaras and mansions seemed flimsier than movie sets and props, the only tangibles the emptiness in my bed at night, the silence that answered my whispered questions when I was alone with only my typewriter for company.

Still, I counted myself among the fortunate ones in this cruel paradise. Every night I thanked my lucky stars for my life, tragedies and all, because they had forced me to take a different path, one not blessed and cursed with a grand winding staircase like the one I was now ascending, the chandeliers glittering like ice, the velvet draperies plush, designed to keep real life firmly at bay.

Slowly climbing—good Lord, had these steps always been so steep?—I glanced into the famous drawing room off the entrance hall. There, over the fireplace, hung the iconic portrait of Mary Pickford, the Girl with the Curls, captured forever in the full flower of her youth and beauty, the face that, at one time, had been worshiped and adored by everyone in America—including me.

That portrait. That idealized little girl. *She* was the reason Mary was currently hiding in a dark room, afraid of the sunshine, afraid of a light unforgiving, unfiltered; that same light that had so loved and flattered her when she was young. Mary once confessed to me that her face felt odd, cold, when not bathed by arc lights and baby spots; the heat of the studio lights had become so familiar, actual daylight seemed dim by comparison.

Now, if the gossip was to be believed, Mary Pickford only emerged at night, sometimes standing in front of her portrait, staring up at it. Sometimes playing with her fabled doll collection, down on her knees arranging Lilliputian tea parties, or cradling one particularly lifelike baby doll in her arms and rocking it, crying softly.

"I ought to pull that damn portrait down with my bare hands,"

I declared, not caring who heard. I talked to myself all the time; I considered it one of the perks of old age.

Finally I reached the second floor, my limbs trembling from the exertion, my blouse stuck to my skin. For a moment I couldn't catch my breath; the air seemed to press down upon my chest. Oh, for the days when I had tagged along after Mary as she jumped nimbly about the set, playing pranks, the two of us giggling like little girls as we made our movies together.

Seventy-eight. I was now seventy-eight. Even Chaplin had started to slow down in his seventies. I took one more deep breath, smoothed the front of my blouse, felt my clammy forehead, then continued down the carpeted hallway, which was lined with more portraits and photographs of Mary—Mary in *Pollyanna,* in *The Poor Little Rich Girl,* in *Little Annie Rooney* and *Coquette,* or *Sparrows.* Photographs of Douglas Fairbanks in costume, his white teeth gleaming in his tanned face, his eyes crinkled with dashing merriment.

No photographs of Buddy Rogers, however. For the hundredth time, I wondered how Mary's current husband put up with the ever-present image of his predecessor. She sometimes called him "Douglas." And Buddy always answered with an eager smile that made me slightly ill.

Finally I reached the end of the hall, where I confronted a closed door. I hesitated a moment—a moment long enough for me to stoke up my anger and resentment and remember all the times Mary had not been there for me. A moment long enough to consider turning back one last time. Then in another one of those memories that might have been a movie, I heard myself saying, long ago and in vastly different circumstances but with the same amount of false bravado, *"I've never turned back in my life."*

So I knocked firmly on the door, loud enough to banish the memories and ghosts so that I might have at least a passing chance of saving the living.

"Mary? Mary, it's me. It's Frances. Why haven't you returned my calls?"

"No!" That rusty voice, so unused now it really did sound like a little girl's, high pitched, uncertain, quavering. "No, go away, Fran, dear. I'll call you tomorrow."

"I'm coming in, Mary. I want to talk to you. Right now."

"No! I'm not—Squeebee's not vewy well today, Fwan!"

Grimacing at the baby talk, I grabbed the door handle. "You're perfectly fine."

Pushing open the door, I had to pause when I crossed the threshold. The room was so dark, I felt as if I'd suddenly gone blind. Only the smallest sliver of light had managed to penetrate the tightly drawn curtains and in here, there was dust; particles drifted and danced through the weak sunrays. There was also a familiar odor: the sharp, sweet smell of whiskey and the juniper scent of gin.

Finally, I made out the enormous bed with its draped head-board. A tiny figure was propped up against the pillows, only a shadow, really. It took a long minute for the detailed image to emerge from the gloom. When it did, my heart twisted first with horror, then with pity. I took a step backward, retreating into the safe embrace of another memory, a memory I hadn't managed to banish, after all.

A memory of a different time, a different door, the same tiny figure emerging from the gloom of a darkened room.

SPRING 1914

"MARY? HEY, MARY, HERE'S THAT GIRL ARTIST I WAS telling you about."

Owen Moore knocked on the door, cocked his head, listening. He held up a finger. "Hold on, she's cutting," he informed me dismissively. "Wait here. She'll yell when she's ready."

"Are you sure this is a good time?" I patted my long skirt, sneezing as reddish brown California dust came flying out of it, and I touched my head to make sure my cartwheel hat was still pinned into place. Oh, if only I could have brought my sketches! But the Santa Anas had been too fierce this morning. They would have blown my sketch folder right out of my hands, and of course I didn't own a car so I'd had to take the trolley, and I had no idea what number to telephone to postpone the appointment—and I wouldn't have done so anyway, not for the world.

So I'd had to leave my sketches behind, and I felt as if I'd misplaced a baby, so used was I to having something in my hands—a sketchpad, a diary, a book, knitting. *Restless hands,* Mother had always scolded. *Daughter, you have restless hands to match your restless mind.*

"Sure, sure, it's a good time." Owen could barely contain his impatience; I knew he'd regretted setting up the meeting the moment he suggested it. "Mary?" Owen hollered again. "Come out when you're ready. I gotta run—they want me on set."

Still no sound from behind the closed door, until gradually I became aware of a whirring, clicking mechanical noise. Owen Moore—Mary Pickford's devilishly handsome husband—patted his smooth, rosy cheek. On his delicate white hand, a ruby ring twinkled from his pinkie. I had to bite my lip to keep from laughing. What a ridiculous dandy!

"My wife thinks she's God's gift to movies." He rolled his eyes nearly to the heavens, a movie actor's exaggerated body language. A *bad* movie actor's, at that. "She's merely a pretty Irish girl with an adequate little talent, hardly cerebral, if you ask me."

"I didn't, actually. Ask." Shifting my feet, I tried to find a stance that showed my disapproval but didn't offend him. I couldn't stand Owen Moore from the moment he'd sidled up to me at the party, flashing that ridiculous ruby ring, and I loathed him even more now. To talk that way about his own wife! He was just another small man afraid of an intelligent woman—the world was full of such fools. Yet my future was held in this particular fool's over-manicured hands.

"Well, it's the truth."

"I think she's a major talent." I couldn't hold it in any longer. "I've always loved her movies, even before I knew she had a name. Even when she was only the Biograph Girl, little Goldilocks."

"You would," Owen sneered; he had not liked it when I turned down his advances at the party, but still, he'd managed to get me the invitation I coveted. With one last exaggerated grimace of disgust, he turned and stalked off toward the "set"—whatever that was.

Left alone, I had to pinch myself; I'd never been in a movie studio before. *Studio.* That was quite a fancy word for what was really a collection of flimsy barns and sheds, so obviously hastily built I was surprised that they were still standing in the force of today's winds. When I'd arrived, I'd given my name to a disinterested man, makeup visible behind his ears, who served as a sort of gatekeeper. After consulting a list, he told me to go inside the largest of the sheds to wait for Owen.

This shed was a maze of rooms partitioned so haphazardly that there seemed to be no real hallway. From one corner of the cavernous building I could hear hammers assaulting nails and saws chewing through wood; from another, violins scratching out *Hearts and Flowers*. Bare light bulbs swung from long, fraying cords. Shouts rang out from every corner; cries to "Watch that flat!" or "Are the damn Indians shooting craps again?" or "Is Sylvia wearing that costume we need for Lita's dream sequence?" Outside, through windows and open doors that let in enough dust to coat every surface nearly a quarter inch thick, I glimpsed a row of tall cubicles, each with three walls but, oddly, no ceiling save a gauzy sheer fabric draped over some ropes, like a canopy. Each was done up in a different fashion—a living room, a bedroom, a Western saloon, a Victorian dining room. In front of some of these cubicles, where the fourth wall should have been, stood clusters of people huddled around one single camera being cranked diligently by a man. Next to the camera, men or women clutching megaphones bellowed directions as people with ghostly painted faces—pale, almost white skin tinged with an undercurrent of yellow, but dark, dark eyes and mouths—moved about stiffly in the odd, ceiling-less rooms illuminated only by the reliable California sun. Owen had headed out a door toward one of the cubicles; that must be the "set."

"Hey, are you an outsider?" A man, barely taller than me, poked me on the shoulder.

"I—yes, I suppose I am!"

"What are you here for?" He narrowed his eyes, and I blushed as if I'd been caught trespassing. Were normal people not allowed in movie studios? Had Owen only been toying with me? Was this revenge for rebuffing him?

"To see—to see Miss Pickford?" I detested the question mark in my voice, but this young man, despite his short stature, looked capable of picking me up by the scruff of my neck and tossing me outside to be swept away by the wind like the rest of the trash.

"Mary? She don't like outsiders. Are you sure?"

I took a big breath, remembering who I was, why I'd ever thought I had a right to be here in the first place. "Y-yes. I'm quite sure."

The boy took another step toward me, but I held my ground, although I did grip my reticule in case I needed to clobber him over the head with it. The boy's eyes were blue and hard and not a little bit menacing—until I detected a gleam dancing behind them. The promise of mischief, perhaps? That dancing light won out; his face relaxed and he was no longer a menacing thug but a laughing leprechaun with a surprising dimple in his cheek.

"Well, okay, then. I guess you'll do. Mary's in there." He pointed to the closed door. Odd; this boy had acted much more protective of Miss Pickford than her own husband had. For when you got right down to it, Owen Moore had no idea who I really was, or what my intentions might be.

"I know, Mr. Moore told me."

"Owen!" The boy grimaced. "So, Miss Outsider. You like it here?" He jerked his thumb in the general direction of the set area.

"Yes, yes, I do!" And I surprised myself with this answer. But I *did* like it here, chaotic and strange as it was. I had suspected—

hoped—that I would, but even so, hearing it out loud, in my own voice, was stunning. It was as if I'd agreed to dive head first into a shallow pond.

Movies.

The first time I'd heard the word, it was used to describe people and not those flickering, mesmerizing images on a screen. *We don't take no movies here,* landlady after landlady told me when I'd first arrived in Los Angeles two years ago.

"What's a movie?" I'd ask, bewildered.

"You know, them people who are running all over the place with those cameras, makin' those flickers. Those *movies*. You're not one of them, are you?" Always a suspicious, squinty-eyed glare as I struggled to look as un-movie-like as possible, because I desperately wanted the room. Still, the back of my neck twitched and I thought, for a moment, of answering in the affirmative; how appallingly prejudiced these landladies were!

"No. Not a movie," I'd confessed, practicality winning out over solidarity with the downtrodden.

"Fine, fine, then you can rent the room," and I'd be allowed to inspect such modest abodes, barely furnished with dusty, moldy Victorian furniture and threadbare Oriental rugs, that I had to marvel that the owner could afford to look down on anyone, let alone one of the mysterious *movies*.

I was a native San Franciscan, born and bred, and everyone warned me that I'd take one look at Los Angeles and turn right around and catch the next train home. "It's a wild and wooly town full of heathens!" "There's not a single museum there!" "I heard they drive cattle down the streets, and you can kill yourself on the cacti!"

Mother, especially, pleaded for me to stay put.

"Why you would want to go to such an untamed place is beyond me," she had sniffed. "There's plenty for you to sketch here, Frances, if you're still bent on becoming an artist."

I refrained from reminding Mother that my husband—husband number two, a number that definitely stung and so was best not mentioned—was being sent to Los Angeles to open up a branch of his father's steel company, and it was my obligation to accompany him. It wasn't that I was exactly thrilled about moving; I loved San Francisco. I loved its hills, its stately new buildings springing up from the earthquake just six years before, its museums, its theater and opera houses, its determined genteel quality, even if most of its residents were only a generation—or less—removed from the gold rush.

But as soon as I disembarked from the train in Los Angeles, I was utterly enchanted. Far from being a barren cow town, the city was drenched in color, red and yellow and purple and white flowers spilling out of every window box, embracing every street lamp. I couldn't stop gazing at the tall pepper trees, with their languid, lacy green leaves dripping with clusters of red berries, providing much-needed shade from a sun that rarely found a cloud behind which to hide—something this native San Franciscan thought she would never find tiresome. Orange groves dominated the mountainous landscape that sloped to the beckoning sea, the air so perfumed that I immediately craved the sweet, tangy fruit that I'd never really cared for before.

Everywhere I walked I encountered quaint little squares lined with small, adobe-style homes like ones I'd seen in pictures of Mexico; colorfully tiled fountains usually centered the squares and people would lounge about, napping or reading or simply savoring being outdoors in shirtsleeves in the middle of February. At first, this drowsiness seemed to embody the town to me, threatening to lull me into a dreamy slumber, as well—sleepwalking through a marriage to a man I didn't know, nor, I now realized with exceptionally bad timing, did I care to. Dutifully I sketched away at my job, doing commercial art for an advertising agency, but it was rote now, not at all challenging or fulfilling—how many different ways could I depict a necktie? After the initial enchantment wore off, it seemed to me that I'd come to Los Angeles to sleep my way through a disappointing life I didn't remember choosing.

Sometimes I'd try to rouse myself with a good, old-fashioned scolding. *What happened to your early ambition to create, to make something lasting, something worthy, my dear? Weren't you going to be the next Rembrandt or Chopin? Weren't you going to set the world on fire? Make your mark, cast a big shadow?*

Stupidity, my dear; that's what had happened. Two—not just one, but *two*—impetuous marriages I could only chalk up to idiocy. Every time I encountered a setback on the road to becoming the next Rembrandt or Chopin, I blindly said "yes" to the first person who asked. Yet as soon as I'd mumbled "I do," I'd immediately rebelled against being a conventional society wife to the conventional society husbands I found myself married to.

But for the life of me, I couldn't figure out what I wanted to be *instead*—oh, I couldn't figure out anything, *do* anything other than fall into miserable marriages in order to put off, for a time, doing or figuring out anything—it all went round and round and managed to dull my early ambition until its edges were harmless and easy for a confirmed sleepwalker like me to ignore.

In the evenings, after a silent meal with the stranger I'd married—truly, I'd stare at Robert, his features still so unfamiliar to me that after two years of sharing a bed I would have been hard-pressed to sketch him from memory—I would lean over the window sill. Dreamily, I'd inhale the perfumed air, feel the warm breeze carrying salt from the ocean, gape at the beauty around me but even so, none of it *roused* me; none of it reached my soul. That remained dormant, waiting. For someone—or something.

One morning, late for work, I scurried around a street corner only to encounter a cluster of people. "Excuse me," I muttered, holding on to my hat with one hand, my portfolio clamped beneath my other arm as I attempted to elbow my way through the crowd, which stubbornly refused to part. "Please, let me through!"

"All right, bring on the cops!" I heard someone shout.

Finally, I pushed my way to the front of the crowd, only to stop and stumble backward. Right there in the middle of the normally busy street stood a man barking through a megaphone, while another man turned the handle of a camera perched atop a wobbly tripod. I glanced around nervously; it was as if I'd stumbled upon something *unlawful,* perhaps. Like a bank heist.

And maybe I had; most of my fellow onlookers had grim, disapproving expressions on their faces as they glared at the spectacle being played out in front of them.

Suddenly a gaggle of men in rumpled police outfits burst onto the scene, skittering around a corner and toward the camera, jumping about, falling down on their behinds, slapping each other with nightsticks. In the middle of the wide, unpaved street stood a narrow fence gate. Only the gate, no fence. And to my glee, instead of running around the gate—the obvious visual effect—the policemen fumbled with the latch, then patiently took turns spilling through the now-open gate, one by one.

The smallest of the police, a slight young man with curly black hair, didn't simply tumble through the gate; he leaped into the air, turned a somersault, and landed on one foot, the other leg extended in a stunningly graceful arabesque. I couldn't help it; I clapped wildly.

The little man turned to me; I could see his eyes gleaming impishly. He tipped his hat, wiggled his nose and hitched up his baggy pants before sprinting after the rest.

When he did, I felt an unexpected tickle inside my belly. Perhaps it was the radiant sun that I should have been used to by now, but still wasn't. Perhaps it was the silly men, the graceful little clown who could do ballet. Perhaps it was the dawning realization that I was watching people joyfully working together, to create while the camera turned steadily, recording the result—*movies*. Finally, I had seen them for myself, these people whom the landladies all deplored; they did exist, after all. And they were doing *something*, something magical, right here, right in front of me on this ordinary street I walked down every day.

Whatever it was, my skin tingled as if someone had slapped my cheeks; I heard myself giggling, a sound so foreign that I almost cried. It had been so long—so unbearably long—since I'd felt anything close to joy. Since I'd felt anything at all.

Of course, I didn't cry; who could watch these funny men continue to tumble about and make silly faces and clobber each other with their nightsticks without laughing out loud? My cheeks actually ached, in a delicious way, from smiling so much; I was having the time of my life and I didn't give a hoot that others in the crowd turned their noses up at me. I actually stuck my tongue out at one glaring gargoyle—until a jalopy careened around the corner, heading right toward us all.

The cops scattered. So did my fellow onlookers, suddenly not so dignified as they whooped and leapt back, dropping parcels and handbags; they were just as funny as the fumbling cops and I laughed at them, too, as that jalopy tumbled closer and closer. Even as I jumped up on a sidewalk, the man with the camera and the man with the megaphone remained at their posts as the car hurtled toward them. I could only watch, unable to tear my eyes away from the impending disaster.

MELANIE BENJAMIN has written the *New York Times* best-selling historical novel *The Aviator's Wife*, the nationally bestselling *Alice I Have Been, The Autobiography of Mrs. Tom Thumb,* and *The Swans of Fifth Avenue*. She lives in Chicago with her husband, and far enough from her two adult sons not to be a nuisance (she hopes). When she isn't writing, she's reading.

melaniebenjamin.com

Look for Melanie Benjamin on Facebook.

@MelanieBen

To inquire about booking Melanie Benjamin for a speaking engagement, please contact the Penguin Random House Speakers Bureau at speakers@penguinrandomhouse.com.

This book was set in Fournier, a typeface named for Pierre-Simon Fournier (1712–68), the youngest son of a French printing family. He started out engraving woodblocks and large capitals, then moved on to fonts of type. In 1736 he began his own foundry and made several important contributions in the field of type design; he is said to have cut 147 alphabets of his own creation. Fournier is probably best remembered as the designer of St. Augustine Ordinaire, a face that served as the model for the Monotype Corporation's Fournier, which was released in 1925.